DEMIGOD 12

BY GAIL CARRIGER

Tinkered Starsong
Divinity 36 | *Demigod 12* | *Dome 6*

The Tinkered Stars
Crudrat

The Finishing School Series
Etiquette & Espionage | *Curtsies & Conspiracies*
Waistcoats & Weaponry | *Manners & Mutiny*

The Parasol Protectorate Series
Soulless | *Changeless* | *Blameless* | *Heartless* | *Timeless*
prequel: *Meat Cute*

The Custard Protocol Series
Prudence | *Imprudence* | *Competence* | *Reticence*

Parasolverse Tie-in Books & Novellas
Poison or Protect | *Defy or Defend* | *Ambush or Adore*
Romancing the Werewolf | *Romancing the Inventor*
How to Marry a Werewolf
Dear Lord Akeldama (direct from Gail only)

AS G. L. CARRIGER

A Tinkered Stars Mystery
The 5th Gender

The San Andreas Shifters Series
The Sumage Solution | *The Omega Objection*
The Enforcer Enigma | *The Dratsie Dilemma*

Newsletter exclusives: *Marine Biology* | *Vixen Ecology*

DEMIGOD 12

TINKERED STARSONG BOOK 2

GAIL CARRIGER

GAIL CARRIGER, LLC

WARNING

This work may contain implied contact of a romantic and carnal nature between members of the same sex, opposite sex, sexless aliens, or more. If love (in its many forms) and love's consequences (in even more varied forms) are likely to offend, please do not read this book. Miss Carriger has the tame young adult Finishing School series, which may be more to your taste. Thank you for your understanding, self-awareness, and self-control.

Version 1.0
9781944751722

For my steampunk besties, you know who you are. You who support me even as I stray from the ticking path into the tinkered void.

Thank you for the light you bring and the laughs you give and the safe spaces you provide, for me and and all those who set their brass compasses by your tea-saturated stars.

In the beginning, the Dyesi created the domes and the divinity.

Or did they?

1

AN ACT OF ASTERISM

When Phex woke up, he was a completely different color. He found himself staring at his own arm in mild confusion. Had he always been that… metallic? He twisted from the shoulder to catch the light – muted dark blues and somewhat silvery. Cute.

He was in the biggest surgery room on Divinity 36. Three of his pantheon were lying in beds around him: Kagee, Tyve, and Berril. Their two Dyesi members were missing. Phex checked the infonet on his ident. It felt like only a few minutes had passed, but it turned out to be over twenty hours since he had been made a demigod.

A medic shuffled over and helped Phex up. An acolyte led him, naked, to stand in front of a large mirror.

"You'll have plenty of recovery time," it said, tone formal and crests neutral.

Phex wondered what that meant. They hadn't had a day of rest since they arrived on Divinity 36 over a year earlier. They were demigods now – he doubted things would slow down or get quieter for him and his pantheon.

He stared at himself. All his skin, which had originally

been a brownish color, was now tinted gunmetal black with silvery blue overtones. He'd expected something like that. Most Sapien gods got tinted metallic. The Dyesi were very into metallics.

What startled him more were the clear sealant bandages over large parts of his torso. They'd removed his blade scars. Or, perhaps more precisely, those scars weren't actually *visible* anymore. It felt as if they were still there but had been covered over and were now phantoms lurking under a pretty metallic facade, shimmering memories of past mistakes. Phex wasn't sure how he felt about that. It wasn't as if he'd liked his scars, more that he'd thought of them as mementos of childhood, a concrete connection to his own past. He did not touch the place where they had once been, only noted the slight discoloration they'd left behind, like dust streaks on a pane of glass. It probably wouldn't be visible on the dais.

They'd reshaped his ears – pulled out the lobe and pointed the tips, so they were slightly larger and more crest-like. The Dyesi had deep feelings about ear shapes. The new tips seemed to glitter and shine, drawing attention, as if they were not so much crests as crest buds. Phex thought they too was cute, but that was how he felt about Dyesi crests, too.

The rest of his face and body seemed largely unaltered. Although his eyelashes and eyebrows had been thickened. He'd been given dark blue and black hair extensions interwoven with his own vibrant blue hair, all the way down to his hips. He moved his head about, enjoying the silken swish and weight of it – the ends tickled his skin.

He looked like a god.

Phex didn't say anything, just clicked at the nearby medics to acknowledge their skill in making him look exactly as he should by their standards.

He pulled on the robe that an acolyte handed him and

wandered aimlessly around the room, waiting for the others to wake up. He wasn't surprised to be the first – tinkered genetics meant he processed drugs of all kinds faster than most.

Kagee was next. He sat up quickly, looked instantly down at his empty hands, then glanced around for threat, relaxing the moment he saw Phex.

"They're in that bowl next to you," said Phex.

Kagee, sharp face neutral and jaw firm, put on his rings, carefully, one at a time, each on its proper finger. Then he twisted each to sit in exactly the right way.

Once he had finished, Phex helped him stand and walk to the mirror.

The medics had worked with Kagee's natural grey coloring, tinting him a silvery lilac, so he was a light to complement Phex's dark. Exactly as one would expect from the two cantors of a pantheon. Kagee already had long silver hair but they'd added volume and purple strands. He had bandage seals at the sides of his eyes and was squinting in pain. The surgeons had opened the lids and reshaped them slightly, the Dyesi prized large eyes. His were already big but they'd been made even bigger and up-tilted at the outer edge, leaf shaped. His long oval face, high cheekbones, and sharp features remained the same, although they had pointed the tips of his ears, like Phex.

Kagee looked at himself silently. Like Phex, he was unashamed to be naked in that moment.

"I look pretty," he said, genuinely awed.

Phex grunted. "You were always pretty, now you look like a god."

Kagee tilted his head and blew his reflection a kiss. "I do, don't I?"

The acolyte handed him a robe. Kagee turned away from

the mirror, took in the big room, then looked at Phex, newly darkened brows peaked in confusion.

"Over twenty hours," Phex answered the unspoken question.

"Where are Fandina and Jinyesun?"

"I don't think they've been told we're awake."

"Your sifters are packing the dorm," said the acolyte.

"Without us?" objected Kagee, forgetting his formality of speech.

"For you," replied the acolyte, unperturbed.

"Why?" asked Phex.

"Because you are leaving Divinity 36, of course." The acolyte sounded like Phex was crazy for asking.

Tyve woke up then. In classic Tyve fashion, she woke up sort of singing and giggling to herself.

Phex and Kagee went over to her bed.

She grinned at them "Am I gorgeous?"

"Absolutely stunning," said Kagee.

She evaluated him. "Likewise. Phex, I like the blue, very moody. Aren't you two as lovely as a deep-ocean resort? Or one of those wiggly, flowery sea creatures."

Kagee said, "If you feel like standing, there's a mirror over there."

They helped Tyve up and escorted her over to the mirror.

The aestheticists hadn't done much with her coloring, keeping the dark magenta, which now coordinated with Phex's midnight gunmetal. They had given her a rosy sheen, more pearl than metallic. Tyve twisted about and angled herself in front of the mirror. Her nose was bandaged and reshaped. She had naturally curly black hair and they had relaxed that into long waves, threading through strands of magenta and pearl so that it looked almost wet.

Their two absent sifters, the other members of their

pantheon, being Dyesi, were already a matched set. Jinyesun's iridescent skin leaned toward teal, and Fandina's was a purpled blue. The acolytes were turning all six of them into a spectrum of cool, watery sunset colors.

They sat together on the edge of Phex's former cot and waited for Berril to wake up.

As soon as she started to stir, they all rushed to her three beds. Her wings, spread to each side, each took up an additional bed.

She sat up, looked around.

Phex watched in profound relief as she automatically folded her wings, tucking and arranging the fine membrane behind her easily. Those wings had been terribly burned with acid a day before.

"How do you feel?" asked Tyve.

"Fine, actually," Berril smiled at them, her face shiny with various bandages. Her jawline had been shaved and her lips plumped, her eyes and nose both reshaped. Most of her face was shiny with the breathable repair bandage. She'd been given a full head of hair. It was long, of course. Phex thought it would take him a while to get accustomed to Berril with hair. It was not at all realistic-looking. The divinity had intentionally given Berril something synthetic and very lightweight so it almost floated around her head. Phex wondered if it could light up, like a holiday decoration.

"She'll need to keep the face bandages on for a week," explained the medic. "While you travel."

"Travel?" said Berril and Tyve.

"Fandina and Jinyesun are apparently packing for us," explained Kagee.

"Where are we going?" asked Berril.

"What's happening?" Tyve twitched her head about.

Phex and Kagee didn't know, so neither of them answered.

Instead, Phex said, "You want to see yourself, birdie?"

Berril smiled small and stiff under her bandaged sheen.

Phex helped her up and over to the mirror. He could easily have carried her but she wouldn't want that right now.

The Dyesi had taken away all her peach fuzz and tinted her skin, as Phex had expected, a silvery pale pink, the counter to Tyve's dark magenta. She looked frail and ethereal, like some sprite creature from ancient folklore.

"Oh!" said Berril, tilting her face around, staring in awe at her entirely new image. Her ears were already pointed, so they were two of the only things on her head that hadn't been substantially changed. Then, automatically, she unfurled her wings.

What had been done to those wings was truly amazing. Using a similar material to her hair, they had given her wings paper-like scales in a feathered pattern. Those scales must be incredibly light in order for her to still be able to fly. They started out the same silver pink as her skin at the top of her arms and back and then brightened into white at the bottom edge.

Berril twirled in front of the mirror.

Everyone gasped.

Berril said, "They're whole! I thought I'd have permanent holes, the pain was that bad."

The medic made a scoffing noise. "It was nothing to repair the acid burns. Now, you trying doing over ten thousand tissue-mica implants."

Berril fluttered her wings. The scales shimmered. "Is that what those are?"

"Yes. And it has a mixed polycarbonate filament ceramic micro-deposit coating."

"What does that mean?" asked Berril, eyes huge.

Kagee said with a sarcastic grin, "They're acid-resistant."

"But still delicate and easily ripped and injured like before," explained the medic. "But yes, most acids shouldn't be a problem. Also heat."

"I'm *fireproof*?" Berril gaped at herself.

"Fire-*retardant*. But the scales can shatter in extremes of temperature. Think of them as a little like glass fiber."

Tyve said, reverently, "They're really beautiful." They glittered in the light of the medical bay. They'd look absolutely amazing under the dome.

The acolyte helped Berril on with a halter wrap. "Enough admiring yourselves. You all look exactly as you ought. It's not like we haven't done this many times before. Come along, then."

But the medic on duty stopped them from leaving, interposing itself in front of the acolyte. Which surprised Phex. He hadn't known medics had authority over acolytes. "No heavy lifting, UV exposure, or gravitational stress for any of you, understood? You are still in recovery, even those places on your bodies without bandages need extra care. A full tinting is no minor procedure."

They all nodded.

The acolyte's crests went slightly back in annoyance – it hissed impatiently.

The medic ignored it and continued, consulting a small wrist screen, which probably had a discharge checklist. "What else? Ah, yes. You've all been sterilized. Not that the divinity" —a gesture at the annoyed acolyte— "lets you do anything that might cause procreation, but there it is."

The acolyte made a humorless huff noise.

Phex was surprised. "I wasn't already?"

Kagee seemed upset on Phex's behalf for some reason. "What?"

Phex looked around at everyone else. "You mean you weren't? You could just *get* pregnant or something?" He gestured at Tyve and Berril.

Tyve grinned. "I don't have those parts, but yes. Why is that odd?"

Phex shook his head. "Procreation is a privilege, not a right, the inner Spokes decide who breeds on the Wheel."

Kagee was appalled. "That's barbaric!"

Phex was genuinely confused. "It is? But this is space, air is limited, you can't just go around spawning, can you?"

The medic tapped at the screen. "Oh, ah, I see. You all already were sterilized before you came in. That's why the procedure notes are odd. How interesting. All four of you. That's never happened before."

Berril said primly, "Shawalee have an overpopulation problem, all teens undergo compulsory surgical birth control at puberty." She looked around. "Like Phex, I thought that was normal."

Tyve said, "Not compulsory for me, just encouraged in noncombatants. I took the option when I was getting my true-self surgery."

Kagee was deadpan. "I was born sterile."

The medic looked up at him without much interest. "No. You were not."

Kagee went pale under his new tinting. "Yes, I was."

The medic was not interested in arguing facts. "It was done in infancy but you show the standard vasectomy given to S-class Sapiens with male genitalia."

Kagee did not look well. Phex moved close in order to support him if he stumbled.

"I… What?" Silver eyes darted about as Kagee couldn't seem to process.

"Don't look so crestfallen," said the medic. "It's reversible, if you leave the divinity. We can do that for you easily, even if we didn't do the original sterilization procedure. I'm sure the divinity would cover it either way. No problem there. I'll make a note in your record."

"Wait, what?" Kagee seemed a little hysterical.

Phex exchanged worried looks with Berril. She shifted closer to their high cantor, put a comforting hand to his waist. "Mine is reversible too."

"All four of you are classified as temporarily sterilized. But no reversing the procedure until you leave the divinity, okay?" The medic was not interested in identity crises or personal revelations – they refocused on the discharge instructions. "Moving along. You have all also been given appropriate travel inoculations and boosters, as well as treatments to ward against most exotic infections and diseases. Gods do *not* get sick on my shift, thank you very much."

"Can we leave now?" asked the acolyte plaintively, only slightly rude in its inflection.

"Oh, am I inconveniencing you?" The medic sneered at it. "Yes yes, go away, why don't you?"

The acolyte did not reply. Merely gestured for the pantheon to follow it out of the surgery room.

"Where are we headed?" asked Tyve, as they were clearly not going up to their residential dorm.

"Toward ground transport, of course." The acolyte's crests twitched slightly in annoyance.

"What?"

"Right now?"

"But we just got out of surgery."

Phex guessed that was what had been meant by *time to*

recover. If they were about to go on a long space trip, they'd have plenty of time in transit to rest and heal.

The acolyte did not feel compelled to explain itself.

Berril plucked at Phex's sleeve. "We made it, right? We're demigods?"

Phex clicked agreement.

She looked furtively around. "So, what are we called?"

"What?"

"Our pantheon, do we have a name?"

Phex shook his head – he had no idea.

The acolyte stopped, turned around, and blinked huge purple eyes at them. "No one told you?"

All four of them clicked.

"Asterism."

"What's *that* mean?" asked Tyve.

"Sounds like a type of philosophy," said Berril.

"Or some kind of moss growing under a rock," joked Tyve.

Kagee answered, "It's geological. A star-shaped refraction of light."

"Oh, that's nice," sighed Berril happily.

"Still think it sounds like a kind of moss," grumbled Tyve.

Fandina and Jinyesun were waiting for them inside the grand entrance to the building on the ground floor. The two sifters crested in interest and flushed blue and shimmery with pleasure at the pantheon's newly upgraded appearance. The two Dyesi abandoned a small mountain of luggage to rush toward them.

Dyesi weren't by nature particularly physically demonstrative, but any pantheon with Berril, Phex suspected, would become so. After half a year living in close quarters together, Fandina and Jinyesun were affectionate even by Sapien standards. However, they could see the sheen of bandages on their fellow demigods, and so they limited themselves to small pats and an abundance of enthusiastic clicking.

"You all look so pretty!" said Fandina, high praise indeed from a Dyesi.

Phex supposed they had been tailored to Dyesi aesthetics, so of course their sifters would appreciate their new appearances the most.

"Beautiful," added Jinyesun, reverently.

"Look at my wings!" crowed Berril, deploying them right there in the middle of the hustle and bustle of the entrance.

Everyone around them, mostly acolytes coming and going about divine business, paused to crest and click in awe at the beauty of those wings.

"Oh, they're amazing! And you are healing well from your injuries?" Jin asked, sounding formal and worried.

Berril nodded and clicked.

"Thank you for protecting us on the dais." Fandina's crest flattened back in agitation and sincerity. Berril had used her wings to shield their Dyesi from the acid attack.

"It would have been the end of us," admitted Jinyesun. Dyesi skin could not be repaired so easily as Berril's wings or Phex's scars. And a Dyesi who could not sift could not be a god.

"Which would have been the end of the pantheon," added Tyve. "We are all grateful for Berril's quick reflexes."

Berril dipped her head, embarrassed. "It was pure instinct. You'll tell me what happened next? I don't remember much except the pain."

Jinyesun said, deadpan and informative as usual, "Phex

nearly killed the fixed that attacked us. Tyve threatened the acolytes with her claws. Kagee doused you in fruit juice."

"What?" said Berril, glaring at Kagee.

"It's a long story," said Kagee looking at the pile of baggage. "You two packed for all of us?"

Fandina clicked. "I hope we chose the correct items. Phex, I regret to inform you that we could not bring your kitchen equipment. All apologies."

Phex nodded. "Hardly any point when traveling. What will happen to it?"

"The acolytes said they would put it into storage for you."

Phex was startled to realize he had enough pots and pans and cooking utensils to warrant *storage*. "Should just leave it in the dorm for the next potential pantheon to use."

"But they're *your* special utensils," said Berril, surprised. Possibly because Phex was so proprietary about his pots and never let others into his kitchen, let alone touch one of his sacred spice racks.

Phex didn't respond. He wasn't really like that about stuff, just territory, but it didn't seem worth arguing about.

"So, we are called Asterism?" Tyve shouldered her bag. An acolyte instantly took it away from her, reminding her that after surgery, she wasn't supposed to lift anything.

Fandina and Jinyesun exchanged a look.

Fandina said, "Yes, we helped decide the name. Does it sound all right to you?"

"You have been busy while we were in surgery." Kagee sounded skeptical, but then, he always did. Kagee's baseline mood was mildly grumpy and dissatisfied with the universe.

"Did we overstep?" Jin speckled opaque with worry. Fandina's crests twitched.

"Naw, it works fine for me," said Kagee quickly.

"I like it," said Berril.

"Me too," said Tyve.

They all looked at Phex.

"Is Asterism a six-pointed star?" he asked.

"Depends on what's being reflected," said Jinyesun, who would have done all the research.

Phex nodded. "Asterism." It felt awkward on his tongue. But new words were often like that. He supposed he'd get accustomed to it.

"Phex likes it too," said Berril, interpreting his neutral response.

"So, do you know where we are going?" Kagee asked their two sifters.

Fandina gave the Dyesi huff-laugh. "Divinity 36 is a satellite moon, where is there to go but off of it?"

Jinyesun added, "Into space, of course."

Kagee and Phex exchanged exasperated looks.

Berril played in to their game. "Yes, but *why*?"

Jin brightened. "We're going on tour."

"Already? But we don't have any godsongs."

"More, we don't have any worshipers."

"Or performance experience."

"Or anything that would warrant a tour, really."

"Don't demigods usually spend another year on Divinity 36 practicing before they officially debut?"

Fandina looked at Jinyesun for help with all the questions. Jin was their explainer of all things mysterious and Dyesi- or divinity-related.

Jinyesun only flattened its crests back in worry. "We don't know either. We were only instructed to pack for everyone for a long tour, nothing else."

The acolytes interrupted them by appearing with a large team of escort guards in tow.

Phex was surprised by the number. His pantheon was only

demigod-rank – by rights, they didn't need that much protection yet. Then again, they *had* already been attacked by a fixed – perhaps such measures were necessary. He certainly wasn't going to complain.

They were escorted to ground transport, which then carried them through rather ugly streets of Divinity 36. It was a contrast Phex had never entirely gotten used to, the rocky, organically shaped, and boxy, uninspired buildings of the moon contrasted to the glory of the ring in which it sat and the pretty but angry green planet they revolved around. It looked exactly the same as it had when Phex first arrived, only a great deal less alien. Or maybe more so, because the Dyesi were so invested in aesthetics, so precise about how spaces looked on the inside and how people looked on the outside, it was odd that they did not care about the exterior of buildings. *Cave dwellers*, he supposed.

The transport stopped in front of an exclusive high-security docking bay. That was different from before. When they'd arrived, it had been in the crowded public-access area with dozens of other potential gods, excited and scared and ordinary.

Now they were there, special.

Onlookers had been kept away. There were no reporters or worshipers. Which was odd. Generally, the divinity welcomed media coverage, on the theory that all publicity was potential worship. But this time, it was just them, their escort, and one very high-end and rather ostentatious spaceship.

It was a luxury divine cruiser. The kind that boasted practice rooms and maybe even a mini dome – big and flashy.

In stark contrast to the moon, the cruiser could only be described as *garish*. It was mostly fish-shaped, and it had also been painted like a fish, with scales that covered the full color spectrum, red at one end and blue at the other. But this rainbow paint had moved all the way from metallic to outright glitter, making the whole thing rather eye-searing.

Kagee said nervously, "This can't be for us."

Yet the acolytes led them firmly toward it.

"This looks like Tillam's boat." Tyve's eyes darted covertly. Their weirdly silent surroundings were putting her on edge, too. "What's going on?" She glanced at Phex.

He grimaced.

At the bottom of the ramp, the acolytes and guards all stopped, and one of them gestured them inside.

"Go in, the manifest has been recorded and your paperwork is in order. You won't be performing for a while, since you need at least three original godsongs before you're allowed on a public dais. And, of course, time to recover from your surgeries." It consulted its ident. "There is a note that you'll have at least one bodyguard assigned to you within a few months. There are three acolytes and six bodyguards aboard to assist you in the meantime. Shared with the other pantheon, of course. Practice well, demigods, this is a rare opportunity. May the divine grace your colors and beauty sing your domes." The acolyte bowed and hurried away, assuming Asterism would board as requested. The remaining escort quickly loaded their bags and then left as well.

"Apparently, this flashy ship *is* ours," said Kagee, leading the way aboard.

"*Other* pantheon?" said Fandina, crests up.

Phex lingered so that he was the last to board. He paused at the top of the ramp, turned to look back out over Divinity 36. His home for a year. Technically his home forever. He was a Dyesi citizen now, so they *had* to take him back. Even if everything failed. Even if his pantheon collapsed. Even if he never became a great god. The Dyesi had to keep Phex.

They'd committed to it. He belonged to them now and this alien moon.

Plus, they had all his cooking utensils.

He turned and followed his pantheon into the divine cruiser.

Phex was probably the only one not surprised to find Missit waiting for them inside that spaceship.

"Welcome to Tillam's tour cruiser," said the rose-gold god, grinning his asymmetrical, mercurial smile.

"Oh, hell no," said Kagee.

Berril whacked Tyve. "Why didn't you tell us?"

"I *said* it looked like their boat!" protested Tyve.

Fandina and Jinyesun chorused, before anyone could yell at them, "We were only told to pack!"

Missit glommed onto Phex's side and grabbed his arm. The god looked up at him in a manner Missit no doubt thought was winsome.

Phex brushed him off, but when the god just came right back and grabbed his hand this time, Phex ignored him.

Everyone was looking at him.

"What?" Phex glared.

"Did you know?" Kagee seemed hurt.

"No."

"But you aren't surprised," pointed out Berril.

"Well, this kind of fancy obviously wasn't for us. Had to be for a major pantheon. Do you know of any other great gods about to go back out on tour? Had to be Tillam."

"Smartass," said Tyve.

Phex tried to extract himself from Missit again.

Kagee looked thoughtful. "And you need *him*."

"Who needs who?" wondered Berril.

Fandina's crests went flat to its head, wide open and looking extra fin-like after experiencing the fishy outside of the spaceship. "Careful, Kagee."

"No one else is going to say it? Why not? Because he is standing right there?" Kagee glared at Missit.

"Moi?" said Missit, coy. "Of course I *need* him. Have you seen this man's body?"

Phex narrowed his eyes and forcefully extracted his hand from Missit's and backed away.

"Like the acolytes would allow *that,* let alone plan for it." Tyve glared at Missit, defending Phex's purity or something equally ridiculous.

Phex heaved an internal sigh. This was about to get messy.

"Oh, no, right. You need Phex's voice, don't you?" Berril understood what Kagee was saying at last.

Missit looked around at them. Fellow gods now. Still inferior to him. Only demigods. Not at his level. But hostile toward him in a way he'd likely never experienced before, not from younger godlings. It must be shocking, to be taken to task by his juniors.

Phex wanted to comfort Missit in that moment. But this was his pantheon and they were protecting him from being taken advantage of. Or that's what they all thought they were doing. He could not comfort an outsider under those circumstances. Also, he was nervous. He had no idea where he and Missit stood with each other anymore. Not that he had before. Missit had slept in his bed for a while, for comfort and maybe for something more. But that time had long passed. Missit had Fortew back. Did he need Phex in that way anymore at all, or did he just need him to sing?

"We are only here, on this fancy-pants cruiser, so Tillam

can use Phex as an understudy because Fortew is sick. Right? That's it, isn't it?" Berril looked somewhat pleased with herself for having put it all together.

"What's *understudy* when it's a god?" Tyve asked, tone crisp and harsh.

"*Underworld*, maybe? Like Phex is Tillam's god of the dead." Kagee was intentionally trying to hurt with that suggestion.

It worked – Missit visibly flinched.

Phex was moved to speak. "Enough, Kagee."

Kagee glared. "But they'll tap you for Tillam, Phex. The divinity will sacrifice us so you can go with them instead. Don't you get it? You'll be rehearsing with both pantheons. This is *our* debut, and they are going to use you to fill a hole for old gods while simultaneously pushing you to be a new one. How can you do both? How could anyone?"

"I'll figure it out," said Phex, because he would.

"You can't be in two pantheons at once." Fandina finally also understood what was going on. The sifter was opaque with concern.

Even Jinyesun looked Dyesi worried, crests low and trembling, a hint of opacity about its cheeks and neck.

Missit said, tears in his voice, hunched protectively, "Fortew is still alive!"

Phex wanted desperately to comfort him – his body ached with it. But they were no longer in a private practice room where he could hug liquid gold close and revel in being needed by a god. Things were different now. *Everything* was different now.

Phex's pantheon did not care in that moment about the pain of elder gods.

Kagee was looking at Phex closely. "How can you be so calm about this?"

"The divinity is making use of me." Phex stated the obvious because he had learned, with his pantheon, that they did not always see the universe like he did. They did not always find the same things obvious.

"But you're a *god* now," said Kagee, still confused.

"Yes, but I am *their* god."

Berril launched herself at Phex and wrapped him in a hug, sniffing and unhappy. As if he needed comfort, not Missit.

"What's this, birdie?" Phex stroked her fluffy new hair very gently, confused. It crackled a little under his touch.

"How come she gets to hug him?" objected Missit.

Berril whirled around, glared. Berril, who was about as fierce as an overcooked noodle. "He's accustomed to this, our Phex. Being made use of. Don't you see? He's not surprised at all. He expected it."

Phex was confused by her shock and her sadness. "Of course. Didn't you?"

"So, you never had faith in any of it?" Kagee looked faintly impressed by such skepticism.

Phex shook his head at their naivety. "Gods don't have faith. We exist to encourage faith in others but hold none in reserve for ourselves."

He looked at Missit out of the corner of his eye.

Missit looked like he agreed that this should be obvious.

"Aren't you worried you'll be overworked or have to choose between pantheons or…" Kagee was spiraling into anxiety.

Phex didn't know the complexities of Kagee's past, but he knew the high cantor did not want to go home. Kagee believed that the pantheon was all he had and all he wanted. This, Phex being loaned out to Tillam, even if it was only as an understudy, threatened his safety net.

Phex gently extracted himself from Berril and approached

Kagee. Wondering if he was right in this. He tentatively opened his arms just a little to see.

Kagee slammed into him, hugging hard. Not minding the bandages over Phex's scars. Phex didn't mind either. He thought Kagee was probably leaving a handprint in the sealant over the one on his upper back, heavy with deadly silver rings, and he kind of liked that idea. Phex squeezed back, made his own handprint.

The rest of his pantheon crowded around. They were worried. Worried about surviving as a pantheon when they had only just become one. But more, they were genuinely worried for Phex.

Kagee pressed a thumb to Phex's cheek, forced him to look down into those newly up-tilted silvery grey eyes. "You're sure you can do both?"

Phex sighed. A little annoyed that he kept having to remind them. This was all easier for him. Everything about the divinity was easier than the Wheel, easier than his past, easier than his childhood. He had survived. Everyone always thought it was about Phex's voice, but it wasn't. It wasn't even about his triggered genetics. What Phex really excelled at was survival. Two pantheons at once? That was just another thing he would have to survive. And he intended to do so.

Missit said, from the outside, "Oh, I see."

Phex reached out an arm from the center of his pantheon, dragged Missit in, too, cupped the back of the god's neck.

"I'll be fine," he said. And when that didn't seem to help, he added, "We'll all be fine."

2

HAVE SPACESHIP, WILL SING

The spaceship proved to be every bit as glamorous as one might expect of a tour bus for the most famous pantheon in the galaxy. It had all the amenities, including several practice rooms, shifting booths, a dance studio, and a mini gym for the graces and bodyguards. There was also one very small dome – smaller even than the copula over Phex's cafe back on Attacon 7. This was still a spaceship, after all, so the dome had to be on the tiny side, but Phex found its presence comforting. Phex, who had no home, always felt at home under a dome.

Inside it was an interesting combination of the close quarters and space efficiency needed for space travel, the Dyesi inclination for soft fabrics and furnishings, and all-out celebrity glitz. Phex wouldn't say the three elements existed in harmony, but they did their best. The seating area in the galley, for example, was comprised of the requisite couch puffs, but they were all smaller and closer together than back on Divinity 36, and they were all glittery copper in color. The throws were Dyesi fiber art, but instead of restful blues, these were woven sunsets of pinks and oranges and yellows.

Like on Divinity 36, all the doors were covered by skin curtains, although Phex had noticed that important sections of the ship did seal off for safety reasons. It was still a space-faring vessel, after all. On the ship, however, the dracohor-hide flaps had been painted in bright colors matching to their different rooms – copper for the kitchen, silver for the mini dome, and so forth.

Asterism were to sleep together in a small dorm facility with a magenta door flap – six beds in one little room decorated in purples and pinks. There were three cots to each wall that folded down, one above the other. Everything was compact and multipurpose, allowing the space to be reconfigured as needed. But the bedding was Dyesi-soft. Phex was too tall for the beds, but he was accustomed to sleeping on his side and curled up, so he figured it would be fine.

There was an equally small, equally pink attached combination waste-and-hygiene chamber that they would have to use individually on rotation. Tyve was annoyed – she liked to spend a lot of time primping and fussing with her hair, but they no longer had that capacity.

Phex felt more at home than he had on Divinity 36. Travel-sized accommodation pods were fine with him, comforting even. It would be harder on Berril and Kagee since they were planet-born. He wasn't sure about the Dyesi – since they were raised in caves, they might be used to tight quarters or prefer something more cavernous.

Tyve's final judgment was "Well, it's luxurious by spaceship standards."

"That's right, you're space-born. Zil too?" Berril looked at her fellow grace.

Tyve pressed at an apparently innocuous panel next to where her bed folded down, and a storage compartment popped open. "All *three* of us. There's an annoying little sister I try to forget about." Her tone was all affection.

"Will she be joining the divinity too?" asked Jinyesun.

"Hardly."

"Kagee, is this too tight for you?" wondered Tyve, clearly remembering that he grew up on a planet among the elite. Also, he had liked to sprawl around their living area back on Divinity 36.

Kagee certainly didn't look comfortable, but he said, "I'll manage. No worries. Phex, you gonna miss your kitchen?"

"I saw him eyeing the galley when we got the tour," said Tyve with her carnivorous grin.

"There's a proper chef in charge." Phex defended himself. "I plan to formally introduce myself."

"What, you still planning to cook in all your copious free time?" Kagee sounded bitter.

"We gotta eat."

"You're okay with this?" Tyve asked.

Phex looked around, found nothing worth complaining about. The colors gave their quarters an odd fleshy feel, like being inside a bruise, but it seemed cozy, he had his own bed, and it was warm. "I like it."

"You *like* it?" Berril was shocked. "It's so small, I can't even spread my wings, and you're huge."

Phex shrugged. "I find the atmosphere kind of reassuring. Remember, I spent my childhood in air ducts on a space station. Then I lived in a small bubble pod on Attacon. I'm not accustomed to a lot of space."

"You're weird." Kagee was looking at him.

Phex folded down his bed, the lowest one nearest the door. It partly blocked that doorway when it was down. Phex liked that. Anyone who tried to get into their room at night would have to go over him first. Tyve took the bunk directly above his, and Jinyesun took the top one.

Phex had only a small pack with a few outfits and personal items. His favorite paring knife was there, one particularly nicely shaped spatula, and his preferred cooking chopsticks, but that was it. He clicked his delight and approval and looked up at Jinyesun. "You chose these for me?"

"I did good?"

"Exactly what I would have packed."

His Dyesi friend flushed bright blue with pleasure.

Phex was amused with himself, too. Without his amassed cookware, it seemed that a year as a potential god on an alien moon hadn't resulted in him collecting much more than he had originally arrived with.

He pressed at the wall around his bed until another storage shelf popped out, stuffed his pack in there.

The others puttered about doing the same.

Phex sat on his folded-down cot, expecting Kagee to come over. The silvery boy kept looking at him.

Phex waited patiently.

Eventually, Kagee sat next to him but at the other end of the cot.

Tyve looked at them upside-down from her bunk above.

Phex gestured at the door with his head.

She flipped out of the bed, threw an arm around Berril. "Let's explore some more. Fandina, Jin, come on."

"Oh, but…" Jinyesun objected mildly.

"Let's see if we can find my brother and the rest of Tillam."

"Oh, really?" Jin looked starry-eyed.

"Yes, really." Tyve hustled the bulk of the pantheon out, leaving Phex and Kagee alone.

"She's not very subtle," complained Kagee.

"With Dyesi, she doesn't need to be."

"Fair point. I know they are custodians of the most popular entertainment in the galaxy, but sometimes the Dyesi strike me as awfully childish."

Phex privately agreed but he thought that it might just be culture conflict and was probably something that shouldn't be discussed.

"We don't have much time. What's up?" he said, not being very subtle himself.

"You think Tyve can't distract them for very long?" Kagee picked up Phex's assigned Dyesi blanket and petted the cable-knit texture, following the three strands along with grey fingers.

"I think Missit will probably come looking for me." Phex picked up the other end of the blanket, subjected it to a similar fiddling scrutiny. He wondered if Dyesi knit was always so soft because they had particularly sensitive skin.

"Are you ever going to explain about your relationship with that god, or whatever it is?"

"You want to talk about Missit and my problems?" Phex shifted to sit cross-legged, noting the way the cot, which was almost more like a hammock, swayed with every little movement.

"At least you acknowledge that he's a problem. But no."

"So, speak." Phex didn't look at Kagee. He'd noticed the Agatay didn't like directed eye contact unless he initiated it and then only under specific circumstances. Instead, Phex swiveled to look across their new room and out the porthole window at the vastness of space. They had left Divinity 36 behind but were still coasting through the Dyesi sector. No FTL yet. Everyone needed to be settled first. Plus, the ship had to find a void. He'd never get over how absolutely silent space travel was.

Kagee took a little breath, then said all in a rush, "You don't mind that the Wheel sterilized you without asking? You wouldn't mind if the divinity had done it?"

Phex tried to understand the situation from a non-Wheel perspective. In this he found himself feeble and confused. It just seemed stupid to him that anyone could breed. He found himself thinking about all that flirting back in his cafe on Attacon 7. Suddenly, those teenagers draped over each other all the time took on a sinister aura.

"I'm sure it was in our contract somewhere, that they would sterilize us upon godhood if it hadn't been done already. The Dyesi clearly carry a lot of taboo around children. They wouldn't want to confuse us on this matter."

"But without directly asking?"

"I'm not upset." Phex answered the original question. "Even if it was the divinity that did it to me. Who knows what my genetics might do to others, unfettered."

"But?"

"Your people did it to you and then lied about it." Phex took an educated guess as to what was really bothering Kagee.

"I was supposed to be born this way. A Protan. A dud. It's the excuse for everything they did to me. Delineation. Proxy training." Kagee wiggled his deadly rings at Phex. "Why did they stop me from having children and then punish me for it?" Kagee looked so sad. He stopped playing with the purple blanket and began fiddling with his rings, staring at them as if they could explain everything. "Me training to be a body double, that was the excuse. Not able to contribute to society any other way. Not useful for the lineage. Not capable of giving anything else to the family. Not worthy of marrying into the elite."

"Is that why you left the planet?" asked Phex, gently.

"Of course. How can I live protecting a thing I want but cannot experience myself? How can anyone live that way?" Kagee's grey eyes were childish and pleading when they finally met Phex's. "Now I learn that I could have had it, they just denied me. What else did they lie about?"

Phex thought about the Wheel. He thought about adults in general. He thought about the divinity, and the Dyesi, and the acolytes, and the medics, and the past year of hard training, and countless tests, and tiny assessments. He smelled memory, the acrid scent of crud in this sterile spaceship.

"What *don't* they lie about? The ones in power, aren't they always made up of demands and denials?" he wondered.

"That is not very comforting."

"For comfort, you should have gone to Berril," said Phex.

"True." Kagee smiled suddenly. "I have something I need to tell the pantheon."

"Asterism." Phex reminded them both they had an official name now.

"It's a stupid name," said Kagee. "Sounds like a medical disease."

Phex agreed that it did. Or a religious movement. But he kind of liked that aspect.

"Call a meeting? Now?" he asked. "We just got rid of them."

Kagee shook his head. "No, we still need to settle in, figure out what's going on here. How to protect you from overwork. What exactly the divinity wants by putting us on tour with Tillam so soon. Of all the pantheons they could pick, why us, a brand-new one? Right now, my dumb past can wait."

Phex nodded. "Does it affect the integrity of Asterism?" Phex was worried about what he should be worrying about. Would they be okay? Was Kagee going to be okay? Did Kagee want to leave them and return home now that he knew what had been done to his reproductive organs? Did he require a confrontation? Did he want to go home and have kids now? Did this negate his wanting to be a god? Kagee had a planet and, clearly, a family back home. Kagee had options. He did not *have* to stay with Asterism.

Kagee laid all of Phex's fears to rest with one sentence. "No. It has to do with the dome."

Phex felt his shoulders relax. The dome could be dealt with later during practice – Kagee was right. "Okay. Good. Are you hungry?"

"I love you too, Phex."

Phex wrinkled his nose. "Cheesy."

Kagee grinned. "Oh, good idea. Do you think there's any cheese on this spaceship?"

The captain of the ship was a round, exceedingly chipper Sapien with a mellow demeanor and high spirits. She reminded Phex a little of his old boss at the cafe, if Del had undergone a personality transplant that converted her into a gregarious type with a propensity to knit and inclination to gossip. Which is to say, they weren't at all alike but something about their general aura of tiny dictatorial capability made them seem like sisters separated by stars.

He liked her immediately. Unfortunately, the feeling was not mutual.

An acolyte showed them to the bridge, and the captain

instantly took over as soon as they had entered and greeted the space.

"Welcome! Welcome, Asterism. Exciting to have a second pantheon aboard. We are built for two sets of gods, did you know?"

Without pausing to have her question answered, she continued. "There's six of us as a crew aboard. For the bridge, there's me, my first mate, and our bosun. Off the bridge, we have an engineer, a medic, and of course our chef. All of us are trained to pilot the ship solo should it become necessary for any reason, so don't you worry about a thing. For emergency purposes, I must ask: are any of you trained in spaceflight or medical aid? It's always good to know what additional talent we have access to on a long tour like this one. Although I doubt we will have need. We're very efficient."

"I carry level-two pilot's creds for Coalition space," said Tyve.

"Level two? Bulk transport, really? No combat training like Zil?"

"Zil is ex-military, I am not. But family tradition sees us all train up to handle large freight and big guns."

The captain brightened. "Most wonderful. Zil is an excellent pilot. Having two of you can only be better for everyone. Unless you two fight? My sister and I can't be in the same room for more than ten minutes together."

Tyve grinned. "Ah, siblings. But no, fortunately, Zil and I get along fine. He's better with his claws but I'm actually a better gunner. Even Jakaa Nova freight carriers go armed. But that's information I'm sure you won't make use of."

The captain glanced quickly at their acolyte escort. "Certainly not."

This was a divinity-hired ship and the Dyesi were strict

pacifists. The cruiser would only have defensive capabilities like heavy-duty shields and high speeds, no weaponry.

"I can pilot, but only within gravity," said Kagee. "I don't know what class that would be or if your instruments would match anything I'm accustomed to in a cockpit. I also have basic survival training, but I'm only good with trauma – physical injuries, some poisons, and the like, and only for Sapiens."

The captain nodded. Phex realized she was recording this information with her wrist ident.

"I can fly," said Berril, grinning cheeky.

"Oh? What level?" The captain looked at her with interest.

Berril unfurled her beautiful wings.

The captain clicked and clapped happily. "You sure can, how pretty! Not exactly useful to me, but thank you for the look-see."

Berril grinned and tucked her wings back away. "I know, but I just got them redecorated and I can't resist showing them off."

The captain clicked again. "Understandable. You'll talk to the chef about your diet? I know chiropterans require specialist cuisine."

"Phex will," said Berril, with complete confidence.

The captain turned to Phex hopefully. He was the only other Sapien who hadn't claimed any kind of spacefaring or medical ability. She knew Fandina and Jinyesun would have nothing practical to add – these weren't traditional Dyesi skills. Which was fair. It was the reason she had a job with the divinity in the first place.

Phex said, "Oh, I can't do any kind of piloting, sorry. Nor am I trained for illness or injury. But I can cook and I'm a decent barista."

"And you enjoy it?"

Phex nodded. "Very much."

"Our chef goes by the name of Korpuna, she's Cotylan. I'll make sure you're introduced."

"Phex will be busy," said Tyve, before the captain could get too excited. "You can't assign him prep duties."

"Of course he'll be busy, he's a god," agreed the captain.

"Twice over," grumbled Kagee.

The captain ignored that, presumably because it did not make sense but possibly because Kagee was using Galactic Common.

"I understand your lot will be practicing more than we are accustomed to with Tillam. The crew will not interfere with you in any way unless your safety is at risk." She glanced quickly and deferentially at the acolyte standing in stoic Dyesi observation nearby.

Phex was moved to curiosity by this dynamic. He understood that the captain was employed by the divinity, but she treated them with such reverence.

"Are you a worshiper?" he asked.

The captain nodded and clicked. "This crew is chosen from worshipers only." That explained why they all spoke in Dyesi.

The acolyte added, "We have found that it is more effective to recruit from within. They acclimate to the divine standards of language and behavior better."

Phex frowned.

Kagee, clearly following Phex's concerns, said, "You aren't worried about the fixed?"

"Why do you think there are bodyguards aboard as well?" The acolyte wasn't being defensive – this was said with cool calmness.

The captain, however, looked deeply offended. "My crew

is not insane! Or likely to become so! Certainly not for a demigod debut pantheon!"

Phex was pretty darn sure that was not how becoming fixed worked. The dome simply pushed some personalities in that direction. Any increased exposure to gods performing just made it worse. Some particularly amazing dome featuring the god they believed in most, and they tipped into madness. But he didn't want to argue with the ship's captain.

So, he asked, before Kagee could start a fight, "Do any of them worship at the dais of Tillam?" Phex was pretty sure he could guess at the answer.

Both the captain and the acolyte said firmly, "Absolutely not!"

Phex nodded. As it should be.

Kagee wasn't going to let it drop, though. "To whom are you most devoted, Captain?"

The captain looked both pleased and wary at being asked, as if Kagee were testing her, which he kind of was. "Xillon," she said, without hesitation.

Kagee relaxed a little.

But now Phex decided to push – he was Asterism's sun, after all. "You'll keep the crew from believing in any one of us?" He said it to both captain and acolyte.

"Of course!" said the captain.

But the acolyte said, "You know very well that belief cannot be controlled to that extent. People believe in who they want to believe. But we will keep watch, and we have incoming reinforcements."

The captain looked even more upset. Much of her good humor had evaporated under Phex and Kagee's accusatory intensity. Phex realized that he and Kagee had basically ganged up on her, but she seemed more threatened by Phex. Well, he was a lot bigger and meaner-looking. Kagee came off as grumpy but also cute and delicate, like a disgruntled murmel.

"Aren't you overly demanding for demigods who haven't even debuted yet?" The captain crossed her arms and glared. Her arms bulged with muscles Phex hadn't noticed before.

And there it was. He had made an enemy of the person in charge of their spaceship, and they'd only just boarded. Phex wondered if he should apologize. Wondered why he'd even bothered to speak when, clearly, his speaking never helped matters.

The rest of his pantheon flanked him.

Fandina seemed moved to explain. "We've already had our first fixed encounter, Captain. Phex is very protective."

"He's your sun?" The captain frowned hard.

"And he trains with the bodyguards." Tyve sounded rather proud of Phex.

Phex glanced at her, confused.

"And he can kind of fly, only it's bouncing off walls and things," added Berril, although Phex had no idea why she felt the need to mention that. She seemed to just want to brag about him.

"He's our low cantor but he can also grace," added Jinyesun, smug.

Phex thought they were using his skills to defend his attitude. But that was, at best, only a distraction.

"I thought he was a *cook*," said the captain, wistfully.

Since the captain didn't seem to get it, Phex turned to the acolyte.

"Phex." Fandina's tone was all caution.

Phex ignored his sifter. "You keep a very close eye on this crew."

"Is that an order, demigod?" The acolyte's tone was neutral and its ear crests revealed nothing.

"You want *my crew* under security supervision from *acolytes*?" The captain's tone rose in serious offense. "We are seasoned professionals! We tour with *Tillam*!"

Phex gritted his teeth.

Kagee jumped back into the fray again. "There's a dome aboard this ship and we'll be using it a lot. Keep your people out of it."

The captain bristled further. "My crew has duties. They don't have time to watch six fledglings prematurely yodel."

She had no idea what she'd allowed aboard her ship. Phex supposed he would have to work to keep her in ignorance.

The acolyte looked equally confused. Perhaps Phex was overestimating his pantheon's worth, but he knew they were good. Powerful. They already had fixed even though they hadn't debuted. He was scared *for* Asterism, but he was also scared that Asterism was dangerous to worshipers. Extra bad at corrupting and causing fixed.

Phex had looked up their numbers shortly after getting aboard the ship, and they were much higher than the average growth for a new pantheon. No longer a potential, Phex had greater access to the infonet and the divine forums. The forums loved stats and comparing pantheons. The divinity hadn't commented directly, but Asterism hadn't even released its first godsong and already interest was spiking. Not to mention the fact that they'd been put immediately on tour. Phex knew his role as Fortew's understudy would be kept secret for now, but that was only part of the push toward fame.

The divinity clearly thought it was on to something big with Asterism. But *big* meant *danger*.

Phex said to the acolyte, "You don't think caution is warranted?"

The acolyte was Dyesi, and the Dyesi did not handle

violence well. If at all. "We're adding another bodyguard just for Asterism. We've never done that for a demigod group before."

"Just one? Tillam has six." Kagee wrinkled his nose in annoyance. He had a background as a proxy. Phex had never learned the details, but he was pretty certain that *proxy* was Agatay for *part bodyguard, part assassin.*

The acolyte's ear crests went back in annoyance. A reaction at last. "They are *Tillam*. You are not."

Phex understood then that no one in the divinity was going to take his pantheon's safety as seriously as he did. He vowed to resume his bodyguard training as soon as possible. He wondered how much sleep he actually needed to survive.

"Bossy sun you've got there." The captain, still annoyed with Phex's slurring her crew's integrity, seemed bolstered, knowing Phex's mistrust extended to the acolytes.

"The bossiest," agreed Berril proudly.

"You should be honored," said Tyve with a sharp grin. "I don't think Phex has ever even talked to even *us* this much in his life. Let alone a comparative stranger."

"Taciturn, is he?"

"Very," said Fandina, with feeling.

"Good," said the captain. She turned to the acolyte. "If that's all, we should get back to winding up for FTL. I understand Syrunid Prime is our first port of call?"

The acolyte clicked.

The captain glanced back at Asterism. "You have three weeks to practice during transit, demigods. Let's see if your dome is as strong as your ego. It was nice to meet you. Have a pleasant fold. I'll see you on the flip side."

Asterism took that as the dismissal it was and quickly left the bridge.

The acolyte, who was a tall, very thin Dyesi with skin

leaning toward the purple end of the spectrum and particularly fragile-looking long crests, led them briskly back to their quarters. It showed them the netting to strap down for FTL one person per bunk. It then supervised them all being secured.

As annoyed as the acolyte was with Phex and Kagee's behavior, it knew that a new pantheon was an expensive investment that must be cared for. They were still gods, after all. An acolyte must always act for the good of the divinity.

"Well done, you two," said Tyve as they settled back, feeling the big ship vibrate as it flushed the DMP and wound up for FTL. "You managed to upset both the captain and our assigned precatio."

"I talked too much." Phex was annoyed with himself. The acrid smell of crud filled the sterile ship's air – this time, it was not his memory.

"Certainly more than usual." Fandina's agreement was not approval.

"Nothing new for me," said Kagee, unruffled. "I always piss people off."

"You think the acolytes are not taking it seriously enough?" said Jinyesun. "The danger to our pantheon? The acid attack. The fixed."

"Berril was *injured*." Phex thought that was reason enough.

"We won't let it happen again." Tyve poked a claw through her netting and over the edge of her bunk so Phex, below her, could see it.

Phex thought about how important it was going to be to fit more bodyguard training into a schedule he didn't even have yet. "It might not be up to us. That's why I pushed."

Fandina said, "I will talk with the divinity seriously on this matter."

“We understand the danger,” added Jinyesun.

Phex said, just to make certain, “Do you really? Asterism can’t risk having worshipers aboard this ship, let alone one of us getting an actual believer.”

“If you keep acting like such a jerk, we won’t have any worshipers at all,” replied Tyve. “Remember the old adage, fans start one-on-one? Seriously, Phex, Kagee is more than enough asshole for one pantheon.”

“I’ll take that as a compliment,” said Kagee, sounding genuinely amused.

“So, what are you doing, influencing Phex with *your* bad attitude?” asked Tyve.

“Everyone is going to hate us,” added Berril somewhat cheerfully.

“Result!” Kagee crowed.

“I need to cook something,” said Phex. But the net around him went stiff and FTL kicked in at that moment.

Space folded in and warped around them, and the bottom dropped out of the universe.

Tyve had once explained how FTL worked to them, back in their big dorm on Divinity 36. She’d picked up one of the many throw blankets and used it as a prop. “It processes dark matter into energy and uses that as fuel to dimensionally fold space. Pretend this is two dimensions.” She tucked two hands under the blanket, one at either edge, then brought the two edges together. “Now just imagine it’s inside three dimensions and the fold is into four. I know it’s difficult, but essentially that’s how it works. That’s why it has to be done in a void, if there’s too much stuff floating in space nearby, it’s like crumbs on this blanket, gets carried along or even dropped out of space entirely.”

“To where?” asked Phex.

Tyve shrugged. “Who knows.”

"Okay." Phex hadn't really understood. Suspected he would need way more smarts and education to do so fully, but he grasped the basic principle in play.

"Just like that, you accept it?" Tyve was impressed.

Phex shrugged. "It's like Missit."

"What?"

"Have you never noticed that he folds the space around him?"

"I think that's just for you, Phex."

"Is it?" Phex had then wondered if he was the blanket that Missit took with him intentionally, or if he were one of the crumbs accidentally along for the ride that would end up lost in the folds of Missit's life.

But now, now they were on the same ship, folding the same space. It made Phex think Missit was a lot more intentional than he first realized.

He had believed Missit was a chaotic, capricious god – willful and feckless. Yet somehow Phex was now an understudy for Missit's partner, and their pantheons were on tour together. How much of that was Missit's doing? How much of it was the divinity? How much of it was the acolytes trying to keep Missit happy and Tillam functional?

Phex lay on his tiny cot and looked up through his net at the underside of the bunk above, swaying slightly. Knowing Tyve was there gave him comfort. But knowing that Missit was nearby gave Phex *more* comfort. And he couldn't process why. His feelings around Missit were soft and squishy and difficult to grasp hold of and analyze.

So, he stuffed them down and trembled with the ship as space reconfigured itself around them.

It was not Phex's first fold. But that didn't mean he enjoyed it. He knew it was something he would have to grow accustomed to. As gods, Asterism would travel around much of the known galaxy. So, he better learn to tolerate FTL as soon as possible.

It was odd, though. Phex had lived all his life in space, but it was only during FTL that he became fully aware that there was *something* ever present around him. It was like becoming suddenly aware of an internal organ, his liver, for example, except it was all around his body rather than inside of it. The dark matter, and Phex assumed that is what it was – or maybe it was the dark energy – folded down and inside of itself, and in doing so dragged Phex's cellular makeup and consciousness along with it.

It was like being unmade all the way down to his atoms and then reformed, but a little bit changed, wrinkled. Phex always felt, reemerging light-years away in another part of space, as if he needed to be smoothed out. It always took a while to resurface into reality. In class, a teacher had once said that folding space was like dividing the human body by zero, undefined and imaginary at the same time. Speculative. Partly, this was because the brain could not conceive of infinity, but it could survive becoming infinite, for a finite moment in time.

That same fold – the one that buckled space – it also bent time into a loop on itself. In order to move great distances, one had to lose time, be everywhere and nowhere, every-time and no-time at all – simultaneously.

Very few minds could understand it. Phex didn't bother to try. It was better not to fight FTL travel. So, he attempted to relax and let himself expand and contract again. Resolving to deal with all the wrinkles later.

3

THE PHEX OF THE MATTER

They resurfaced slowly. Phex felt the net relax around him first and then everything else followed. He wasn't sure where they were, but at least they were once again *somewhere.*

Tyve, the most accustomed to FTL, was the first to get her mind back. She tumbled out of her bunk, and Phex watched it fold away into the wall above him.

She looked down at him out of friendly red eyes. "You good?"

He grunted at her.

She stood on the edge of his bunk to look into the top one. "You okay, Jin?"

"Can you check to see if my brain is oozing out my left crest?" asked the Dyesi, sounding only half-joking.

"First fold?" asked Tyve, sympathetically.

"That obvious?" replied Jinyesun.

Phex couldn't see, but he guessed that the sifter's ear crests were very wilted.

"Stay lying down for a bit, okay? It will take you a while to get everything back in order."

Tyve jumped down and turned to Fandina in the middle bunk on the other side. "Your first, too?"

Fandina clicked at her, weak and pathetic-sounding.

Phex unstrapped himself and stood, ignoring his own unsettled balance out of concern for his Dyesi. He looked at Jin – definitely wilted – then stood next to Tyve. "You look a bit pink, Fandina. Are you okay?"

A slightly stronger click.

Phex pursed his lips.

Tyve had the emotional calluses of a longtime traveler. "You'll be fine. Kagee?"

Kagee had the lowest bunk in the other row. He was grey and sour-faced by habit, so it was difficult to tell if he'd been adversely affected by the fold. He wasn't the type to show it, even if he were.

"Move, you big lugs, lemme up."

Phex rotated toward the door and Tyve toward the porthole so Kagee could unstrap, stand up, and fold away his bunk.

If he wasn't fine, he was making a good-enough show of it for Phex not to care.

Berril poked her head over the top bunk above Fandina and smiled down at them.

"Birdie?" asked Tyve with a pointy grin.

"I'm hungry!" Berril, looking far too cheerful for a recent FTL survivor, made big eyes at Phex. "Feed me!"

Tyve lifted her easily down, using one of their regular grace maneuvers. It was now quite crowded with so many standing and other bunks still down.

Phex figured now was a good a time as ever to try annexing part of the galley for his own, so he led the way toward the galley.

To Phex's disappointment, they had to find and wake up

the ship's chef to fix something for them. He wasn't allowed to just rattle about the tiny kitchen on his own. Luckily, the crew of six all quartered together, and Asterism knew where from the tour.

Phex was suitably apologetic and used it as an excuse to obtain direct kitchen access in the future.

Chef Korpuna – "Just call me *chef*" – was a curt older Cotylan. That meant she was an HS1-class Sapien. Her tinkering was just subtle enough to be difficult to distinguish from *regular* Sapiens. To Phex, she simply looked like a slightly odd non-Wheel human of the type he would have meet any day on Attacon 7.

She dismissed their obsequious apologies for disturbing her with a wave, saying everyone had their own stomach schedules, and she was accustomed to rockstars. Then marched them double-time back to the galley.

Phex offered to help, and while she declined, she seemed pleased to have been asked. He made plans to keep doing it until she let him into her kitchen.

She prepared them a quick cold meal of Dyesi staples that they were all too familiar with at this juncture, plus some dried fruit and nuts, and water to drink. A healthy nutritional meal for demigods recovering from surgery and FTL.

When Phex gently pressed Berril's chiropteran needs, the chef showed them where snacks were kept for future reference and indicated the meal plan and posted schedule.

"Oh, it's the middle of nightshift," said Tyve. "Sorry about that, chef."

"You didn't know," repeated the chef with a soft smile.

"We won't do it again," said Berril in a small voice, looking pathetic.

The chef was not immune to Berril's charms. "Don't worry about it, sweetie. I know how your lot get. Tiny bones, fast metabolism, and hungry all the time. You saw there was a sweets section just for you?"

Berril gave her a winsome look. "I did. Thank you so much for looking out for me. It's all very tasty."

Phex thought she was laying it on a bit thick, but the chef lapped it up. He understood. Nothing was better than having the people you were feeding feel spoiled over being fed.

The chef instructed Phex in how to clean and put away the utensils when they were done and then thanked him sincerely for his future diligence. She then retreated, presumably back to her bunk.

They were left alone to eat together unsupervised in the small seating area. Tillam were still asleep – apparently, they'd already taken pains to adjust to the ship's cycle. Phex wondered if his pantheon should try to set themselves on the swing shift so they didn't have to share facilities with the great gods. Or if it would be better for crew if they were on the same schedule? He thought maybe he should ask an acolyte about that.

Tillam's bodyguards were off doing whatever they did when their charges were safely sleeping. Phex hoped to meet them all later. He knew, and liked, a few of them already. Itrio, Fortew's guard, had given him defensive training. Skills that had helped his pantheon once already. He owed her and Elder K, Zil's guard who had arranged the whole thing.

Asterism would get their one pathetic bodyguard at some point during the tour, hopefully before they debuted. It wasn't considered necessary until they began appearing under domes. Until then, Phex would do what was needed. Checking in with the bodyguards was at the top of his mental to-do list.

"I have an announcement to make," said Kagee, about halfway through their meal. "I'm sorry I never told you sooner. I was embarrassed. It is a terrible thing, on my planet."

"You don't have to tell us anything you don't want to," said Berril quickly.

"It's not that, because it's all out in the open now. It's the sterilization thing." Kagee stared at their two Dyesi with accusation in his eyes. "The divinity would have done it to us without asking."

Jinyesun and Fandina both crested at Kagee, waiting and curious.

Finally, Jinyesun asked, clearly mystified, "You are *upset* about this?"

"You wanted offspring *and* godhood at the same time?" Fandina was also confused.

"That is not allowed." Jin used the Dyesi formal language indicating moral imperative.

"Why?" wondered Berril.

"Divided loyalties," explained Fandina.

"I get it," said Kagee. "But you still should ask verbally before giving sterilization surgery. It is not a matter of aesthetics like the rest of what you do to demigods."

"It's in your contract," protested Jinyesun.

"Told you," said Phex, chewing and untroubled. He figured this was all an excuse Kagee was using to get around to what he really wanted to talk to them all about.

"Phex doesn't look like *he* minds," said Jinyesun. It turned to Tyve and Berril. "Did you?"

"Like Phex, we both already were," said Tyve.

Jin looked closely at Kagee, trying to understand the nuance of Sapien behavior. "You alone were upset by this?"

"I was also already sterile. Only, I thought I was born that way. Turns out not. Turns out it was done to me without my knowledge by my own people."

"And this is what upsets you?"

"Of course!" Kagee looked at all of them as if he could not understand why they were not freaking out.

"But isn't that a good thing? Now you know it's surgical, it can be reversed if you want it later, or what have you?" Tyve was also confused.

Kagee glared at her.

Phex could see this devolving quickly. Kagee was terrible at expressing himself and Tyve was feeling feisty. They didn't need an argument – they needed Kagee to get to the point.

"So, it is something to do with the dome?" he interrupted.

Everyone stared at him. Phex so rarely took a role in guiding discussions, and this comment seemed to be a total non sequitur.

Phex was embarrassed. "Kagee warned me earlier he'd be discussing this with us."

"What does you being involuntarily sterilized prior to divine intervention have to do with our performance in a dome?" wondered Jinyesun, now even more confused.

"Because on Agatay, if you are born with protanopia, you are also supposedly born sterile. But I guess they just *tell* us they're genetically linked and then sterilize us as babies, instead."

"Protanopia?"

"I'm blind to colors."

"Your people *made* you *color-blind*?" Fandina looked like it was about to be sick. To a Dyesi that was true horror.

Kagee frowned. "No. Well, I doubt *that*. Wouldn't your medics have noticed? No, I mean they made me sterile *because* I was born color-blind."

"To prevent you from spreading the genetic defect?" Jinyesun looked as horrified as Fandina, but in classic fashion, Jin was more interested in understanding than shock.

"Completely color-blind?" wondered Phex, because how could Kagee understand the dome at all under those circumstances? Had he been faking it? How?

Kagee visibly shrank in on himself, glancing around at them warily. "No, just parts of the spectrum and levels of intensity. It's an accident of colonization. Too many color-blind humans in the original landing party. A high percentage of Agatay males, especially among elite families, are born with protanopia. I'm not entirely trapped in grayscale, but it makes distinguishing color nuances nearly impossible."

Tyve grinned. "Ex-core fucks up? How funny."

Kagee glared back. "Like being tinkered means you have no genetic abnormalities?"

"Touché."

"Wait. So, you're telling us that you can't experience the full range of the dome?" Fandina was still processing, crests flat back and cheeks clouded with opaque concern.

"That's terrible!" said Jinyesun, meaning it.

To the Dyesi who had built an entire economy on the colorful beauty of domes, to not see the full scope of the art that they displayed would seem a major tragedy.

Phex said only, "Makes sense." He was thinking about the time he had blasted the dome with orange and frozen the Dyesi where they sat. He'd managed to shock all the other aliens there, too. Only Kagee had been unaffected. Phex had thought it was because Kagee was too Sapien – now he knew Kagee just hadn't seen that color as *that* bright. Kagee was immune to Phex's vocal power and also Phex's mistakes. Phex kind of liked that. "You see the patterns, though?"

Kagee nodded. "If they're contrasted strongly enough."

Phex choose to be practical over being sympathetic. He wouldn't want pity – he assumed Kagee felt the same. "So I will help you compensate. You help me stay on top of patterns and songbruise. Deal?"

Kagee gave a small tight smile – it was genuine, though, it crinkled his eyes. "We already do a lot of that. You aren't mad at me?"

"Why would I be?"

"I lied by omission."

Phex considered. "It would have been nice to know sooner. But now I think it will make the dome a lot easier for us going forward."

"That's it?" Kagee looked around at the rest of them.

The other four didn't seem angry at him either.

The two Dyesi clearly just felt sorry for him. That he was limited in his ability to appreciate the dome, but they weren't upset at him.

Berril stood and approached Kagee sideways, like he was a suffering animal who might lash out. With any of the others, she would have instantly hugged him. But this was Kagee, so she just put a small hand on his arm. "Was it tough for you there? Did they abuse you for it? Your planet? Or…" She hesitated, then added, "Your family?"

Tyve suddenly looked like she wanted to kill someone. "Who needs to bleed on Agatay? Why would they hurt you for something you were born with?"

Kagee, of course, lashed out. Understanding was one thing, but pity was painful. "You are less interested in fighting than most Jakaa Nova, right? Were you not punished for that?"

Tyve looked confused. "But I've no physical defects. I'm just less aggressive than others of my species."

"And you don't think you were born like that? If violence were entirely a learned behavior, wouldn't you have acquired it from your family?"

In a quiet voice, Tyve said, "I never thought about it that way."

"Even if your inner spirit has no direct medical test that does not make it any less *you*."

Berril looked at Phex. "Why are we talking about Tyve and the Jakaa Nova all of a sudden?"

"Deflection," said Phex.

"Oh! Uh, Fandina? Do something."

Fandina, of course, did. "Thank you for telling us this, Kagee. Phex will help you compensate in the dome, and we will do whatever we can to help as well. Should we keep this information private to the pantheon?"

"You're willing to hide my defect from the acolytes?"

The two Dyesi exchanged crest wiggles.

"It could be argued that genetic testing for visual defects should be implemented as part of the intake medical exam. We should perhaps tell the acolytes *that*?" Jin was never one to voluntarily limit information exchange.

"They might ask *why* we recommend it, though," said Fandina.

Jinyesun clicked. "So, we wait until we are established gods with unshakeable worship bases, or even later, until we retire from the divinity?"

Phex filed away the interesting fact that Dyesi gods expected to *retire* eventually.

"I'm surprised they missed it," said Tyve.

"Why would they even think to test for it? Color blindness is such a throwback," said Kagee, "It's only planets like mine that even have the defect anymore. And there aren't many ex-core colonies who've survived into the modern age."

Fandina stiffened its crests in a decisive manner. "If it doesn't impact the divinity as a whole, the acolytes do not need to know." Its crest swiveled to point at Kagee. "Unless you think mass recruitment from your planet is likely?"

"Gods, no," said Kagee fervently.

"Then we wait to tell the others," said Fandina.

Jinyesun clicked agreement. "You are turning me into a rebel like you," it accused the other Dyesi.

"Loyalty is an interesting emotion," replied Fandina, as though it had considered only the practical repercussions of choosing between pantheon and divinity.

Kagee looked annoyed by the philosophical bent the conversation had taken but was also, clearly, relieved.

Jinyesun asked Phex, "Is there something else we should do or say for Kagee's peace of mind?"

As if Phex should know.

But Phex was still curious about something. "Do you really think Agatay did this to you because you're color-blind? Sterilization, I mean?"

Kagee frowned. "That's what I'm afraid of. We're taught the one leads to the other. Protans are born infertile. Only, we aren't. So, why do that to us? To me? Just so we won't breed? Or do they want proxies that much? In which case, why did they let me escape?"

"Those answers are all only available on Agatay," said Phex. Because what was the point in asking them such questions?

"You would have to go back to find out." Tyve sounded scared, like she thought Kagee actually would abandon them. Just up and leave Asterism, because of some mystery in his past.

Jinyesun crested at Kagee. "Is this an instrument of mortality? Will you abandon godhood to return home now?"

Fandina went opaque with worry.

"Never," said Kagee, firmly.

Phex would have guessed he'd say that. Because Phex understood. He was never going home again either. They were exiles together, him and Kagee. More similar than he'd ever realized. Phex had been outcast because his brain rejected an implant, because his genetics had been triggered so far, his body overreacted to intrusions. Because, by Wheel standards, he was defective. Kagee was the same – defective.

They were both demigods by accident of genetics. But then, wasn't that the nature of godhood? Even Fandina and Jinyesun were there because their skin was better at sifting than other Dyesi's. More sensitive. More receptive to cantor. Stronger at projecting onto the dome. Traits that once might have cost them survival and were now highly prized.

"None of us are going anywhere," Phex said firmly.

Fandina crested at him. "Quite right. Instead, let's go practice."

Tillam's cruiser eased into Syruni space gradually and after only the one FTL fold required to traverse between star sectors. Which meant Syrunid was comparatively close to Dyesi space. Phex supposed that was all intentional. Better to start a tour gradually. Especially as Asterism was new and recovering from surgery and Tillam was limping along with Fortew unwell.

Phex didn't know much about the Syruni, but it was better to enter alien space with either caution or fanfare. As gods, they used both. They would progress through the local star systems sedately, and the Syruni news would report excitedly on their progress.

Tillam was coming.

Tillam would arrive soon.

Wasn't Syrunid lucky?

Tillam would be performing for them.

Tillam.

And a small but increasingly vocal group of worshipers made certain everyone also knew that a new pantheon, Asterism, would be debuting as Tillam's opening act. Mysterious but highly talented, the misfit demigods of the divinity, Asterism already had a reputation merely by virtue of their membership. To have a chiropteran was unique enough, but Kagee was ex-core. The first ex-core god ever. And no one knew what Phex was, but rumors of his crazy voice were rampant.

Then the divinity leaked the fact that Tyve was Zil's younger sister, and excitement went into supernova mode. Zil, as Tillam's dark grace, had millions of believers. There was something about a sibling relationship that gave all of his worshipers tacit permission to also believe in Tyve. Normally, believers were devoted to only one god, but apparently, exceptions could be made for genetic relatives.

Had the divinity known that would happen? Were they *that* manipulative?

The Dyesi had different notions of family, so Phex wasn't sure they were that targeted or intentional. But Tyve's sudden popularity certainly gave Asterism a major boost, pushing their graces to the front as the most searched-for and believed-in gods of the new pantheon. Phex wasn't sure he should be grateful, but he was relieved it wasn't his name as the top keyword anymore.

Even if he wanted to, there was nothing Phex could do to stop any of it. The word was out about Asterism. The divine forums buzzed with speculation. Over the space of one sleep cycle, their popularity surged. An acolyte told them excitedly that they had the fastest worshiper onboarding of any demigod group in the history of the divinity, and they hadn't even debuted yet!

Meanwhile, they practiced.

They had only three weeks, so they practiced with unprecedented intensity. Even though they'd been told to rest, they could still rehearse cantor and sifting that first week.

As Kagee said, "They didn't futz with our voices."

"Or our skin," added Fandina.

So, Jinyesun, Phex, Kagee, and Fandina camped out in the sifting booths and practiced tons. Kagee even began scribbling away at a new original godsong. He had, as it turned out, a gift for composition. The graces were pretty bored, although they came in with the others, just to make sure they knew the songs. An acolyte did spend time putting them through physical therapy and mild weight training to make sure they didn't get too out of shape. Then they made Kagee and Phex do it too.

As soon as they were officially deemed *medically recovered*, Asterism started in on the most rigorous schedule they'd ever had. That was saying a lot, since things had been very intense at the end of their potential training on Divinity 36.

Asterism was going to debut with half original godsongs and half covers of other pantheon's work. They had no other choice. They wouldn't be re-sifting any of Tillam's songs, of course, but instead had selected three from lesser-known gods. They were also given three original songs to work on, and they had to practice hard to turn these into something not just beautiful on the dome but quintessentially theirs. For Asterism, this meant switching roles around and having Phex grace while Tyve sang cantor and exploring all the ways they could turn their unique abilities into Asterism's signature.

Perhaps that was ambitious. As Fandina took pains to remind them, this was only their first public dome and they were opening for Tillam. Really, they just needed to be passing pretty, inoffensive, and not muddy Tillam's colors.

Phex had thought Asterism would practice during one of the off shifts, but instead, they practiced part of day shift at the same time as Tillam, and all of swing shift, and occasionally into the night as well. One of the three acolytes aboard was always on hand to monitor them. Phex wasn't sure if that was to push them or stop them from pushing themselves too hard. Either way, the acolyte on duty always made suggestions, tweaking their performance subtly one way or another.

The three acolytes aboard the ship with them had clearly been chosen with this express skill set in mind. They were nameless, like most acolytes, and rather difficult to tell apart, but Jin said with confident pride that they were all specialists, or diefthyn acolytes, who focused on the artistic side of the divinity. Apparently, it was an honor to have three of them, as the three were chosen expressly to provide the kind of help Tillam did *not* need. So they'd been assigned to the ship because of Asterism. Phex thought that this all sounded very expensive.

All three were confident in their direction and suggestions for choreography changes or singing and composition adjustments. It was actually impressive. Asterism stretched and improved markedly under their focused guidance. But it wasn't easy on anyone.

It was physically exhausting and mentally taxing. The acolytes were there to push Asterism to perform as well and as quickly as possible – they barely concerned themselves with Tillam at all.

Not that they needed to.

Tillam had been dominating domes for over a decade. Why interfere with perfection?

When they saw Tillam at all, Asterism were all so tired, they couldn't even manage awe, just the general respect due to elders in the same professional sphere.

Tillam didn't seem to mind, thank goodness. To be fair, Missit and Zil had hung out with Asterism semi-regularly back on Divinity 36, and Fortew was generally easygoing, when he wasn't on bed rest. Tillam's light grace, Tern, was mild-tempered and rather shy, and their two sifters seemed mostly just cool and indifferent.

What it came down to was that if Tillam was already in a practice room or the baby dome, Asterism used other facilities. Otherwise, they barely saw each other.

Tillam didn't need to practice much. They'd been doing this a long time and hadn't added anything new for this tour. It was a pickup from the tour they'd had to cut short when Fortew got diagnosed a year before. Besides, Fortew couldn't manage new content. They did, however, need to practice with Phex on occasion.

This was done seamlessly. Occasionally, when he was practicing with Kagee, or in the sifting room, an acolyte would simply appear and escort him away and to the small dome.

Whoever he left behind would go find the rest of Asterism, and Phex would spend a few hours on the dais, singing color with Tillam in Fortew's stead, while his own pantheon made do without him.

Phex had to learn to accommodate and meld with Tillam's choreography so he didn't break the graces' rhythm, but he drew the line at learning Fortew's part exactly. His voice wasn't Fortew's, it was his own. He already knew the songs by heart, Tillam was famous for a reason, but Phex wasn't the same kind of low cantor, so the dome that resulted was never going to match Tillam's original dome style. He wasn't a vocal mimic. Phex with Tillam meant something else. Something new. So far as Phex was concerned, everyone was going to have to learn to accept that fact. Including the legions of worshipers.

The acolytes seemed to be okay with this. They knew that Phex was a patch for a terrible situation. They hoped they wouldn't actually have to *use* him on Tillam's dais. But they weren't so stupid they didn't realize that he might be required and that he must be trained and prepared. It was just they didn't like it.

But Tillam's sifters were not so relaxed about the situation. Yorunlee and Melalan didn't like that they had to practice with Phex. They *really* didn't like that he refused to simply be a poor imitation of Fortew. Even Zil and Term seemed to find his presence irritating and tiring.

In fact, nobody liked the situation.

Phex didn't like being taken away from his pantheon who desperately needed him to prepare for their debut. Asterism wasn't Tillam – seamless elder gods who had been performing for over a decade. Asterism was new and nervous and they needed their sun.

Phex also didn't like the hostility, real or imagined, that Tillam gave him in exchange for his time. He was doing them a favor, in his mind anyway. He was physically capable of doing what was required but Yorunlee and Melalan acted as if it were his fault Fortew were sick. As though he wanted to be there, the poor shadow of a great god rather than a demigod in his own right. They blamed him for not being Fortew.

Except Missit.

Missit clearly missed his cantor partner but also never once tried to hide how happy he was to have Phex share a dais with him.

Because Missit could sing a dome no matter what. Sing it

in a way that was as close to magic as art could get – effortless. Phex wasn't Fortew, so he didn't balance him or hold him back or mute him. He didn't honor Missit's voice with temperance. He wouldn't even know how. Instead, he amplified it. Phex was a low cantor with power. Like Missit, his strength as a vocalist was in the colors and their saturation rather than the pattern. The two of them singing together often – too often for the acolytes' comfort – maxed every spectrum out on that tiny dome.

The sifters, aged and experienced, could handle it. The graces too – Zil and Tern were sometimes mildly amused by the vibrancy. But the dome shuddered under the weight of the intensity, and the acolytes, when that happened, got scared. Phex and Missit, singing together, were too much. While everyone knew it had to be done – Missit and Phex *had* to learn how to produce a viable dome just in case Fortew failed – no Dyesi liked watching that experiment in action.

An acolyte would put Phex into play on the dais. Missit would be all smiles and the rest of Tillam all enmity. And that acolyte would be crests-back and opaque skin before they even started. And it never stayed to watch, that acolyte. It poked its head in briefly to observe once or twice, but it never stayed in the dome like it did when Phex practiced with Asterism.

And it made it absolutely clear to the bodyguards that they and the crew were to stay far away from that dome.

Phex enjoyed that part of it. The fear of his voice. Not sure what it said about his personality that he felt pleasure in acolyte terror. But he always tried to follow their notes when they were issued afterwards.

Pull back, Phex. Tone it down. You too, Missit. You should know better. It's not good for the dome. It's not good for the divinity.

"Why?" Phex wanted to ask.

But he didn't. Because in part, he could tell. Even as the notes left his mouth, he knew they were too much. He remembered all too well what had happened when he and Missit first sang like that together under a larger dome.

There had been an audience then. No real congregation, just an audience of mostly Dyesi. All those acolytes, just sitting, frozen into immobility and paralyzed by song. What he and Missit could do under a dome might not be good for that dome. And it might not be good for the divinity. But it *definitely* wasn't good for the Dyesi.

Phex managed the extra practice better than he thought, partly because with Missit it was a lot less work. It was even a little bit fun. For a slightly bonkers god, Missit had excellent control. Phex didn't have to monitor himself as closely as he did with Kagee. He could just sing those old familiar godsongs, the ones he had heard a million times back when he was a lowly barista on a forgotten moon.

He didn't brag about it or comment on it to his pantheon, but even with the extra understudy work, he never got as sore as they did. Sometimes, it even seemed like he had more energy by the end of a shift. The genetics that had betrayed his youth were now working in his favor.

Still, when Missit tried to get him alone after practice or drag him off to the side at mealtime to flirt, Phex pretended exhaustion. It was this that pushed him too far, this that made it all too much – Missit wanting to be yet another thing Phex had to handle and keep safe. Missit wanting him, not for his voice but because he saw something even more valuable in Phex. Worth that Phex doubted existed at all.

If Missit took that as a rejection or a coolness, he didn't show it. He kept up his relentless flirting, as if any wall Phex erected was just a dome for him to bounce his colors off of.

"You're exhausting," Phex said to him one night when all twelve of them were having dinner together, slightly overwhelming both the chef and the galley capacity.

Missit arched coy golden brows. "But in the best possible way, of course."

Phex pushed some water at him – the boy never seemed to be hydrating properly.

Missit cocked his head in a way that indicated he was about to be outrageous. "We sing well together, how well do you think we dance?"

Phex reached for more pickle. "You've seen me grace."

"Not grace, *dance*. Proper partner dancing. You know, like normal people do at weddings, and funerals, and the like. *Dance* dancing."

"Missit, darling, I don't think people dance at funerals," said Fortew, mildly amused. Phex noticed he never ate very much, but he seemed to enjoy socializing, even though he was obviously more frail and tired than anyone else each night.

Kagee said, quietly, "We dance for the dead on Agatay."

"And does that confer sufficient honor upon the deceased?" wondered Jinyesun.

"Depends on the quality of the choreography, I suppose" —Kagee paused— "and the dancer."

Phex was still genuinely confused. "But what does it *look* like, if not grace?"

Tyve laughed and pulled up a vid via her ident. "Like this." Two Sapiens of some ilk did a thing together that was kind of like grace partner work but more exactly rhythmic and clearly not designed to influence the music or have any effect on a dome. More passive reaction to sound being played. It looked pretty but not all that complex.

Phex wrinkled his nose. "Why? What purposes does that

serve?" He looked over at Kagee, not wanting to insult him. "If no one has died, of course."

Missit was not to be dissuaded. "It doesn't have to have a reason, Phex. Sometimes, we dance just for enjoyment. I think it would be fun. Obviously, you have a great sense of rhythm, so we should dance together, like people do outside of the divinity. Like we're normal Sapiens, you and I."

"But we aren't normal."

Zil and Tyve both laughed. Siblings, same sense of humor.

"You need to broaden your perspective, Phex," insisted Missit.

Phex thought that was rich, coming from someone who'd been raised inside the divinity since he was a child and never once left it.

"You're big enough to pick me up and flip me around and stuff," Missit added, seeming charmed by the idea.

"Because Phex needs more to do when he's already filling in for you and practicing with us." Kagee no longer felt any awe at all in Missit's presence. Not that he'd had much to start with. Still, his tone was almost informal.

Yorunlee flattened its crests at him.

Fandina put a hand on Kagee's wrist to urge caution.

Missit narrowed his eyes at the grey boy. "Is he training with Itrio too?"

Kagee looked suspiciously at Phex. "Not that I know of."

Phex stood and went into the galley. He was only managing a half hour or so each day with the bodyguards, but he *was* getting in some time with them. He didn't want to slack off. But he also wanted to do whatever would make Missit happy. If Missit wanted to dance with him, whatever that meant, Phex would eventually dance with him. Of course he would.

The chef casually began sharing the cleanup workload with him. They performed their own dance together in that tiny kitchen, putting things away. Phex enjoyed it and found it restful. He and the chef were getting along so well, she'd designated a small upper part of cabinet space just for him. There Phex could store a few spices and eventually, he hoped, utensils. She'd even taken to putting one or two ingredients in there for him to find and enjoy when she wasn't around. He was honored by her thoughtfulness.

"You're not avoiding this that easily, Phex," said Kagee, swiveling to direct his voice at the kitchen from the sitting area. Not that he needed to in such a tiny space. "Fess up. Do you have time to dance with Missit, or are you overbooked already?"

Phex was a sucker where Missit was concerned, and he knew it. "I guess I could take one evening off from bodyguard training."

Missit looked pleased.

Kagee growled.

Fortew shook his head, chuckling softly.

"See? He *was* adding in fight training. Pay up," Tyve said to Kagee as if they'd already had an argument about it.

Kagee passed over his portion of their mutually favorite dessert with an annoyed look. Well, more annoyed than normal.

Missit and the rest of Tillam watched this action with interest.

"Your sun is hard to control?" wondered Melalan, expressing interest in Asterism for the first time.

"Very," said Kagee, annoyed.

"He is powerful," said Yorunlee. It wasn't a compliment.

"But easily manipulated," said Zil, grinning at his sister and pointing at Missit with one claw, as if he were proud of his friend's ability to convince Phex to do whatever Missit wanted.

The chef patted Phex's big shoulder in a consoling way. Phex made a sad face at her. She grinned.

"Is that manipulation," wondered Tyve, "or being led around by his—"

Zil interrupted before she could finish that remark. "Careful, sister mine, little Dyesi have big crests. The divinity is always listening."

Tyve closed her mouth and rolled her red eyes.

"So, that's settled. We dance, old-style?" pushed Missit. Because he was nothing if not pushy.

Phex continued puttering about the kitchen and didn't answer.

"That is really annoying, you know?" said Missit, losing a tiny bit of his cool.

Phex stayed quiet.

"Tomorrow? Same practice room the bodyguards use, we'll just kick them out for a bit?"

Phex clicked agreement. Because what else could he do? He was going to fold eventually – he might as well get it over with.

4

THROUGH HELL AND HIGH CANTOR

When Missit made up his mind he wanted something to happen, it happened. Gods were like that. Accordingly, at the end of a long double shift, Phex found himself in the grace's practice room with a high cantor who wanted to dance and music playing.

Just music. Not godsong.

It was some kind of Sapien-invented something or another with instruments and singers. Phex had heard music before, of course, but he wasn't particularly familiar with the art form. He'd heard very little of anything on the space station of his childhood and worked in a divine cafe on a moon after that, so that had all been godsong. Of course, there was stuff in the infonet and such, but music simply wasn't his thing.

"My parents are musical anthropologists," explained Missit, even though Phex hadn't asked. Perhaps he looked curious. Phex thought that was unlikely – he hadn't that kind of face. Missit just liked to explain things to him.

"That is how we ended up on Dyesid Prime in the first place, back when I was a baby. They wanted to study the cultural music practices of the cave dwellers and ended up being in at the start of everything."

"And they put you into the divinity?"

Missit clicked agreement. "Best way to understand what was going on was from the inside out. Since they themselves were considered too old, it had to be me."

"Oh, it had to be, did it?" Phex considered this. "Do you still report to them about what it's like to be a god?" *After ten years? Like a cultural spy?*

"Not anymore. We're still in touch. I don't blame them or anything."

"Blame them? For what?"

"Of course you wouldn't find it objectionable or confusing."

Phex didn't think that deserved a verbal answer. He wished that he had crests so he could wiggle them sarcastically at Missit.

Missit made a funny face at the silence, wide mouth twisted. Then filled that silence. "I was ten when I sang my first godsong, that idea doesn't horrify you?" His sharp up-tilted nose was so cute when it wrinkled like that – too large by Dyesi standards, but Phex still found it cute.

Phex shook his head, the long weight of his new hair swishing about heavy and silken and still unfamiliar. "I was six when I ran my first blades. The dais is a whole lot safer. You're a god and were always treated as one. Why should your age or origin matter?"

Missit huffed in surprise. "Sapiens often find it objectionable to start professionally entertaining so young. It's not considered very nurturing."

"Do *you* feel bad about it?" Phex wondered.

"I've been told I should."

"But do you actually?"

"I don't…" Missit paused, frowning hard, the mannerism so entirely not Dyesi, it almost sat ill on his face. "I don't know."

Phex decided to change the subject. "So, this music. We dance to it?"

"Ah, yes, let me show you how. My parents taught me as a child. They thought it was important to give me a thorough education in the musical arts. It's their field of research, after all. You know I can even play a few stringed instruments?"

Phex blinked at him. That seemed arbitrary and somewhat useless as skill sets went. But he thought that saying so might be considered rude.

Missit shook his head. "Is there anything you find admirable? Gods, you're hard to please."

Phex thought that was unfair. He admired lots of things about lots of people. He liked lots of things about lots of people, too. Especially his pantheon. Especially Missit. It was possible he liked too many things about Missit.

The golden god beckoned him over. "Come on. Stand up and come here. I put the music on a loop. Let's just see what we can do."

Phex did as commanded.

It wasn't all that different from gracing, or it was different, but Phex could use grace training to learn to dance. Instead of catch-and-release and perfected moves the beat and motions of which became godsong, he and Missit moved together with the song and with each other – reacting rather than contributing.

Missit taught him about something called *the frame* which employed a body-resistance technique. Phex had to learn how to fold against and follow where Missit led and then to lead in turn. Once he got the pattern of it and the way he could mold and lean their bodies against one another, it was, as Missit had said it would be, a lot of fun. A little like Berril's cuddling, only in movement form. There was a kind of joy in moving his muscles for no other reason than to follow an established rhythm. His body had no work to do for the song like when gracing, and no work to do for the blades, as it had had when a crudrat. His body just had to play with Missit's and with the music.

Missit issued an instruction to the net feed to the room, and so the music changed to something new. Phex followed him into a different kind of dance, different pace, different pattern to the steps, faster with sharper movements. Center of gravity higher up, movements lighter. And from there into another, different one, deeper in the knees, slower and with more liquid movements.

In a way it was a bit like sparring with one of the bodyguards. Just like when sparring, Phex used Missit's momentum to roll them both into something else. In a fight, this would have been a throw or block, but in dancing, it became a lift or a twirl. He could pick up Missit and spin him around, as if he were Berril. Or sometimes he would support Missit into a leap or a jump, as if he were Tyve. They became each other's springboard at times, or traded weight to mirror or synchronize. They were communicating in a private language that was neither spoken nor sung.

It was as if they were making gentle mockery of each another with their bodies. There was certainly some grace to it, the old-fashioned kind – in the fluid extension of limbs and the float of fingertips, in the curl of toes and the stretch of legs. The curve of Missit's neck and the arch of his back was all grace, painful in its subtle beauty of contorted form. Phex liked all of it – in that way anyone likes a new thing because they are good at it without trying.

Phex's bones had been crafted for action, and this was

action as art, no purpose but showing off his remastered genetics in motion and the flesh that made him formless.

Missit moved against him at one point, and the music paused them into a clutched shape of whimsy. At the silence, Missit collapsed all of his weight onto Phex, so Phex had to catch and support him using his whole body.

At first, Phex thought this was injury, but then he realized it was intentional. Missit desired to be pressed fully against him, warm and curved into complementary shapes. It was lovely, to rest like that in an intimate space were bodies were molded but minds were still free floating from the pleasure of creation.

Too lovely.

Phex brought himself back to the reality of a practice room on a spaceship and a god in his embrace.

Missit was looking up at him with huge, begging eyes.

Phex jerked away, but that made Missit unstable and likely to genuinely fall. So, Phex caught the golden god back up and supported him. They stopped dancing, frozen in that moment while the music continued on without them. It felt dimensionless and lonely.

Missit was amused. “You can’t even get repulsed by me properly. Always driven to be the support.”

“You’re testing me?”

“I’m testing your resolve.”

Phex didn’t get that, but he did know that he was weak in the face of whatever Missit wanted. Which is why he was now in this awkward position – supporting a god in a room together while music he did not understand reminded him of all the things he did not know he wanted.

Phex put Missit firmly back onto his feet and let go.

Missit could fall if he wanted. But this way, it would be his choice.

The god stood strong, head tilted. Swaying his arms slightly, as if when the music played, it was impossible for him not to move some part of himself with it.

Phex realized then that they had been dancing for a long time. They were both glossed with sweat. He was very thirsty. Missit was probably thirsty too, except he always forgot to drink. Phex also realized that he was a little turned on, which was inconvenient at best and embarrassing at worst. Not illogical, though – he defied any creature in existence to spend time holding a god close in one way or another and not *want* something from it. Even the Dyesi, who apparently felt no sexual desire, still desired things of the gods. Gods brought with them sensuality, for all the Dyesi could not see and did not understand. That was part of the appeal.

Phex's desire for Missit was obviously just proximity to a god and a side effect of full-contact dancing.

Phex told himself this firmly. Almost managed to convince himself. He was, after all, of an age when desire leapt forward because of nothing more than a hand touch or a nice smell, and he and Missit had just been doing a lot more than that. It wasn't like he could control either of their instincts.

Phex should probably get accustomed to this kind of thing, as they were on tour together.

Then Phex realized that they had an audience.

The curtain at the entrance of the practice room was pulled back and faces were poking in and around the frame.

Tyve and Zil were there, plus Berril and, of all people, Fortew, who wore a funny half-pained expression, mixed in with what could only be called *awe.* His eyes looked very tired, bruised in his pretty heart-shaped face, as if that awe was the only thing that kept him able to focus. The chef and the captain of the ship were there too, and Itrio, Phex's bodyguard friend, stood toward the back. All of them looked impressed and entertained. Phex was enough of a performer to be pleased by this. There were no acolytes or sifters present, not even Jinyesun, who was generally curious about other cultures. Apparently, music and dance that were not godsong did not rank as interesting to Dyesi.

"That was *amazing*," breathed out Berril, high-pitched with delight.

"Phex, I thought you said you couldn't dance." Tyve looked equally impressed.

Zil said, "Oh he probably couldn't until they started. Missit is like that."

But Missit, being Missit, didn't care that they had an appreciative audience, didn't even look at them, just stood grinning up at Phex. "Did you like it? Dancing?"

"They liked it. Isn't that what matters?"

"No, it isn't. Not here. Not on a dais or under a dome, either." Missit pressed two fingers gently into the notch at the base of Phex's throat. "You have to love it or none of it works. *You* do. Not them."

Phex thought about this statement. He had enjoyed dancing with Missit, but he didn't like how much his body had enjoyed Missit's proximity, and that was beyond his control. And he didn't really like the fact that others had been watching them, which was also beyond his control. It felt like something intimate they'd been doing together that had been intruded upon. It made him feel dirty. He certainly didn't want to experience a sensation of being exposed in every performance in front of millions. He really hoped a big dome wasn't at all like dancing with Missit.

"Did *you* like it? Dancing with me?" Phex asked the god.

"I liked the lifts. They felt like flying. I liked the way we move together. It's easy to sync to you, even though we are not the same size – it feels more like a shell or a reflection than a pair." He raised up on his toes, leaning casually on Phex's shoulder. They had been touching nonstop for over an hour, but this felt different, proprietary. His voice was warm gold in Phex's ear. "I like this."

Phex glanced at him, suspicious. What did Missit want from him now? What new form of trickster was this facet of the golden god-boy? Like a prism, Missit seemed to have so many.

Missit just stood still and silent for a change, almost holding his breath, staring at Phex from right up close. His sharp nose like a blade, his wide mouth slightly open, full lips parted.

As if… *what*?

As if Phex were something multifaceted and surprising too?

As if Missit was scared by what Phex could do?

As if Phex were the godly one.

As if Phex were the risk.

The threat.

Phex rubbed at the side of his neck. Confused and a little hurt. What was going on? What did Missit really need from him? Phex would figure out a way to give it to him, of course, but he needed to know what it was first. Was this hunger? He wondered if he'd stashed snacks anywhere. They may have missed a meal at some point, which might explain the chef in their audience.

He found himself cupping the back of Missit's head, beneath the coiled silken hair. Like one might comfort a child. If Phex had any experience with children. Which he didn't.

Missit moved even closer, still on tiptoe. Reached back himself and cupped the back of Phex's head, mirroring him.

Phex's hair was down and tangled now, heavy and little sweaty, but it hid the intimacy of that hand.

Missit leaned his whole body against him. Phex braced himself easily to support the weight – it was second nature after their dance.

Missit's lips were a surprise. Warm, and smooth, and briefly pressed to his, hesitant in a very un-Missit-like way – he who wasn't hesitant about anything.

Phex flinched, ducked his chin, then tilted his head back. Wondering if this all had been a terrible mistake. Still feeling the soft slight dampness of unexpected lips.

Missit responded by jerking away, but Phex was still providing a frame, so he couldn't get far.

Phex processed that Missit wasn't hungry, not for food, anyway. He wondered at that. At the sensation of being wanted. His first kiss. He'd liked it, what little there had been – the spiced salt of someone else's skin. He wanted to taste again. Badly.

The intensity of that sudden, unadulterated *want* terrified him. Phex, who had never really wanted anything or anyone before, or if he had, would not remember the sensation for the repression that automatically followed.

Not this time. This time, there was someone else to consider. He examined Missit's face. It was… *what*? Tired, crestfallen, embarrassed, uncomfortable.

What a ridiculous creature to think anyone would ever reject him.

But also the cost, to do this in front of an audience.

Phex considered his options – the sweat cooling on his skin itched and prickled. Or maybe that was the gaze of watchers.

He wondered if this was just another risk being taken by a capricious god. If Phex was yet another mistake Missit wanted to make. Like walking around without a bodyguard. Or climbing into a stranger's bed. A new means of testing old boundaries.

Phex decided he didn't care if he was a lapse in godly judgment, since he was holding the divine. He dug his fingers into Missit's hair, urged him forward, as if part of a dance, before a roll or a spin. He leaned down, tilted both their heads in a counter movement for a better match of shape, then pressed his lips to Missit's – full and parted.

It was probably the biggest mistake of his life. But he was going to make it anyway. For no other reason than he wanted to, he who never wanted anything for himself, wanted this moment.

If sound had color, surely so did flavor? The god in his arms tasted of salt and sunshine, syrup and metallic gold. Phex breathed out and opened down into him, pressed until Missit gasped – sipped at surprised flesh, careful of tenderness over teeth. This way was better – he decided. Tilting Missit's head a little more, feeling him shudder and arch, like they were dancing again, like Phex should brace Missit's lower back so he might catch and dip them both to fall and swirl together.

Phex expected Missit to move away. He wasn't sure why – he just did. He expected one of them to be in control. But the god squirmed closer, opened his mouth more, made a funny half-whimper noise – eager and lost.

So it was up to Phex to pull back, relax his grip. Give over exploring that wide honeyed mouth. His ears filled with a buzzing beating fuzziness. Surely if *that* had color it would be white and pink.

Missit stayed close. His eyes were shut. He let out another whimper, more contrived this time, collapsed forward, and bumped his forehead onto Phex's collarbone.

"You're so unfair."

Phex didn't understand, so he didn't say anything. He stayed as still as he could, like a pause in their dance, holding some precious fragile musical creature – trying to grasp it close, even knowing it might fracture in an instant. Trying to show no desire at all, for fear it would fly away to someone more disinterested.

It was the precipice of affection.

Phex didn't know what to do. So, he did nothing. A wanting ache was lodged in his throat, and a need like pinpricks of hot stardust spiked through his veins – both new to him and terrifying. For this was Missit, the most unattainable of the gods, a divine truth that was as undeniable as it was cruel.

"What are you doing?" The sharp voice of an acolyte.

Missit glanced over at the entranceway, shine and glory. "It's just the way the dance ends."

"Is it?" The acolyte was clearly suspicious. It occupied the center of the arch. Only Zil and Fortew were brave enough to still be watching. Phex's pantheon and the crew had vanished from view.

"Are you challenging me?" Missit snapped back, his Dyesi perfect, his slide from polite to impolite exactly balanced to imply unworthiness with the *you* pronoun.

The acolyte's crests flattened back and its cheeks speckled with humiliated opacity.

"What could we possibly be to one another, more than partners for a single dance? He is a baby demigod and I am one of the greatest gods of all time."

Which was, Phex thought, a very fair assessment of their situation – an excuse, of course, but also the truth.

And really, how perfectly fitting for the tenor of his life, that when Phex finally felt desire, it was for the impossible.

Missit kept his distance after that. Perhaps he was actually scared of the acolytes. Or perhaps he was scared of Phex or for Phex. Since if there were fallout from that kiss, it surely wouldn't be on Missit's head. The divinity would do everything in their power to keep Missit from descending back to the mortal realm.

Or perhaps Missit was just distracted by their upcoming show.

He was still very much present and very much Missit whenever they happened to eat together or pass each other in the hallways or practice rooms. It wasn't that big of a spaceship, after all, so they did run into each other.

Phex was glad not to have to focus on anything more than his own debut with Asterism and his role as understudy to Tillam. Adding Missit's focused flirtation into the mix might have broken even Phex's genetic resolve. He'd been engineered to withstand most stresses the universe could throw at him, but even the best genetic enhancements could not account for a force of Missit's caliber.

There were other things making those three weeks before their debut even more chaotic than anything prior. Since they were now officially demigods, they were being beamed more and more out across the galaxy. Not just bits of their practices but sometimes their meals and lounging in the galley. Chef was always mildly thrilled when publicity occurred in her territory and would try to appear in the background looking *capable and efficient*, as she said. Phex thought that was cute. He wondered if he should give Asterism's believers a tour of his little galley cabinet, the one with his special cooking supplies in it. But then they might be encouraged to send even more offerings, and the small space was already packed with fun things the chef had found for him.

Occasionally, the divine forums hosted them in pairs, taking live questions or answering ones chosen ahead of time by the acolytes.

Asterism was starting to gain real worshipers on a much larger scale as a result. A few of them even had believers. Berril was popular enough to get digital offerings regularly. Apparently, people loved her *persona* – Fandina's term for it, not Phex's – and how she cuddled the others all the time. She was hugely popular with other chiropteran species, since they felt like the Dyesi tended to snub them as potential gods due to their looks. Her whole planet was behind her, and that was *a lot* of people. The Shawalee were a highly procreative species.

What Phex couldn't quite understand was that he'd also gained worshipers. Fandina, who spent the most time in the forums curating their brand, said Phex had a reputation for *being a badass*, and this had certain appeal among harder-to-reach demographics. As if Phex being grumpy and quiet was an asset of some kind. People also liked that he enjoyed time in a kitchen, as if this were an appealing softening to his hardened image.

Fandina was interested in the mechanics of godhood in a way that was slightly mercenary and very Dyesi. So, Phex supposed he had to take its word for what was happening. Fandina thought this was a good thing and that the divinity would be pleased with Phex because of it. Which, after that kiss with Missit, Phex could only hope was true.

Phex thought the idea that Berril was worshiped because she was likable and he because he was a grouch was ridiculous. Why base a preference within the auspices of art and religion on personality rather than skill? It would make more sense if they were worshiped based on appearance, considering how much thought the Dyesi put into aesthetics. But to be worshiped because of one's character? Odd. Still, if Phex had to lean into playing the *dad* of Asterism, at least it came naturally to him.

They did get physically worshiped, too, of course.

Kagee was particularly popular. There was something about his grayness that was hugely appealing to Sapiens. He was so unique to the divinity. In a place that traded on color, he was predominantly colorless, even with the lavender tinting. His vibrant temper and sharp wit contrasted to his innately sweet and pretty countenance and his delicate frame, which made him a sensation. Everyone wanted to marry him, to rescue him, to soften him. He got multiple proposals a day, some of them quite rude.

"I guess everybody loves a bad boy," he said, when they were comparing supplication numbers one evening in the sitting area attached to the galley. "This one says he's deeply in love with the way I tilt my head right before I say something particularly nasty. Do I do that?"

Everyone clicked at him.

"Well, okay, then." Kagee flopped back into the copper-colored couch poof. He rolled to one side and pointed two ring-bedecked fingers at Phex. "How many proposals have you gotten?"

Phex hadn't bothered to count. He looked over at Fandina, who kept their stats.

"Two dozen or so today," said the Dyesi checking their local infonet.

"What archetype is he?" Kagee wanted to know.

"Wounded warrior," said Fandina, without looking away from its holograph.

Phex huffed at that. "But they covered over my scars."

"It's still your *type*," insisted Tyve, apparently agreeing with Fandina.

Kagee waggled a hand at her. She threw a bright red fuzzy throw at him, from a small pile at the end of her poof. Kagee shook it open and snuggled into it.

The little sitting and eating area was very similar to the one back in their dorm on Divinity 36, except everything was a lot smaller and closer together. It all had a very Dyesi feel to it, albeit glitzy. Phex didn't mind, it felt comforting.

"What archetype are you, Tyve?"

"The lovable trickster," she answered, with a shrug.

"I'm the cute one," added Berril, somewhat proudly. "Or, if this supplication is to be believed, *a tiny perfect ray of sunshine without which all would be darkness and they would have no reason to go on*."

"Very poetical," said Tyve, patting Berril's head.

Berril listed against her and seemed suddenly shaken. "It feels surreal sometimes, how did I get this lucky?"

Tyve said, "I find it inspiring, energizing, even. Zil used to say that about supplications. Especially at first."

"The last thing you need is more energy," grumble Kagee.

"I suppose Tillam gets too many now to read them themselves anymore?" Phex looked over at Tyve.

She clicked affirmative.

It made Phex a little sad.

Kagee continued, "This one says she falls asleep to clips of me singing, so I will always appear in her dreams. Should I be flattered or creeped out? Oh, wait, she wants to know why I don't show up in her dreamscape naked. So, I guess – creeped out."

"Send that one to the sacerdote," suggested Phex. "The acolytes in charge of worshiper management should dissect it for fixed tendencies." Then, to change the subject, he asked, "What archetype are you, Fandina?"

"It's harder for sifter gods to gain sympathy as archetypes. We Dyesi are a bit too alien to tap into the ancient narrative tropes."

"Fandina is obviously the mastermind," said Tyve, overruling said mastermind confidently with her choice of archetype.

"The leader," added Phex. Because he might be the sun, but it was almost always Fandina who made the final decision for their group.

Fandina clicked and went a little opaque in amused-yet-embarrassed pleasure.

"And what am I?" Jinyesun asked, ears crested in genuine curiosity.

"The mentor figure," suggested Tyve.

"That's a terrible role. In mythology, that character always dies," objected Kagee.

"But Jin always has the answers and knows the most about how the divinity works." Tyve defended her choice.

"How about the wise fool?" suggested Berril, terribly amused with herself.

Jin looked like it wasn't certain if it should be honored or offended by that one. So, it returned the conversation back to their digital supplications. "Like you, Kagee, some of the messages I get are quite rude and sexually graphic."

"Sapiens love Dyesi looks. We think you're really hot. I'm afraid it's always gonna be confusing for you," said Kagee. "Honestly, it's the only way the divinity has made inroads on my planet at all. We don't have domes. We simply believe sifters are sexy."

Jinyesun and Fandina both flattened their crests in disgust.

Phex wondered how the Dyesi procreated, if they didn't have sex. But he also knew enough now not to ask that impossibly rude question, even with Dyesi friends and members of the same pantheon. Even Jin drew the line somewhere. Phex didn't need to ask anything to know that line was drawn firmly around Dyesi sexuality.

The Dyesi did not do sex, they were not interested in it, and they entertained neither offers nor discussion. It was one of the things the rest of the galaxy had learned right away upon Dyesi entry into the Galactic milieu. With the popularity of the divinity, it was now one of the things all species knew about the divine. Relationships were forbidden. The Dyesi might be to your taste but they were *unavailable*. For many, this only added to the allure of the gods.

It certainly didn't stop worshiper supplications from pouring in to both Fandina and Jinyesun, full of sexual innuendo and outright proposition. There were sensual prayers, vows of devout celibacy, and praise creeds laid down on the virtual altars of both of Asterism's sifters. Fandina was disposed to find it all amusing, but Jinyesun was unsettled by this kind of worship. Jin was much shyer than Fandina, and all the attention might have been tolerable if it weren't so graphic.

Kagee, who still got the most propositions by a long shot, was also the most philosophical about it. "Presumably, we will all get accustomed to it."

"You don't seem too shaken," said Phex.

"This may shock you to hear, but on my planet I'm considered quite sexy. You know, as the hottest member of the pantheon – it says so right here – I feel bound to inform you that you're allowed to enjoy this part a little, Phex."

Phex said back, "This one says she thinks she now likes boys because of me. Is that flattery?"

"Well, yes."

Phex made a face. Maybe it was kind of sweet. He felt himself softening a little.

"When supplications are good, though, they are really *good*," said Tyve. "This one said I changed her life just by being myself as a pantheon member. Said she wasn't confident in her identity until she saw me grace."

Berril agreed, leaning back against Tyve's knee. "I love those ones. I got one yesterday that said he didn't realize someone who looked like him could be a god. Now he feels like even if he can't make it as a potential, he at least can do something in the entertainment industry, whether he looks the part or not. Isn't that amazing, that I could do that? Just by flying under a dome. And this one says they think I'm the sweetest girl in the galaxy."

"Well, you are," Tyve said, stalwart in support of her gracing partner.

"Isn't that why we do it?" wondered Jinyesun.

"No, it's why we perform. I think I would grace and dance whether someone wanted to watch me or not. But this is my reason for doing it *in front* of other people," said Tyve.

"In front of millions," said Kagee, clearly thinking about their upcoming debut.

"In front of *millions*," agreed Tyve. "*That* is because I want to touch strangers with my art."

"Make them believe in you?" suggested Fandina, like a true member of the divinity.

"No," said Tyve, waving around her ident projection filled with supplications from worshipers, "Help them believe in themselves."

"Is that a more noble undertaking?" wondered Fandina.

Kagee laughed at the Dyesi confusion coloring the question. "Ask not what the divinity can do for you but what you can do for the divinity." He thought he was being funny.

"That is the guiding mantra for acolytes, not gods," grumbled Jinyesun.

Phex looked up then. He'd been half-listening to the conversation, half-processing his own supplications. Running them through various algorithms to divide them out. Searching for signs of obsession and signs of the fixed. But also reading a few, awed by the love these strangers were giving him because of how he looked, and how he acted, and how he sang under a dome.

"What is the mantra for us gods, then?" he asked. Hoping he hadn't missed something during all their training.

"There is none," said Jin.

"We *are* the divinity, it is not for us to do unto others or ourselves. It is just for us to be the best we can under the dome. That is all we need give and all that can be expected of us." Fandina spoke reverently.

Phex thought that was patently incorrect. He felt lousy with divine expectation and restriction, so many rules governed his existence – no romance, no sex, no violence, no scars, no ears too close to the head, no short hair, no singing at full strength, no kissing Missit. He wanted to be mucking about in a kitchen and not sitting reading about unwarranted love on a tiny projection. He missed the clatter of his own pots and pans back on Divinity 36.

He stood.

"What are you up to?" asked Tyve.

"I need to make tea. You want?"

"That bad, is it?" said Kagee.

Phex only gave him a look.

Kagee nodded.

His pantheon let him putter in the galley undisturbed.

He was grateful.

The chef did come in at some point, but Phex didn't mind her. Technically, this kitchen was her sanctuary – he was just borrowing it for a time.

He'd been humming softly, trying to puzzle out how to better balance Kagee in one of their new original godsongs, but he stopped at her arrival.

She gave him a sweet smile and said, "It's lovely, please continue."

So, while his pantheon lounged about, absorbing the praise of strangers that he felt they richly deserved, Phex hummed and made tea. Maybe even if he didn't really deserve the supplications himself, but if he were very good he might eventually deserve his pantheon.

5

GRACE SOFTLY AND CARRY A BIG ALIEN

Syrunid Prime offered up their very best dome, in one of their most famous capital cities for Tillam. Of course they did. This was *Tillam*.

The tour ship did not conduct a fanfare atmospheric flyover before it landed, but it did fly in to land over the dome. Phex and the others had already seen plenty of holos of Syrunid's famous Dome Precept. Of course they had. It was probably the most famous dome in the galaxy.

It was different to see it in person from the sky.

Dome Precept was a masterpiece of engineering. One of the first domes ever constructed. Because Syrunid was so close to Dyesid Prime and its dome was built so long before, more of the special materials required to build the interior had been used in this one dome than in any other two combined.

Dome Precept was the first major outpost of the divinity, a cathedral of sift and color – iconic. The divinity used Dome Precept as publicity all the time because of its all-round beauty. It combined Dyesid technology with Syrunid's famous passion for architecture. A trading planet for as long as anyone could remember, Syrunid was always open to new experiences and other cultures. The Syruni specialized in inviting the very best architects from other species to their home world specifically to build the biggest most impressive and most ridiculously artistic buildings.

The Dyesi did not do architecture – they only left the naturally formed caves of their home planet to take to the moons in the rings around it and spread the divine. Their buildings were either underground or brutally utilitarian. Divinity 36 had proved that in spades. Dyesi buildings off-planet were brutalist at best, mostly just slap-dashed warts on the natural landscape. For them, the dome was only interesting for its interior. Dyesi cared for the colors they could bring to the insides of things. For aestheticists, they were terrible about building structure.

But Syrunid's famous Dome Precept had been designed by a local artist and devoted worshiper of the divinity who had been inspired by the swirls and colors of skinsift when forming the exterior. It looked like a dome under godsong turned inside out, grown by cantor and grace into swirls and points, pinnacles and spires. It was anodized and iridescent, symmetrical yet organic, seeming to move and shift as the sun and shadows played over it. Parts of it were designed to move and twirl on windy days.

"It looks like a psychedelic sea anemone from Hydrab or something," said Tyve, who opened her mouth some days and pure nonsense spewed out.

Apparently, this wasn't nonsense, though, because Phex looked up *sea anemone* on the infonet and she wasn't far off.

Immediately after landing, the acolytes announced Asterism was to host their first congregation – right there in the open air. They weren't expected to perform or anything, just stand and bow and wave as a group. A divine visitation, nothing more.

Apparently, they hadn't been informed of this sooner because the acolytes didn't want them to worry. Considering how nervous he suddenly was, Phex thought that was probably a good choice. They went into hair and makeup for less than half an hour before they were hustled out onto the ramp of their cruiser in front of the local press and some select thousand or so Syruni worshipers.

It was also Phex's first time on an actual planet.

"What *is* that smell?" he asked, low and shocked.

"Natural air," explained Berril.

It was hard to describe how different the experience of being on a world was, and not just the smell. Phex had lived and breathed the stale recycled air of space his whole life – space stations, space ships, artificial cities on satellites and moons. He was a creature of ducts and forced air – everything he'd breathed until that moment had passed through artificial tubes of some manufactured material or another.

"Yes, but what *is* it, exactly?" Phex was confused by the range of scents hitting his nose. It was a little like cooking with lots of different ingredients, except none of them were designed to go together.

"Animal, vegetable, and mineral," suggested Tyve.

"Flora, fauna, and fungi," added Kagee, unhelpfully.

Phex wrinkled his nose. "Is there any way to turn it off?" He sneezed.

Planetary air seemed to have a life of its own, too. There was no regulation or pattern to it – sometimes it was moving and messing with his hair, and sometimes it was still. Very unsettling. It was also warm and a little wet. Odd to think of wasting water inside air like that, just letting such a precious substance float around all willy-nilly.

On the other hand, the weight of the planet's gravity felt good. Nice on his bones. It was only a tiny bit heavier than the spaceship and certainly no more than Attacon 7. Phex was grateful for the steady weight of it – otherwise, he would have a hard time with his grace parts tomorrow. He wondered if there were performance domes on heavy-gravity worlds or if the divinity had found a way around that.

He sneezed again. Squinting into the bright natural light, he noticed that there were tiny semi-reflective particles of something floating about in the air to go with all those smells. Really, natural atmospheres were *wild.* "There's stuff in the air as well as odor. Dust?"

"Probably pollen," said Kagee.

"Plant matter?" Phex frowned. "Is that normal?"

Kagee laughed. "How else do they, you know, pollinate?"

"I thought that's what bugs were for."

"No, sweetie." Missit popped up next to them at the top of ramp. Luckily, so did his bodyguard. Asterism already had Itrio and Elder K accompanying them. Tillam's bodyguards had been borrowed for Asterism's congregation on the ramp.

The landing green was segregated off but still entirely in public view. There was a huge crowd – Asterism's congregation, Phex could hardly believe how many there were – kept at bay by some kind of high fence. People in uniform, who Phex assumed were local security, patrolled to stop anyone from climbing up or over that fence. But none of this was far away.

The crowd set up a screaming roar when Missit appeared.

"Go back inside," grumbled Phex. "They can still throw or shoot things at you."

"But it's okay for you to risk it?" Missit asked, cheeky.

Phex thought that a god like Missit should understand how expendable a new pantheon like Asterism was. "We need the publicity, you do not."

"You forget" —Missit was cool and poised, smiling and

bowing to the now very excited congregation— "I enjoy this part. And I do it all the time." He winked at Phex. "But thank you for worrying about me."

He waved at the assembled masses.

The crowd undulated and yelled at him in paroxysms of excitement.

Phex sneezed some more. He wondered if his crazy over-engineered immune system was so aggressive, it was forcing him to sneeze so it could exit his body and do battle with the pollen outside of it, like some sort of military coup.

Berril snuggled up to Phex's side. "Poor baby, do you have hay fever?"

Phex touched his forehead – his temperature seemed normal. What was she talking about?

Missit glommed onto his other side. Now he was trapped and neither of his arms were free to defend anyone.

Phex shook them both off. "Hay fever?"

"It's a respiratory response to pollen," explained Kagee.

"Then shouldn't it be called pollen sniffles?" wondered Phex.

He looked at Missit and Kagee, suddenly worried. "Won't this wet air with all its moving about full of particulates cause—"

"That's *wind*," Missit explained.

"Fine, whatever, won't wind and pollen impact our voices?"

Missit said, "It's all kept out of the dome."

Phex thought that this was the *air* of this *whole* world, how was *that* possible?

He looked desperately at Jinyesun. Fortunately, the Dyesi was paying attention to their conversation and came to his rescue.

"The atmosphere inside all performance domes is tightly

regulated to match the original caves back home as closely as possible," Jin reassured him. "So, when we go into Dome Precept, it should feel exactly like we're back on Divinity 36."

Phex nodded, relieved.

Missit shook his head at Phex's unnecessary concern. "Nothing is ever allowed to mess with live godsong. Nothing."

Jinyesun added, "The god is correct. Every mote of dust and speck of pollen is removed from the interior surface of the dome, and the air within is clean and sterilized."

Phex's nose had started to run, and this was embarrassing, since he had nothing to wipe it on and there were thousands of raving worshipers in line of sight.

"Should we go back inside the ship now?" he suggested hopefully. It felt like they'd shown themselves off for long enough. They weren't performing – what could the congregation possibly want from them?

"Did you see that you have believers?" asked Missit, before Phex could go anywhere.

Phex scowled at him.

Missit gave him the dimple and gestured with his pointy chin.

Phex crumbled and turned to look.

Held up against the restraint barrier at one end was a very large banner, done in blue, presumably to match Phex's hair color. It was written in Galactic Common, the script bold and slightly too square to his eyes, which were now accustomed to swirly Dyesi lettering.

Welcome to Syrunid, Phex, our beloved blue koel!

"What's a koel?" he asked.

"A kind of songbird," explained Jin, consulting the infonet.

Phex gave the people holding the banner a timid wave. One of the ones at the end fainted or pretended to faint. It was a very dramatic collapse and Phex appreciated the artistic execution.

"You should blow them a kiss," said Missit, standing on tiptoe to whisper in his ear.

Phex shivered at the sensation and gave Missit a brief side glare. "I have no intention of being *that* kind of god."

"Oh, so fierce."

"Well, I do," said Tyve. She proceeded to blow multiple tiny kisses in a rather charming old-fashioned way to a different group of believers holding up a red glowing sign with her name and well-wishes scrawled all over it. Or presumably it was well-wishes, because her name was in written in Galactic Common and then again in Dyesi but the rest was in languages Phex did not know and he assumed were local to the planet.

Phex was beginning to get uncomfortable. Even with the three bodyguards at his back and not-insignificant amounts of space between them and the congregation, he still felt exposed. And his nose would not stop running.

"Can we go back inside now, please?" he begged.

Kagee gave him a click of approval, but the rest of the pantheon and Missit were still enjoying themselves.

"I forgot how much fun debuting was," said Missit, wistfully.

"What are you talking about? They yelled the loudest when you appeared, not us." Phex grumbled.

"Yes, but not because I'm some new exciting thing but because of who I already am."

"Exactly. So, go away," suggested Phex, desperately trying to keep an eye on both him and Berril, who was jumping up and down at the back and waving like a mad thing. Fandina and Jinyesun had their crests puffed up with pride and were flushed opaque with embarrassed speckled pleasure and distraction. Those four couldn't defend themselves even if they *were* paying attention.

"Can't you just enjoy yourself, Phex?" wondered Missit.

"What's to enjoy?" Phex wondered right back.

"You're as bad as a bodyguard." Clearly, Missit thought that was a grave insult, but Phex took it as a compliment.

"Should I show them my wings?" Berril asked, bouncing in excitement.

"I don't think that's a good idea." Tyve was warrior enough to realize that would just turn Berril into one huge target.

"I won't fly away, I promise. They're so pretty now. Fandina, can I?"

"Of course you can, cutie." Fandina used the Dyesi diminutive for something small and charming.

Berril stepped away from the group slightly, making Phex even more nervous, unfurled her wings, and lifted them up so they fanned out behind them in broad glittering glory.

The congregation screamed in renewed excitement.

Phex made desperate eyes at Itrio. The bodyguard moved to shadow Berril, disappearing from Phex's view behind her wings.

Berril fluttered them. They sparkled under the sun and lifted her slightly off her feet and above the rest of them. Making her even more of an easy target.

"Berril! What do you think you're doing? Put those away immediately!" said Phex, losing his cool.

"You sound like someone's maiden aunt," said Kagee, amused.

Phex had no idea what an unmarried female relation had

to do with anything or why Kagee was suddenly bringing her up.

"I don't like their energy," he explained, gesturing with his chin at the assembled worshipers.

The congregation on the other side of the barrier was boiling like water did right before Phex dropped noodles into it. Kagee had assassin's training – he should know how to read a crowd. But mostly, even Kagee seemed to be enjoying the adoring enthusiasm.

All Phex could see was that barrier. While it was a tall fence, it wasn't as tall as Phex thought it should be. There was no additional protection at the top.

"We have bodyguards right here. You are being paranoid, Phex." That was Fandina.

"You should start to get accustomed to this kind of thing," said Jin, moving to stand next to him. "This is only the beginning."

Then, at the back of the crowd, two new sets of wings unfurled. They weren't special, not augmented or made sparkly with Dyesi aesthetics, but they were huge, much bigger than Berril's and softly colored browns and yellows.

Chiropterans.

Syrunid Prime wasn't supposed to have any chiropteran residents.

"There are flyers in the congregation," Itrio barked, presumably to the other two bodyguards and into her ident.

Phex responded immediately. He moved to simply push Berril back inside the ship. She bumped back to ground but wouldn't budge. Normally, it was no issue picking her up and moving her around – she was a tiny thing compared to Phex. Plus, they practiced with him as dark grace all the time, so she was accustomed to trusting his lifts. But she had her wings open and even flapped them for leverage to counter him. She was his little birdie, but those wings of hers, once deployed, were incredibly strong. And she was using them against him.

Phex couldn't move her. "Berril!"

"No, Phex, I want to meet them!"

"Get inside."

"Those are *my* people. Those are Shawalee!"

Desperate and unable to find words to argue, Phex made a split-second decision and changed targets. He hooked an arm around Missit, who was still right next to him.

"You, get in!"

"So demanding," said the god, not fussed.

Phex glanced desperately around for Missit's bodyguard, wishing he knew their name. The armored cyborg appeared out of nowhere, and Phex practically hurled Missit at them.

Missit's bodyguard didn't waste any time, just carried the passive god back inside. Missit waved at Phex casually as he was hauled away. Or maybe he was waving at the congregation. Phex had already turned back to face the threat.

Berril had actually flown over their heads and down to the end of the ramp to meet the two Shawalee. As Phex suspected, the barrier was no barrier at all to winged aliens.

Itrio was leaping down the ramp after her, heavy-gravity tinkers giving her that unnaturally long, high, bouncing stride. Phex and Tyve dashed after her – although they were less bouncy about it. Elder K, the other bodyguard, stayed with the rest of Asterism on the ramp. Phex figured Kagee could also help if needed and fervently wished they would all just go back inside.

But right now, Berril was the one most at risk.

Again.

The two visiting Shawalee landed and were approaching Berril slowly.

On a level with her, it became clear that they were either much bigger than average or Berril was much smaller, since she looked like a child compared to them.

One of them began speaking rapidly in what Phex assumed was a Shawalee native tongue. It was a sharp, pretty, chirpy kind of language.

Phex skidded to a stop slightly in front of Berril and to one side, so he had some maneuverability to pivot and either shield her or lash out with his legs at the enemy, whichever was required. He was already calculating where the weakest physical point might be on a winged hominin. Did they have external genitalia? Their ribs were probably very strong in order to brace the wings, so not a great option. Neck might be the best target, and Phex's legs were long enough to reach, so long as they stayed grounded. But a kick to the neck could kill. And there was a crowd watching, recording, and beaming this whole confrontation.

The divinity would love those headlines. *Demigod kills worshipers right before debut.*

The congregation was rhythmically chanting something now, but Phex tuned it out. He couldn't think of them anymore. He tapped the ship's infonet for machine subs, held his chip to his ear. The translator wasn't great, but it was better than not knowing what was being said between Berril and the chiropterans.

"—so we bought you this rock," one was saying. He reached into his vest.

Itrio and Phex tensed.

Berril said, in Dyesi to Phex, "No, really, it's okay. This is culturally significant to my people. You must let them do this. We are being live-streamed. At this point, not allowing the ritual could cause an international incident."

"Berril!" Phex could not believe this was happening.

"It's okay, Phex, trust me. This is important." She turned back to the two Shawalee with a sweet smile and shy dip of her head.

The Shawalee in the vest handed over a perfectly ordinary-looking rock. The kind one might pick up right there in the landing port. Or on any satellite moon. It was roundish, and grayish, and fit inside the palm of Berril's little hand.

Berril examined it reverently. "It is a very nice rock." She sounded very somber and formal, for Berril. And that wasn't just because of the crappy translation chip.

"We will await your answer after tomorrow's performance. We have obtained passes for private visitation rights afterwards."

With that, the two Shawalee turned and flew away.

Berril clasped both hands around the rock and watched them with an impressed look. "They're so fast and powerful. High *eyrie*. What an honor."

She turned to Phex and Tyve and Itrio, entirely ignorant of the crazy panic she'd just caused.

"They gave me this rock!" she announced proudly. "Me!"

Phex looked at Itrio. "Tell the acolytes we're done here."

Itrio nodded.

Phex pointed at the ship and sang out, with all the strength of his very powerful voice. "Everyone back inside, now."

He sang it in Dyesi. The congregation assumed they had been blessed. Collectively, they fell to their knees in awed silence.

Fandina and Jinyesun skin-flinched at the power of Phex's voice. Kagee looked amused or something. Berril was still excited about her dumb rock. Only Tyve seemed at all aware that something awful had just happened.

Phex felt the horrible urge to scream at them all, at the top of his voice, without any musicality. At Berril in particular. In Galactic Common. And wondered what was wrong with him.

Phex and Berril had been together since the beginning. They'd gone through it all *together*, survived being potentials *together*, they were demigods *together*. This was why the Dyesi set everything up the way they did. Training made them – Phex struggled for the right word – *friends*, he guessed. Maybe more than that. Maybe family. Maybe Asterism was Phex's home, or as close to one as Phex would ever get. If that was the case, he could see why the progenetors of the Wheel did what they did to protect the sacred lines. Phex knew now, without a shadow of a doubt, that he would modify his children for his pantheon. He would change his own genetics from the core out if that was what they needed from him. He would do anything for them.

But that also meant when they made stupid mistakes, he suffered for it, and he *hated* that. He hated that he had become someone so easily damaged by the behavior of others. That someone else's choices ruined him. Home, it seemed, came at the cost of autonomy. He had made that trade without realizing it at the time. Because one day, a long time ago now, Berril had hugged him, a stranger at a party. And Kagee had insulted him. And Jinyesun had explained things. And now he cared far too much about all of them.

The acolytes took Berril and her dumb rock away for a little chat as soon as they were back aboard the spaceship. Phex wished them luck but doubted they'd be able to talk sense into her any more than they could that rock.

Phex and the others sat in their quarters in silence. Fandina and Jinyesun were clearly confused by the tension.

Kagee was smug about something. Tyve was giving Phex little worried glances. Phex just focused on suppressing a very weird urge to scream and maybe throw something.

Berril came back alone and annoyed. "They lectured me about safety! Tillam's bodyguards did. Do they have the right to do that? I'm not even officially their charge. The acolytes recited ritual regulations. I know them all already. But there's cultural exceptions built into our contract. My people gave me *a rock*, for goodness's sake. They must have traveled half the galaxy just for that! It's the highest honor for a Shawalee. Why would they..." She trailed off, finally taking in the quiet, awkward stillness of the room.

Phex thought Berril had never before acted like such a child. He was so frustrated and worried, he almost vibrated with it. He, who rarely spoke, had many things to yell at her but didn't want to say a single one of them. Because he knew his words would be cutting and cruel, and he also knew how much power he had over Berril. His jaw ached from clenching it so hard.

Fortunately, Tyve was not so reluctant. "Berril, that was *very* dangerous. Haven't you been hurt enough already? How could you take such a risk?" Her voice was full of sorrow.

"I didn't mean to. But to be fair to them, I did spread my wings, that's an invitation."

"Did you know they were in the congregation?" wondered Fandina.

"No, but that doesn't technically make a difference."

"Even so, how could you fly down and meet them face-to-face like that?" Tyve remained upset but calm.

"You don't understand. This is a rock from the highest eyrie in the whole world!" Berril held up the small, innocent rock as if it were something glorious.

"But we aren't on *your* world," stated Jinyesun flatly.

"That doesn't matter. It's like" —she looked desperately at Kagee— "getting invited to become one of the ruling family. They're elite!"

"Those two Shawalee were royalty?" Kagee was genuinely curious but clearly in full sarcasm mode, which meant he too was actually stressed about what had just happened.

"Not exactly. More like royal guards but still *a rock*." She waved the rock at them as if it explained everything.

Kagee said, tone cutting, "I think you should hold out for a rock from *actual* royalty, birdie dear. After all, you're a demigod now. You deserve a higher standard of… rock."

Realizing Kagee too was no ally in this matter, Berril turned desperately to Phex. "It wasn't that bad, was it? Meeting with them?"

Phex thought about the precedent she had just set. She had done that in front of thousands of people – millions because of the live beam. Did every Shawalee in the universe now expect to be able to personally hand Berril a rock? He thought about how dangerous it had been – complete strangers, unvetted, possibly insane, and so close to his Berril. Their light grace. There was no species immune to fixation. One or both of those Shawalee could easily have been fixed. Could easily have killed her.

He thought about the fixed who had thrown acid at Fandina and Jinyesun less than a month earlier. Remembered Berril writhing in pain on the dais.

He could never not think about the fixed. They were always there now, in every crowd, at the fringes of his peripheral vision. He thought about those two Shawalee crazed and tearing into Berril's beautiful wings. He thought about blood and glass feathers littering the ground of his first planet. He remembered being forced to put Missit first, turning away from Berril and prioritizing getting the golden god to safety – having to make *that kind of choice* in a split second.

Over and over and over again he saw in his head how close those two strangers had been to Berril because he had been distracted. He should have held on to her and kept her from flying to meet them.

Phex was scared but also so angry. Angry with Missit, who had forced him to choose. Who shouldn't have been there *at all*. Angry with the bodyguards, who had not simply shot the threat out of the sky the moment it appeared. Angry with those two Shawalee, who had thought, somehow, that the normal patterns of behavior from their stupid home planet still applied to demigods. Still applied to Berril, who wasn't even one of them anymore. Still applied on a world that wasn't theirs. With gods who risked everything every time they went out into public.

He was so angry with Berril for not understanding any of this. For being rash with her own safety. And with Missit for doing it again. And *again*.

And again.

Angry with both of them for being important to him.

That anger couldn't go anywhere, so it settled into his gut and reformed itself into bile and lava. Like old times, before he'd had a pantheon, when all he'd had was fear.

He ignored Berril's stupid question, got up, and went into the hygiene chamber, where he threw up most of what he'd eaten that day. When he came back out, everyone was very quiet and staring at him.

"Don't start *that* back up, Phex. We'll figure it out," said Kagee, silken voice soft, grey eyes worried in that arrogant, sharp face.

That night, the night before their debut, Berril crawled into Phex's cot and hugged him as tight as she could, with arms and wings, and whispered over and over that she was sorry and she wouldn't do it again, until he finally fell asleep.

Everything was different on a performance day. There was a lot of strategy and transport to discuss, so the bodyguards were very much among them for a change, even at breakfast. Both pantheons were on exactly the same schedule.

Phex took the morning nosh and mingle as an opportunity to have a private word with Missit's bodyguard.

As usual, the cyborg was an impassive wall of armored efficiency. Or attempted efficiency – Missit sure didn't make it easy.

"He gives you a lot of trouble, doesn't he?" Phex said, following the guard's gaze to where Missit sat, curled half in Fortew's lap, eating some kind of local sticky-bread treat. Fortew looked happy to have him there but also listless and exhausted. Phex thought he should still be in bed.

The cyborg glanced at Phex briefly. A glance that was all mechanical swiveling. One eye was augmented and pixelated, probably with an infonet readout, so that even when it moved to focus on Phex, it didn't entirely feel like it was focused. Phex assumed the bodyguard was classified as full cyborg with that many visible augments. It was rude to ask, though, in this part of the galaxy, anyway. The bodyguard re-centered their gaze entirely on their charge, watching Phex only peripherally, if that. It was as if they could never relax, not even on a battened-down spaceship. "The worst. But he is also the best at what he does. Sometimes, we get to hear stuff no one else ever will. Always, we get to know about it first. Counts for a lot."

"Why is he like that?"

"Spoiled and entitled in some ways but not others? Your guess is as good as mine. We both know the same history. Too much of the wrong attention too young? No freedom *ever*? He has been a god, one way or another, his entire life."

"Or he simply doesn't care for his own safety."

"You think he's self-destructive or depressed?" The augmented eye flashed red.

"You should at least consider the possibility." Phex didn't say *Please, just keep him from turning up in strangers' beds. Keep him from turning up in mine. Keep him from kissing me after dances. Stop him from constantly pushing the limits of his own safety. Keep him from killing himself.*

"He didn't used to be this bad."

Phex took an educated guess. "It's gotten worse since Fortew's diagnosis."

"That or..." There was a note of something like accusation in that perfectly auto-tuned voice.

"Or?" Phex pushed.

"You. He's gotten worse since *you* showed up."

Phex scoffed at that ridiculous notion.

The bodyguard seemed to realize this was a conversation with a demigod that probably shouldn't be happening right there with acolytes circling nearby.

"You're very mature for your age."

Phex rolled his eyes and shook his head. "Keep him safe or I'll do it myself."

"What does that mean?"

Phex wasn't sure. But he knew he would do it if he had to. It was okay to admit such a thing to a bodyguard, because they had the same instincts.

He turned away to find Itrio standing on his other side, arms crossed, amused expression on her face. "You telling us how to do our jobs now, kid?" Behind her, Chef stood still in the galley, stirring something and listening in with interest.

But Phex was annoyed enough to say for anyone to hear, "You know how many times I've run into that god off leash, alone, and at risk?"

Itrio looked interested. "No. You never told us about it."

Phex shook his head. "Since the very beginning. It can't be that hard to keep one god protected."

Missit's bodyguard actually laughed, metallic and brittle. Phex didn't know a cyborg could laugh. "You have *met* Missit, right?"

Phex said, with feeling, "This revival is going to be a nightmare."

"They always are," said Itrio. "We're deafened when we go with them under the dome" —she gestured to all the bodyguards— "for the pantheon's safety, but it limits our communication."

"Wait, how do you handle it?" Phex hadn't thought about that angle. Of course the bodyguards wouldn't be allowed to actually hear godsong – even just seeing it could be considered risky.

Itrio said, "We use sign language and eye contact, checking in with each other every six minutes. It's not ideal, but guarding gods is a crazy business. One of the things we sacrifice is godsong. We can't allow ourselves to be even slightly affected by it. So, yeah, no sound allowed when a bodyguard is inside a dome. Even so, there's a risk we might get distracted by the beauty of the colors."

They must have tremendous self-control not to stare at the swirls but instead stay focused on the gods producing them.

Phex had wondered. After all, nothing could possibly be more dangerous than a bodyguard becoming fixed. During practices and in the normal course of things, bodyguards always stayed outside of the dome, but on an alien world, with thousands in the congregation, the guards must protect their gods *inside* the dome. It must be nerve-racking for them.

"So, I have the advantage?" said Phex. Because he was a god himself, godsong would have no effect on him. Gods did not become fixed – they were immune.

"You'll be watching Missit's show?" Itrio looked confused.

Phex nodded. "I have to. I'm Fortew's understudy, remember? I must be prepared to step in at any moment. So, I'll be there, and I'll have both my ears and my eyes in full working order."

Itrio and Missit's bodyguard both looked at him with something like relief.

Phex inclined his head. "I can be your understudy, too."

Itrio made fun of him. "You sure you want to be a god? I could offer you a great job as a bodyguard. The hours are weird, and the pay is only passing decent, but it's important work, and you get to see the universe."

Missit's guard slapped her shoulder. "Cute."

Phex felt that it was about time he outright asked, so he faced the cyborg. "What's your name, anyway? I can't keep just referring to you as Missit's bodyguard."

The cyborg looked surprised. "Oh, sure. You can call me Bob."

Phex nodded, expression neutral. "Nice to formally meet you, Bob."

6

FALL FROM GRACE

Phex was alone in the dressing room about an hour before Asterism was supposed to rise onto the dais and debut as a pantheon. He was struck by how different this moment was from being under a Dyesi dome. Here they had an actual room, with a proper door. On Divinity 36, everything had been communal – privacy was something be hunted down at the expense of society, not the other way around. It felt odd to be alone in a room with a closed door, like he was in trouble or being punished. It was actually simply that the rest of his pantheon was still in hair and makeup. He'd been declared *done* and dismissed early.

"Why mess with perfection?" the local makeup specialist had said.

He'd returned to their dressing room and decided at the last minute that he needed to switch his socks – one of them kept bunching up. You'd think modern technology would fix the universal scrunching-sock problem, but there he was, about to perform in one of the biggest domes in the universe, and still… his sock kept falling down.

The door crashed open in such a way that made Phex

pretty certain he knew who had come in. He didn't even look up from his sock quest.

"Hi, Phex."

Phex stood and turned slowly. "Missit."

The god launched himself toward him. Accustomed to such things as a trained grace, Phex automatically caught the god's weight and twisted him to land sitting next to him on a soft couch puff. Much of furniture in this waiting room was pretty and sculptural, symmetrical but organic with plenty of excessive curlicues, like the outside of the dome, but there were still puffs. Phex didn't trust the thin, swirly furniture to hold his weight, so he was relieved that it seemed puff couches were as ubiquitous as domes.

"What are you doing here?" he asked the god now happily cuddled next to him.

"I wanted to wish you luck on your first big show. Are you nervous? I was so nervous my first time. I think I fainted."

"You were very young."

"True. But still, you don't seem nervous at all." Missit's wide mouth twitched at the corners, like it was hoping to smile. "Does anything get to you?"

Phex didn't know how to answer that question. Everything got to him – he just didn't show it. What good would that do?

Not that he was given a chance – Missit nattered on. "Where's the rest of Asterism? Why are you here alone? Not that I mind. What's up with your sock? Can I see?"

And suddenly, Phex had the golden god kneeling at his feet, playing with his sock. Which Phex did not like. He didn't like Missit debasing himself, and he did not like that it made them both feel dirty. He wasn't sure why he reacted so strongly, but it came out in his voice.

"Stop that! Get up."

Missit bounced back up to sit next to him again.

"You're very barky. Should you be shouting at a god like me? Maybe you actually *are* nervous and you just get grouchy about it. Well, grouchier then normal."

"What are you doing here, kid?" Phex used the Dyesi diminutive because Missit was being such a brat, he felt like he'd earned it.

"Hey. I'm older than you."

Phex gave him a look that perfectly transmitted his doubt of that statement. Missit might be older, but he certainly didn't act like it.

"Are you hiding from Bob again?"

"How did you know?"

"Why do you insist on constantly taking risks with your own safety?"

Missit widened his eyes and leaned in, pressing his weight against Phex's side. "I think you're sexiest when you're all growly. Did you know that? Is that why you do it?"

Phex had no idea what to do with that information. He did not want to be sexy to Missit, but he could hardly stop himself from growling at him, or being grumpy – both seemed to be his natural state, especially around the god. He would just have to avoid contact altogether, he supposed.

Phex gave the golden god a critical once-over. "Are you taking care of yourself since we started the tour? You look less skinny but still tired." He was thinking about the time before, when Fortew returned to Divinity 36 for treatment, and Missit had crumbled with fear and uncertainty. He'd become a frenetic wraith, trying to distract himself with risk and Phex.

Missit knew exactly what he meant. He also knew why it was coming up for discussion now, their first moment of complete privacy together. He was surprisingly honest. "Much better. I miss it, though."

"Miss what?" Phex was perhaps injudicious in asking.

"Your bed."

Phex didn't want to be reminded of Missit curled up against him all night, and he didn't like it when Missit felt he had license to flirt. He searched for a way to put them back into safe territory. Then he realized Missit was probably doing all of this to distract him from being nervous about his debut.

"I'm really okay about going up on the big dais."

"There's over half a million people out there." Missit played with the back of the couch puff, petting the blue velvet material. It was almost the same color as Phex's new hair, and Missit's gold skin seemed to glow against it. It must look that when they danced together.

"Are *you* nervous?" Phex asked, since Missit would keep fidgeting.

Missit laughed. "I've done it so many times."

"But not with Fortew this frail."

"You'll be waiting just in case."

"I'll be waiting and watching," agreed Phex, because he would be.

"It'll be okay, then." Missit shook his head. "How are we talking about me all of a sudden? This is Asterism's first performance. Your first godsong."

"Did you forget? We did it together once."

"No. I didn't forget. Is that why you aren't worried?"

"I have the voice, Missit. That's never been in any doubt."

"No, the doubt is whether you have the will, isn't it?"

Sometimes, this childish, capricious, beautiful creature was nothing but perceptive. Like an actual ancient omniscient god, he knew things he shouldn't. Sometimes, he seemed to understand Phex even better than Asterism did.

Phex thought about his pantheon. "They depend upon me."

Missit wondered, "And that will be enough up there?"

"Of course."

"Explains why you aren't nervous."

Bob slammed open the door. Spoke into an ident chip. "Found him." The cyborg looked at Phex. "Of course he's here."

Phex shrugged. "I warned you."

"At least we have a good idea where to start looking, going forward."

Phex arched a brow.

"Wherever you are," said the bodyguard, with feeling.

Phex didn't want to think about that. He went back to hunting for better socks. "Sock technology leaves a lot to be desired," he said to no one in particular.

Missit said to Bob, "See, I told you he could be funny."

"Let the demigod have some peace and quiet, Missit. Come away."

"Bye, Phex! Bob is going to let me watch your show from the observer niche. I'll be rooting for you."

Phex wasn't at all sure how he felt about that.

"When did I say that was okay?" barked the bodyguard.

"Oh, but Bob! Please. It's Phex's first time."

"You're nothing but trouble, you are." But the cyborg's voice was all affection, even with the augmentations and mods. The bodyguard was relenting already.

"You always say that," replied Missit, knowing he was winning.

Their voices faded away and Phex finally found some better socks.

It was amazing.

Performing there, under a dome, in front of half a million worshipers. Not doing it in front of acolytes judging and taking notes (although there were probably a few of those sprinkled throughout), but real honest divine worshipers. Sure, most of them believed in Tillam, but Phex thought Asterism held their own even as a new baby pantheon stacked up against elder gods.

They didn't try to be like Tillam. Who could? They tried to be themselves and still spectacular instead.

They could do things Tillam couldn't. They were younger, healthier, and with nothing to lose. It was a lot easier for them to take risks under a dome. Asterism graced like no other group. They used Berril to the maximum her wings allowed. Tillam had no wings. Asterism could swap parts. Phex would run up the sides of the dome, flipping back and causing the congregation to gasp with the surreal unexpectedness of a cantor in motion. Worshipers of Tillam had seen grace and cantor share movements, sing together, even, but they'd never seen them switch around so readily and so seamlessly in the middle of godsong. Phex and Tyve were so good now, they could use their flexibility to highlight a pattern and yet never break it.

Asterism was one of those pantheons where the congregation wanted desperately to watch both the dome and the dais, because the dais was just as much a performance. It made them particularly exciting to witness live and in person.

Phex thought the sound of thousands of people gasping at the same time just because he flipped was probably the best sound in the universe.

More magic than godsong.

He wondered if those gasps could be predicted, if they could roll them over Jinyesun's skin and incorporated that into their song color, or spin the indrawn air against Fandina's skin into a pattern. Like speckles over the dome. Could they use the congregation itself for godsong? Had any pantheon ever done *that* before? Would that not be the most magical thing of all?

He wondered if worshipers could become part of the sound, the way his cantor grace could be part of the dome.

They did make a few mistakes. Of course they did. It was their first time.

The rest of Phex's pantheon was very nervous. Even Fandina showed a little opacity right up until Phex blasted out their opening note.

But Phex still thought they did really well despite their nerves. Six songs in full, and there was no fear visible on the dome, just pride up on that dais. Just exhilaration. In the end, this was what they had trained for. This was it – all that they knew and had known for over a year. Even when nerves might have made them forget, their voices and muscles and skin remembered what they were supposed to do. And so they did it. Like a true pantheon.

And they did create godfix.

All three of their original pieces went over well, but Phex knew they had a real hit with "Blue Mirror." It was the slowest of their godsongs, but it built into a spectacular crescendo that took full advantage of the explosive power of Phex's voice and Berril's wings. It was the kind of song that other pantheons would struggle to cover. It was entirely theirs, like a signature mark across the dome, and it would define their worshipers with its unique style. The awed hush when they ended was filled with unspoken prayer. A congregation of thousands was simply grateful to have been there, under *that* dome, listening to *that* song for the first time in divine history.

Phex knew it.

He glanced at Kagee, who looked terrified.

Tyve and Berril, still in their kneeling positions from the ending grace, were wide-eyed at the all-encompassing quiet of the response.

But Fandina and Jinyesun were standing tall and Dyesi-elegant, crests up, huge eyes joyful.

They knew.

The Dyesi knew what they had done.

Then a roaring wave broke over them and the dome. Phex lifted his head, schooled his features because he remembered that millions were watching the beam, and this song, their song, would be on rotation in domes all over the galaxy come morning. The divinity would see it done.

Certainly, "Blue Mirror" was their best of the night, and he was glad they closed with it, but all their songs went as smoothly as Phex might have hoped. Of their original songs, the other two also caused at least some moments of godfix.

As they exited the dais, Phex was happy with what they'd accomplished. Content, like after a successful blade run, that his best had produced the best possible result.

But below the dais, in the waiting room, away from all the eyes, he also realized that he was tired down to his bones. More tired than he thought he would be.

Something about the number of people there, watching them in person, had eaten away his energy. Like he had to hand out bits of his reserves to each and every one of those worshipers. It had taken more out of him than all-day performing under a practice dome ever had.

Tyve put it into words. "That was amazing, and scary, and exhausting all at once."

Kagee looked out of character, hesitant. "We did good, though?"

Phex looked at them all and gave them warmth. He was their sun, after all. "We did great."

Tyve was grinning, sharp and broad "Did you see their reaction to 'Blue Mirror'?"

"Did you *hear* it?" Kagee's sharp face lit up with a rare answering smile.

Berril slammed into Phex's side and he hugged her with one arm, although they were both sticky with cooling sweat. She was shaking slightly.

"You did good, birdie."

"We were gods up there. Actual proper *gods*," she said, awe in her voice.

"We really were," agreed Tyve.

"You okay, Jin?" Phex moved quickly to support, of all people, Jinyesun, who looked suddenly shaky and slumped forward.

"I just never actually believed I would ever get here, to this moment, after wanting it for so long." The Dyesi's crests were limp.

Fandina clicked in agreement. "It seems unreal."

"Just imagine being in the congregation, then?" said Kagee, covering his own discomfort with sudden arrogance. His grey eyes were shining. "That was our first time! And we did it. Godfix! Several times."

Phex let him crow – he'd earned it.

"That was indeed well done, Asterism." An acolyte appeared suddenly. The local sexton of the dome. "Debuts usually struggle to generate true godsong their debut dome. You are the fastest adapters I've ever seen put on the dais. No wonder they rushed you to release." This meant a lot. The sexton of Dome Precept would have seen plenty of pantheons make their debut, so it knew what it was talking about.

It was high praise indeed, but Phex also felt slightly as if it were a threat.

The acolyte gave a funny little bow, a habit on Syrunid that the Dyesi sexton had clearly picked up during its time stationed there. "You must be tired. Let me escort you back to your dressing room."

"Not Phex," said Kagee.

Phex sighed. Kagee was right. He had to stay under the dome.

"He is to watch Tillam from the observation niche," explained Fandina, using highly formal Dyesi to communicate the official importance of this obligation.

The acolyte crested sharply. "Really? How extraordinary. Is your sun not tired? Not to mention he should be with you for the fall from grace."

"Fall from grace?" Kagee was confused.

So was Phex – he'd not heard of this.

The sexton cocked its crest and used another term: "God drop?"

They all looked at each other.

"No one warned you?"

"My brother has never mentioned it." Tyve was clearly annoyed about this.

"After a major dome like this one, most gods experience a severe drain of energy. It generally helps if the sun remains with the group under those circumstances, for support."

"How do you know he's our sun?" Berril wondered.

"How could anyone not know? You turn your faces to him, even now, like flowers to the light."

Phex said, "Will they be all right without me?"

"It's not just them, demigod, it's also you. The sun holds

the group together on the dais. Keeps the gods centered and burning brightly. Those who cannot find fuel in the congregation will use you for kindling instead. Are you not exhausted? Do you not want to stay with them?"

So, that was the sensation as he left the dais. *God drop.* No wonder Phex felt dimmer than usual – the world a little fuzzy and far away. Numb with mental, physical, and emotional exhaustion. And he did kind of want his pantheon around him, but he also thought it wouldn't be so bad to watch Tillam next and not feel things as deeply as he normally would. To watch Missit without wanting him. To be numb right now was no bad thing.

Kagee said, voice cold. "Consult your schedule, acolyte. He is still on the clock."

"On the— What are you speaking of, high cantor?"

Kagee waved a ring-bedecked hand, looking very much like an annoyed god.

"Phex is still working," explained Berril.

As if summoned, Itrio appeared. "You ready, kiddo?"

Phex looked at his five friends – they seemed to be fine. Tired and exhilarated, euphoric and pleased, but fine. He made a decision and chose a delegate. It might have been Jin, but the Dyesi was still out of it from shock. "Fandina, you will look after them?" He used formal Dyesi.

Fandina seemed surprised that it was the one chosen. "Of course."

"Don't forget to hydrate. And for goodness's sake, make sure Berril eats something. You know how she gets. Come to think of it, no one ate very much before we came here. You should all have snacks." He stared hard at the sexton. "You'll see it done?"

The sexton clicked with alacrity.

Berril said, "We love you too, Phex."

Tyve was looking at him, clearly worried about god drop.

"I'll be fine, Tyve. I'm built for this."

"Someday, even you are going to stretch the limits of genetics."

"But not today," replied Phex, who really was already feeling a little better. A little less fuzzy. Like the act of knowing Fandina was willing to take charge of their pantheon was good enough. Like the act of having named what was happening to him gave him confidence. He wondered if, like everything else, he processed god drop faster than other species.

"Come on, then," said Itrio. "You won't want to miss the opener, it's 'Tillam's Lament.'"

"Starting on a downer?" said Phex, because he always found "Five" such a sad song. More so now that he had a pantheon that he was scared to lose.

"It's transporting."

Phex remembered that his first and only godfix had been with 'Five.' Wondered if Missit's ballad of loss could still drive him into a trance. Now that Phex was a god, it shouldn't be able to, of course. But this was Missit. And Phex *was* kind of out of it.

Phex bowed to the sexton, clicked supportively at his pantheon, and followed Itrio off toward the secret observer niche, recessed between dome panels where he could keep eyes on the dais if not really the dome. A place from which he could run fast to get onto that dais if necessary.

Itrio saw him settled and handed him a bottle of water and a stick of some kind of compressed protein, probably with salt and carbs and other nutrients. It was absolutely disgusting. Phex ate it all, too quickly.

The bodyguard checked his face closely. "You seem alert. Are you really okay to go back up there, if necessary?"

Phex clicked.

"Remember your promise? You're our backup, too."

"There are fixed in the congregation." It was not a question.

"This is Tillam. Without a doubt, there are fixed here. Be careful yourself now, though. You increased your worship base a thousandfold this evening, three solid godsongs, they say. One with full godfix. You'll have your own legions of fixed soon enough."

"Oh, what blessing is ours." Phex was all sarcasm. "Do you know how it happens? *Why* it happens? Getting fixed?"

"Of course not, no one does. But I know *that* it happens."

Phex took a long swig of water and regretted that there wasn't time to wipe down and freshen up. He felt salt-crusted and sweat-clammy.

Itrio seemed to understand that. "I'll send an acolyte with cleaning cloths and a change of clothes. It'll match Tillam's costumes. Should be more comfortable, too, their outfits are a lot looser than yours." Her tone seemed to imply, in a motherly way, that she found Asterism's very tight bodysuits a little too revealing.

"I'd be grateful," said Phex, meaning it.

Itrio looked at him. "Not as much as I am. In case none of the acolytes have ever said it. Or Tillam, for that matter. Thank you for doing this for them. You didn't ever have to."

"Yes, I did." Phex considered Tillam and the empty hole Fortew would leave in the hearts of millions. He considered one small capricious golden god who hurt so hard for the inevitable loss of his low cantor, for whom Phex would likely do anything anyone asked of him.

"This niche is secure. You're safe so long as you don't leave it and only allow acolytes to enter. The lock is here." Then Itrio was gone.

Fortunately, Tillam's performance also went off without a hitch. Phex did not fall asleep, or cramp up, or lose focus. He did slow stretches and watched the masters of the dais in mild awe and gentle appreciation.

He no longer experienced godfix.

Or perhaps that was the result of being inside the niche with only limited view and exposure to the dome. But "Five" was even more amazingly sad in person, with the dais performance live and right in front of him. Possibly more so then when he'd first experienced it. Or maybe that was what kept him grounded, the constant aching worry for the faltering in Fortew's steps, for all it never entered his voice and was invisible to everyone but Phex, who knew exactly what to look for. Fortew held himself together, his mellow voice strong and solid as ever, but there was a fragile delicacy to his movements.

Phex found himself humming along with Fortew's part throughout the show. Twelve beautiful godsongs, each one transcendent, each one causing godfix. But Phex spent every moment prepared to crack the niche's door and direct his voice where it was needed.

He realized then that he would never get to truly experience godsong ever again. He would never get to just enjoy it. Now he could only generate it.

After Tillam left the dais and the congregation left the dome, Phex's obligations to the divinity still had not ended.

There was a press meeting and a special VIP interaction. Not for Tillam, of course – that would have been unprecedented access to major gods. Especially when Fortew needed to get back to the ship as quickly as possible.

No, it was up to Asterism, the new pantheon, the young ones, to keep the divinity alive. To meet the obligations of public-facing godhood. To keep worshipers happy and extend their reach out into the universe.

But by the time that VIP event rolled around, Phex really was completely exhausted. The others had clearly napped and eaten during Tillam's performance. Kagee had a slight wrinkle on his face from whatever couch puff he'd slept in.

Phex could barely keep his eyelids open – apparently, he'd finally reached the limits of his much-vaunted stamina. But they had divine obligations. From some deep part of his psyche, some blade-cut and scabbed-over place where his safety once depended entirely on alertness, Phex found reserves and dug them out enough to stand upright and keep his eyes mostly open, if glowering.

Thank the gods this was his public persona already. As low cantor of Asterism, Phex did not actually *have* to answer many questions or really say anything to the press. Asterism had already established their spheres of divine representation and communication. Phex was the god of silent glares, and even thoroughly exhausted, he was master of that realm.

Fandina, Tyve, and Berril did most of the talking for Asterism. They'd basically self-delegated as the pantheon's heralds early on – live-streaming and doing infonet chats with worshipers. Kagee could talk if required, but it was never easy to predict what he would say. He liked to deviate from the divine script, get sarcastic and cutting, so the acolytes thought it best to keep him from speaking as much as possible. Jinyesun came off as cool and calculating. And Phex simply didn't enjoy talking.

Between them, Berril, Fandina, and Tyve could cover multiple languages and most questions. It was unusual not to have a cantor also acting as herald, but not unprecedented.

So, Phex stood, looking grumpy, and Kagee stood, looking smug, and Jin stood, looking confused, and they all were really just trying to behave themselves and be pretty while the other half of the pantheon did the real work of entertaining.

After the usual run of lip-service praise and mundane questions, all of which were beamed out into the universe live and unedited, Asterism was ushered out of the press room and in to meet with the VIP congregation.

Tillam's security were on deck for this. They'd seen their primary charges back to the cruiser and then turned right around and come back to Dome Precept to protect Asterism. Phex could not be more grateful. The six bodyguards seemed alert and wide awake.

The two rock-bearing Shawalee were waiting among the VIP congregation, as promised. There were twelve total VIPs, a combination of diplomats, politicians, and local celebrities who had been hand-picked by local acolytes as ideal believer representatives and avatars of divine significance. Phex might see all twelve as a threat, but clearly, the Dyesi saw them as a blessing.

The two Shawalee had shining eyes full of worship. If anything, they seemed even more interested in Berril than yesterday. Phex found himself constantly checking their faces for signs of avarice and their body language for signs of violence or obsession.

Fortunately, with all of Tillam's bodyguards present, no one was getting within grabbing distance of Berril. Still, Phex stayed flanking her, just in case.

He turned on his infonet audio translator and made it public so the whole room could hear what was being said among the three Shawalee. He was taking no chances – threat could also come in the form of words. As well as rocks.

With a glance at Phex and after getting a click of

approval, Berril went up and spoke to the two Shawalee. She kept a careful distance, well out of arm's reach. Phex was aware of how fast these two could fly, but he thought the ceiling might be too low for them to really maneuver or deploy their wings properly.

"Your rock is lovely and I shall treasure it with all honor," said Berril, sounding formal, although the translator did nothing to indicate Shawalee register, if their language had any.

All the acolytes around the room froze and crested in her direction. But then clearly accepted that some other culture had taken precedence over the usual ritual of a VIP confessional.

"But?" Of the two Shawalee, one was slightly larger and slightly yellower than the other. Linguistically, they gave no clue as to rank, name, title, or gender. So, Phex continued to label both of them as *them* in his brain.

Berril took a breath and straightened her shoulders, fluffing back her wings and facing the two much larger chiropterans. "*But* I am at the beginning of this flight, I must beg your patience and restraint."

"The home world summons you back and you ignore the call?"

"Since when has the High Eyrie spoken for the whole of my world?"

Phex was proud of Berril – her voice did not shake. She had learned something of cantor during her time as grace.

"The little chick has strong wings indeed," said the slightly smaller of the Shawalee.

"You refuse our rock?" The larger one sounded both sad and offended.

"To keep and treasure is not to reject." Berril's voice remained calm.

"It is not to accept, either."

"The High Eyrie lacks patience?" Berril went on the attack. Now, that was something she had learned from Kagee.

"We would join you on this flight."

Berril took a step back, a significant movement, as it separated her from them even more distinctly. "My pantheon is six and six alone. For now, they are also my eyrie." She gestured with her hand at Asterism. Unconsciously, Phex and the others had fanned out behind her, as if they were on a dais.

"A strong claim. And who will carry you if your wings fail, when all your eyrie is flightless?"

Berril turned her back on the two Shawalee without fear and pointed to Phex and Tyve, closest, one to either side of her. Like bodyguards.

"They will." Her eyes were pleading.

Phex and Tyve quickly exchanged glances and then both nodded and clicked. They would play whatever part she, and her culture, needed them to play.

"Wingless and unworthy," spat the smaller of the two Shawalee.

Berril did not deny what was clearly a grave insult. "Yes, but you saw them on the dais. They both still fly, in their way."

"The High Eyrie calls you. You have our rock." The larger one was stubborn.

Berril remained calm. Tyve would have lost her temper by now. Kagee would have said something cutting and flounced away. Phex was proud of Berril. "But I have already answered a prior call. What I do here is not for the good of the High Eyrie but for the good of all Shawalee."

"You *are* our first god." The larger one acknowledged the importance of her representation.

"So, let me be that alone, please. It is the highest flight possible in this lifetime."

"Higher even than our eyrie?" The smaller one was suspicious but no longer angry. Berril had made some kind of significant point.

"Higher still." Berril fluttered her wings, not unfurling them but reminding her visitors of their unprecedented beauty and sparkle. Reminding them that she was different. That aliens had made her into a god.

The smaller one finally relented. "Agreed. But not forever. And when you return to us, remember, ours was the first rock, we have the prior claim."

Berril looked profoundly relieved. "Agreed."

"Heart sister, then?" The larger one held out his arms.

Without pause, Berril trotted over and stepped into them.

"Berril!" said Tyve sharply.

Phex felt his adrenaline spike in a way he would not have said was possible moments earlier. Clearly, he was not so tired that he could not fight.

Bob moved to separate Berril from the Shawalee.

Berril's voice was muffled against the softness of another Shawalee's wings. "They will not return. Let me have this once more before the choice becomes entirely mine and they never come again."

Bob looked at Phex.

Phex signed and clicked at the cyborg. They both shifted their stances but remained tense.

The smaller Shawalee moved to join the hug. Solid and supportive, the three were grounding each other in a way only those who knew flight could. Berril relaxed into the embrace of her people as an infant might. In a way that she had never fully relaxed with her pantheon, not even Phex.

Phex envied her that. The knowing certainty of home and

place in the universe. Even there, light-years away from that planet, they *wanted* her back.

He still saw only risk in the flex of the big Shawalee's hands and the smaller Shawalee's strong wings. But they were not fixed. He had to remind himself of that. They loved, in their way, and worshiped, too. They believed in Berril. And they wished to possess her, but it had not gone so far as to enter madness.

For now, his Berril was still safe and still his. Still theirs.

The two Shawalee left after that.

The rest of the VIP congregation was actually a joy. Mostly Syruni, they were happy and sweet and calm, almost soporific with the lingering impact of the dome still inside them. Their open pleasure at meeting Asterism was contagious and joy-filled. Phex ultimately left the event feeling rejuvenated. Feeling worshiped.

It was a nice sensation.

That night, Berril put her rock away and Phex slept like he had died with no worries and no deeds left unfinished. As if he were the one with wings.

7

ABIDE WITH KAGEE

The second stop on their tour was not too far from Syruni space, no FTL needed, and another S1 colony world.

Everything went smoothly there, too. Phex even sneezed less on the planet. It was a peaceful place, and if the security seemed a little too lax for Phex's taste, at least Tillam's bodyguards became more vigilant as a result.

The dome was smaller and so were the crowds, but they were told this meant that the sexton had turned away thousands. So, the divinity added a second night of performing to keep the worshipers happy.

Back-to-back performances turned out to be very challenging indeed. Even Phex was sore after the second show. Fortew looked like he might keel over, even to the untrained eye, and no amount of makeup or Dyesi aestheticists could improve appearances. Tillam was amazing up on that dais, though, even tired – gods in truth, ten years in the making.

To compensate for Fortew, Missit took pains to draw the bulk of the congregation's attention. He gave away to his worshipers so much of himself in cantor form, Phex marveled that there was anything left to be sunshine and capricious cheer the next day. It was a miracle he was not a wraith, wasting away like Fortew, for no other reason than that Missit was a martyr to his performance, riveting to all who watched him. Even Phex.

Asterism, opening for that kind of show, did their very best. Surprisingly, that seemed to be good enough.

The VIP congregation after the added performance had a much different feel from the ones prior. Security was tighter and Phex felt happier about the whole thing. Believers were separated by preferred god, and lined up in an orderly manner. Phex had his own set of personal believers patiently waiting just for him, who genuinely seemed to love him, their eyes shining with worship. He felt better about everything as a result.

"Your voice is amazing," said one woman, looking at him as if he hung the stars in the night sky.

Phex marked her ident chip, not quite smiling because she seemed so genuine and surprised by her own enthusiasm for his singing. His signature mark was scripted in Galactic Common. He supposed as a Dyesi citizen now, he should use their language, but the Galactic Common mark looked more his.

"I have a present for you" —she glanced at the bodyguard behind Phex— "is it okay?"

Itrio signaled for one of the acolytes, who came over to receive the tribute. Gods were not allowed direct physical contact with worshipers.

"It's a whip scarf," she explained, shyly unraveling it into the acolyte's elegant purple hands.

It was a long, thin woven scarf with an intricate swirling pattern of silver over black.

"It's very pretty," complimented Phex, because it was.

They were speaking Galactic Common. Hers was better

than he might have expected, as if she had learned in school or for business purposes. He wondered idly what she did for a living.

"It's warm and soft and also protective. Those crystal ends, they're very sharp. It's heavier than it looks."

Phex looked at her, noticed her stance and the movement of her arms away from her sides. "It's a weapon?"

"Yes, it works as an actual whip. You are the protector of your pantheon, I've seen it in vids. You're a little scared of us." She gestured to make it clear she meant Asterism's worshipers. "I understand. You've had fixed already. But it makes me sad that you have to be afraid of those who love you, when you give us so much on the dais."

Phex was about to click but instead he nodded. She was perceptive and smart – he liked her. "You recognize my concerns, are you ex-military?"

She nodded. "I used to be diplomatic corps." That explained why her Galactic Common was so good. "Violence in diplomacy was made redundant two years ago, thank the gods. I work with kids now, using art to help them process trauma. After finding the divinity, I wanted to do something kinder with my life. That scarf was mine when I was enlisted. I think, now, you need it more."

Phex thought that this, like the cooking utensils believers sometimes sent him, was tribute he might genuinely make use of.

"I want it back," he said in Dyesi to the acolyte.

"Of course, Demigod," it answered.

And he would get it, after it had been checked thoroughly for malware, spyware, and tracking devices and sanitized to prevent biological or chemical contamination. The Dyesi took no chances with offerings.

Phex returned his attention to his believer. She was being gestured away to make room for the next supplicant.

"It is a thoughtful gift, thank you," he said, in Galactic Formal.

"It is my pleasure, and a small thing in exchange for how much you have moved me. Divine colors changed the course of my life, no doubt yours will do so for the next generation." She bowed her head and backed away.

Phex felt, for the first time, actually honored. Maybe he could do something genuinely *good* with his voice. Maybe it was already doing good. That had never occurred to him. Often, he felt he was taking advantage of the dome for his own autonomy, for survival, but it seemed he could actually produce something that would make a difference in strangers' lives.

Some of the potentials had said that was why they wanted to be gods. For the first time, Phex understood their motivation.

"You're in an odd mood," said Kagee, when they were back aboard ship and getting ready to sleep.

"Ever heard of a *whip scarf*?"

"I have," said Tyve. "Very rare these days, although they were once quite common in this sector before the last big war ended. When was that?" She looked at Jinyesun.

"About a decade ago," answered the Dyesi without having to look it up on the infonet.

Tyve continued. "It used to be a high military honor, a mark of valor. But these days, there aren't any more wars around these parts, so they don't get given out."

"I got given one."

"A weapon?" Fandina looked disapproving.

"Defensive," said Phex… defensively.

"But still, is that a good thing, to give a weapon to a god?" Fandina wondered.

Phex considered the question seriously. "It is if I learn how to use it properly."

"Ask Missit's bodyguard. Cyborgs have readily installed training programs for most hand-to-hand combat weaponry in the known universe. Bob can teach you how to wield it properly," suggested Tyve.

Phex nodded. "It's also pretty. I could wear it, at congregations, and no one would guess what it does."

Berril perked up. "Pretty and deadly, like Kagee's rings?"

"Like Kagee," said Tyve, amused with herself.

Kagee swatted her without malice. He looked at Berril, grey eyes soft. "You think my rings are pretty?"

Berril grinned. "Very."

He nodded. "They're heavier than they look."

"I can wear them for you sometime," suggested Berril, not meaning it.

Phex thought that was not the kind of heaviness Kagee meant. Those rings were heavy with responsibility and, probably, guilt. Both of them knew protecting the others was an obligation, but Kagee did it out of habit, while Phex did it out of need. Still, it was nice to know the burden was, somewhat, shared.

An acolyte pushed the curtain aside. "It's late, demigods, you should sleep now. We have FTL first thing in the morning."

They all murmured agreement.

The acolyte killed the ambient lighting, turned to go, and then paused and turned back, uncharacteristically hesitant for a precatio rank. This was a new acolyte to their spaceship, just picked up in this sector. The three acolytes initially assigned to their tour ship had been rotated out. Phex couldn't figure out why. This one seemed new to the divine in general, younger even than Jin.

"I perhaps should not tell you this, demigods, it may make it difficult for you to sleep. But I have very good news for you. Asterism now has the fastest rising number of registered worshipers in divinity history. Congratulations."

It clicked at them its approval and then left the room, arranging the curtain to drape carefully over the doorway behind it. Berril and Tyve squealed in excitement. Fandina and Jinyesun had puffy crests and they trilled slightly. Even Kagee was grinning. Phex could just make it all out in the now-dim room.

He didn't know what to feel. He was probably more excited about the whip scarf than about Asterism rising in the divine ranks and recruiting new converts, but still, at least they were pulling their weight and the divinity was pleased with them.

It did take them longer than it should to get to sleep after that.

Now that the tour was in full swing, the two pantheons were given matched schedules by the divinity. It behooved the acolytes to calculate energy levels and ensure that both pantheons were assigned the best circadian rhythms, so that when it came time to perform, they were at optimal levels. Since the cantors, as S1s, were the most sensitive, not to mention Fortew's illness, they matched to Sapien schedules. It meant that Tillam and Asterism regularly mingled in practice rooms and the galley at mealtimes.

Perhaps this was also the result of almost a month traveling together, but Asterism had mostly lost its awe of Tillam.

Maybe occasionally one of them would find themselves staring in shock at a major god sitting casually next to them on a brightly colored puff, but at least they were building up a tolerance to the sensation. It was difficult to entirely forget the shine and glory of the great gods, but it was certainly easier now than it once had been.

Phex managed to squeeze in some practice time with the bodyguards, and Bob was, if not happy, at least not opposed to teaching him how to use a whip scarf. A weapon didn't come as naturally to Phex as simply kicking did. But the whip scarf extended his reach considerably. There was something to be said for being able to take out an enemy from a full body length away. Not to mention clearing space around him and his pantheon or, if necessary, strike a chiropteran out of the sky.

Also, Phex liked it. He liked the way it looked and felt when he was wearing it. It was reassuring.

Missit was funny about it. Annoyed or something the first time he saw it wrapped around Phex's neck. "What is that? A love token?"

"Tribute," explained Phex.

"Favoritism? You shouldn't do that. Your other believers will get jealous."

The two pantheons were sitting around, talking in the galley. Only half of Asterism was there, but it was still crowded. Berril and Tyve had gone off to do some grace work because they had an idea for a new move, and Fandina had gone to watch.

But for the others, it was after dinner and there was a lazy feeling to the gathering. Phex had no outside obligations for a change, and no one else seemed inclined to go anywhere either.

Their third tour stop was imminent, so the acolytes were

off reviewing logistics. Even the bodyguards were away training. The gods were unsupervised and at their leisure for a change. Well, Chef was there, tending to a big pot of stew in the galley, but Chef and Phex were close enough now that she was treated as part of the family.

"It's a nice scarf," said Zil, unexpectedly coming to Phex's defense.

Missit sneered at his dark grace for daring to contradict his ire, and then returned to glaring at the innocent whip scarf.

"No, it's tacky," he pronounced.

Phex felt himself flush with embarrassment. "Is it?"

His pantheon often teased him for his lack of style. He still owned only a few jumpsuits and an odd assortment of practice clothes. He wasn't exactly a fashion maven. The divinity dressed him for congregations and performances. But gods were technically supposed to be leaders and arbiters of taste. Phex was unequivocally not.

"Good for keeping your voice warm?" Fortew suggested an excuse in a placating manner, accustomed to mollifying Missit. He was sitting at the end of one of the couch puffs, looking small even in a small puff. For all the metallic tint of his skin, it was sallow and ashy.

Phex unwound a bit of the scarf, fingered the dangling ends. "I thought it was pretty." He liked the whip scarf and didn't want to give it up. But if Missit really thought it was ugly, perhaps there was something seriously wrong with it. Missit never made a single fashion misstep.

Missit looked angry. Everything got momentarily awkward.

Fortew nudged him.

"Stop looking so crestfallen, Phex. I'll buy you a hundred prettier scarves," Missit grumbled.

"But I like this one," insisted Phex, because this one was also deadly.

"Why are you so difficult?" wondered Missit, and then, looking at Fortew, asked "Why is he so difficult?"

"You never did like simple or easy things, hon." But Fortew was looking at Phex curiously. "Phex you're S1, right?"

"Mmm," Phex nodded.

"May I be a little rude? I don't know much about the Wheel. But are you still growing, still in your adolescent life stage?"

Missit's annoyed expression cleared and he too looked curious. He seemed to forget about the scarf and leaned back against Fortew's side. He was bigger than Fortew, but Fortew was older and clearly liked mothering his high cantor. Often petting Missit's head. Although, when he wasn't focusing, Fortew's hands trembled slightly.

Phex watched Missit close his eyes and lean in to the caress. He was a little like Berril, always happy to snuggle up and touch his pantheon. The golden god didn't have Berril's cultural excuse, though. This made Phex wonder what had happened to turn Missit so clingy.

Phex didn't understand why Fortew was asking him such a question, but he also didn't mind answering. "By galactic legal standards, I'm an adult Sapien, but my body hasn't completely settled yet." Phex knew that sometimes the ache in his bones was them still growing, rather than just all the constant practicing for grace and dais and bodyguard duties.

"Did you ever worship, as a kid, I mean?" Fortew asked, still curious.

Phex thought back to the kids in his cafe on Attacon 7. He always considered them younger but they had mostly been about his age. But the way they had *felt* the dome had been different. Different from him and different from mature adults of the species. The way godsong moved them into extremes of emotion. It was like there was a blade inside them, sharp and close to the surface – ever ready and gleaming. Compared to them, Phex had always felt emotionally older, already blunted and dulled by use and time.

"No. I never felt anything as deeply as they did."

Missit leaned forward, using Fortew's knee for leverage. Lips soft and eyes widened with taunting. "Nothing?"

Phex supposed there was *that* to consider, too. All that aggressive flirting of his peers, jumping through emotions, wild with hormones and desire, until the dome acted to calm them down. Had he ever been like that? No, not really.

Not until Missit. He thought about Missit's tight performance costume.

Missit gave him a lazy half-smile.

"Whatever it was seems to have stopped working." Phex sat back into his own puff, unconsciously putting distance between him and the desire to drag two fingers over the gleaming skin at the base of Missit's throat.

He crossed his legs and tried not to think about that time he'd danced with Missit. The want sparking through his body like hot particles of star dust. The way they had probably looked together, gleaming gold and gunmetal blue. He clenched his hands to stop them from trembling like Fortew's did, but for an entirely different reason.

Phex coughed to cover a sudden itch in his throat.

Missit narrowed his eyes. "They keep pushing you, are you getting sick? You were sneezing planetside."

Kagee gave a humorless laugh. "Him? Never."

"Why's that?" asked Fortew, interested for obvious reasons.

"Phex has an aggressive immune system," explained Kagee, haughtily.

"Does he?" Fortew looked understandably wistful.

Kagee was looking at Tillam, more specifically Missit. "The acolytes never told you?" The elder gods were relaxed and casual. Tillam's sifters, Melalan and Yorunlee, were barely even paying attention to the conversation.

"Kagee," warned Phex.

But Kagee was on a roll. He was oddly proud of Phex's genetics. As if it were a point in Asterism's favor – Phex being a manufactured freak. Plus, Kagee liked to shock people. If he could shock major gods, all the more social victory for him. He didn't like how Melalan and Yorunlee were ignoring them.

"He's massively tinkered," he explained, smug.

"Triggered," corrected Phex. "When it's done at the fetal state by enhancers, it's called *triggering*. Tinkering is a somaform nanotech-based system. It's from the before times. Even the Wheel can't do *that* anymore. Wouldn't risk another singularity even if they could. Not even the Wheel is that crazy."

Phex felt the need to explain because Kagee who was ex-core and thus naturally adapted to his home planet – he wouldn't have had an education in genetic vocab. But also, the Wheel was weird.

Zil sat up, interested all of a sudden. His red eyes scanned over Phex as if looking for a visual clue. "You were genetically altered *before* you were born?"

Phex clicked agreement. He really wished he could make noodles right now. Everyone was staring at him. But also, everyone had already eaten, and Chef was right there, stirring stew. Noodles weren't necessary.

"Wheel-made," said Tern, who seemed to fully understand what that meant. Tillam's light grace curled his lip. "What the progenetors do with their pregnancies is objectively disgusting."

"How do you know?" wondered Phex.

"Cotyla," explained Tern, pointing at himself. "I practically grew up next door to your lot." Cotylan Mainspace was the governing system that buffered the Wheel against the rest of the galaxy. They didn't have it easy.

Phex winced. "Sorry about that."

"Not your fault your people are xenophobic alienist assholes."

"Is that how you sing the way you do?" asked Melalan. Phex thought maybe this was the first time the sifter had ever said anything directly to him. But even Yorunlee seemed interested. Kagee's plan had worked.

Phex clicked again.

"And grace the way you do?" asked Zil.

"That's partly upbringing." Kagee was back, ready to shock them some more.

"I thought Phex used to be a barista," said Missit.

Phex wondered who had told him that, or if he'd looked up Phex's god stats on a forum somewhere. He wondered if he could use that as an excuse to go make drinks right now. Missit looked thirsty. Phex needed to do something with his hands. He wanted this all to stop.

"Oh, did I say *upbringing*? I meant *servitude*."

"Kagee, stop," warned Phex.

But now Jinyesun was also in on it. The Dyesi all had this obsessive disgust of child labor. Jin could barely talk about it, it was that taboo. But, then again, the fact that Phex had survived was a point of pride for both of Asterism's sifters.

Jin said, "Phex was a *crudrat*," taking pains to pronounce the alien word properly.

Zil nodded. He was from the Kill'ki Coalition – like Tyve, he'd heard the moniker before. "Explains the blue hair."

"What's *crudrat*?" asked Missit and Fortew at the same time.

Jin said, "They force unregistered children to clean DMP out of their air ducts on the Wheel. Children!"

"It's dangerous, too. Before the acolytes got hold of his body, Phex had all these scars all over," Tyve added.

"Three," said Phex, defensively. "Only three big ones. The rest were pretty small."

"The *rest*?" Missit sat up, lurching away from Fortew. He was looking really upset about something. Again.

Phex checked his scarf – nothing had changed there. He supposed, since Missit had been raised among the Dyesi, he probably had the same phobias around child labor.

Phex tried to be reassuring. "They're all hidden now. You can't see them anymore."

That didn't seem to calm Missit down. He leapt across the small space and knelt in front of Phex's seat, two hands on the top of one of Phex's knees.

"What are you doing?" hissed Phex.

"What happened to you when you were a kid, Phex? What was done to you?"

Phex never knew what to say to that kind of question. *Now* he understood how bad it had been, but he still didn't really *feel* that way. His childhood had just been his childhood. It was what it was. A matter of adrenaline and survival. It wasn't something to be picked at or grieved over like a badly healed wound. He hadn't lost anything, because he hadn't known that there was an alternative. What point was there in regretting a thing that had already happened and over which he had no control? But he couldn't transmit that feeling to others, so everyone tended to pity him when they found out about his past.

He didn't want Missit's pity. The shoulder of Missit's top was slipping, and Phex almost reached out to tug it up. Of course he stopped himself, but there was terror in knowing that he possessed that instinct. Especially around Missit. Why was his reaction to care, and to care for Missit in particular? Phex swallowed down fear – fear of caring about anything.

"He does not like to talk about it," explained Jinyesun in a very practical tone, for which Phex was grateful.

"Trauma?" Fortew asked, sympathetically.

"No," said Kagee quickly. "He's just weird about it. Like he doesn't think there was anything really wrong with being a crudrat, but he knows everyone else does, so he doesn't want to embarrass us with his indifference."

Phex wished he had ear crests that he could lay flat back against his skull to indicate annoyance.

Missit was still pressing his knee, staring up at him with big gold-flecked eyes, now filled with worry.

Phex tried an evasive maneuver, a verbal blade dodge. "There were plenty of others who had it worse. At least I escaped."

Missit looked like he was going to cry. "But Phex, that's how abused kids talk."

"It was work," Phex defended, annoyed, "not abuse."

"Hazardous work, for no pay, starting at six years old, that leaves lasting physical, mental, and emotional scars is *abuse*," said Kagee, flatly. Then to the rest of Tillam, sitting there full of pity: "See, he just gets like this."

"But it gave you grace?" Melalan's crests were interested, and it was Dyesi enough to try to understand.

Phex licked his lips. "Apparently."

Missit said, squeezing to get Phex's attention. "We aren't done. What exactly happens to crudrats?"

Phex said, "You can look it up on the net. Last I checked, the description was basically accurate." It was relatively new information, too, available to anyone with the right search term. A listing for *crudrat* hadn't been there a few years earlier, before he became a potential. But he'd checked for it after he got aboard the spaceship. He wasn't sure why he'd bothered. And he really didn't know why he'd been happy to see a listing, and a definition, and accuracy. Like somehow the presence of the word *crudrat* on the galactic infonet validated his existence. Phex supposed it must have come out of the Kill'ki Coalition and their crudrat-extraction program. Maybe he was happy because it meant there were enough crudrats escaping the Wheel to make it necessary for the rest of the galaxy to know about them. Maybe it was just that now he knew for certain he wasn't alone.

The divinity had kept *crudrat* out of his demigod bio. Divine forums had him officially listed as coming from Attacon 7, nothing more. His believers were left to assume that he'd been born there, blue hair notwithstanding. Phex thought the Dyesi did it because they wanted to protect him, or protect the child that he'd once been. It was oddly endearing. Phex was grateful. He'd hate to have to explain his background to Asterism's worshipers. Then what? A million people would pity him.

Tillam's pity was bad enough.

Missit's pity was worse.

"But I want *you* to tell me," insisted Missit.

Phex looked down at golden perfection and wondered that Missit didn't melt with the strength of Phex's embarrassment. He would try to give Missit anything he needed, but Missit didn't *need* this. Phex wasn't going to make himself vulnerable in front of someone so capricious, no matter how sweet his lopsided smile or how beautiful he looked in a tight bodysuit. In fact, largely because of that.

Phex's background was ugly. Someone like Missit shouldn't have to deal with that kind of ugliness. Phex certainly didn't want to watch Missit's gorgeous face as he learned how cruel and indiscriminate the universe could be.

So, he told the god, a great god, "No."

Then he purposefully looked away from Missit and pointed rudely at Kagee and Jin. "Don't you two start, either. Enough now. Missit is perfectly capable of reading about it on his own."

Missit pressed his lips together and looked away from Phex. Then stood and retreated back to Fortew.

"It seems I have research to do," he said, offering his friend a hand up.

Tern stood as well.

Without further fanfare, the three gods left the galley.

Zil, Melalan, and Yorunlee moved to follow. They made proper and polite goodbyes to the three demigods.

Of all the members of Tillam, it was Yorunlee who stopped because it had one final question on the subject. Yorunlee, who seemed to drift around in a cloud of arrogance and disinterest, and, when it did speak, tended to be casually cruel.

It looked down at Jinyesun, ignoring Phex.

"Was it that bad, young one?" Dyesi informal, so casual as to be almost familial and definitely rude. Phex wondered if these two were from the same cave.

Jin replied without hesitation, "As bad as it is possible to be. I recommend against reading about crudrats. I found it extremely upsetting."

"The divinity saved him," stated Yorunlee.

"I saved myself," protested Phex. To be fair, he'd merely escaped, run away like a coward. Left the other crudrats behind. Survival was like that.

"Or did the Wheel let you go like a virus to infect us?" Yorunlee's crest remained neutral.

Jinyesun's crests flattened back. "He was a child!"

Kagee was even angrier. He leapt to his feet, chest out. "I didn't tell you so you could use his past as a weapon against him!"

"Then why did you tell us?"

Zil moved quickly to interpose himself between Kagee and Yorunlee. It was comical. Kagee was substantially smaller than the Dyesi and the Jakaa Nova. But also, he was wearing all his rings. Tyve would have told her brother what those rings could do.

Melalan flushed opaque with shame, turned quickly to Phex, body hunched in embarrassment. "Apologies. Yorunlee is extremely irritable these days."

Yorunlee allowed Melalan to hustle it from the room.

Zil shook his head. "You might have rolled that information out differently, demigods. We are friends, after all."

"Are we?" Wondered Kagee, still postured and angry.

Zil slapped his grey shoulder companionably. "You're an angsty little nodule, aren't you?"

"You have no idea," said Phex, with feeling.

"Oh, we got our own troublemaker. So, I kind of do. Sorry about Missit earlier, his curiosity gets the better of him. Especially with you."

"Why is that?" Kagee wanted to know.

Zil shook his head, red eyes gleaming. "My sister has her work cut out for her, I see. Goodnight, *friends*." Then he too left the room.

Silence reigned until everyone was sure Tillam was out of

earshot.

"I wonder if Yorunlee is close to instar. There is an edge of instability there." Jin sounded philosophical. "Did you see any yellow in its eyes?"

"Yellow? In a Dyesi? Of course not," Phex answered, because Kagee wouldn't have been able to tell. "You think maybe it's not just Fortew's illness setting them all on edge?" Phex was grateful for a change of subject even as he wondered what *instar* was.

Jinyesun blinked a moment. "Never mind. I shall talk to the acolytes about it." It turned to Kagee. "You sure can kill a companionable atmosphere."

"It's my one true gift."

"Not cantor?"

"No, I'm far better at assholery than I'll ever be at singing."

Phex was deeply annoyed that his past had been brought up at all. Plus, Chef had been right there all along, so now she knew his past as well. The last thing he wanted was pity in the kitchen. Having nothing nice to say to Kagee on the subject, he decided to maintain a stony silence.

The rest of the pantheon noticed this once they were reunited before bed.

"Is it just me, or is Phex even quieter than normal tonight?" Fandina fluffed its blankets before climbing in.

Kagee said, "He's mad at me."

"What did you do this time?" asked Tyve, assuming, quite rightly, that it was Kagee's fault.

"I told Tillam about his past as a crudrat."

"Why?" wondered Berril. "Phex hates that."

"Because it's not something he should be ashamed of."

"Is that for you to decide?" Fandina wondered, seriously.

Kagee was really upset about the whole thing for some

reason. "He should be proud that he made it out alive!"

Phex wondered if pride was a matter of survival on Agatay.

"But you made him seem weak in front of *elder* gods," protested Jinyesun.

Phex thought that it wasn't that, either. Well, maybe a little. He certainly hadn't liked appearing lesser in Missit's eyes.

"Why *weak*?! He survived, remember? Isn't that the very definition of strength?"

In actuality, it had never been a matter of strength or weakness, of will or ability – it had mostly been dumb luck and desperation. Now it was just shame and regret that he couldn't come from a normal planet with a normal background like a normal god. That his past had to be trotted out before others like godsong, a creature of overwrought emotion – something that titillated with its uniqueness.

He wondered if Missit would research crudrats and then make a song about it. About him. He wondered if Kagee already was.

He hated that idea.

There were some things in the galaxy unworthy of godsong.

Finally, carefully, he said, "There is nothing honorable or noble about my childhood. It is not something to be bragged about. It was just crud and blades and now-invisible scars. Thinking about it" —he shot a quick glance at Kagee— "*talking* about it, makes me feel like I'm unworthy of being a god."

Kagee swore and looked at the ceiling.

Berril sat next to Phex and hugged him from one side. Tyve did the same from the other. But this was more for their comfort than his.

As he often told them, he was fine.

Phex wondered if his saying such a thing somehow justified the Dyesi taboo around child labor. He glanced over at Jinyesun and Fandina. But they just looked sad, their crests slightly wilted, like limp, translucent lettuce leaves, their huge eyes fixed on Phex. He hadn't meant to hurt them.

"It's just the way I feel. It's not really important," he said, to fill the awkward silence.

Kagee launched himself directly at him, knocking Phex back and landing to lie on top of him, freeing Phex from Berril and Tyve. Kagee hugged him hard, surprisingly strong and wiry, the cool metal of his deadly rings pressing into Phex's skin.

Phex sighed and patted his back.

Kagee's face was damp were it touched Phex's neck. "I'm sorry, Phex." His voice was muffled.

Then, just as quickly, he jumped away, rubbing his eyes angrily. "I don't agree with you. I think it's amazing that you made it out. Everything that happened to you only makes you a better god. The best, really. But I'll not talk about it again. Not in front of anyone."

Kagee nodded once, sharply, not meeting Phex's eyes. Then he climbed into his bed, pulled the blanket up over his head, and curled into an angry ball. He was mad at himself, though, not Phex. They all knew that.

Berril and Tyve flopped back to cuddle next to Phex. The cot was far too small to do that for long, but it was nice while it lasted.

Phex realized then that Kagee was a little wonderful for taking the thing Phex found most shameful about himself and admiring it so much that he thought the universe should know. Weird, but wonderful. With that realization came forgiveness.

8

TWO GODS WITH ONE TONE

It would take them two weeks and two FTL folds to arrive in the sector of space destined to host their third tour stop. A few days after their awkward conversation about Phex's past, and a little before their second FTL, the acolytes made an unusual request.

Missit had been uncomfortable and cautious around Phex. He'd clearly read the entry on crudrats. Phex wanted to grab him by the shoulders and shake him and explain that really it hadn't been that bad, but instead, he ate his stewed grains in sullen silence and left breakfast as quickly as he could. Only an hour or so later, an acolyte came and took Phex away from his pantheon.

Kagee was annoyed. "Tillam needs him again? Right now?"

"Is Fortew not feeling well today?" Phex wondered.

"Nothing like that, younglings," said the acolyte. It seemed a bit friendlier than some of their other handlers had been. "The divinity has a small scheme in mind. We will explain shortly."

The scheme involved Missit, because that was who waited, alone, in one of the cantor practice booths.

The acolyte got straight to the point. "We want the two of you to sing together as a special offering. Under the dome. And maybe dance, too. Like in an old-fashioned Sapien way."

"That seems risky," said Phex. To be in close proximity to Missit, encouraged and supervised by the divinity?
Please, no.

Missit gave him a look.

Phex quickly added for specificity, "Won't it diminish us in the eyes of worshipers, performing without color?"

The acolyte crested at him in confusion. Its crests were particularly large with an unusual shape, like butterfly wings.

"No sifters and no graces, will we not look small and insignificant up on the dais alone with a dark dome around us?" But Phex was thinking that yet another thing to practice meant pulling back on bodyguard training even more. Why was it always a war, one way or another, between Missit and his pantheon, between pleasing the divinity and keeping everyone safe?

The acolyte puffed out a Dyesi laugh of genuine amusement. "He is Missit. You are Phex. Given the current standings, *insignificance* is no longer possible."

Phex looked to Missit for help, but the golden god seemed more interested than cautious. Could he actually be entertaining the idea? He was the one who had the power to nip this in the bud.

The acolyte pressed. "It would just be a special thing. During *this* tour."

Missit cocked his head and picked at a single loose thread at the end of one long sleeve of his silky jumper. "Why?"

"Our gift to them."

Missit hissed disapproval. “The divinity collects tribute, it does not dole it out. Phex and I are not alms to be distributed at your whim for some kind of musical charity.”

Phex wondered if that were true. He thought that was what gods actually did under a dome. Gave of themselves on the dais, in exchange for worship. That was why performing was so exhausting.

Missit, god that he was, used a Dyesi formal mandate on the acolyte. “Give us a better reason.”

“We want to get the worshipers accustomed to seeing you two performing together.” This acolyte knew when it was no longer a good idea to be cagy.

Phex understood the nuances of that statement. The divinity really didn’t think Fortew was going to make it through the end of this tour.

Phex wasn’t actually an understudy – he was being groomed as a full replacement. His stomach knotted.

Regardless of his feelings, such a jarring shift would be too much for worshipers of any pantheon, let alone Tillam. The acolytes wanted to get everyone comfortable with the idea. Familiar with seeing Missit and Phex singing and their dynamic on a dais together. This was a priming tactic. Like preheating the oven.

But they had no idea what they asked of Phex to practice one-on-one with Missit. They understood the danger Phex and Missit singing together could cause, but without sifters from their perspective, that would be negligible. But they could not possibly comprehend the price of Phex and Missit dancing together.

Phex felt his skin prickle just thinking about it. He had a good deal of restraint, but when faced with constant physical contact just the two of them, Missit in his arms, over and over?

And had the divinity even considered what they asked of Missit? He was a major god – would this not be debasing, to perform with a demigod and no sifters? Did it not tarnish his glory? Shouldn't Missit feel insulted?

Missit had a funny look on his beautiful face – mixed emotions. Sadness for Fortew, of course, but also anticipation, even eagerness. Phex stopped himself from huffing out a breath of annoyance. The boy probably just wanted an excuse to flirt. This was going to be hell.

"Are you *certain* it will not curtail Missit's divinity?" Phex pressed. "I am only a minor cantor. I am not worthy."

"We think it will be perceived as something special, a window into your unique friendship. The elder god and the young demigod he's graciously taken under his wing."

Phex wondered if the acolytes really did see them like that, or if they had run polls and tests in the divine forums to try and understand the reception this kind of display might garner.

"It would be a way for you to honor the origins of the art form as well. An exploration of humanity's deep past. Old-fashioned song and dance."

"I bet the idea tested well with S1s," said Missit.

The acolyte wiggled one crest slightly. "We will record you practicing, too, beam that. Let them get used to you being with Phex as grace first. Less threatening that way. And then we can slowly introduce Phex as cantor."

Phex wondered if he could control his reactions to Missit in front of a beam. He'd have to if they were going to be dancing together, streamed onto the net while doing so.

It sounded like a nightmare.

Missit said, "One song and only one. We get to choose. And the practices are done in private – no acolyte supervision, no beaming, no interruption. Divine bond on all three conditions."

The acolyte considered. "You're sure about the privacy requirement?"

Missit glanced quickly at Phex. "Nonnegotiable."

Phex, embarrassed, felt compelled to add, "We will make many mistakes. It would be too embarrassing to be watched." But he was thinking about how aching and lost Missit made him feel when there was too much of his skin against him.

The acolyte nodded. "Very well." It turned expectantly to Phex. "What are your conditions?"

Phex was surprised that, as a demigod, he got to set any. "If, for any reason, and at any point, you wish to add graces or sifters into this special performance, they must be taken in equal parts from both Asterism and Tillam."

The acolyte looked momentarily shocked but clearly didn't think that would happen. "Agreed. Anything else?"

"The divinity must make this request official. I want it on record that you asked this of us, we did not offer."

"Of course."

"One final request."

"You're very uppity for a demigod."

"Careful," said Missit, sounding unexpectedly cool and deadly with very formal Dyesi. "Three requests each is sacred and contractually sanctified."

The acolyte flattened its crests back, cowed by a great god's ire, changed its body language to be more respectful.

Phex framed his third request carefully. "I want to be approved to practice with the bodyguards. The acolytes know I'm doing it. I want official dispensation. I want it in my record and stats. I want it known."

Missit gritted his teeth and said, "*That's* your final condition?"

The acolyte flushed opaque and its crests rose back up. It seemed to be having a bit of a war with itself. "Among ourselves, we acolytes did agree that it's a good idea to have at least one god in a pantheon who has battle training. Although we are not convinced that you are the correct choice for Asterism. And the violence inherent in the process concerns us deeply."

"I understand that the Dyesi are pacifists. But I am not." Phex did not give any quarter, just acknowledgment.

"But, technically, Demigod Phex, you are Dyesi."

Missit interrupted. "What does *that* mean?"

Phex explained, quickly, "I carry Dyesi nationality. They accepted me as a refugee, and once I was elevated to godhood, I became a citizen."

"Oh? Oh!"

Phex focused on the acolyte. "This is a condition, not a request."

The acolyte clicked. "I must consult the divinity on this. Your voice, you understand, you are already a risk. To officially train you in violence? Even riskier."

Phex clicked. He knew that under the dome with sifters, his voice was considered dangerous – paired with Missit, doubly so. For the Dyesi, Phex's voice was already a weapon, and now he wanted permission to turn his body into one as well. Phex was doing deals with safety again, his pantheon's for the Dyesi's.

The safety of his own heart was in play too. He was parlaying what Missit could do to him against how important his pantheon already was to his emotional well-being. He was scrabbling for control of an untenable situation, and bound to lose either way.

"You'll let us know?" said Phex.

"By tomorrow."

The next day, the answer came back in the affirmative. Apparently, the divinity really wanted Phex and Missit to perform together – all six conditions were agreed to.

So, the divinity added a new form of torture into Phex's day. He still spent most of his time aboard ship practicing with Asterism. That was lovely. He really enjoyed his pantheon. And he still, occasionally, was stolen away to observe and sing with Tillam in Fortew's role.

But now, in the evenings, he and Missit spent hours alone together in one of the grace studios. He let Missit choose their song – after all, the kid came from a family for whom music was everything.

Missit decided on an older ballad from an obscure colony in some remote region of space. It was haunting and sweeping and a little sad. When sung, it took full advantage of Phex's range and Missit's honeyed sweetness. It was a good choice since it was all about their voices. Had it been sung at sifters, the pattern would be too simple and the colors too bold. There was very little dome to it at all. It was meant to be sung directly out into the void, not at skin and into visual existence. It was old music, the kind designed for ears alone. Because of that, there was no danger in Phex simply singing to the extreme of his ability. He need not worry that it might burn or bruise any Dyesi present.

Phex liked the song and found himself humming it as he puttered about the galley while chef grinned in delight. He learned it easily and Missit sang it with him well. They laid down old-fashioned recordings of their voices in harmony instead of their voices as visual instruments. They planned to sing some parts live and dance to others recorded, interposing bodies with vocals since they could not interweave the way a pantheon did. They would have to switch between singing and dancing for the sake of stability, but Phex kind of liked that idea. It was like some ancient musical put on before a city forum on a stone stage, from a time before there were Dyesi, when domes were colored only by firelight.

It took them only a few days to perfect the song – no surprise there, they were cantors, after all. But the dancing, that was another thing entirely.

Phex had to rely on Missit for the choreography – all he really knew were crudrat tricks and grace beats. Missit did make use of those, stepping back to sing a high note while Phex would flip backward over him.

“It will be more spectacular this way,” Missit explained, watching Phex take a casual leap at a bulkhead and bounce into a backflip.

Phex landed one knee down and panting. “Why would that be?”

“Because they will have to focus on you with no colors to distract.”

That’s if they could tear their eyes away from Missit, Phex thought but did not say.

“Okay,” said Missit. “Let’s practice some of the partner parts.”

It had to be done, but it was torture. Phex could not be stiff about it, this was dancing, but he also could not forget that this was Missit. The moment he got Missit in his arms, there was wanting. It wasn’t like the golden god made it easy on him.

Sometimes, when they stopped, holding a pose in order to examine it and get body position correct, Missit would simply lean against him, all his weight outside of the frame. It was a kind of affection expressed only with his body, and it was all temptation. Phex wasn't certain if Missit even realized what he was doing, like he just could not help himself.

"Stop it." Phex made his voice low and blurred, like a fuzzy line of dark charcoal slashed over the dome.

"Don't you want a hug?"

Phex hissed in annoyance.

"You let Berril hug you all the time."

"Because she's Berril."

"Tyve, too. Is it because they're female-identified?" Missit straightened only so he could press his nose into the side of Phex's neck.

Phex flinched away.

But when Missit looked hurt, Phex leaned back in, because he was weak.

"You prefer boys, right?" Missit could be blunt too. Always blunt – after all, gold did not hold an edge. Missit might be the greatest god in the divinity, but there was no steel in him – he did not cut, he only warmed. Burned sometimes, if Phex got too close, but no cutting. Missit was never cruel – intentionally or accidentally.

Missit's breath branded Phex's neck. Phex wondered if such a thing left an invisible scar, like the blades had. Blunt or no.

The heartbeat in Phex's ear, like the *thump thump thump* of grace, reminded him that they were entirely alone together. That Missit had bartered his skill for their privacy. Of course, there was no locked door between them and the rest of the world – this was still a Dyesi spaceship. But Phex ached because of that aloneness – it made him feel hot and itchy with selfish need. The beating in his ear was about risk, not exercise. He wanted to kiss Missit again so badly, his own heartbeat was punishing him for it.

Phex stiffened and moved away. They were definitely not

dancing anymore.

"Someday, you'll actually like me," warned Missit, looking a little odd, almost sickly.

Phex wondered if Missit simply wanted him to admit to the attraction, or if he genuinely didn't realize how much Phex adored him. But because he couldn't risk giving him touches, too afraid he might never stop, Phex gave him words.

"Holding you is like holding sunshine."

"I didn't know you could be poetic." Missit glanced down at his feet, smiling shyly at them. Was he embarrassed? How cute.

"I won't do it again."

Missit widened his eyes intentionally. "See that you don't. But what do you mean?"

Phex sighed. "I read somewhere that once, a long time ago, they used to say you should not fraternize with the gods. They burn."

"But aren't you a god now too?" Missit moved in close again, emboldened, bumped Phex's chin with the side of his head. Some of Missit's long gold hair had fallen out of its customary bun – strands stuck to the skin of Phex's neck.

"Not a god like you're a god."

Missit pulled away and looked up at him, gave him that smile, the one that lit up worlds. The one that made Phex's throat ache. "No one is like me."

"Exactly." Phex turned away. Because he never got to have anything, so he assumed he did not deserve it. Certainly not sunshine or the burn that followed.

For some reason, at that moment, Phex remembered something he'd read in a psych article back on Attacon 7, sitting alone in his cube after some revival at the cafe.

You must want something in order to feel threatened.

But that statement was wrong. The act of wanting Missit wasn't threatening – it was terrifying. It was like having a pantheon.

For the first time in his life, Phex had things he could lose. And the act of holding too tightly on to one could cost him the other. He couldn't afford to love Missit, not how he really wanted to, because, as Kagee once forced him to realize, that put his other love at risk. His pantheon.

"Shall we try that move again?" Phex asked, steeling himself. Because there might be no sharp blade of steel running through Missit, but Phex contained more than his fair share. The real, greatest risk was that he might be the one to cause pain and damage to both his pantheon and Missit.

Phex and Missit were ready with their special performance by the time they reached Cotyla Mainspace. Phex could sense that it was a *good* show, too. Not good in a way that the dome would tell them. They would get no feedback from the colors. *Good* in a way that would impact an audience, congregation of worshipers, or some other kind of audience. When they finally did their song-and-dance routine for the others – pantheons and acolytes, crew and bodyguards – under the ship's tiny practice dome, it ended in awed silence. No godfix there and no risk of it, but simple appreciation for entertainment as art. Like seeing a beautiful painting or eating a delicious meal.

"That was truly lovely," said Itrio afterward.

Phex was sparring with her and Bob, whip scarf at the ready.

She added, "I forgot what it was like just to watch a show rather than experience the divine."

"It has its merits," agreed Bob, in an acerbic way.

Itrio snorted. "Well, yes, for one, we could actually both watch and listen to the darn thing without risk."

"Your voice is very good, Phex," said Bob. "I understand now what all the fuss is about." The cyborg, no doubt, was particularly appreciative of the trueness and clarity of Phex's range. They had both been modified and manufactured in their way, and like valued like.

Phex took the compliment as something important and genuine. "Thank you, it is the work of prior generations, but I am no longer ashamed to be the beneficiary."

"And why should you have ever been ashamed of your talent?" The cyborg's eyes ran bits across them, calculating.

"Because I did not *work* to earn it."

"Is that why you do this? Learn to fight? Because it is something that you can earn through personal cost and time well spent?" Itrio cocked her head at him. Her huge arms braced, her stance firm. She was playing the attacker today and was even more padded out than usual to withstand Phex's sparring.

Phex whipped out his scarf, trying to use it to wrap around and yank her legs out from under her. He missed. "Maybe. I never thought of it that way. But sometimes, it feels like this time I spend with you is more honest than what happens under a dome."

"Makes sense to me." Bob sounded very much as if it did, in fact, make perfect sense.

They finished up their training session. Afterward, Phex was happy to be with them, wiping down in companionable silence.

"Is your lot ready for your first solo performance?" Itrio asked, casually.

"I'm sorry, *what*?" Phex set the towel down and stared

at her.

"Oh, the acolytes haven't told you? My bad. Maybe plans have changed recently."

"I doubt that," said Bob.

"What do you mean, *solo*?" Phex pressed.

"Well, obviously, they'll have you and Missit do your pretty little couple's piece. But otherwise, Tillam won't be performing at all in this sector. The dome is only going to Asterism."

"What!"

Bob made a cutting hand gesture at Itrio. "If the acolytes haven't told him yet, it isn't for us to do so."

Phex went for his scarf.

"Don't threaten us, youngling. Bob is right. I shouldn't have said anything. But you should definitely ask them tomorrow."

Phex resolved to do just that at breakfast. After all, their next dome was only a few days away, and apparently, Asterism was going to perform in it alone.

But it turned out he didn't have to ask.

"Where are we, again?" asked Fortew. He was curled in a puff in the galley, looking tired even though all they'd done was eat breakfast. There were bags under his eyes that even all the skills of the divinity could not fade.

Tern gave his low cantor a funny look. "Cotyla."

Fortew sat up, clearly shocked. "Your home?"

"No. Mainspace," corrected Tern.

Fortew sat back. "We aren't performing, then."

"No, just Asterism."

Phex had been warned of this by the bodyguards, but it

was news to the rest of his pantheon. Well, the ones who were there – Berril and Jin were still in bed. As were Melalan, Yorunlee, and Missit.

"Wait. What?" That was Kagee.

Tillam ignored him. Which Kagee did *not* like.

"Thank heavens for that," said Fortew with feeling.

Tyve tilted her head at Fandina. "We are the only ones going under the dome this time? Really?"

Fandina had its crests back in shock.

Kagee pressed the matter with Tillam since there were no acolytes around. "Why wouldn't you perform in Tern's home sector? Shouldn't Tillam be massively popular here? Even more than elsewhere."

"Oh, we are. And I am indeed Cotylan, but I'm from Cotilax," answered Tern, as if that explained everything.

"Really? The acolytes keep *that* pretty quiet, don't they?" Understanding dawned over Tyve's face.

Tern shrugged, unperturbed. "They didn't understand when they took me on. Frankly, they still don't. Conflict, especially political conflict that's been going on for generations, is mysterious to the Dyesi. You know they've never been at war, had civil unrest or invaders."

"No one has ever tried to take Dyesid Prime," pointed out Fandina, looking smug. It was an amusing expression on a Dyesi, crests neutral and half-flappy, big eyes a little squinted, chin up.

"Well, who would want it?" asked Kagee.

"Fair point," replied Fandina, even more smug. The Dyesi were realists about the sinister nature of their home planet. After all, there was a reason most of them took to the stars as acolytes – to spread the divinity, of course, but also to get away from home. But that didn't mean they weren't proud of its harsh reputation.

"Odd that no one even came after your tech." That was Tyve, full of idle speculation.

"The domes?" Zil wandered over with a bowl of porridge, bumped his sister aside to join her on a puff meant for one. "Entertainment is a pretty stupid reason to go to war. Especially when the technology only works with Dyesi sifters."

"Fair." Tyve shoved him back but not so hard he spilled his breakfast.

Fandina was still confused, fortunately for Phex, because he also didn't get what was going on. It piped up with a polite but insistent "I still do not understand why Tillam cannot perform in Cotylan space."

"Cotilax used to be the capital, did you know?" Fortew explained, presumably so Tern didn't have too.

"No." Fandina's crests perked.

Phex was a little shocked. Cotilax was talked of in a positive light, a safe, industrious, ultra-modern planet, but small and not exactly a power player in galactic circles. It had always been a strong ally to Attacon, though, probably due to its central trading position.

Tern said, "It's regrettably complicated, and frankly, most of my generation doesn't care anymore. But the elders tend to think of Cotilax as the only *real* Cotylan homeworld while Mainspace and the colonies are *the rebels*. Mainspace, of course, believes the opposite. The end result is impasse, since Mainspace is bigger and stronger and refuses to recognize us as self-governing. But I can't go there to perform, because if they host a god from Cotilax, it's too validating for my planet's independence."

Fortew added, sounding sad for his friend, "And we can't do Cotilax, either, because Mainspace would label it favoritism and Dyesi allegiance."

Fandina clicked agreement. "The divinity can't risk a

Cotylan ban, it's the third most devout area of space."

"Doesn't that upset you, Tern? Never getting to perform for your people?" Kagee asked.

Tern tilted his head, thinking. "They can't keep Tillam's godsongs out. I'm still there, even if I never get to go in person. The domes are everywhere. It's enough that they know I exist, and no one can forget about Cotilax because of Tillam, even if they wanted to."

"You aren't worried they'll come after your planet?" asked Kagee.

"There's been peace between us for as long as I've been performing. I think the younger generations all feel the same way, Mainspace or Cotilax."

"And what's that?" Kagee leaned, pretending disinterest but his eyes were intent on Tern.

"Indifference. None of it is worth fighting over. It's the previous generation's hang-up. We are more alike than we are different. Who cares for some ancient conflict over ideals and principles? Unity or independence no longer matters. I don't see that changing anytime soon."

"Things aren't tense anymore?" Kagee, from a land of conflict, was curious.

"Sure, between the governments. If they weren't, Tillam could perform wherever we liked. But they are becoming *less* tense as the older generations die off and everyone forgets why the fight started to begin with."

"Will it happen in your lifetime? Will Tillam ever get to perform for your people?" Kagee pressed. Phex had never seen his high cantor this curious about anything.

Tern looked sadly at Fortew. "I doubt it. But *in my lifetime*? Maybe. Cotylans live longer than Sapiens."

"You aren't S-class?" Phex was surprised, Tern looked a lot like him in physical build and appearance. Or at least enough like Wheel for Phex to have assumed humanity, erroneously, as it turned out.

"No, HS1. I know we look untinkered, but we're altered for space travel, longevity, gravity, and few high-grade somaform hallmarks of early colony survival. Enough to render us no longer strictly human."

"Such an old-fashioned way of thinking about it," said Fandina.

Tern smiled for a change. His face suddenly transformed into something younger, prettier. Divine. "I am still Cotylan. You know we have the reputation for being old-fashioned and traditional."

Phex said, "I imagine that's how you tolerate being next door to the Wheel."

"Or the Wheel tolerates us." Tern examined Phex closely.

Phex thought it was a very good thing that the Wheel didn't know the Cotylan carried an HS designation. They'd hate that. His home sector might trigger their own children into freakish absurdity, but they were purists about expansion tinkering. They hated so-called *aliens* with a passion.

"I guess you'll never get to perform for your homeworld either, Phex." Tern's voice was sympathetic but also a little indifferent. Phex kind of liked that.

"No actual homeworld, plus I wouldn't bother, even if I could," said Phex fervently. "I can't go back but I don't want to. Fortunately, neither does the divinity. Smart decision."

Tern clicked at him. "Asterism has an advantage in this."

"Really?" Phex was confused.

"The Wheel is out, but the rest of you have no complicated alliances or politics among your membership's planets. Yet you are multicultural enough to appeal to a broad range of sectors and worshipers. I suspect that somewhat accounts for the rising popularity of Asterism. And it's possibly one of the reasons the acolytes put you together." Tern seemed to be the one of his group who, like Fandina, was interested in popularity and strategies for expanding divine reach. "The divinity has gotten a lot smarter about this kind of thing since we debuted."

Phex considered his pantheon. He'd never thought of them from the perspective of market capacity. That seemed awfully manipulative.

"Not my planet."

Tern looked at Kagee. "No?"

Kagee snorted. "I take it you don't know anything about Agatay?"

"Do they participate on the galactic stage?"

"Not for lack of trying, but we're cursed by internal conflict."

"Civil war?"

"And how." Kagee clicked fervent agreement.

"Messy." Tern wrinkled his nose and sounded somewhat condescending.

Kagee laughed. "The elites of my planet would boil in their soup if they knew how easily the rest of the galaxy dismisses them." He twirled his rings. "So, we are about to put on our first solo performance. Yet the acolytes still thought it important enough to come all the way to this sector. Does that mean Asterism is particularly well worshiped among the Cotylan? Or does the divinity have some other agenda in Mainspace?"

Fandina checked their demographics. "Ooo, look, we *are* extremely popular with Mainspace! Want the breakdown? You're in first place, Kagee. Apparently, your visuals are particularly admired."

Tern evaluated Kagee with a critical eye. "I can see that. My people would find him quite pretty."

"Tyve is in second."

Tern nodded again. "Yes, Zil is second-ranked after me for Tillam. Cotyla has been trading partners with the Jakaa Nova for generations. They're considered sexy. There's a lot of interspecies unions between Cotylan and Jakaa Nova."

Phex looked at Fortew and Zil. "How about the rest of Tillam? Ten years must have taken you home at least once."

"Jakaa Nova have no domes, but we've done a few satellite revivals in Coalition space that were attended by my people," said Zil.

Fortew added, "Countless times for me. I'm from Syrunid. Dome Precept is *my* dome." Phex wondered that they hadn't stayed longer there, if it was Fortew's home sector. But perhaps he did not have affection for this home. After all, something had happened in his youth to make him sick now.

"What about Missit?" Phex asked.

Zil combed fat-tipped fingers through his sister's new long wavy hair, working out a knot. "Tillam has done Hucore a few times. Western spiral arm is a weird part of space. Old and absent-minded. Out of touch. Couple of really nice domes and enthusiastic attendances. Can't complain. You know he wasn't raised there, though?" He gave Phex a hard look.

Phex nodded. Missit's upbringing on Dyesid Prime was a matter of divine record, after all.

Tern gestured at Asterism in a friendly way, seeming to have finally softened toward them a little. "Will you make it home to a dais, do you think?"

Tyve said, "Same as Zil for me. I assume we'll do a Coalition event eventually. Or at least visit some large satellite that my people gravitate towards."

"And your messy little homeworld?" Tern asked Kagee,

genuinely curious.

"Agatay? No way. No domes and no interest. My people are pretty xenophobic. I imagine I'm a planet-wide embarrassment because while Agatay *knows* about the divinity, it's considered frivolous childish entertainment. We *are* tapped into the infonet and the galaxy at large. We aren't as bad as Phex's Wheel. But I used to have to sneak illegal copies of Tillam's stuff when I was a kid. Listen to secret recordings with my friends when no adults were around."

"That makes me feel old," said Zil, glaring at Kagee.

"We *are* old," replied Fortew.

"Ever thought about just stopping?" wondered Phex of Tillam.

Fortew looked over at him. Or, more to the point, Fortew hadn't really stopped looking at him. Phex wondered why Tillam's high cantor was finding him so interesting today. "Us? What else are we good for?" He sounded bitter.

"Speak for yourself," said Zil gently. "I always wanted to have my own ship. This – touring – has always been my favorite part."

"You're originally traders, right?" asked Fandina, crests curious.

"Originally, more just freight transport, sometimes people, sometimes stuff," said Zil.

Tyve added, "But then our parents co-married a pair of surgeons six years ago, converted our freight whale into a medical ship, and have been serving support for natural disasters, search-and-rescue missions, high-conflict sectors, and the like ever since."

"An ambulance ship? That's brave work." Fandina looked genuinely impressed, and it took a lot to impress a Dyesi with something that wasn't godsong.

Phex wondered that they'd never talked about this with

Tyve before.

Tyve and her bother exchanged a look that Phex couldn't decipher. Then she said, "Especially when they both gave up military connections to do it. It's not really considered honorable by Jakaa Nova standards. But who are we to talk? We both became entertainers. That's basically the bottom of the barrel."

Zil squeezed his sister's hand. "Our uncle is pretty high up in the Kill'ki Coalition military, so he's still bitter with the shame of us all at this point."

"I used to be his favorite." Tyve pressed her lips together, then licked them and said, "And now our little sister might follow in our parents' footsteps, even skip being a warrior altogether. Before I left, she was talking about opting for conscientious objection and medical training over military service. It's not considered an honorable path, but" —Tyve flexed and extended one very sharp claw— "Jakaa Nova make truly excellent surgeons. Sharp scalpels are attached to our hands, we have multiples we can work with at a time, we're very dexterous, and we come with a numbing agent."

Zil grinned with sharp teeth. "And most of us are ambidextrous." He looked at his sister. "She'll do well."

Tyve nodded. "Yeah, she will. Little brat."

"Will it be hard for her?" Phex asked, knowing that Tyve hadn't had it easy because she didn't enjoy fighting and then worse when she'd opted out entirely to become a god.

"Easier than either of us did. Things are changing with the Jakaa Nova."

Fandina's crests puffed with interest. "Really? In what way?"

Tyve shrugged. "I don't know exactly, my sister and her age mates, they just seem less violent than we were as kids. They don't seem to care to prove themselves like previous generations. Like Tern was saying about Cotyla, things are different now."

Zil nodded. "I notice this in the supplications I get. The kids that are coming after us, they think less about planets and species and more about the galaxy as a whole. Less about what separates them and more about what's shared."

"And about revivals and the divinity, of course," said Fandina, proudly. "Because that's very much shared."

Zil laughed. "Yes yes. Never forget how important we gods are to the galaxy."

Phex thought Zil actually sounded a little bitter.

But Fandina clicked affirmation and *clearly* did not think it was a joke. To the Dyesi, the divinity *was* important, as important as a medical ship or stopping political upheaval from devolving into civil war.

Phex stood and went into the galley, took down some tea powder from his special cabinet. Silently blessed Chef for her thoughtfulness in replenishing it. He boiled water and wondered how much of his pantheon had been selected for the new species the Dyesi could reach, and how much was based on skill and compatibility.

He wondered if he represented not just the Wheel but all the disenfranchised refugees of the stars. How many of his believers were young kids who felt they didn't belong and loved him because they saw themselves reflected in his loneliness? Had he let himself become a tool for divine recruitment? Did that make him a bad person, or just one more human who was trying to survive as best he could? Was the divinity a benefit, a distraction, or something worse? And what could Phex do if he learned the answer to that question? What *would* he do?

As Fortew had said – being a god was now all he was good for.

9

MORE FUN THAN A BARREL OF MURMELS

So it was that in Cotyla Mainspace, Asterism took to the dais alone. But Phex and Missit did their partner piece together first.

Certainly, Phex suspected the divinity of designing this intentionally as a way to use Missit when they couldn't use Tillam.

It worked.

It was the debut of something entirely new, a unique style and an original pairing. Worshipers went wild for the novelty of it. The Cotylan felt honored by the privilege rather than insulted by the absence of Tillam. No doubt that was why the divinity chose this place and this moment in time. Cotyla was getting something extra for having come only to see Asterism.

The crowd was still massive. Even believing only Asterism was to perform. Which was not to say they didn't go wild when Missit appeared unexpectedly on their dais. It's possible they were more gracious about the partnership since they came to the dome believing in Phex and his pantheon – Missit was a blessing and a bonus, but Phex was no deficit or distraction next to him. The divinity had turned a disadvantage into an honor for all concerned. Except maybe Missit.

Although the great god seemed to have a grand time. Certainly, he was happy to continue torturing and flirting with Phex given any opportunity, even in front of hundreds of thousands of worshipers.

Their old-fashioned dancing to an ancient obscure song went over unbelievably well. Certainly, a large part of that was getting to see Missit live, since Cotyla would never have had the privilege before.

But not all of it.

Some of it was the charm of the dated nature of the performance. The simplicity of two small figures on a dais, enchanting an audience with only the power of their voices and the movements of their bodies.

The crowd gasped at all the right moments and stayed riveted throughout. They cheered uproariously at the end. When Missit took his solo bow, the noise was deafening. He left the dais with a causal benediction, and Phex was beyond relieved to see Itrio right there waiting to escort him back to the ship.

Then the rest of Phex's pantheon joined him and they put on their first major solo performance. Fortunately, no comparison could be drawn to what had come first, since one utilized the dome and the other had only performed inside of it.

Asterism learned that it was a lot harder on the body and energy reserves to hold a dome alone and not simply as an opening service for a more famous pantheon. They practically tumbled off the dais at the end, knees weak and heads heavy, having given themselves wholly to the dome. Fandina and Jinyesun had wilted crests. The yearning, roaring cries that followed them meant they should have returned for an encore. But they were still too new. They only had six songs. They had nothing more prepared. There was nothing further that they could do or give.

"We need more songs," said Phex, doing his cooldown stretches, as they gathered in their dressing room before yet another VIP congregation.

"Additional originals. Godsongs that belong to Asterism," agreed Fandina.

"I'm on it." Kagee waved off an acolyte and leaned forward to touch up his own makeup.

"You're writing another one already?" asked Tyve.

"Good, Kagee!" Berril praised. "Go, high cantor, go."

Kagee gave her an exasperated look.

An acolyte appeared. "You kids ready for the next bit?" Highly informal for addressing gods, but Phex was too tired to care.

Fandina's crests went back. "Kids? Kids!"

The acolyte immediately prostrated. Although it didn't seem entirely genuine in its shame. "Demigods."

Asterism struggled to their feet, slumped. Only Fandina and Jinyesun seemed to have found a bit of energy, possibly from the insult. Phex wondered if that was why the acolyte had done it.

Bob commented on it while helping them navigate the back tunnels to the VIP vestry. "You kids don't look so good."

None of them objected to Bob using casual diminutives with them. The cyborg had earned the right. Plus, Bob was easily double any of their maturity levels.

"It takes a lot out of us, the dome," explained Tyve.

Itrio said from behind them, "Tillam was like that too at the beginning. I remember it well."

"You don't?" Kagee asked Bob.

The cyborg shook a well-armored head. "I wasn't with Tillam at the start."

"No? What happened to Missit's first bodyguard?" Phex tried to sound more casual than curious.

"Died," said Bob, shortly.

"Fixed got her," explained Itrio sadly. "She was good, too. Early days, though. We didn't know."

"Didn't know what?" Phex pushed.

"How bad the fixed could get."

Kagee glanced at Phex's face, then said in an annoyed tone, "Could we not have this conversation right before a VIP congregation? Meet-and-greets already freak Phex out."

Itrio handed Phex his whip scarf. "Here. This'll make you feel better."

Phex draped it around his neck in the ready position. "Yes. Thank you."

Kagee fiddled with his rings.

Berril and Tyve looked exhausted but untroubled, but then, neither of them were big worriers.

"Okay, then, last crest, everyone," said Fandina trying to rally some kind of enthusiasm.

Berril fluffed her wings and nodded.

Tyve brushed at an invisible wrinkle in her stage costume. "Let's do this thing."

Kagee strode forward, taking point into the room.

Jinyesun looked at Phex. "You ready?"

Phex nodded. He wasn't, but this was what they did. What they had to do. He brought up the rear – it was becoming his favorite position.

It went better than expected, partly because this time, the VIPs were mostly celebrities themselves. There were lots of politicians (including asteroid, moon, colony, and planetary leaders and their families), and then some actors, musicians, orators, authors, and other local implements of entertainment.

Cotyla did not permit just any old worshiper to pay court to the gods – only the extremely privileged got access. The divinity usually allowed local regulators the primacy of choice, so long as the gods got maximum exposure and protection. In fact, it had been argued that acolytes actively cultivated local authority figures. It increased divine exposure when local luminaries came to worship.

There was definitely a different feel to the VIP assembly as a result. These people were famous in their own right, accustomed to threat and renown. Also, since the Cotyla quadrant of space abutted both the Kill'ki Coalition and the Wheel, the assembled VIPs were familiar with both Tyve's and Phex's cultures. Several even greeted Tyve in her native language. Now, Phex's public record didn't state his Wheel birth, but it became evident that some of those present had sussed the truth. Probably because of his crud-blue hair.

The last person in the lineup for official diplomatic greetings was the prime minster of a strategic and, as it turned out, mineral-rich moon who was a particular believer in Phex.

An older gentleman with stiff mannerisms, he nevertheless lit up with delight at getting to meet Phex in person, apologizing profusely for not knowing the correct Wheel protocols.

Phex assured him that Cotylan politeness was more than sufficient to show respect, and the man flushed with pleasure.

"We have a special tribute for you, Demigod Phex. Please excuse the informal presumption about your history, but we have been assured of acolyte approval, and we know better than many the suffering of your people."

"My people?" Phex wouldn't describe most of the Wheel as necessarily suffering.

"The crudrats."

"Ah."

"We have assured the divinity of our understanding of your background."

Phex felt quite awkward. "Um? Okay. Very good?"

The prime minster gestured autocratically and a young lady came running in with what seemed to be a shrouded barrel.

The barrel was shrieking very loudly.

It was a tone and sound with which Phex was all too familiar.

Phex waved the bodyguards off and moved almost automatically to the cage, for that was what it was. He lifted the covering to expose a fuzzy blue creature, half-monkey and half-cat, locked within. Phex knew the signs of mammalian genetic manipulation now, but he hadn't before Attacon. As a child, he'd known them only as murmels – the lifelines of Wheel space stations and once upon a time his constant workmates.

Crudrats carried and cared for murmels because the creatures ate and disposed of crud. Murmels were entirely necessary for Wheel space survival. This particular beastie was lean and small, still young, an adolescent. And from the tenor of her screams hungry.

"Have you any crud?" he asked the handler.

The girl looked confused. Phex realized, startled, he'd defaulted to Wheel low tongue. The language of his childhood. He switched to Galactic common. "Flush? Do you have any flush?" When that still didn't work, he tried for Galactic technical, "Have you any dark matter particulate or DMP cleaning fluid?"

"Waste wash? Of course."

"Fetch some, please."

The youngster glanced at the prime minster, who was looking at Phex and the murmel with great approval. "Get the god whatever he wishes."

Berril approached eagerly. "Oh, aren't you just the cutest little thing?" She went to stick a finger through the bars.

Phex swatted it away, even as the murmel snapped very sharp teeth at her.

"This one is wild," he explained.

"What is it?" Kagee wanted to know. "And can you get it shut up?"

The prime minster said, still sounding very pleased with himself, "Did you not know your god-mate required a symbiont?"

Phex had never heard that word before. "A *what*?"

Tyve was looking at Phex like he'd suddenly grown ear crests. "Are you mad? I've known him for over a year. He's never pined for anything."

Kagee said, soft and snide so that the acolytes lurking nearby couldn't hear, "Except maybe Missit."

Phex glared at him, shook his head slightly. He tapped up his indent chip, looking for the entry on crudrats.

There it was, buried deep. The general Wheel classification was S1, but under the crudrat listing was now an addendum, added by the Kill'ki Coalition for legal reasons. It was a very clear and entirely erroneous statement.

Crudrat variant, classification: S1 + symbiont. Symbiont = murmel. Murmels are genetically engineered Animalia Chordata Mammalia Primates Haplofeli Felidae. Crudrats will emotionally wither, and possibly die, without murmels.

Will we indeed? Phex arched a brow at the entry. Clearly, some very enterprising escaped crudrat had convinced the Kill'ki Coalition that they should be allowed to keep their tame murmel as a permanent pet. Phex had known some 'rats 'round tunnelside who bonded closely with their murmel workmates. He had never been like that, never bothered to tame one specific blue fuzzy companion. Never been chosen by a murmel, either, because largely, murmels did the choosing. But he wasn't particularly surprised to see the *S1 + symbiont c*lassification. Crudrats could get very attached and wouldn't hesitate to lie on this matter.

He looked to the nearest acolyte. "The divinity approved this tribute?"

The Dyesi genuflected. "The divinity is embarrassed that we did not realize we were failing to provide you with an ingredient vital to maintenance of a healthy psyche."

Phex only just stopped himself from displaying exasperation at this absurd situation.

The murmel screamed, possibly at such an outrageous statement.

The prime minster added, rebuke in his tone as he addressed acolytes in the room, "It is considered cruel for a crudrat to have no murmel."

"Is it?" said Phex, deadpan.

The young handler reappeared and passed Phex a soup container of bright blue liquid. Crud flush.

Phex unsnapped the lid and set it in front of the murmel.

She stopped shrieking immediately and began lapping it up, making cooing trills of pleasure.

"Phex, the creature matches your hair almost exactly," said Berril in delight.

"Yes, she would, same root cause," answered Phex.

"What are we going to name her?" asked Tyve, crouching down next to Berril to look at the murmel on her level.

Phex was a still a little confused. "I am expected to *keep* her?"

The acolytes clicked.

"With me, at all times?"

More clicking.

"On the dais?"

The acolytes looked suddenly worried. "Is that necessary?"

Phex was going to say that none of this was necessary, but the leader of a major moon was standing right there. To refuse this gift might cause an intergalactic incident. Not to mention the fact that the crudrat record on the infonet was falsified, and he didn't know who would suffer if he told the truth.

"No, not necessary," he said, meaning everything, but actually just addressing the idea that he would have to carry a murmel with him everywhere he went. Wrapped around his neck instead of the whip scarf, impeding his movements, screaming willy-nilly and generally becoming yet one more fragile creature he had to protect.

"So, Asterism has a pet?" said Tyve, looking excited about it. "This is awesome. My family has always kept ship's cats. Zil is going to be so jealous."

Berril clapped her hands.

Kagee rolled his beautiful eyes but didn't look as upset as Phex might have expected. "So long as she doesn't yell like that all the time."

Jinyesun said, crests worried, "Phex, why did you never tell us you were suffering for lack of a symbiont?"

Phex needed to put a stop to guilt inherent in the question, "I'll explain everything later."

Jin clicked and Fandina looked like it might understand a little of what was actually going on. Both sifters stepped quickly forward, next to Phex.

"Prime Minister," Fandina said, all formal politeness, "we are so honored that you would recognize a need in Asterism that even the divinity did not see. You are a true believer. Asterism is particularly honored by your worship. Thank you for looking after one of our members as if he were your own. We are not worthy of such focused regard."

The prime minister blushed with pleasure. "It was nothing. To provide for such a god. I assure you the honor is all mine."

Phex stood, glanced down at the murmel. She had almost finished with her container of liquid crud. He turned to the nearest acolyte and said in quick, slightly rude Dyesi informal, "It would be better if we could be done here quickly." Murmels did not have very big bladders or a particular interest in self-control.

The acolyte clicked, taking him seriously. "I will make our divine excuses."

Phex flipped the shroud back down over the murmel's cage just as she finished her meal and started shrieking again.

"Seriously?" said Kagee.

Phex gave him a look.

Back on the ship, the murmel was an immediate sensation, despite the lateness of the hour. Phex passed her off to one of the acolytes, instructing it to liaise with the captain and make sure all the DMP flush was preserved for her consumption henceforth – murmels ate a lot. He also explained that her excrement was copious and toxic but useful for certain spaceship repair jobs. The acolyte looked primarily confused – he could only imagine what the captain would look like after a Dyesi-style explanation on the matter of murmels. Phex added that since she hadn't bonded with anyone, it would take a while and consistent handling to get her tame enough to actually leave her cage.

He wondered if he could recruit the bodyguards to the cause.

Back in their room together in exhausted and blessed silence, he explained what had happened to his pantheon. "The infonet is incorrect in this matter."

"What?" said Jinyesun, mind blown. "That's not possible."

"Don't tell me everything in the public record about the Dyesi is accurate, let alone complete," snapped Kagee.

Jin huffed a laugh, taking no offense at all. "Well, when you put it like *that*."

Fandina's crests perked.

Kagee glared at Phex. "So, *not* a symbiont?"

"Definitely *not*." Phex only just stopped himself from rolling his eyes.

Berril clapped her hands, apparently even more pleased than before about this. "So, we really did just get a cute pet?"

Phex didn't want to burst her bubble but… "She is going to be a beast to train. Without a regular run and blade work, not to mention other murmels, she will require lots of attention. Also, they tend to bond with one person, and she doesn't want me."

"How novel for you." Phex took Kagee's dig as rote. The grey boy never could leave an insult aside if the opportunity presented itself. At some point, Phex had started to find it less annoying and more endearing, not that he would ever say that to Kagee.

Tyve crossed her arms. "And you'll train this beastie when, exactly? In between practicing with us and practicing with Tillam and practicing with Missit *and* bodyguard training?"

Phex gave her a look. "Apparently, it's *vital to my mental health*."

Kagee grimaced. "How do you get yourself into these situations?"

At that juncture, the acolyte returned with the murmel in her cage. Deposited her with evident relief and left. The little creature was docile, belly distended. She'd clearly been fed her fill. Phex was relieved – nothing calmed a murmel like a full meal.

She caught sight of Phex and gave him a whisker-twitch. He leaned down close enough for her to touch him, if she liked. She looked sleepily into his eyes. Blue gaze meeting blue gaze. She gave a little chirp and reached through the bars, petted a strand of his blue hair. He wiggled it at her and she batted at it in a condescending way, too lazy to really play.

"Can we let her out?" asked Berril, charmed.

Phex hissed a negative. "If this place had doors, sure, but once she's out, she could get anywhere on this ship. Did you see her hands? Curious as a cat but with opposable thumbs." Phex had meet a few cats on Attacon 7. He had always liked them because they reminded him of murmels, but he wasn't about to underestimate either species.

He added, "Murmels are independent by nature. She'll set off on her own to explore the moment she can. We have to make certain that she knows who feeds her and where the warmest bed is first."

A cry of delight came from the entranceway, "Oh, my

stars, what is *that* adorable thing? And why does it look so much like Phex?"

Missit announced his relationship to the room quickly and came inside. Even with everyone in their cots, the addition of the murmel's cage and Missit made the quarters that much more crowded.

The murmel yanked at Phex's hair, dragging his gaze away from Missit's delighted face and adorable smile, and back to her.

"Yes?" said Phex.

The murmel chittered at him in a questioning way.

The golden god crouched next to Phex, squeezing in tight between the folded-down cot and the hygiene-chamber entrance. "Look at you, aren't you pretty?"

"Missit," said Phex, tone warning, "don't touch."

Missit was, apparently, smarter than that. Instead, he gently extracted the long lock of Phex's blue hair from the murmel's grasp. "Pretty things shouldn't damage other pretty things," he told her sternly.

He leaned in and whispered soft to the murmel, so low only Phex could hear. "You are a super cute little beastie, but this one is *mine*."

The murmel stared deeply into Missit's golden gaze and then trilled at him. It was the courting trill, an expression of affection. Of course she would like Missit best. Everyone liked Missit best. Phex felt oddly indulgent. He rocked back on his heels, let them flirt. She reached both paws entreatingly through the bars. Missit glanced at Phex, and when he clicked approval, the god gave her a finger. She squeezed it and chittered at him delightedly.

Phex wasn't worried. If she didn't like Missit, she would have already bitten him.

"Gods, you're precious." Missit's golden voice was even warmer than normal.

The murmel made a cooing noise. Apparently, she had found her person. It happened sometimes with them. Murmels couldn't be fully tamed by others, but they did sometimes voluntarily tame themselves.

Phex shook his head. Apparently, even murmels couldn't resist Missit's allure. He wondered if there were more than one, if they would all follow Missit around like a pack of tiny blue worshipers.

"Well, there it is," he said. "We can probably let her out now."

"Why?" asked Berril.

"She chose Missit."

"*Chose*, what do you mean, *chose*? I thought she was your symbiont." Missit had clearly been doing some reading on the infonet.

"No such thing," explained Phex, annoyed. "The classification is wrong."

"Oh." Missit looked back at the murmel and said almost inaudibly, "I thought you needed one and that's why you were so lonely."

Phex was genuinely confused, so he ignored Missit's mumbling. "She wants you." *Don't we all.* "Looks like you got yourself a pet."

"But I thought she was ours," protested Berril.

"No one owns a murmel." Phex was relieved not to have the additional responsibility. "Mostly, it works the other way around."

Missit clutched his hands together and looked at the little creature with shining eyes. "Really?"

"Really." Phex said it just to see how wide Missit's smile could get.

"You'll teach me all about her? How to care for her? All that?"

"You seem remarkably unfazed."

"I love animals," admitted Missit.

"She'll want to sleep with you."

Missit gave him an arch look. "Only her?"

"Stop," said Phex, cracking a smile.

"Phex, did you just *smile*?" Tyve almost fell out of her bunk, trying to see.

"Amazing," said Kagee. "Surprised he didn't strain something."

"I didn't know he could do that," said Jinyesun. Sounding very much like Jin had actually thought Phex didn't have the facial muscles necessary.

Missit was on a roll – he clutched Phex's arm and looked up at him. "Honey, our first child!"

The murmel hissed at this in annoyance.

Phex smiled fully at Missit's offended look. "She's hissing at me. Murmels are jealous creatures. She doesn't like you touching me."

Missit clutched at his chest and lectured the murmel. "Now, now, pretty lady, none of that, you can share Daddy, can't you?"

Phex added, enjoying Missit's ridiculousness, "She'll want to sleep curled next to you. Murmels like to share warmth."

Missit gave him big eyes. "And how about crudrats?"

Phex figured he'd walked right into that one. He cleared his throat and straightened, suddenly realizing Missit was mostly draped over and against him in order to see into the cage properly.

"We'll keep her here tonight. Easier that way." Phex was thinking there was a lot to explain to Missit about murmel care, and better to handle it himself for now.

Missit said, "If I'm her chosen person, shouldn't I stay too?" He glanced meaningfully at Phex's cot.

Phex coughed. "I think it'll be fine for one night."

"Spoilsport," said Missit, pouting.

Bob appeared in the doorway. "Of course you're here. Bed now."

Missit said, "Darling! I got a murmel."

"Well, I'm sure the medics can fix that for you," replied the cyborg. "Come along now."

Missit trotted away, already explaining the murmel to his bodyguard, leaving Phex feeling somewhat wrung out. Like he'd just been through a highly personal version of FTL.

He turned back to the room, realizing he had been guilty of giving Missit the full force of his attention.

Jinyesun and Fandina were crested at him in complete confusion. Tyve and Berril were both grinning.

Kagee was looking disgusted. "Well, well, well."

"Don't start," Phex said to all of them.

The murmel belched loudly.

Phex pointed at her. "You either."

She gave him a look not unlike Kagee's, her whiskers twitching. Then she yawned hugely, showing all her razor-sharp little teeth, turned around three times, and curled up with her back to him ostentatiously.

The next day, Missit named her Dimsum and paid very close attention to Phex's instructions on the care and feeding, as did Bob. Dimsum moved to Tillam's quarters, and Phex figured between Missit's enthusiasm and Bob's practical efficiency, Dimsum would never want for anything. It did seem to be the case, as she spent most of her time riding around on Missit's shoulders, which, frankly, Phex envied.

She learned quickly that she wasn't welcome under a

dome or in pantheon practice. Fortunately, as she had taken against godsong. She was a believer in Missit but not a worshiper of the divine. Cantor caused her tail to lash and the occasional annoyed hiss. And if the best cantor in the universe couldn't convert her, nothing would. Apparently, murmels were immune to the divine.

Phex didn't think Dimsum was qualified to have an opinion on the subject, given how grating her voice was. But the end result was that she, like the bodyguards, was generally to be found outside in the hallway if Missit was inside, being high cantor. She preferred to sit on Bob's massive armored foot as if it were her tiny throne.

So, a murmel entered their lives, Missit's shoulders, and Bob's feet all in one fell swoop. As murmels were wont to do.

They were delayed getting to their fourth tour stop because Fortew had a relapse. The ship diverted to a peaceful planet known for its relaxing beaches and excellent carborg augmentations (and several highly discreet medical facilities).

Their worshipers were informed that the tour was delayed for reasons of fatigue. Asterism dropped promo vids and live streams almost every day to keep up the momentum, also some inside-studio beams, and processed a lot of supplications. Kagee worked on a new godsong.

They had a small local dome to practice in, and Asterism put on two special elite performances for local dignitaries, which were extremely well received.

Phex and Missit took it as an opportunity to really work on the dance part of their duet, since the local planet's dome was a thousand times better for staging than anything on their spaceship. Also, Phex wanted to keep Missit distracted, with Fortew back in hospital.

They were under the dome together almost every day for two weeks, to the point where the acolytes stopped caring about their persistent exposure to outside risk and only required Itrio and Bob to escort them. The dome was isolated on a remote island free of all civilization, almost too perfect and pristine. But ideal for gods who wanted to practice without being disturbed, and without any risk from fixed.

Some of their respective pantheons came to watch occasionally. The graces were always appreciative, and even Kagee accompanied them to have a look-see a couple of times. The sifters, however, came only once each and then left quickly.

"You don't like it?" Phex asked Jin one morning. "Missit and I, under the dome together."

Jinyesun looked to Fandina for support, but it was Melalan who explained. "It's not exactly ugly, but it is very unsettling. Uncanny."

"Because it's only the two of us?" The numbers were off – Phex knew that.

"There is an innate wrongness to it. The way some purists feel about cyborgs, that is what it feels like to see you two bastardize a dais." Yorunlee was nothing if not blunt.

"You're insane. They're amazing together." Tyve came to Phex and Missit's defense.

Missit was listening in but seemed mainly amused by the conversation, not insulted.

"Perhaps if they were on any other stage in the galaxy. But a dais and a dome? It is somewhat… grotesque." Yorunlee wasn't trying to persuade them, just stating facts.

Phex watched Fandina's crests. It had a hard time hiding its feelings, and it seemed that it too felt similarly.

"You don't have to watch," he said to his two sifters.

Jinyesun speckled white with shame and its crests wilted. "We would like to be supportive."

"It is particularly hard on sifters, you understand?" said Melalan. "You waste your song on nothingness with no one to sift it into color. It feels pointless."

Jinyesun added the old saying, "A sift is sung into existence and danced into submission, there are no colors without cantor, and no music without grace."

Fandina explained further, "What you two do is the opposite, cantor and grace without color. It's unnatural."

Phex lowered his eyes, understanding. "When we use the dome without Dyesi, the dome itself becomes an anathema."

"It's almost like you don't need us at all. But also, there can be no worship."

"And it must always be about worship, because what else is there?" Missit's golden voice was flat. He stood, brushing bread crumbs off his hands. "On that note, shall we go practice, Phex?" His eyes were bright with annoyance, as if the Dyesi had challenged him with their dislike.

"You feel insulted?" wondered Phex, soft and careful.

"Everyone *else* likes our dance." Missit pouted, truculent.

Phex looked away quickly, hiding a smile. "Come on, then, maybe someday the Dyesi will come around too."

"I doubt it," said Yorunlee, fervently.

Missit stuck his tongue out at his sifter.

Phex put a hand to the god's back and hustled him from the room.

Phex had thought their original performance was pretty good, but with practice under a true dome, they got even better. Despite what the sifters felt, Phex and Missit singing together was always going to be amazing, but now their dancing was becoming amazing too. They were using the full scope of the dais. Their lifts and synchronized movements were smoother, and the way they slid together, matched or reflected, started to balance despite their size difference. Missit was so much brighter and smaller when contrasted to Phex's bulky, somber blues. Sometimes, Phex thought he was there to be Missit's shadow. Long, arching limbs flung about the space, leaping up the walls of the dome and flickering off to the sides, as if Missit were casting light and Phex were the darkness racing away before him.

But it was fun, and Phex was even getting accustomed to Missit's constant flirtation. Learning not to take it seriously. Which he thought was probably the key to surviving this whole relationship, whatever that relationship may be.

And it worked.

For the first week, at least.

But then, early on in the second week of constant practice, Missit started to change again. The god didn't stop flirting, but he did start occasionally shifting his bodyweight around during the dance. No less a kind of communication than Missit's clever words and longing glances, but a language Phex couldn't so easily dismiss as he did the other two types.

Frankly, Phex didn't think he could take something new and capricious from this trickster god. Missit was stretching him and testing him all the time. Phex felt close to snapping in a way he hadn't when it was just him and his pantheon, pushing into all the different directions required by godhood.

The first time Missit did it, Phex figured it was unintentional. Phex was supposed to pick Missit up from behind and lift him to one side, at which point Missit would swing his leg outward and arch-leap away. But Missit kept missing the push-off, and instead, he'd curl and press back against Phex, and wriggle slightly as if to get comfortable. It was erotic and Phex was getting distracted.

Carefully, he set the god down. He moved away, crossed his arms, and tried to damp down on any hint of arousal. But Missit was looking at him with blown pupils and pinched hunger.

So, Phex guessed it was all intentional. "What are you doing, Missit?"

Missit skittered up to him, looking eager but also a little embarrassed and ashamed.

"Could I just *have* you? I mean, I know you don't like me very much, but I like you loads and I'd really love to be with you. Just have you, for a bit. Or you have me. I don't care which. I don't know which, either. Blast it, I'm making a mess of this."

"And how many divinity rules and regulations would that violate? What about your contract? What about mine? Screw the contracts, how deeply offended would the Dyesi be? Our friends in our pantheons, your sifters, mine – what happens when they find out? It isn't *allowed*, Missit."

Missit plucked at the end of Phex's sleeve, tight to his skin on the outer wrist of his crossed arms. Ran a hopeful finger from there up to his shoulder. His breath did a funny catch, and then that mellow perfect voice begged, "Please?"

Phex tilted his head back and looked at the dome above. "We should stop practice for the day."

"No. No. I'll behave, I promise."

Phex wondered how bad Fortew was this time. If Missit was destined to act out in new and enterprising ways every time his low cantor's symptoms grew worse. How much of Missit's interest was genuine and how much was a distraction? For certain, there was a sincere need for comfort driving Missit, but sex was not the right outlet, and they both knew it.

Not that Phex wasn't tempted or that Phex didn't want him – desperately, even. But one of them had to keep a cool head.

Both heads.

"Missit, I'm just at the beginning of godhood. If we were to be found out, the trouble wouldn't fall on you, it'd fall on me and Asterism."

"That's unfair and fatalistic. We won't be found out."

"And that's overly optimistic." Phex's tone was sharp. "It's my pantheon that would be disbanded, not yours."

Missit sighed audibly. "Not that mine is going to be around much longer."

"Now who's being fatalistic?" Phex hated Missit pleading with him. It made Missit seem desperate, when he was a god who should never need or want for anything.

"Look, Phex, Asterism is already a big deal. The acolytes aren't going to do anything to jeopardize that at this juncture."

"How do you know?" Phex was genuinely curious. Did Missit have some kind of special insider information from having lived among the Dyesi for so long? As a great god, had the acolytes told him something that they didn't tell demigods? So far as Phex knew, the rules against fraternization between gods were pretty darn proscriptive – it didn't matter what rank or level or classification that god was.

"That is not the point." Missit's golden voice was full of frustration but his eyes were still pleading. "I know that the Dyesi probably wouldn't even recognize what was happening. And even if they did, I could argue them out of it. I've done it before."

Phex didn't like that at all. Missit went around kissing demigod boys under the dome regularly, did he?

Missit put up both hands. “Not like that. Don’t make that face.”

Phex ignored this. “And what would be *happening* between us, *exactly*? Distraction? Amusement? Relief?” Phex scrubbed at his face in exasperation. Missit was such a child. He saw a thing and he wanted it. The murmel. Phex. And who cared about the consequences?

But Missit looked sincerely hurt. “That’s not fair,” he whispered. “I’ve always made my intentions clear. When have I ever not been genuine with you?”

Phex looked around at the grey, pearlescent curve of the dormant dome above him. It was still beautiful, even without skinsift, but it was also dead. Inert and sad, as if it were no longer waiting but had irrevocably given up on all the colors it could be.

Please don’t risk our pantheon on his instability, Kagee had said.

How could Missit not realize that his sincerity wasn’t the point? “You’re asking me to *choose,* Missit.”

“Between me and the Dyesi?” Missit asked, voice small.

“Between you and my pantheon.”

“But I can help you protect them.”

“No god, not even you, is more powerful than the divinity as a whole. The entire system is set up that way. There will always be more pantheons. And the worshipers may mourn for some small amount of time when a god becomes mortal, but they will move on because it is the divinity they need in their lives, not one god or one pantheon. Not even Tillam is that powerful. You should know that. Of anyone, you should know. Right now, isn’t that why you’re clinging to me?”

Missit took a shocked step back and put a hand to his own mouth, gasping. “You think all this is because of Fortew?”

He gestured at the two of them, standing, breathing heavy

and tight. Both of them warm with dance and desire. Both of them hot with need and fear.

Phex gave him a look that said he wasn't stupid and of course it was because of Fortew.

Missit licked his lips, gaze intense on Phex's face. "Do you know what I thought the first time I saw you? In that crowd on Divinity 36, among all those other potentials?"

Phex rubbed at his arms, suddenly cold.

"I thought you were already a god. I thought there was no way you were a mere potential. Just the way you walk, it's as if nothing matters to you. You were like some rock dropped into that crowd – solid and unbending but causing ripples. I didn't see the fixed come after me, because I was looking at *you*. Like I was fixed myself."

"And that was it, you wanted me."

"Yeah, fine, I wanted you from the start, but what's wrong with that? Why is desire bad? Regardless of what the Dyesi say. Besides, you wanted me too."

"Yes, but the difference is I know it's a terrible idea."

Missit gritted his teeth. "You know what else I thought?"

Phex shook his head. Apparently, he didn't have a choice – they were hashing this out right now under the dome.

"I thought you were terribly lonely. I thought I'd never meet anyone more lonely than me, and then there you were. And I just wanted to fix it. I wanted to make you smile."

Phex closed his eyes. Swore in his own mind. Because what could he say to that? What could he do when Missit had seen in him a thing he hadn't even realized himself at the time?

Because, back then, he *had* been lonely. But then he'd found his pantheon.

Now what was he supposed to do? Missit had recognized in him the one thing he couldn't reason his way out of.

Truth.

The god was shaking with it, his gold-flecked eyes huge. Not cocky or confident or flirty. Just crazy and brave and exposing – to say such a thing openly to another person. To communicate that level of risk in a desperate bid for understanding.

Phex knew himself to be in the wrong then. All along, he had been trying to trivialize this thing between them. That way, he could also trivialize Missit and dismiss the god's feelings. And, similarly, dismiss his own. Make their mutual yearning small and insignificant, blame need on other things like youth and hormones – formulate excuses that pretended to be logical. All because Phex didn't want to have to choose. Because if what Missit offered was capricious and insincere, then the choice to reject him was obvious and easy. But if that wasn't the case, well, then they were in real trouble.

10

FEAR ENDS WHERE FIXATION BEGINS

"Couldn't you tell what we had together? Back then, on Divinity 36, when you were hugging me late at night?" Missit twisted his jaw, dipped his head then quickly brought it back up. A move like the twitching of an ear crest, full of discomfort.

Phex looked down at his feet, encased in high-quality practice booties that the acolytes had purchased for him. His legs covered in a high-tech practice suit the divinity had provided to him. Even his skin and his hair were of their making. He was their creature – the Dyesi had manufactured him, as his family had done first, tailoring him to fit their needs. Like the Wheel, the divinity would cut him loose based on some arbitrary fatal flaw that they alone decided upon. He knew this for certain. Because they already had.

They had made him feel wanted and then rejected him. Was all his fear of Missit based on the premise that this god was doing the same thing?

Phex did remember all too well. He remembered curling with Missit in the old practice studio on Divinity 36, hugging him close as if it were the only way to keep a god from breaking into stardust. "I thought it was a crazy, special, momentous thing, to hold a god because he needed me. And that it would never last. I never let myself expect more than that."

"You thought I was *using* you?" Now Missit looked very hurt, flecked eyes filling with tears.

Phex realized he was messing everything up. And maybe he should have pushed that messiness forward intentionally, letting the thing between them get distorted and broken. But he couldn't bear Missit's face in that moment.

As if Missit had been betrayed.

As if Missit were the lonely one.

"I like to be useful," Phex said, timidly. "I don't mind being made use of."

"You can be a little cruel, can't you, when you eventually speak?" Missit tugged on one ear. Missit's ears had been adjusted into perfection by Dyesi medics just like Phex's. Had they made Missit feel wanted and then rejected him?

What was it like to be ten years divine, constantly altered to their needs, paying tribute with one's body for the privilege of having talent?

Phex sighed and stepped to the god, pulling him close and feeling Missit instantly melt. Breathing out against Phex's shoulder as if his flesh were a safe place for someone else to inhabit.

Phex couldn't see a way to make this work, but he also knew he would let Missit win if that was what it took to make him happy. To wipe that sorrow away and replace it with the reassurance of his arms had already become instinct. Missit was right – this was more than desire, there was something else there that Phex had been intentionally ignoring. He'd been forming excuses and building walls out of Missit being too great a god, or too capricious, or just too much.

Maybe Missit was all those things, and he was certainly a great risk, but Phex had ignored the *familiar* in Missit. The familiar parts of Missit that felt like Berril's hugs or Kagee's glares… only *more*. Like Jin's need to answer every question and Fandina's courage to step forward to lead when necessary… only *more*. Familiar things in this strange package of golden great god that Phex should not be ungrateful to receive as a gift. Because they were special, and Missit had granted them only to him.

Phex *had* been lonely for most of his life, and so he could not dismiss love, whatever form it took. That he did not know exactly how to give it in return was no excuse for being harsh when it was offered. Even if it was dangerous to him and to his pantheon and to everything they worked so hard to achieve.

Perhaps, in the end, he didn't really have a choice.

Phex folded down to the dais and backward, taking Missit with him. Putting them both at a disadvantage. Draping Missit over him like a confused but not reluctant blanket, his hands bracketed around the god's slim waist.

Missit's body was vibrating with leftover tension, or fear, or something else.

Phex circled his thumbs on the small of Missit's back and just breathed. Tilted his head to rest one cheek on the dais, a strange kind of obeisance to Missit's pleading.

The golden god stared down at him for a long moment, disbelieving, and then crumpled from his shoulders forward and onto Phex, pressing his face into Phex's neck, chin against his shoulder. His nose, a little too big and sharp, always reminded Phex of a blade. He wondered that the Dyesi had never altered it, but he supposed Missit became godly before standards were set. Now it was too late.

Missit inhaled Phex, there like that. Despite the sweat

cooling on Phex's skin and the fact that he hadn't visited the hygiene chamber yet that day.

Missit clearly liked that spot. Phex's smell. Phex.

Phex raised one hand, tentatively, and stroked it over Missit's gold-tinted hair, but the god didn't like that – he shook Phex off, reared back, grabbed at his wrists, and pushed them to the ground, holding him down with all his weight.

This was insignificant to Phex. It would be more than easy to roll out from under Missit and get away. But Missit wanted something from him, needed something, and Phex wanted to give him whatever that was.

"What's wrong?" he asked, not in Dyesi but in Galactic Common, informal, the language of friends.

"Please," said Missit, his flecked eyes wild, shifting over Phex's face.

"I can't read your mind."

Missit gave a humorless chuckle. "You sing and dance with me sometimes like you can."

"Missit."

"Not this," the god said, and then, "I want—" But he cut himself off, bit at his lip, closing his eyes as if praying for help from some ancient god, the kind that didn't exist anymore.

Phex forced himself to relax even further, dropped his core into the dais, lost his frame, melted back, making himself as soft and unthreatening as possible. Didn't try to fight, only to welcome and accept.

"No," said Missit in response, "not that either. I don't want you passive."

"Then what do you want?"

Missit shook his head, clearly frustrated by Phex's inabilities. His tough, corded hands twitched and tightened around

Phex's wrists. Then Missit launched himself forward and down, pressing the whole length of his body against Phex's.

He was turned on and eager. They both were. Phex hadn't considered that Missit would want to act on anything *now*. But clearly he did, because his lips were moving over Phex's skin, kissing his neck in between desperate gasps for air.

Missit's face was wet too.

Phex jolted with the realization that Missit wanted him, not a little bit, or just because of their dancing, or the way Phex looked in a jumpsuit. This was a desperate black hole of desire that came from somewhere else, something like time spent yearning, or years spent hungry, or a deep need to possess.

Phex knew what drove most gods. The talented ones and the beautiful ones and the bright shining creatures that overwhelmed planets. The attention-seekers, the high-energy performers, beauty or grace or song. There were some who did it for the way it touched and transported strangers, a way to reach out and connect. There were some who did it to show what they could do, to impress and to charm. But in the end, it all came down to one thing: they wanted to be loved. By millions of complete strangers. But still, just be *loved*. That was all gods wanted.

What Phex hadn't realized was, in Missit's case, he wanted to be loved by Phex *specifically*. He wondered if it was just the way Missit was with those he treasured, so much a natural flirt that it took this form of extreme need. But Phex didn't really mind that idea. Missit was Missit, no changing that. And if Missit craved him, now in this moment, and wanted him, who was he to turn away a great god for the terrible sin of loving him?

Phex liked Missit. Liked his bright, ridiculous, shiny ways. He respected his insane talent and his dedication to his work. In this, the physical, Missit wasn't asking for much of Phex, just a bit of himself.

Missit cut himself open and bled under the dome for millions, had done for a decade – why shouldn't he get something back?

"Oh, I see." Phex surged up easily, shaking off the hold on his wrists. Sitting, he pulled Missit as close as he could get, encouraging him to wrap long legs about his waist, press so tight that they might share skin, mixing metals.

He dug one dark blue hand into Missit's gold hair, clashing and making a mess of the bun, not at all gentle. He tilted Missit's head, arranging the god at an angle he liked, and then kissed him. Not kindly but with real need, showing him in return that his desperation would be matched, that this wasn't one-sided.

Because that's what gods got all the time under the dome – one-sided love. Worship and adoration, yes. But only from one direction. Missit wanted it exchanged, balanced like cantors. Harmonized. He wanted to feel it in hands, and mouth, and muscle. Like their dance.

Phex figured he was correct in this assessment because the god calmed almost instantly the moment he took control. Missit melted upward, still trembling, but not with anxiety anymore. Phex tasted salt on his lips, swallowed down whimpers, used passion to gentle Missit until he was a mess of shivering desire curled in his lap.

Phex hugged him close, still kissing. Deep and hungry until he felt it in his bones, a different kind of love, still wanting, still a need to possess but one that was warmly returned. The flavor of Missit changed, from salt to sweet, from desperation to relief.

But they were making out in an empty grey dome on an

alien planet. An acolyte or a bodyguard or a member of the pantheon could still come in at any moment.

So, Phex pulled away from their kissing, hoping to encourage Missit into mirroring him. He softened his hands in Missit's hair, not too much but enough to indicate reason.

Missit whimpered in protest. "No no no, you can't stop now. You were going to let me have you."

Phex bumped his forehead. "Open your eyes. Look at where we are. We can't do this here."

"You're not stopping for good?" Missit was radiant with hope.

Phex gave up.

This boy was going to destroy him. Because no one got to hold a god for very long, but Phex wasn't strong enough to resist temptation anymore. His choice, in this moment, was Missit over his pantheon. He tried not to think about Kagee's pleading or Berril's small, hopeful face.

Phex wasn't like the others. He didn't take to the dome because he wanted the kind of love that came with worship. But that didn't mean he didn't want love at all. This, it turned out, was his weakness. Missit. Salt in kisses. Desire so potent that a god trembled with it. Trembled for Phex. In the end, it was not something he could dismiss, or avoid, or ignore.

Funny that, so easily, Phex minded not one iota the adoration of millions. But one gold-tinted boy with a lopsided smile, and Phex lost his integrity and loyalty and crumbled himself into bite-sized pieces to feed someone else's hunger.

He stood, Missit still wrapped around him. Ridiculous.

"Where do we go where acolytes and cameras do not find us?" he asked.

Missit uncoiled his legs and slid to stand, staying pressed along the length of Phex's body the whole time. Confident now in getting what he needed.

Phex thought they would have this one time and that he wanted it to be fun and glorious, but he knew almost nothing about what to do. So he would have to make it up as they went along, and like their duet, he could only hope that the end result was beautiful. He grabbed Missit's hand and led him out of the dome.

The murmel waiting back on the spaceship for Missit to return shrieked at both of them. Phex was pretty darn certain she was correct in her offense and insult. Well deserved, that scream. There was a large part of him that also felt like screaming.

Late that night, Phex met Missit alone in the smallest of the cantor practice booths. The one at the end of a hallway where no one ever went except cantors. Phex let himself in, arranging the curtain to drape carefully behind him.

Missit was already waiting, coiled and eager.

They didn't use that booth to sing – it was more like a dance. Graceful and beautiful, and also awkward and uncomfortable – and brave, because it was their first practice of this kind. There were moments of perfect rhythm and coiled power. And moments of aching joy and synchronized connection. And moments of clumsiness and confusion, and bumps and bruises in the tiny space with amused laughter at the absurdity of the whole situation – where gods must act like criminals for the sake of kisses.

At some point, naked and sticky and fumbling and eager, Missit said the thing Phex never expected, and mostly dreaded hearing.

"This is love, isn't it?"

Phex wasn't sure if he was more scared that it *was* love or more scared that it was not. So he gave no answer. Also, his mouth was occupied at the time.

Their unexpected mid-tour break ended after the second week. The tour ship folded into FTL and unfolded near the fourth stop of their tour.

When Phex ran into him at practice or in the galley, Fortew looked better. Rested. But he was also getting skinny in a way that wasn't the lean muscle of a performer or the manufactured lines of Dyesi medical aesthetics. There was something inside of him that was eating away at his body. Something that could not be stopped.

They were heading into a sector of space where the divinity struggled with reach but where Asterism was unexpectedly spiking in popularity and Tillam was eagerly anticipated, never having visited before. It seemed they had something Fandina referred to as *good crossover believer demographics*. This was a sector that the divinity eagerly wished to convert utilizing those demographics.

They hoped to build more domes soon, but in the meantime, the biggest of the few that existed hosted the two pantheons with much fanfare. It was the only dome on the premier planet of the sector. A planet rather unimaginatively named Earth 10. It was a large industrialized world full of political upheaval but which had called a complete cease-fire under the auspices of a divine visitation.

The Dyesi demanded this as a prerequisite for their visit. Gods did not grace places torn asunder by politics or war or both.

When they arrived, it was to find everything locked firmly down and suspiciously quiet. Divine mandate was a powerful thing.

Earth 10 was not a planet that allowed large assemblies of worshipers to gather and wave banners or put on light shows at a docking bay. There were no groups of fans waiting for them to land. But when Asterism took their greeting position on the ramp to liaise with the local press, the resident acolytes, at least, could not hide their delight. Earth 10 had a larger complement than normal in this regard. Most domes boasted only one sexton, some newer domes had three, but Earth 10 had six. With puffy crests fluttering in the wind and faces changeably blue with pleasure, these acolytes were the most animated Dyesi that Phex had ever met. Practically effusive in their welcome.

Fandina said something dismissive about them being *regrettably youthful* in their mannerisms. Phex found them charming. They reminded him a little of Berril.

Tillam and Asterism had two massive performances, the first of which went very well.

After their unplanned tour hiatus, intergalactic worshipers were even more eager than ever to tune in to their beam and gain enlightenment. The acolytes even discussed that perhaps little delays like this on future tours were not a bad idea – if they ultimately resulted in such high levels of believer anticipation and enthusiasm.

Phex and Missit danced their song in between the two pantheon shows this time – to great acclaim and roaring approval. It was considered a privilege to witness, since it wasn't beamed out – anyone who watched it would cherish the honor of knowing they were among some of the few in the galaxy to do so. Certainly, the duet was recorded and distributed to the infonet by congregation members with wrist idents, but that was shoddy production and nowhere near as expansive as a dome performance, and nowhere near as good as seeing them live.

At least, that was what one excited VIP told Phex breathlessly afterward.

"You and Missit are amazing together. It's magical!" Her topaz eyes sparkled with delight. "I was lucky enough to see your debut in Cotyla. I immediately knew I had to see it a second time. So, I followed you all the way here."

Phex said nice things back and made his mark on her arm. She said that she would get it tattooed there along with a stylized image of one of his and Missit's most spectacular lifts.

Phex was relieved when she was shunted onward.

Because of Fortew's limited energy levels, they weren't going to do any domes back-to-back anymore. So, they had a day of rest before their second performance on Earth 10.

Well, Fortew rested – the rest of them practiced.

Then came time for the next show.

It all started out normally enough.

The two pantheons were lounging together beneath the dome. Earth 10's dome was designed more communally and, as Jinyesun said, *authentically,* so it didn't boast separate dressing rooms, just one underground vestry under the dais.

They didn't really mind. At least, Asterism didn't. Tillam might have found this lowering, but they were all so comfortable with each other at this point, Phex suspected not. Yorunlee was looking especially crabby, but Phex had learned with that particular Dyesi never to take personal offense. Yorunlee was just a big old curmudgeon of a god.

There were local snacks set out before them, which was new. The diets of gods were usually better controlled than that. But the six local acolytes insisted the food had been vetted for both safety and nutritional value.

Phex was pacing and stretching idly. He found movement calmed him before taking to the dais.

Missit gestured at him imperiously from where he sat with the snacks. "Come here, try this."

Phex was suspicious. "Why?"

"Just come here. It's good."

Phex wandered over and crouched down next to the puff.

Missit tugged Phex forward by the front of his jumpsuit and fed him a bite of something salty and a little sweet and crispy. It was nice, and Phex's stomach made an interested rumble.

Phex realized, at that moment, that he'd been so busy back on the ship making sure everyone else ate before this performance that he'd forgotten to eat himself.

"It is good," he confirmed.

Missit nodded, fed him another bite. "Eat more."

"It's yours."

Missit rolled his eyes. "I chose it for you. You know I don't really like sweet things."

Phex did know that. Missit's tastes were often rather Dyesi for a Sapien.

Phex put his hand out to take the rest of the yummy stick-shaped thing.

Missit ignored this, just tugged him again and fed him another chunk.

Phex sighed and let him. Quirky boy, why did he want to do such a strange thing as feed him? Phex was grateful, though – he hadn't realized how hungry he was.

"You don't get grumpy like other people when you're hungry," Missit pointed out, after Phex dutifully ate the last bite.

Phex gave him a disbelieving look.

"Fine, well, you don't get any *more* grumpy than you normally are."

"How do I get?" Phex poked about the snacks, trying to identify something with protein.

"A little spaced out, lost. Quiet. Well, quieter than normal.

If that's possible. Docile. Like now, you just allowed me to feed you."

Phex nodded – that sounded about right. Normally, he would have gotten upset with Missit for doing such an outrageous thing. Instead, he found it oddly sweet that Missit had bothered to notice such a thing about him.

"Perhaps I should starve you to get you to do what I really want," suggested Missit, looking cheeky.

Phex snorted at him, because what a ridiculous thing to say. Phex would do whatever Missit wanted whenever he wanted it – starvation was not required. How could Missit be so stupid as not to realize that?

Missit reached past him for a small white ball coated in herbs. "Here, this is protein, try it."

Phex took it from him and popped it into his mouth before Missit could feed it to him.

Missit pouted.

"What exactly are you two doing?" Kagee was glaring at them from the large puff opposite – his voice was low and he was speaking Galactic Common.

"Eating," replied Phex, popping another ball into his mouth. It had an odd texture, almost too creamy, but it tasted fine.

"No, you're flirting, and this place is crawling with acolytes. Are you crazy?" Kagee was correct – there were nine acolytes milling about, the three from their ship and the six local sextons. It was *a lot* of acolytes in one place.

Phex glanced furtively around. Fandina and Jinyesun were playing some kind of ident game together on a nearby puff. Berril and Tyve were stretching in a corner. Most of Tillam were huddled together around Fortew in a separate sitting area. The acolytes seemed mostly concerned with whatever was going on there.

So, it was only Kagee who'd seen Missit feed him.

Missit bristled. "Are you jealous?"

Kagee looked at him like he was completely insane. "Seriously, Missit? What game are you playing? Do you *want* Phex kicked out of the divinity? Are you trying to sabotage Asterism? Or are you just totally incapable of being subtle?"

Kagee was angrier than Phex had ever seen him. It was probably the tension of an imminent performance, but also the risk to Asterism if Phex got caught. And Kagee was right. It was one thing to sneak around late at night on the spaceship. It was quite another to act publicly as if they were lovers.

Phex stood and stepped away from the god. "He's right."

"But, Phex!" Missit whined.

Although Phex would realize, later that night, that in his own way, he was almost as bad as Missit. He was weak for him, in manners and body language. Visibly so to anyone who cared to notice. It was just that the acolytes didn't want to notice.

Phex was tucked away with some of the bodyguards and acolytes in an observation niche, low in the dome, watching Tillam perform on the dais. This particular niche was soundproofed and had intentionally limited visibility so no one inside could become fixed by godsong. As a result, there were a few local security officers present as well.

Phex had met most of them already. Then a new one came wandering in halfway through Tillam's second song. He was a massive Sapien. Phex would have suspected heavy gravity tinkers except he didn't bounce as he moved.

Itrio intercepted him and checked his credentials before

he could get anywhere near Phex.

Phex remained mostly watching Missit and Fortew, half-wary of the new stranger in their midst, even one brought in by an acolyte. But staying focused on the dais.

"Who are you here for?" asked Itrio of the newcomer. Since, like the bodyguards, local security was supposed to focus on only one god at a time.

"Zil." The man gestured to the dais where Tillam's dark grace landed a perfect beat at the end of one of their most famous godsongs. At least he was well-researched enough to know who was who in the pantheon. He moved to stand next to Phex for an unobstructed view of the dais.

"Which one is your charge?" he asked Phex, politely. "Missit?"

Everyone, except Phex, laughed at him. The new guard crossed big arms over an even bigger chest and glared at them like they were children.

Phex gave him a half-smile, pleased to be taken for a bodyguard rather than a god, before refocusing on the performance.

Phex listened to the conversation after that, not participating in it and not taking his eyes off Tillam. He was a little sad that he couldn't hear the next song. It was "Five," and no matter how many times Phex heard it, he always loved it under the dome. He suspected he always would. "Five" had been his first, last, and only experience of godfix. Now that he was on the dais and making the song, he would never get to truly experience it again. Still, there was something about the haunting sadness that he adored. Perhaps he was secretly a maudlin personality? "Five" was one of the few songs he actually hoped to get to sing with Missit under a dome someday.

"Phex is a demigod, not a bodyguard," explained Itrio,

amusement rich in her tone.

The newcomer's voice was tinged with mild disapproval. "So, why is he here? Is he a believer in Tillam? I didn't think gods got that way about other gods."

"Don't worry about Phex. He's fine where he is. Let us go over your duties for escort after the final godsong, shall we? You know Tillam has to be relocated back to the ship as quickly as possible, right?"

It turned out, however, not to be Tillam who was in jeopardy.

Phex found out later that after their last bow, Tillam had been easily transported back to the spaceship. There had been no security breaches and no issues at all.

Not so, Asterism.

They were moved early to the VIP room, while Tillam was still performing. All except Phex, of course, who had to stay in the observation niche right up until the very end. Even if it was the last part of the last godsong, if Fortew failed, someone had to step in.

Fortew didn't fail.

Tillam finished clean and pretty. All their dedicated bodyguards dashed off to escort them, leaving Phex behind in the soundproof niche with only the locally provided guards to act as his personal security. And three acolytes who, while very pretty and useful in their own way, had absolutely no defensive capacity. They were, after all, only Dyesi.

They left the niche to find an unexpectedly crowded hallway. Somehow, someone, somewhere, had opened the underground access halls of the dome to the general public. Or *some* of that public.

Neither Phex nor the security detail were prepared for

this. They were inside it and surrounded by a large crowd of worshipers before they realized what was happening. There was no returning to the safety of the niche – it was too late.

It was instantly a complete mess – an enclosed area, crowded with worshipers, Phex slightly taller and definitely more blue and spectacular than anyone else there. He was also in a performance costume, and not Asterism's but one that loosely matched to what Tillam had been wearing. He had no hood or cloak to hide under. There was no disguising anything about him. Plus, he had three Dyesi acolytes accompanying him.

He was, in a word, godly.

The divine was not easily hidden under the best of circumstances. Phex was made instantly aware of how that fact explicitly applied to him. He stood out like a beacon. He was a god, after all, and gods were designed to stand out.

Someone recognized him instantly and started screaming.

Hands were out and grasping, enthusiasm spiking so quickly, it was near to hysteria in seconds.

For one horrible moment, Phex actually thought they might physically tear him apart. And these weren't fixed, or at least he didn't think they were. They didn't seem crazed, just high on the excitement of an amazing show and the transporting influence of the dome. They were overcome with ecstasy and awe in the presence of an *actual* god, even just a demigod, who was walking among them. It was simply too much for an average worshiper to withstand.

Phex was tall enough to see ahead and down the hallway. He thought he saw blurs of grey and dark red emerge at the far end. Kagee and Tyve? Even they wouldn't be stupid enough to leave the safety of the VIP room to come get him, would they?

The crowd surged like a wave and began roaring even

louder with excitement. Hysterical screams and paroxysms of delight.

Phex was hampered in his ability to move or to fight because he was surrounded by the local security team and three terrified acolytes. The Dyesi were practically opaque with fear, crests flat back and eyes enormous. The security had closed ranks around him protectively, but also, they severely limited his movements. And their own. They were almost too tight together now. He couldn't even reach up to unwrap his whip scarf, let alone get off a good flick. Not that he had a target or thought that adding blood to the mix was a good idea. This was a soup pot packed too full of need and joy, and it was overheating with enthusiasm and about to boil over.

His training had not prepared him for this particular situation.

Then there came *that* face. A face so familiar but simultaneously so unexpected and out of place that at first, he didn't recognize her.

"Chef?"

"Don't worry," said Chef, eyes wide and darting every which way, body movements oddly jerky. "I can save you, beloved."

The horror of it hit him then. She had been inside the dome.

Crew was *never* supposed to enter their domes, not for the pantheon they served with. Certainly not *Chef,* who was around Phex all the time.

Around Phex, his churning stomach told him, *far too often*.

Around him when he was puttering happily in the galley and humming to himself. Singing.

Around him so often, she knew his taste and filled a

cabinet for him in her kitchen.

A special cabinet.

Full of *offerings*.

Phex realized in that horrifying moment that he thought of Chef as a friend. But she had come to *believe* in him. He had never noticed.

And now, he felt her jerk his surprised body into her arms, coiling herself tight around him.

She was freakishly strong.

"You're so delicious," she said. "Is it so wrong, how much I just want to eat you up?"

Her teeth scraped gently against the costume-covered muscle of Phex's upper arm. He shrank away instinctively.

He wanted to throw up badly, in a way he thought he'd moved beyond. In a way that purged the anxiety and the pain and the guilt of having befriended someone, anyone, who he was now responsible for corrupting.

What to do with that friend now? Where did he direct *that* feeling? Did he strike out at her? Fight Chef? *Hurt* Chef?

It was almost a relief when there came a sharp prick and sting in his side. The decision to bodyguard himself was taken away from him. He looked down, meeting the crazed eyes of someone familiar who had become the monster that he did not understand.

Chef licked her smiling lips and braced to catch him.

He wondered how he had missed this or if he was just naturally careless with his own safety. Having once never trusted at all, did he now trust too easily? Had she planned this or tipped into being fixed like a switch, after sneaking in to watch the dome? Had too much Phex made her insane? Would too much Phex make anyone insane?

He felt terribly cold.

The arms and the crowd around him were so warm.

His brain was entirely made up of this funny, woozy, fuzzy feeling. Even with the loud din of the hallway, he thought he could hear Kagee yelling over the shrieking of the crowd. Kagee was just *that* loud. But also, Kagee was a trained cantor – when he wanted to project that amazing voice of his, he very much could.

But Phex's messed-up brain thought that was totally normal. Kagee was *always* yelling.

Then he thought he heard Tyve yelling. His brain did not want to believe that. It couldn't be Tyve, because she rarely raised her voice.

But if it *was* her yelling? Well, then, something was seriously wrong. He needed to go help her. But his body would not behave. *What was wrong with it? What was wrong with him?*

Why was Chef squeezing him so tightly?

Why were there teeth on his neck?

Phex struggled to stay on his feet. Tried to fight his way free of this strangely familiar embrace, through the bodyguards and the acolytes and the crowd to get to Tyve. Had something happened to his pantheon? Was it Berril again? Was one of their sifters in danger?

He thought he might be throwing up.

The buzzing in his head was now the real enemy. It crept in from his ears all across his mind, scrambling everything into blessed silence. Blessings. Huh.

A blood-red darkness closed in around Phex… After the colors of the dome and the noise of the crowd… After the wooziness in his gut and the embrace of a trusted monster… After the acrid taste in his mouth and the danger, danger, danger…

The muffling sensation was a profound relief.

Phex slid gratefully into nothingness.

11

BETTER THE IMAGO YOU KNOW

Phex woke up in a massive medical facility that was both entirely unlike any he'd been in before and also exactly like all of them – because hospital rooms had a *type*, and that type was always immediately identifiable. Usually by smell. It was that precise combination of cleanliness meets the biological fluids that the cleanliness tried to cover up.

No doubt even the Galoi, widely considered the weirdest and most alien of all the tinkered species, still had hospitals that looked and smelled exactly like this one.

Phex was also surrounded by his pantheon.

"Flaming hell, that was a nightmare," said Kagee, loudly, and in a very accusing way.

Phex found himself looking around desperately for Missit, wanting to make sure the god was nearby and safe. Then he got mad at himself because of course Missit was back on the spaceship and not lurking next to Phex's sickbed like some bleeding-heart soulmate.

"How'd—" Phex started to speak but it came out as a pathetic squeak. He panicked, wondering if his voice had been damaged. Someone had been biting his neck – had they ripped out his vocal cords?

"Your mouth is dry," explained Jinyesun, using its own body to lever Phex into a sitting position.

Jin squirmed to sit on the medical cot behind Phex and act as back support. Phex leaned against the Dyesi, grateful for that elegant strength. He was honored Jin was willing to undergo extended physical contact. The Dyesi must be very worried about him.

Fandina helped Phex to sip water from a flask.

Phex was appalled to discover that not only was he feeling extremely weak but his arms were shaky and his fingers were limp and unable to grip anything.

"How'd the VIP meet-and-greet go?" he croaked.

"It didn't happen, of course, you absolute amoeba." Kagee was even more annoyed with him than normal.

"Oh, but—"

"They cancelled the damn meet-and-greet because some low-cantor prick got himself drugged, knocked out, and pretty much eaten alive." Kagee's tone was very high-pitched. He was flapping his hands around his face. His gestures, normally so elegant, were fluttery and confused.

He was also missing two rings.

"Kagee" —Phex tried to sound stern, but that was difficult when he only had a tenth of his voice strength— "did you kill someone?"

Kagee paused and looked at his two empty fingers. "You mean *two* someones? I don't miss. But no. I don't think they actually died. More's the pity. I just knocked them out. Who cares? This whole darn planet can rot."

"Did you lose the rings?" asked Tyve, appearing in Phex's line of sight.

Kagee got truculent. "Of course not." He patted at the

secret pocket of his performance suit. "They're here. A proxy doesn't wear useless jewelry. What kind of sense does that make? I need to know without thinking which are fully functional. Those two are empty, and it's not like I can get a refill of a neurotoxin when I'm, ya know, a gods-damn god. I'll store them in quarters for now. This is ridiculous, why are we talking about my rings?" He was clearly upset and feeling vulnerable, even with eight rings left.

Phex coughed, shifted his gaze to Tyve. "Did *you* kill anyone?" Her hands didn't look bloody, but she would have had time for a post-evisceration manicure while he was out of it.

Tyve sniffed. "No. I would have, but the local guards grabbed me and dragged me back into the VIP room before I actually managed to stick my claws into anyone. I might have accidentally nicked one or two of security, though." She didn't look upset about it.

Even Berril, the sweetest of them, chimed in with "Their fault for not respecting the claws."

"My point exactly," agreed Tyve, extending a claw to emphasize her pun.

The pantheon would blame local security for what had happened to Phex. But what exactly *had* happened to Phex? Wondered Phex.

Still, his pantheon came first. "Are we in trouble with the divinity for cancelling on the VIPs?"

"That's not the point, you unmitigated maggot! Of course we aren't in trouble. It's the planet's fault. It was their security breach."

Except something niggled at Phex – it wasn't all Earth 10's fault. Yes, the crazy mob had been locals, but there had been a fixed there, too. And the divinity had brought that fixed with them. They had brought her on themselves. Phex had brought her on himself. Phex winced.

Kagee continued ranting. “The local VIPs, in fact, have all written multiple apologies to you. You have received wergild from the ruling body of every major nation on Earth 10.” Kagee continued to rant. “Wergild, can you believe *that* nonsense is still happening in this sector?”

Jinyesun interrupted to say, “One of them gave you blood-stock recompense. By which I mean *actual* livestock. You now own a herd of *Capra aegagrus hircus* with specialized myotonia congenita. Apparently, they’re quite popular for their meat, fur, and comedic effect.”

Berril’s head peeked around Tyve’s side again. “Fainting goats, Phex! You own a massive herd of fainting goats now. How cool is that?”

Phex wondered if the goats had been loaded onto Tillam’s luxury cruiser and how *that* would work.

Kagee continued ranting, which fortunately explained matters. “The tour ship is apparently filled with tribute and recuperation wishes from your believers, because at least *they* know to gift you *spices* for goat meat and not *actual* goats.”

“So, my goats will stay on Earth 10?”

“Enough with the damn goats! Phex! The whole incident was beamed, for fuck’s sake! Someone in the crowd had a chip pointed right at your dumb face.”

“You will be pleased to know that you executed a very stylish collapse. You have become a galaxy-wide headline,” said Jin, almost cheerfully, patting Phex’s forearm with one six-fingered hand.

“Your eyes rolled back in your head like some dramatic horror film from Hu-core,” added Tyve and she definitely sounded cheerful. “I’m afraid you did also vomit.”

"You're a bit of a galactic sensation at the moment," confirmed Berril. "It's become a meme."

Fandina added, "Although Asterism seems to be increasing its worship numbers significantly because of it."

Jin clicked wisely. "The martyr effect."

Kagee was still on a roll. "Is that all you care about?" he griped at the rest of the pantheon, then turned back to Phex. "How on earth could you let this happen?"

Phex was still feeling muddy-headed. "The goats?"

"Phex! How could you be the one to be taken down? Of all Asterism, why you? Haven't you been practicing for months with bodyguards exactly so this wouldn't happen? Why would you, of all people, faint?"

They didn't know? They didn't know about the fixed? And the drugs he'd obviously been pumped with. And that the fixed had been one of their own. One of their crew. Phex's friend. Had they not seen? Had they not been told?

Or was everyone carefully avoiding the truth, even Kagee?

"It was Chef." Phex faced it head on.

Kagee was on a roll. "Yes, but Phex, you… *what*? Our chef? Ship's chef? Always with the yummy new tea, pouty lips, cute-auntie *chef* chef?"

"You didn't see?"

"Funnily enough, we had our own problems."

"It's not in that beam recorded by that worshiper or security footage or whatever?"

"Not so as we've seen," said Tyve, looking very serious. "Tell us what happened *exactly*, Phex."

"I don't remember much but it was Chef, and she was definitely fixed," said Phex, as if that explained everything. "I think she'd been inside and seen the dome."

"Crew isn't supposed to be able to do that," said Jinyesun, tone very angry for a Dyesi.

"You did sing around her all the time, Phex. In the kitchen and stuff," said Fandina, and there was accusation in the way its crests stiffened and pointed him.

Phex felt like an idiot. "I should have noticed what was happening."

Kagee was evidently used to betrayal and typically Kagee about it. "She's half your damn size, how the hell did she get the drop on you?"

Phex felt that was the first sensible question anyone had asked. "I'm not trained to cope with mass hysteria or threat from within. Certainly not in combination." Still, Phex felt inexplicably guilty for having gotten himself into the situation in the first place. Especially when he was always the one harping on at his pantheon about safety precautions.

Feeling like it was a wimpy excuse, he said, "A fixed with a familiar face was a shock."

"Plus, your bodyguard training doesn't kick in when you're called upon to protect yourself, does it?" accused Berril, of all people.

Tyve looked with approval at her fellow grace. "When did you get so smart?"

"I might not know fighting, but I know Phex," replied Berril.

Kagee said, still truculent and accusatory, "Was Chef the one who tried to eat you?"

Phex blinked in shock. "I thought I hallucinated that part."

"You had a mouth-sized chuck of flesh bitten out of your neck."

Phex shuddered at the memory, felt his stomach clench.

Focused on keeping himself from trembling, because Jin would be able to feel it.

"What actually happened to me after that?" He nudged Jinyesun, still supporting him.

But Jin didn't answer.

"The fixed crew member drugged you, little one. She would have had to prepare for that. Premeditation. She must have been tilting into insanity before she got fully driven mad by the dome. She used sodorium lorithite. It's a miracle you woke up so quickly. If at all. That's an extremely potent drug on Sapiens." That was a new voice, speaking Dyesi in a tone and style that Phex had never heard before – aggressively informal. It was a weird voice. It sounded like two vocal boxes speaking in combined harmony, blurred and fuzzy. But soothing and humming.

Phex looked around.

They all did.

A massive figure materialized out of the shadows to one side of the room. The medic on duty, maybe? Huge, at least two times Phex's size, but impossibly graceful and… Phex squinted.

Crested?

A Dyesi?

But surely the biggest, most unusual-looking Dyesi Phex had ever seen. It had the same hairless skin, so smooth it almost looked like carved stone. The same roughly humanoid figure but everything overly long by Sapien standards – neck, legs, arms and all with that double-jointed, liquid way of moving. Its face shape, curved and beautifully oval, with those enormous eyes, and massive unfurled crests to either side of its head, looking even more like beautiful fish fins than Phex had ever seen.

It was definitely a Dyesi, just unlike any Dyesi Phex had ever seen before.

Phex touched his lips with three shaky fingers and tried to bend forward in the Dyesi formal greeting that had been drilled into him since the beginning.

"Who the hell are you?" growled Kagee.

The newcomer was so big, it now blocked out the main illumination of the medical facility, making it difficult to see details. What color was this behemoth?

Its crest puffed, seeming almost amused. The light from behind shone through them, making little prismatic sparkles on Phex's bedsheets.

"Did you know fixed are only dangerous to the god they fixate on? To everyone else, the fixed are usually quite passive. Sometimes almost catatonic. I wonder what's actually going on in those corrupted brains of theirs," said the stranger. A divine analyst or Dyesi intellectual of some kind?

"Madness," said Kagee in low register, annoyed with this new person. "I hope Chef has been taken away and locked firmly in a padded cell somewhere very far from Phex."

"Padded cell, like a room made of chair puffs?" wondered Phex, oddly worried about Chef. Worried about what he had inadvertently done to her.

"No. What? Oh, old Hu-core-ism." Kagee waved one delicate hand – it was odd to see it with only four rings.

"Will she be all right?" Phex asked the Dyesi stranger.

"What are you…? You're the insane one. How can you care about her at all? She tried to *eat* you, Phex." Kagee threw both hands up in exasperation and stormed away, presumably only to a different part of hospital bay. He'd still want to hear the rest of the conversation.

The newcomer's crests remained focused with interest on Phex. "You are a strange creature. To answer your question, no, she will not be *all right*. She is not the *she* you once knew. If indeed you ever really knew her. But, little blue, how could you have made friends with a believer?"

"I had no idea she believed in me." Phex was moved to defend himself, for a change.

"No? Well, either way, no one comes back from being fixed. It is the price paid by the divinity for its existence, that monsters happen."

"It seems like they are the ones paying the price," said Phex.

"Perhaps you're right. No doubt she will be kept in comfort and studied, as they all are."

"Why *studied*?" asked Tyve.

"So that maybe, someday, we can prevent fixed from happening at all."

Phex wondered if this was a Dyesi medical professional of some kind. He didn't think they really had healers.

"So, how did I escape?" wondered Phex.

"I got you out," said the newcomer, using a first-person pronoun Phex had never heard before. Was this Dyesi a different gender from any Phex had met previously?

"And who, exactly, are you?" asked Phex.

The stranger lumbered closer, looming over Phex and Jin, still sitting behind him.

Its skin was also different from normal Dyesi, not blue-tinged iridescent but instead a dark grey pearlescent color. It looked waxy and hard. Like it might be cold to the touch. Like it was armor.

"Oh. Ah." Fandina flushed opaque with shame, but its ear crests were pointed in deferential eagerness at the newcomer. "Phex this is Quasilun. Asterism's new bodyguard." Fandina's linguistic register was so formal, it was almost beyond Phex's understanding of the language.

"A *Dyesi* bodyguard?" said Phex for confirmation.

Dyesi were not warriors and this one might be big, but it had the same fragile, androgynous beauty and innate elegance of any acolyte or sifter. Even if it was clearly from a different part of the planet or a high-gravity moon, it did not look deadly in any way.

Jinyesun explained. "Quasilun is an imago Dyesi." Apparently, that made all the difference.

"Just the *one* bodyguard?" Kagee was clearly on Phex's side in this, doubtful.

"One protector imago is all we need," said Fandina with confidence.

Phex did not trust his sifters on matters of defense. He huffed at them.

"I got you out and to safety, didn't I?" Quasilun sounded amused.

Phex stared up into its face. Beautifully perfect and hard and alien but also somehow more relaxed and less stiff than most acolytes and sifters.

Fandina made a gesture of obeisance with its crests. "Quasilun, this is Phex, low cantor of Asterism. He is also our sun, please forgive him his tone, for the worry behind it is sourced in kindness." Fandina was still using that extremely formal register of Dyesi honorifics that Phex had never heard before.

Phex shifted against Jin and whispered. "What form of the language is Fandina using?"

"Frozen register," explained Jinyesun.

Phex had heard it mentioned once or twice when they were being educated as potentials in Dyesi culture. But they hadn't studied frozen register. They were told it wasn't needed. It existed, apparently, only on Dyesid Prime, and in certain legal documents, ancient texts, and the very first godsongs.

"But why a—?"

Shockingly, Jinyesun cut Phex off. Jin, who was always one to explain anything anyone asked, especially about Dyesi culture. Especially to Phex.

"Now is not the time, low cantor. You must pay attention to the imago." The unprecedented amount of respect in Jin's tone emphasized the importance of Phex following its lead.

Quasilun leaned back to stand upright fully, towering over everyone. It looked at Phex and Jinyesun cuddling with those huge eyes, crests curious. Its eyes were also still very Dyesi in shape and expression but with an unusual color to them. Instead of the general blues or purples or greens, Quasilun's eyes were almost gold, yellow metallic, like Missit's skin.

"That was a high dose of a *very* powerful drug, how are you awake so soon, little blue Sapien-child?" asked their new bodyguard, sounding suddenly very like a bodyguard ought, actually. But its Dyesi was so informal, it was if they had known each other for months, or as if Phex were truly a tiny child. Phex was just Dyesi-trained enough to be offended by such profound informality at their first meeting. But Quasilun had used the same tone with Fandina and Jinyesun, and neither of them were taking offense.

So, Phex took his cues from his sifters and simply said calmly, "Was I not out long enough for Jin to explain?"

"Jin?"

"Jinyesun." Phex gestured at his Dyesi backrest.

Jin clicked. "Imago, our Phex is genetically enhanced." Then it explained, carefully and precisely, using frozen register, exactly why Phex could process drugs faster than other Sapiens.

The imago's crests twitched back and Jinyesun instantly

stopped talking. "Ah, of course, I understand. I was informed as to all of Asterism's genetic backgrounds. I did not realize his enhancements would impact his substance-processing capacity, but that makes perfect sense."

Phex asked Jin, "Are imagoes a different subspecies? A biological procreative variant? A different gender?"

"Not *now*," hissed Jinyesun.

Their new bodyguard clicked. "It's fine, youngling." To Phex it said, "There is no Galactic word for my biological state, and you have already heard the Dyesi term *imago* and not understood it. Let's get you back to the ship, shall we? I'll explain there."

Phex glanced around. The facility seemed empty but for his pantheon, one acolyte, and this new bodyguard. But if Phex had been hooked up to anything before he awoke, he wasn't anymore. So, he girded himself to stand, not entirely sure his legs would hold him.

Then the imago stepped forward and simply lifted him up. Cradling him in its arms as if he were an actual child. Phex had never been held in such a way in his life. Certainly not in his living memory, anyway.

It was the oddest sensation. He was pretty certain he should protest it as beneath him, but the imago was impossibly strong and its skin was exactly as hard as it looked. Phex was too weak to do more than flop about and squeak, "Hey!"

"Relax, little blue," said Quasilun, unaffected by Phex's pathetic struggles.

It was weird to think that there were Dyesi warriors, but Phex supposed they did come from a planet known for its challenging surface conditions and carnivorous megafauna. The Dyesi must have developed a means to defend themselves from the predators of their home world. This imago must represent that warrior caste, he guessed.

"Just one bodyguard needed, huh?" Phex croaked, not bothering with formal Dyesi. If the imago wasn't going to use it, why should he?

Quasilun huffed in amusement. "For now, little one. Let us see how powerful you get. So, you rest, I'm here. It'll be fine." Its voice was low and smooth, that double-barreled burr. So soothing. The loving hum of a mother Phex had never known.

"Who's going to cook?" he wondered, worried about Chef.

Kagee's voice then: "Oh, for the love of… just sleep, you chump."

Phex found himself, much to his further embarrassment, doing what he'd been told and drifting off to sleep.

The next time he woke, it was because Missit was having hysterics.

Phex awoke while Quasilun was carrying him up the ramp and into the belly of the spaceship. Missit was blocking the entrance in front of them like a tiny, angry sunbeam. Dimsum was wrapped around his neck – a more animated and more vicious form of Phex's whip scarf. Also more vocal – she was chittering angrily.

"Is that Phex? My Phex? So, he *is* injured. What happened? Where have you been? Why does Phex need to be carried? What took so long? What is going on? What could *possibly* warrant a protector imago?"

Missit's head appeared close to Phex's, and his slim cool hands began petting over Phex's face. Phex stared up at him, cataloguing his skin for damage, his flecked eyes for pain. Nothing there, fortunately, except concern for him.

"Are you okay? You don't look good. You don't look terrible, either. Were you injured? Are you sick?"

"This is an interesting development," said the imago, in a certain tone of voice that spoke volumes without actually being loud.

Phex was sublimely happy to see that Missit seemed to be his normal self and completely unharmed. He forgot, for the moment, that he was supposed be hiding his reactions to the golden god. He shouldn't be so relieved to find that Missit had gotten back to the ship safely. Tillam had six highly trained bodyguards with them, after all. But he *was* relieved.

Speaking of which, Bob's impassive metal-plated face appeared next to Missit's.

"He's fine," said Bob to his god. "Just a little snafu with a fixed who also happened to be a crew member."

The cyborg should have known that was exactly the wrong thing to say.

"What?" Missit looked even more upset. "Crew? Here?"

Kagee, clearly delighted to find someone else sympathetic to his general anger, added more, in order to rile Missit further. "Phex got caught in a crowd of worshipers and nearly crushed to death on his way from the niche to the narthex. Then Chef, who'd snuck away to see the show" —he glared at other crew members present— "how could you not stop her? Anyway, she turned up, turned fixed, pricked him with an ampoule of this highly potent toxin, knocked him out, and then tried to eat him." Another glare. "Yes, I said it! Literally *eat him*."

Phex shivered, his stomach churning.

"I suppose she is a chef," said Tyve, who had a warped sense of humor at the best of times.

"Shut up, Tyve," said Kagee without looking around.

"Everyone was thinking it, right?" asked Tyve hopefully.

Kagee pushed on. "And then your friendly neighborhood imago swept in and rescued him."

Missit said, "I'm sorry, *what*?" And then, apparently having processed everything, started yelling at the surrounding acolytes, at ship's crew, and at anyone else who would listen. "She's boxed, right? Fucking cannibal-level *fixed* and none of you noticed? Aboard this ship? *My* ship? Get us off this planet right now. I want all the crew fully evaluated. Brain scans, body scans, booty scans… *all the scans*! Any others been sneaking domes, or watching practices, or hanging out too much with Phex, I want them quarantined. Fuck it, I want a whole new crew. I want a new ship!"

"Uh, god, we can't just…"

Missit held up a hand, looking cold and oddly deadly. "Meanwhile" —he drew out the word, soft and hissing— "get us out of here. Don't wait for clearance. Inform the authorities that neither Tillam nor Asterism will ever visit Earth 10 again. No wonder they sent so much tribute."

He unwound Dimsum from his neck, which meant the murmel started shrieking almost as loudly as Missit had been yelling.

Crew and acolytes leapt to do as instructed. It was absolute chaos.

Berril said, "Someone gifted Phex with a herd of fainting goats."

"After *he* fainted?" Missit paused. "Is that irony, parody, or insult?" He became suddenly the opposite of what he had been, icy calm and hypervigilant. He grabbed Phex's dangling hand, squeezed it tightly, trotting to keep up with Quasilun, who was still moving fast through the ship's hallways.

"Where is Asterism quartered?" the imago asked.

Missit took a deep breath and pointed with his free hand. "Just down there and to the right."

Phex noticed that he slipped easily into frozen register.

Phex could hear a general excited chatter behind them. He assumed that was his pantheon discussing with Tillam what had happened.

Phex raised his head, worried. "They haven't eaten. Missit, what time is it? How long have we been gone?"

Missit sighed and looked up at Quasilun. "You have to stop a moment, he'll fret himself sick if he doesn't know they're settled."

"Sun. I know how it goes." The imago stopped and turned so Phex could see back down the hallway, crowded with most of the ship's complement and both pantheons.

"Fandina, come here, child," said Quasilun.

Fandina trotted obediently over.

Phex heard Berril say, "Shouldn't we stay with Phex?"

Tyve replied, "You know he'll just get anxious that we aren't looking after ourselves if we fuss over him."

"Let the bodyguards handle it. It's their fault, anyway." That was Kagee, and he meant it to sting. At least the barbs weren't aimed at Phex anymore.

Itrio yelled down the hallway, "We're sorry, Phex. We had no idea it'd be so bad."

"We didn't see the red flags in the chef either," added Bob, who had stuck close.

Phex would have yelled back at Itrio, but he didn't have enough voice yet, so he said to Fandina, "Tell her I don't blame any of the bodyguards. Their first duty is to Tillam, and Tillam is safe. They did what they were supposed to. Guarded who they were supposed to guard. They can't be in two places at once. I was the one close to Chef. If anyone one should have seen her going rotten, it was me." He meant Bob to hear it, too.

Fandina looked from Phex to Quasilun and back. "Anything else, imago?"

"Let your sun bleed out his concern."

Fandina crested attentively at Phex.

Phex coughed, then continued, croaky. "Don't forget you need to eat. We just performed a major dome, everyone's exhausted. Hydrate too. You know Kagee and Tyve are bad about that. Don't let Berril fill up on carbs."

He paused, worried. "Who will cook for them?" Maybe one of the bodyguards could lend a hand in the galley for the time being? Phex winced – he didn't really want to think about the kitchen.

Bob said, "Most of us bodyguards can prep basic nutrition, don't worry, no one will starve."

Phex decided he had no choice but to trust the imago. For now.

He returned his attention to Fandina. "Don't let them stay up late, looking at the infonet and trying to muffle gossip about me on the divine forums. They need sleep. All this drama will still be there when we wake up tomorrow. Unfortunately."

Fandina, clearly a little exasperated, replied politely. Possibly because Phex was ill but more likely because of the imago's presence. "I'll make sure they eat and drink, and we will all follow you to quarters directly. There's plenty of leftovers, Phex, no one needs to cook. You'll see us all soon. I promise."

Phex nodded, relieved. Too tired to remember to click.

So, Missit clicked in his stead and then pressed Quasilun back into motion toward Asterism's quarters.

Fandina took that as dismissal and went to hustle Asterism into the galley for a much-deserved meal.

Missit caught Phex up as they wended through the ship. "It's almost morning. You were away most of the night. The divinity was practically colorless with crisis. I've never seen acolytes move that fast. Apparently, there's *live* footage of you collapsing." Missit bowed, rubbed violently at the wrinkles that weren't allowed to be in his forehead, then pressed on. "Bob wouldn't let me watch. Rumor is that both Cotyla Mainspace and the Kill'ki Coalition mobilized warships to this sector. *Warships!* Because you passed out on a live beam."

"Asterism is very popular," said Quasilun. "And your Phex here is particularly appealing to the more violent civilizations. This is a *good* thing."

"Considering he acts like an idiot warrior half the time, that's no surprise."

"Only half the time?" said Phex, trying for levity.

"Hush, you. Your voice sounds awful, save it. Plus, talking doesn't suit you." Missit frowned furiously at him.

Phex hushed as ordered, feeling warm and pleased for some reason.

Missit looked with big, pleading eyes at Quasilun. "He's really uninjured?"

"Remarkably so. Just weak. Did you know how fast he could process drugs?"

Missit didn't answer, because they'd reached the entrance to Asterism's quarters.

"Here we are." Missit held aside the flap so Quasilun, taking up most of the doorway with its huge bulk, could move inside. Phex worried that the imago would never be able to sleep aboard the cruiser – spaceship cots were far too small.

Quasilun said, "I sleep on the floor, little blue, but thank you for your concern," which was how Phex realized he'd spoken out loud. He obviously was very tired.

"Why are you really here, imago?" Missit leapt to pull away Phex's blanket and then supervise as Quasilun set him carefully into his cot.

"You know why, little god."

"Do I?" Missit tucked the blanket carefully around Phex.

"This one can cause fugue." The imago crossed huge arms over its chest and stared down at Phex with an impassive face but very interested crests.

"*We* can cause fugue, together," corrected Missit. "But that was a while ago. Why would Dyesid send an imago to us *now*?"

"You can ask such a thing after what just happened?"

"I regret to inform you, old one, such a thing as this can happen to any god insufficiently protected on any planet in any corner of the divinity. That is the nature of the fixed."

"But to have a fixed so focused and so fast? To make a fixed out of a friend? Plus, he's doubling doses as a cantor for two pantheons. What happens if he goes up on a dais twice in one night under one dome?"

"He already does. It's just sometimes it's a duet with only me."

"Experimental that may be, but it's still extra exposure for worshipers."

"The divinity guessed this might be a problem?"

"The moment he was recruited."

Dangerous voice, Phex remembered them saying. Was that what they meant? He thought they meant he could hurt sifters. He could freeze Dyesi. But did it mean fixed?

Phex cracked his eyelids – he hadn't even realized he'd closed them.

The imago was wiggling the tip of one crest at Missit. "They sent me here as soon as they could. There aren't many of us available, or even around anymore, you know that."

Missit looked suddenly very wary, which made Phex focus wholly on his face – it was uncharacteristically serious. That wide mouth, usually so mobile and smiley, was set firm. "You would have been here earlier if you could, is that what you're saying?"

"Yes, little god."

"Why?"

Quasilun looked back down at Phex. The expression on the Dyesi's face was strangely caring but also cautious, like the parent of a troublesome child.

Phex felt small and young all of a sudden. He was also inexplicably sad, missing something he'd never had but still, somehow, lost a long time before. A parent, if he'd ever had one, might have looked at him like that.

"There has never been a cantor who can sing both high and low and also grace."

Missit's serious expression cleared. "Oh. I see. He contains within him a power of three. So, are you here to be Asterism's bodyguard or just Phex's?"

"He is the sun, is there a difference?" The imago suddenly lost interest. "I will leave him in your care now, god. He should sleep. I must discuss matters with the acolytes."

Missit said, frozen register but tone very sharp, "Protector imago, are you really here to protect Phex? Or are you here to protect others *from* Phex?"

"Is there a difference?" Quasilun shot back.

With which Phex's new bodyguard left the room and left Phex in the tender care of Missit.

Missit hit him.

Not hard, just on the shoulder, but still. "Ow!"

"Idiot. How the hell could you let such a thing happen?"

Phex might have protested but that wouldn't help. And Missit was right – he had been stupid.

"I'm fine," he said. "I'm here. I survived my first fixed attack. And I'm sorry I worried you." Because what else could he say, really?

Missit let out a long, shuddering sigh, knelt next to the cot, and put his head on Phex's chest, like he was trying to hear his heart beat.

The murmel, who'd followed them, gave a shriek of protest from under Phex's bunk.

Missit said sternly, "Now is not the time, Dimsum."

She subsided into sullen chattering.

Phex raised a hand – at least his arms were responding okay now – and gently petted Missit's head. Careful not to muss his beautiful hair, which was already pulled and coiled back for sleep.

He ignored Missit's tears because that was just relief leaking out with no other possible release.

Phex only realized at that moment that he'd been stripped of his costume and wrapped in a robe, probably at the hospital. They'd cleaned him of performance sweat, but he smelled like a medical experiment, and Missit's lovely face was right there.

Phex tried to sit up.

"What are you doing?" Missit protested.

"Hygiene chamber. I stink."

"You're fine. Go to sleep. You can barely walk."

Phex grumbled at him, sounding not unlike the murmel. "Help me clean up, then."

"That is not a good idea. Your pantheon is coming back soon. You instructed them to do so." The god winced. "We never get any private time."

Stubbornly, Phex swung himself to sit on the edge and then standing all in one movement. His legs weren't doing him any favors. Instead, they were conducting a remarkably accurate simulation of udon noodles.

Missit leapt to his feet to slide himself under Phex arm for support. "Oh, for gods' sake. Fine. I'll help. It's not fair, though."

"Fair?"

"We'll be naked in a hygiene chamber together, and you're too weak to do anything about it."

Phex spoke without thinking. The drug must still be in his system no matter what the imago had said. "True. That isn't fair."

"Did you just agree with me?"

Phex lurched into the wall and sort of rolled along it to get into the hygiene chamber. "Come on."

"Can I sleep with you here tonight?"

"Stop it, Missit."

"Guess those drugs weren't *that* strong, then."

Phex did look up the footage later. Vids of the incident were spreading faster than the divinity. Post-incident psych eval instructed him not to hunt down the beams, claiming it was a bad idea to look up posted trauma about oneself. Phex thought that was ridiculous.

He didn't think he was traumatized by anything more than his own inability to realize what was happening in that crowd and get out of the situation without help. He needed to review the beam as closely and as frequently as possible so as to understand and prevent it from ever happening again.

It turns out that he had, in fact, vomited. Lovely. Oh, well. And Chef was very much *fixed.*

That bit was… not good. That bit always made him look away from the vid. Even though he was supposed to be studying it for flaws he could rectify in the future. He just couldn't look at Chef's face. Even though, if it appeared at all, it was blurred and jumpy, coming in and out of the frame.

"A perfect case study," said Quasilun, noticing what he was watching when it came in with some indifferent porridge. "Eat. It's not good, but it's nutritious and spud-based." The imago wasn't like other Dyesi. In general much more relaxed and willing to talk about anything than even Jinyesun and Fandina. Certainly more than any acolyte.

"I can cook once the acolytes let me up," said Phex, who was, frankly, feeling fine.

The imago's crests flattened in the negative. "It's a full-time job on a ship like this, the acolytes will onboard someone new soon. The bodyguards are doing fine in the interim."

Phex made a face, thinking of those large, violent types in Chef's kitchen.

But then, wasn't he a large, violent type?

And it wasn't Chef's kitchen anymore.

"I found the shrine." Quasilun flipped down Kagee's bunk and sat on it, taking up most of it.

Phex was confused. "Shrine?"

"In the upper left cabinet. Full of offerings of food and a few tools. You didn't know?"

"My special cabinet?" Phex was confused.

Quasilun huffed. "No, *her shrine to you*. You misconstrued worship as friendship. She built you an altar, little one." The imago didn't say that Phex should have realized this, but Phex felt the implication.

How could he not have known? He'd missed the most obvious sign. That cabinet had been full of offerings. Not of friendship but of obsession.

"Sometimes, I sing in the galley when I'm cooking," he admitted.

"That would not have been a healthy thing for her." The imago's crests drooped a little and it looked away. "The dome is always the trigger. But being constantly around you would contribute to any believer's obsession. She may have packed those drugs and thought it was just to be on the safe side. That she wasn't actually going to use them. That she only wanted to watch. That she really wouldn't do anything to you. But then she felt the dome."

"Why?"

"Why does the dome do anything it does to worshipers? Because it is divine. If the acolytes understood how the dome caused fixed, they would have corrected for it by now." The imago sounded tolerant more than anything else. "I'm not surprised it was a chef. The divinity has *kitchen* listed as your sacred space."

Phex nodded. "My believers send me spoons and spices and the like. They think it's cute – a god who enjoys cooking."

"I'm sorry she corrupted it for you. But that too is part of being fixed, to know and become one with your most private and intimate occupations."

Phex did know that. The fixed always said in interviews after being caught that they did it because they wanted to be remembered by their god. They wanted to make their mark on a god's life. They wanted to be *important* to the one they believed in, even if only in a negative way. Thank goodness she'd never found out about him and Missit.

"I think maybe she wasn't quite there until the dome."

Phex tried not to think about that crazed, obsessive look, that unfettered obsession in those eager, grasping hands. The teeth scraping over his fabric-covered bicep.

"But the signs were there, little blue. She built you a *shrine*." The imago was firm.

Phex closed his eyes and tried not to see the truth. He should have known.

He shouldn't have sung in the kitchen where crew could hear him.

He shouldn't have made a friend of a worshiper.

He should have behaved more like a god.

Too late now.

The imago took his half-eaten porridge away, unsympathetic. Phex wanted to cry out that this was all new to him. He didn't know how to act. He was only a demigod, after all. He was doing his best.

But that would only come off as defensive. One didn't argue with a blade. One suffered the wound it inflicted in silence and learned how to better avoid it in future. The blade didn't care for excuses.

It was Kagee who pointed out how sanguine he was. "You're not overreacting and throwing up."

"Overreacting?" Phex was offended by the term.

Berril peeked over her top bunk. "Of course he isn't. *He* isn't one of *us*."

Kagee snorted. "One of us?"

Berril sounded all-knowing. "Worth protecting."

Tyve explained her fellow grace. "Phex doesn't mind risk if it's him, not us."

Phex *had* half-expected to carry the horror of it in his gut. He was a little surprised his stomach wasn't churning. But they were okay– he was the only one who'd been injured. And he had the genes to bear it.

"I can take care of myself."

Kagee huffed. "Evidently not."

"I'm fine," lied Phex.

Maybe he woke up a few times each night, in a cold sweat from a familiar friendly face becoming some nameless nightmare. But the blades had done that to him countless times as a child – it was nothing he wouldn't grow out of. The chef, like the blue crud of his youth, would also pass into dust motes and memory.

So, Phex tried to avoid the chef part when he reviewed the footage even as he kept it on repeat. Compelled to face the fact that his choices, cooking and bodyguarding, had been tested and found wanting. Some vain attempt to understand how he might fix it all going forward. Might fix the mob of worship. Might fix the insanity of fixed. Might fix himself and his choices. Watching those vids, again and again, in hopeless penance.

There was an odd thing after he fainted, a sound – presumably made by Quasilun before the imago appeared on screen, a dark grey blob taking over the beam. The odd sound was a reverberating bellow that had the feel of two voices blurred together. The acolytes within the scope of the vid's audio had yelled as well, or Phex presumed it was them because the yelling was in Dyesi. Perhaps Quasilun's bellow was some kind of Dyesi war cry.

Then, after one of Phex's countless rewinds, he noticed something peculiar. Just before the imago's massive form took over the screen, Phex caught flashes of blue flesh. As if the acolytes had regained their color and were moving around him. That was highly unlikely, so perhaps they were just being pushed by the crowd into the vid's frame? Because everyone knew the Dyesi did not fight, except, apparently, for imagoes.

Quasilun cleared a swath around Phex's collapsed body, folding back the crowd like wilting flowers. It moved so fast, its grey form was never fully visible. It was impossible to see that Phex's savior was Dyesi at all. Instead, it just looked like some massive blur, felling all and whisking Phex away.

Phex thought it was probably no accident that a Dyesi warrior used non-deadly fighting techniques. Still, he watched in awe, as in the time it took him to collapse, one imago managed to clear all visible life from that beam. Including, presumably, whoever was beaming, because the vid's view flipped up to the ceiling of the tunnel and then to one side, as the wrist wearing it flailed and its owner collapsed.

Whatever imagoes were, they certainly knew how to fight.

At least this one did.

Aside from Quasilun, who was brusque, and Kagee, who was annoyed, everyone treated Phex like a precious baby for the next twenty-four hours – including Missit. Kagee made himself scarce, too annoyed to even watch the fussing.

Phex remained confined to his bed with one or another of his pantheon running errands at Missit's insistence. Missit took up residence at the foot of his cot, curled up with the murmel in his lap, insisting on doing silly things like hand-feeding Phex breakfast and reading to him from the infonet, even singing for him on occasion.

"You're totally ridiculous," accused Phex, several times.

"You love it," accused Missit back. Phex wondered if the god realized that his presence prevented Phex from continually reviewing footage.

Since Phex did, in fact, love it, he didn't protest further. Just basked in the odd sensation of being looked after by a flighty golden god who normally would never dream of doing such a thing.

During a lull in the proceedings, Phex even managed to have a decent conversation with that god. "Missit, what is an imago Dyesi, exactly?"

"Ah, your new bodyguard. Do you feel blessed by divine intervention? You should." Missit's tone was all sarcasm.

"Well?"

"One of your sifters might explain it better." He plucked at the woven blanket, eyes narrowed.

"I did think to ask Jin, but I'm worried it's rude, or taboo, or not talked about by the Dyesi themselves."

Missit made a face, wide mouth twisted. "I don't think so, or they'd never have assigned Quasilun to you in the first place. This is the first time I've heard of a protector imago guarding a god, though. It's not normal for imagoes to involve themselves with the divinity. You should be honored."

"Should I?"

"No, not really." Missit looked up at him with big eyes and a funny expression. Maybe concern. He grabbed Phex's foot through the blanket and squeezed it as if for comfort.

"So, it's okay for me to ask Jin about imagoes?" Phex automatically reached down, tucking a loose lock of hair behind Missit's ear.

"Do you want me to go get your sifters for you? I think they're practicing with Kagee." Missit looked like he really just wanted to curl up on top of Phex. But even Missit knew better than to do that in the middle of day shift.

Phex dropped his hand. Fingers still feeling the silk of Missit's hair.

Missit closed his beautiful eyes a moment. "Fine, I'll forgo my nursemaid persona. But I want you aware of the fact that I was prepared to mop your brow, should your brow require mopping." He stood up from the cot and stretched, flashing a gleam of golden skin at his belly.

"Good to know." Phex suppressed the urge to touch that skin.

"Does it need mopping?" pressed Missit hopefully, watching Phex's gaze graze over the gleams of his body.

"No, thank you." Phex cleared his dry throat.

"Why do you never play?"

"Missit."

"Yes, yes, I'm off. But think of me as the man who sacrificed hours of his valuable time to mop your brow." He stroked two fingers over Phex's forehead, which was perfectly dry, and down one side of his face. Phex only just managed to stop himself from kissing them.

"Why is it called *mopping*, anyway?"

"Missit!"

Missit sashayed off, having definitely won this round.

12

ALL THINGS MUST PANTHEON

"Missit told me to come sit with you. Told me I was to *mop your brow in a platonic way*. Is there a special Sapien tool for that?" Jinyesun came in looking cheerful and fluffy-crested.

"He was making a joke, Jin."

"Was he? One would think after so many years among the Dyesi that Missit would have learned we don't get most jokes."

Phex patted the end of his cot, and Jinyesun obligingly came and perched at his feet, in that stiff but elegant Dyesi way.

"Yes, o greatest and best low cantor? If I cannot mop, what can I do for you?" The Dyesi's big eyes were inquisitive.

"Explain something, please?"

"Delighted to be asked to do that at which I consider myself proficient." Jin settled back expectantly.

"Am I allowed to ask, what is an imago?"

"You are allowed. Quasilun is one. But there are actually three different kinds. He is a *protector* imago. The rarest kind. I think less than twelve percent."

Phex knew that Jin tended to approach a topic, especially a unique aspect of Dyesi culture, from all directions at once. So, he let his friend explain in its own way.

"Protector imagoes don't often leave Dyesid Prime, although they are the only imagoes who actually can. Their primary duty is to the breeders and the young, not us nymphs. Quasilun is scary, right?"

"It fights. In the manner of a true warrior. Not deadly but effective."

"Yes, they have other defensive capacities as well, beyond fists and feet, I mean."

"And we are to use frozen register when speaking with protector imagoes?"

"With *all* imagoes, yes. Also, different pronouns." Jin made a subtle kind of shift in tone and emphasis between the *it* that the Dyesi normally used with each other and another, entirely new pronoun.

"What does that mean exactly?"

"Imagoes are not genderless like us nymphs," Jinyesun gestured to itself. "A protector imago outside of the caves is more like the Galactic *they*, genderfluid, but also not exactly. Galactic does not contain the right term for what Quasilun is. You may continue to use the *it* with which you are familiar. Quasilun will not take offense."

"So is imago a subspecies?"

Jinyesun puffed hard in amusement. "No no no. Imagoes are simply in the third life stage. You would say, maybe, *grown-up*?"

Phex processed that for a moment. "So, you and Fandina will eventually become like Quasilun as you age?"

"Not *as we age*. After our next instar," said Jin. "Imagoes come in three variants, the two breeders and the protector. Quasilun is a protector. It's not a common metamorphosis in modern times, but no lesser than the other two simply because it is old fashioned."

Phex didn't understand at all. "So, what stage are you at?"

"Oh Fandina and I are nymphs," said Jinyesun. "Second stage," it added, brightly.

"The acolytes too?"

Jin clicked an affirmative. "Acolytes, softskins, sifters, agents of the divinity, we are all nymphs. That is why we share certain characteristics in appearance, not to mention lack of sexual identity and sexual interest. We collectively are too young to procreate. We do not possess the biological capacity."

"So, you are *children*?" posited Phex, still confused.

Jinyesun went opaque with horror. "Absolutely not!"

Phex frowned, thinking hard, trying to wrap his brain around alien concepts. "How long do you live? The Dyesi?"

Jin looked very smug, as if Phex had finally asked the correct question. "Almost twice as long as Sapiens. And we spend the bulk of our lifecycle in the nymph stage. This one." It flapped a pretty, tapered six-fingered hand at itself.

Phex grappled with that answer, for it meant that the Dyesi lived for hundreds of years.

Jinyesun explained further. "We do not procreate until much later in life than Sapiens. And our breeder imagoes are planet-bound. They even get reclassified by the galactic system as H10. Only protector imagoes, like Quasilun, leave the caves. And us nymphs, of course."

"It seems complicated," said Phex, because it did.

"Just imagine how Sapien romance, courting, and procreation rituals seem to us," replied Jinyesun, pertly.

Phex grinned. He supposed Sapien biology and life patterns would seem very alien to a nymph Dyesi. Let alone sexual interest and flirting. "Very messy?"

Jin clicked a hard confirmation. "You said it, not me."

Phex thought, longingly, about Missit's fine golden limbs wrapped around him in the cantor practice booth. Messy in the best possible way.

"Not to mention all your different sexual orientations and genders. Very, very confusing and, as you said, *messy*." Jinyesun agreed wholeheartedly with Phex's assessment.

Phex thought it might be nice to have sexual desire removed entirely from the equation at this point in his life. He could certainly focus better on being a god. He could focus better on most things since Missit would be a great deal less distracting. Golden limbs and all.

It explained why the Dyesi had regulations against fraternization among gods, though. If nymphs existed in a pre-sexual life state, it would be taboo for the sifters among them to have sexual contact. It made a Dyesi kind of sense to extend that to all other gods as well.

Jinyesun relaxed slightly since Phex seemed neither confused nor disgusted. "Frankly, we have no idea how you do it. How you decide on romantic and sexual relationships? It does not seem easy."

"Is it easy to pick which kind of imago you want to be?" Phex asked in response.

Jinyesun crested in interest. "We have no idea whether choice is even a factor. It happens during instar."

"You can't ask Quasilun about it?"

"No point. Instar is different for everyone. Did you choose what gender and type of person you were attracted to when you became fertile? What type of person and gender you yourself *are*?"

Phex shook his head. He thought it probably wasn't directly correlative, but he understood Jin's point. Carefully, he asked, "Would Quasilun be able to flirt? Have sex? Fall in love?"

"Why? Are you interested?" Was Jin actually teasing him? Usually, only Fandina tried to do that. Jin was by nature more reserved.

Phex frowned as fiercely as he could.

Jinyesun gave a Dyesi soundless huff-chuckle. "As incomprehensible as I might find it, yes. Quasilun cannot produce young but is still an imago and can do *that* kind of thing. If they wanted to."

The Dyesi seemed not so much disgusted as very carefully neutral on the subject of sexual intercourse and romantic attachments within its own species.

Phex figured he should lean in to politeness. "Thank you for explaining, Jin. Will I ever get to meet the other two imago types?"

"Breeders? That would mean going to the home caves. It is highly unlikely." Jinyesun sounded genuinely sad for Phex.

"Yet desirable?"

"They are quite beautiful," explained Jin, "the caves and the breeders. They live the dome and die for it." Which made absolutely no sense but sounded like an idiom.

Phex thought about what he knew of Missit's family history with the Dyesi. Missit's parents had been the first anthropologists invited to visit the caves. Missit had been born on Dyesid Prime and abandoned there.

"Has Missit seen the breeders?"

"He has."

And yet insisted on Phex asking Jinyesun about imagoes. Why? Phex supposed Missit wasn't big on explanations, just chattering uselessly in that endearing and weirdly appealing way. Or maybe it was something more sinister. Perhaps Missit wasn't allowed to talk about it.

"Luck of the gods," said Phex, using a Sapien idiom.

Jinyesun gave Phex a crest-fold of approval for his wit. But Phex was now worried about Missit, who had not been raised among Sapiens. Who did not know how to flirt except as a god. No wonder he was so bad at it. Not that Phex was one to judge, but still.

Phex was even more scared of them being caught together in a compromising position. For he had an imago Dyesi watching him. An imago who could understand desire, unlike the nymphs. Who might pick up on the heated nuances of Phex's interactions with Missit. Who might see the glorious mess they were making of each other.

Or maybe already had.

After one more long sleep, Phex felt absolutely fine. They were winging their way on to their next tour destination. He handled a full day of practice with both pantheons with no issues or feeling of weakness. Chalk one more up to the genetic wizards of the Wheel.

That night after dinner – which Phex cooked for lack of other options – he checked in with the bodyguards. Phex was hoping for a bit of sparring, but Quasilun was with them. Phex didn't know why, but for some reason he felt it ill-advised to insist on training under imago observation. So, he merely waved and went off to have a quiet night hanging out in the galley with the other gods.

Itrio looked hurt and snubbed. Phex hoped she didn't still think he blamed them for what had happened on Earth 10. But there was nothing he could do about that.

Missit squeezed next to him on one of the small puffs, gave up cuddling Fortew for Phex's big broad shoulder.

Seeking to be comforted rather than comforting. Phex didn't think it was a good idea, but at least he knew Quasilun wasn't watching. Plus, Missit was being very Missit about it. So, it came off as his normal loosely doled-out version of godly affection. Phex supposed everyone needed a bit of extra reassurance from him these days. He was a rock they had all seen crumble unexpectedly. Now they knew he too could be damaged.

There was a lively discussion going on about a new virtual game that was sweeping the galaxy, which everyone was playing except Phex. Phex never understood gaming. Real life was already full of enough games to be going on with.

Dimsum was loafing on the back of the biggest puff opposite them, tail lashing, monitoring Missit and how close he was getting to Phex. Her little eyes gleamed with possessiveness. Phex thought she was like a tiny fixed.

He glared at the murmel, not caring how ridiculous that was. Missit did belong to him, at least a little bit. Dimsum had to learn to share.

The murmel made a small growling noise when Missit pressed even closer so he could whisper into Phex's ear.

"Are you better? Would you maybe want to meet me in the booth later?"

Missit was being uncharacteristically shy, making a request rather than his usual teasing demand. Missit being cautious with Phex and about Phex was disconcerting. Phex didn't like it. Was Missit still scared Phex was hurt?

"I'm fine," replied Phex. "I process drugs faster than most, remember."

"I didn't enjoy it, seeing you like that. Weak." Unspoken between them was the now-ridiculous memory of Missit trying to support and clean a very floppy and grumpy Phex in the hygiene chamber. It had been the opposite of sexy, although Missit's body at the time didn't seem to realize that. At which Missit had been embarrassed. As if he could control what Phex did to him any more then Phex could control Missit.

"None of us did," said Berril, reminding them of the fact that they were not alone but sitting in the group and no longer whispering.

The conversation drifted on to other topics.

Later that night in the practice booth, Phex asked Missit about it. Because Missit's hands were too gentle with him. Phex missed the instant need of their first time. Only then realizing it was one of the things he loved best about Missit, how Missit hungered for Phex so desperately.

Missit being tender was scary.

"I'm not going to break," protested Phex. Hoisting Missit hard against him, taking one of Missit's hands and forming it around his shoulder, wanting the bite of fingernails there. Gold dipping into blue.

Missit bumped his forehead into Phex's sternum softly. Frustrated with himself, too, it seemed.

Phex lowered him. Stood with his arms only loosely draped around the god. Waited.

"I keep thinking about the fact that you were almost eaten. I didn't believe that this kind of thing would start happening so fast for Asterism. You're new. And you're an idiot, Phex. You always care for the others first, even me. You need to look after yourself too sometimes, you know?" Missit raised a hand as if he wanted to cup Phex's face or stroke his hair. Then dropped it, clenching and awkward.

Missit was usually the one to move first – to ask first and to incite.

Phex picked up a lock of golden hair and wound it

between his fingertips. "Don't you ever get tired of chasing me?"

Missit blinked at the abrupt change of subject. He made a funny Sapien-meets-Dyesi huffing noise. "You're like some isolated moon that I'm trying to land a ship on."

"Am I?"

"It feels like I'm constantly circling an abandoned world, forgotten and alone."

"You make me sound very mysterious and romantic. And kind of sad."

"Hush, this is my fantasy."

"Go on, then."

"It makes you seem strong and safe. Hidden away and isolated like that."

"Because you have no place of refuge?" Phex thought of Missit living his whole life in the open, in front of adoring believers, scrutinized by millions. He thought of the parents who had left him behind to become a child god worshiped by the whole galaxy, entirely dependent on an alien species.

"If you let me land, just me, it would always be *just me*. Because that part of you is so hard to find, so difficult to get to, that once I make it, it will really be worth something. And I must be *special* for having managed the trip at all."

Phex knew that Missit liked being a god and that he was good at it. It had always been clear that Missit *wanted* to be special and enjoyed *being* special to millions of worshipers. But was it really that, all along, he wanted to be special to just one person?

Phex had been the opposite all of his life. Rejected by his family and his whole society. The opposite of special. Until the Dyesi came along. And he still wasn't certain he wanted it.

Just like he wasn't certain he wanted Missit. Oh, he

desired him, but did he want to let him stay, keep him close? Missit seemed like a lot of *work*, and Phex was cautious and careful by nature. Guarded. Still startled that his pantheon had crept its way into his soul. Five of them had landed on that abandoned moon.

Did Phex trust Missit enough to let him be the sixth person in his heart? The Dyesi would say that six was a significant number. A significant moment. A significant person. And was this even a matter of trust?

It was possible that Phex didn't have the means to form a genuine romantic connection at all. Having never been given a model for relationships, Phex had no idea what to do with this one. Could an empty moon like him – a small, quiet, vacant heart, weak and underdeveloped – be altered forever by one god landing on it?

"It's a good thing you like me this way, because I wouldn't know how to change my nature," he said finally.

"You like it, though? Who you are? The solitary moon."

"I don't know any different."

"That's what I mean. I'd like to know what that kind of safety feels like."

Phex wondered if he was stiff and standoffish because it made him feel safe. Or if it was just habit. Either way, it wasn't safe anymore. It couldn't be only him against the crowd, against the fixed, against Missit. Not really. Clearly, him alone wasn't strong enough.

Missit shifted away from him in the small space, withdrawing physically in a way that made Phex's throat sink into his stomach, forming a sticky, sick knot there. Fear. Missit had never before withdrawn from him.

But the face the god raised was full of hope. "Can I talk about it?"

"What?"

"What started us, back then?"

"Do you need to?"

Fervent nod. Phex thought that how they started was understood between them. Missit had seen and wanted him, and what a god wanted, he got. At least this god.

"I was always trying to be close to you, get you to notice me."

Phex nodded. "I know."

"But just you, Phex."

Phex frowned. "Ah. You knew I thought you were a flirt? Hunting for attention. Anyone's attention."

"Yes, but I don't know *why*."

"Because you needed to fill some void Fortew was leaving behind. Or maybe just because it's in your nature. I was a baby potential back then, remember."

"You're so unfair to me." Missit rubbed the middle of his forehead with one finger, as if trying to smooth out the frown lines that were not there because the divinity would never allow them to develop. "It was just *your* attention. I only wanted you to like me."

"I didn't realize." Why would someone like Missit, all bright and shiny special, like someone as plain and dour as Phex?

"Because you're completely clueless."

"Apparently."

"Should I make it more obvious, going forward? Would you find that reassuring or intrusive?" Missit reached a hand up, cupped the side of Phex's face, petted fingers over the sharp jawbone, and looked deeply into his eyes in a parody of some romantic drama.

Phex fended him off. "More obvious? Don't you dare. You'll get us into trouble. We have an imago aboard now.

Even if the acolytes haven't noticed, don't you think Quasilun will catch us dating?"

"We aren't dating." Missit picked up Phex's hand, traced the line on his palm with one fingertip.

"We aren't?" Phex was grateful for the return of physical contact but also hurt by Missit's words. Not that he had any prior experience of dating, so maybe he had assumed too much.

"No."

"What are we, then?" Phex wasn't a casual person – he thought Missit would have realized that. Perhaps Missit was just so very casual himself that he assumed everyone else was like him about this kind of thing.

"The Dyesi call it heartsound. When you resonate with someone. When you work better together than solo, like singing in harmony."

Now Phex was a different type of uncomfortable. Apparently, Missit was exactly the opposite of a hardened flirt. He was taking things *more* seriously than Phex. Heartsound made their illicit affair seem too much. Too important. Now it was Phex who shifted away from Missit, forgetting how much that had hurt him.

Missit's wide, expressive mouth twisted. "Friendship or romance or family. Whatever form of love it is."

"We are clearly more than friends." Phex wouldn't be hiding out in booths and thinking of Missit's face when he woke up from attempted cannibalism if this were only friendship.

"Yes, that works too. We are okay apart, but together we form something better. So, it's not dating."

"It's a duet?" Phex finished the thought for him.

Missit nodded eagerly. Looking at him with that funny

half-hopeful expression again. Like he wanted Phex to understand something. Understand him. See him differently.

"I'm not sure the Dyesi will see the distinction if they find us rolling around naked together. Rules are rules."

"So, they won't find us."

Phex was skeptical. Missit was not a subtle person – witness the galley earlier that night. Already, it was getting so that when they were together in a group, Missit preferred to be touching Phex. The god had started slowly gravitating toward Phex no matter what the situation. He'd do this during breaks in rehearsals and practices. Missit next to him when they warmed up their voices. Missit sprawled near him on the floor to stretch.

Phex had no doubt Tillam noticed. His own pantheon probably too. Certainly Kagee and Tyve. Probably the acolytes.

It was hard for Phex not to give back the care that Missit craved. When they were not under observation, he often found himself tucking the hair out of Missit's face or feeding him snacks, trailing fingertips casually over one golden wrist. He surprised himself each time, but he didn't question it.

Missit wanted to be special and Phex thought he was.

The god had brought whole planets to their knees with his desire to be loved, but what seemed to make him actually happy wasn't the adulation of millions but was Phex quietly opening the water flask and passing it to him without a word. Phex sitting crossed-legged while they waited, so Missit could put his head on his knee.

The change to duet had happened so recently, yet Missit was already unwilling to give it up. In fact, from his blissed-out expression, he wanted more of it.

"We can be careful." Missit persisted, bumping his nose

against Phex's bicep and then biting him gently there. "We can be!"

"I can. You, I'm not so sure of."

"You didn't notice me chasing you back then."

"I noticed, I just thought you were doing it out of habit and novelty."

"Did you really?"

"Well, yeah – once I noticed."

Missit laughed.

And Phex crumbled.

So late that night, in the cantor practice booth, Phex tried actually loving someone. Tried it on like it was an ill-fitting costume. Meeting Missit with gentle caution, smoothing out the rough edges of his own emptiness, making welcome an abandoned moon. Tested out mixing caring with lust and tenderness with desire. A new recipe Phex was attempting for the first time.

Like cooking, he found it remarkably easy. Tenderness was two steps away from grace. And Phex might be a cantor, but he could also grace.

Something core between them shifted that night. Perhaps it was the gravitational orientation of one small, desolate moon.

They arrived at their next destination in good time to find a very eager and massive worshiper base. This was a profitable sector of the galaxy comprised of a loosely allied but friendly trading consortium of several large planets, moons, and associated space stations. There were hundreds of beautiful domes to choose from and many more under construction.

The divinity was strong and believers were plentiful.

They were open-hearted and kind about it, too. Messages of welcome and congregations full of captivated adoration awaited them. And it wasn't that there weren't any fixed – it was just that at his pantheon's insistence, Phex tried focusing on the fact that the vast majority of their worshipers were actually quite wonderful.

"You're always looking for the threat in a crowd, so you never realize how awesome the rest of that crowd is," complained Berril, justifiably.

"It only takes one fixed."

"We all know that, especially now. You forget, it was you who got taken down last time. But that doesn't mean we should blame all those who aren't fixed for those few who have gone rotten," said Kagee, of all people.

Phex tried to believe that and tried to like Asterism's worshipers a bit more. Maybe he wasn't quite capable of loving them yet. But he had to admit that they did genuinely adore his pantheon. And since that pantheon was full of Phex's favorite people in the galaxy, he and the worshipers had something in common. He had reason to be grateful for that. He might not love them, but at least they loved the same thing.

The divinity had selected six of the biggest domes for them to perform in. With a day or more off between performances, depending on travel times. This was to be a much longer than normal stop on their tour.

The two pantheons geared up and everything went smoothly in the first four domes. Asterism was doing well, the arrival congregations and VIP meet-and-greets went seamlessly. The press adored them. At every new planet there seemed to be more and more worshipers waiting specifically for Asterism.

Tillam's situation worried Phex, though. Fortew only

continued to decline. All the divine skill of aesthetics applied to his face each night could not hide the weariness in his eyes, the thinness of his flesh and his hope. Sometimes, Phex caught him clenching his hands together to stop them shaking, red with embarrassment.

Missit's worry was starting to leak into his performances too. It was as if he were trying, both vocally and physically, to support Fortew on that dais. It didn't impact the dome. In fact, Phex was pretty certain he was the only person in any given audience who ever noticed – except maybe the acolytes. But there was nothing he or they could do about it.

It was starting to impact Phex in weird ways. One night, he saw Missit execute some complicated grace move with slightly less elegance than normal, and Phex almost choked on the worry it caused. An odd overreaction that made him glance around to see if any of the acolytes had noticed. No Dyesi were looking at him, not even Quasilun.

Back on the spaceship, Phex found himself staying up late with Missit. Not in the cantor booth, they had no energy for that on performance nights, but simply because Missit's insomnia was back. It had been so much a part of their beginnings on Divinity 36, and now it had returned with a vengeance. Phex would stay up with Missit in the galley, long after the others had gone to bed, even Bob, waiting for the golden god to fall asleep – usually on Phex's shoulder or in his lap.

No one suspected anything and there was nothing to suspect. Even Quasilun knew this was only a sun's care and light. Fortew had nothing left to give anymore, and of all the members of Tillam, Missit needed centering the most. This was something the acolytes understood perfectly. This was why Asterism was traveling with Tillam in the first place. What Fortew could no longer hold together would eventually fracture. The damage to the pantheon was inevitable. But sometimes, some gods themselves were also held together by the gravity of a sun. Missit was one of those gods. The divinity could not afford to have Missit himself fracture.

Very late, when everyone else was fast asleep, only then did Phex let himself touch Missit without fear. Just his hair usually, stroking it back – or the arches of his eyebrows. They were interesting things, eyebrows, after spending so much time around the Dyesi, who did not have them. Missit's were peaked, one slightly more than the other. A tiny flaw that, for some reason, the Dyesi had opted not to correct.

Phex liked all of Missit's moments of asymmetry, from this eyebrow to that lopsided smile. The smile that had edges, except when it was pointed at Phex. He couldn't remember when he'd last seen it. Asymmetry was something he had no experience with as a child on the Wheel. So, Phex found these flaws precious things that made Missit into art, like his voice. Better than perfect, because perfect was boring.

And maybe Missit was asleep and maybe he was not, but in those moments, there was peace for both of them. It was enough to carry them through, until it wasn't.

The fifth dome on this tour stop was also the biggest.

They'd been told there were particularly important attendees, royalty or some power players like that. Frankly, Phex paid very little attention to the breathy enthusiasm of the press. On every new planet, there was some new set of rulers or politicians or elites gracing a dome with their presence. While he was very sure they were, in fact, extremely important to the people they ruled over, he and Asterism, and Missit and Tillam, would be moving on to some new planet and some new crop of dignitaries the very next day. In the grand scheme of his own life, they counted for very little and impacted Phex's memory even less.

Frankly, they were not so important to the gods as they were to themselves.

But there did seem to be more than the usual number of security around during this fifth stop. Apparently, some of the royals had purchased whole blocks of congregation tickets for their own personal bodyguards. Clearly, they were entirely unaware of the fact that bodyguards lost all effectiveness under the influence of godfix.

Looking out over the sea of worshipers and noticing not just devout believers but also uniformed and impassive military types was a strange experience. The whole congregation skewed older than normal and became a lot more work for the pantheons as a result. Fully grown adults were less easily transported by godsong and less susceptible to godfix.

It took a lot out of Asterism in particular.

"Cold dome," said Itrio when Phex joined her in the observation niche.

"They liked the Missit and Phex duet, though," said Bob, flat voice still somehow sounding confused.

"Yes, they would, it's old-fashioned," said Phex, unsurprised.

Itrio nodded. "It pulls on something different when you two perform together. Some ancient Sapien desires and instincts. Even all of us here are compelled to watch you two, and not just for protective reasons."

Phex looked over at Quasilun. "Even you, imago?"

"Of course," said the imago. "I am not so old I no longer appreciate art."

"But you are unaffected by the dome."

The imago wiggled their crests. "The dome is not art. Not

to an imago. I do not even need to be in this niche. I could go out under that dome and not a single thing would happen to me."

"Not even if Tillam were performing?"

"And no chance of it. Which is exactly why I know that you and Missit dancing and singing together has a unique pull all of its own. Whichever acolyte thought to form an interstitial act out of just you two should be elevated to a divine-power position. As out of balance as the idea of two under a dome might be, what you do up there is a new kind of divinity."

Phex could say nothing to such a high compliment as that, so he just gave the imago a slight bow of gratitude.

They both returned their attention to Tillam's dais.

What happened next seemed to occur in slow motion.

Ironically, or perhaps not, it happened right in the middle of "Five."

Fortew simply crumbled, folded down to the dais like a lock of hair cut off from the scalp.

Tillam had four more godsongs still to go.

But Fortew did not get up.

13

THE DYESI IS IN THE DETAILS

Phex was moving before he even knew it was happening. Itrio right behind him.

They'd planned for this.

Missit, face tortured, just kept singing. The graces moved, breaking the dome pattern with a change of choreography but not fracturing it. They were still gods, after all. They were never not gods. Certainly not under a dome.

The sifters and dome went golden peach under just Missit's voice, the pattern too simple, like some kind of dome-wide reboot.

The crowd gasped and shifted, rustling and coloring the dome with black speckles of discontent.

Missit kept singing. Voice strong. Trained for a decade never to crack and never to falter. His eyes bleeding pain.

Phex burst out of the niche and leapt at the dais like a crudrat. He bounced up and off the side of the dome as only he could, springing backward into a tight backflip and landing in the spot Fortew had been moved from. The graces carrying their low cantor off to the side of the dais, depositing him into Itrio's waiting arms. She was almost as quick to the dais as Phex, if perhaps not quite so flashy about it.

The bodyguard whisked away her charge.

Phex picked up the verse.

The whole transition had taken less than four lines of godsong.

Phex and Tillam finished out "Five" quickly, knowing there was no chance to hold godfix under such circumstances – the change in the colors was too shocking, let alone the change in cantors.

Without pausing for any kind of reaction, the six moved instantly into "Starshine."

It was a great song to be the first one featuring Phex as low cantor, because it was one of Tillam's most famous. It was their second major hit and they had only added it back into this tour because they knew it would be their last tour together. It was easy for Phex to sing and well practiced. It was beloved by worshipers and well known. Phex had once hummed along to it daily at a small cafe on a sad little moon.

He and Missit were good at "Starshine" together. Different from normal, of course. With Fortew replaced, this was no longer strictly Tillam's performance. But no one could deny that Phex and Missit were strong together. Phex pushed the dome a little, half out of nerves and half to force Missit to keep up with him and to distract the golden god from what had just happened.

Phex reminded himself that he only had to hold Tillam together for three more songs after this. He didn't need to really register what he was doing.

It started happening again.

The thing that had happened back on Divinity 36. The acolytes around them, off to the sides of the dais, and standing near doorways or niches become affected by the dome in a way they weren't supposed to be. Not a ton but enough. Dyesi, all of them, frozen in place. Much of the congregation became deceptively still in their seats too.

This was godfix on a massive scale, catching sentience up in the emotional net of the dome's beauty – the irresistibly intense strength of Phex and Missit's voices interweaving.

Missit gave Phex a panicked look.

Phex instantly pulled back. They had nothing to prove this time. He had nothing to prove. He'd only pushed it out of nerves. They didn't need this and certainly shouldn't do it right now.

It wasn't easy to withdraw. Once Phex let the power roll out of him into skin and sift, it was almost too intense to force it to fade back to normal. But Phex could see the strain in Melalan and the annoyance in Yorunlee, and he remembered that these two Dyesi had just lost their sun. Now the surrogate seemed likely to burn them or stun their worshipers if Missit couldn't hold it together. And Missit had just lost his best friend.

Phex didn't shatter the dome by stopping cold or cutting his voice off, but it was a close thing.

He managed to muffle it, gentle himself, and saw the relief on all of Tillam's faces. Phex realized, in that moment, how young he was in this art. Really, what had they expected? Why had they asked so much of him? Why had they pushed him this far? Why had they burdened his voice with their grief? He was only a demigod standing there, holding together a pantheon that wasn't his own.

Suddenly, Phex went white-hot with anger.

Anger for himself for the very first time. Anger at what had been done to him, rather than over the safety of his friends.

Angry at the divinity for using him.

Angry at the acolytes for putting him on tour in the first place.

Angry at Tillam and Missit and Fortew, who could not have simply left him out of their undoing.

He was standing at the edge of a black hole where no sun had enough gravity to hold off the inevitable. Why should it be him? Why did it have to be him, alone? Why was it *always* him who had to be the strong one?

Kagee had been angry on Phex's behalf all along, and finally Phex understood why.

But he was also a god.

He had trained for this – long, hard, stretched-out days of stress and worry. He had thrived under that, in his way. So, even though anger was not something he often dealt with, he damped it down for the sake of the dome and refocused on his duty to the worshipers, if not to the divinity.

Phex and Tillam made it through all three final songs. Certainly, the dome was different, but more importantly, it was still *good* and it was still godsong. Maybe Tillam's true believers felt a little lost by the experience, but they left that performance knowing it had been unique.

Then the infonet lost its collective mind over the whole incident.

Phex did not go to the VIP congregation that evening. His pantheon would have to handle it on their own. If he went, he would be all anyone talked to or asked questions of. In fact, Asterism came back early to report that that had still been the case.

"It was a bust," said Kagee. "Even our believers only wanted to talk about you stepping in for Tillam, and how seamless that was, and how worried they all were about Fortew."

"I guess the divinity will have to go public now with what's really happening," suggested Berril tentatively.

Phex considered. "I doubt it."

"You think they *still* won't make a divine statement?"

"How is he? Did you see?" asked Tyve.

Phex shook his head. "I know nothing. Tillam disappeared as soon as we got aboard."

"Even Missit?"

"Even Missit."

"And they wouldn't let you go with them?"

"Why should they?"

"Well, you are their temporary sun."

"Only on the dais."

"So you say. Like we can't see what you do for them the rest of the time."

"For Missit," interjected Kagee, getting up to putter about the galley, looking for the customary pot of stew that Phex had taken to warming for them after every performance. He wasn't doing the bulk of the cooking for the ship – there was a new, very timid cook. But on their free days between performances, Phex felt the need to reclaim his comfortable relationship with the kitchen. He didn't want Chef to have stolen that from him along with his self-confidence. It wasn't easy. He'd yet to open his cabinet shrine, even though the acolytes had documented and cleaned it out. Phex didn't want to think about it.

Kagee dipped a bit of bread into Phex's stew, pretending to be less concerned than the others. Although Phex noticed Kagee's gaze darting about, taking in the high number of acolytes rushing in and out.

"Did they take Fortew to a local medical facility, or is he in ours?" asked Tyve.

"Here, I think," said Phex. "I imagine we're gearing up to take off."

"Will we be doing the last show in this sector, or going for another break, or…"

Phex shook his head. "No idea. I have as much information as you do. All I know is that I had to get up on that dais and do what they trained me for."

Berril came over and crawled into his lap. "Was it awful?" she asked, cuddling up to him. Phex patted her arm rhythmically, not sure if it was for his comfort or hers.

Tyve came over and slumped onto the puff next to them. She looked at her hands, no doubt thinking about her brother and his pain. Phex stopped patting Berril so he could rub Tyve's back. He rested his cheek on Berril's manufactured hair so she wouldn't feel bereft.

Fandina sat in the puff opposite, crests pointed at them in concern.

Kagee said, since Phex was stuck, "Anyone want more stew?"

No one said anything but he went and started serving out bowlfuls anyway.

Kagee was right. They needed sustenance.

Phex wasn't certain he could eat, though. "It was fine," he answered Berril's question.

"Of course you'd say that," said Kagee, slamming down a bowl in front of him. "Eat, you pushover."

"Stop it, Kagee." That was Fandina, actually sending out an order, voice calm and crests stiff.

Kagee gritted his teeth. "Sorry, Phex."

Phex knew Kagee lashed out because he was worried, not genuinely mad. Or maybe he was back to being mad that

Phex refused to defend himself in the way Kagee expected and wanted.

So, Phex made an odd kind of peace offering. A confession. "I got angry. Up there, with Tillam."

"Did you?" Jinyesun went to help Kagee pass out bowls but sounded genuinely curious. "That's not normal for you, right? To get angry on the dais?"

"Certainly not."

"At who?" Tyve asked.

"I think at the situation." Phex did not want to admit to being mad at the divinity, since one of the acolytes was lurking nearby, keeping an eye on them, and Jinyesun and Fandina wouldn't understand.

Quasilun came in at that moment.

Kagee handed the imago a bowl of stew.

Quasilun looked at it in surprise, possibly startled at being so casually included.

"How is Fortew?" asked Phex.

"Dying," replied the imago, without inflection, crests neutral. "But you knew that, didn't you?"

They all clicked softly.

"The nymphs are in crisis. They've never lost a god like this before."

"At least two have been killed by fixed," disagreed Kagee.

"How do you know that?" Quasilun looked impressed rather than upset.

"Even the divinity can't completely control access to the infonet." Kagee sat, legs crossed and alone at the low dining table, hunched over his second bowl of stew like it had all the answers.

"Whole pantheons have collapsed in the past, too." That was Tyve.

"Certainly, but they did so under their own weight. Or they voluntarily returned to mortality after serving divine time, for reasons of family and procreation. They moved on to their own adult life stages. Things we Dyesi can actually understand. A kind of Sapien instar." The imago looked amused at itself. "This thing with Fortew is different."

The older Dyesi's apparent indifference to Tillam's crisis, Fortew's imminent demise, or even the acolytes' plight and desperation, felt almost insulting.

The rest of Asterism certainly seemed to think so. At least the Sapiens did. Tyve, whose brother was intimately affected by all this, was glaring at Quasilun, red eyes gone sour. Kagee had a new target for his ire. Even Berril was looking at the imago with a kind of disgusted horror on her normally cheerful face.

Phex said, intentionally using casual speech as if the imago were the child in the room, "Tread with caution, elder."

Quasilun looked at him with genuine surprise. "What are you… Oh. Ah. Yes, I see. You are disposed to find me callous?" It ate a bite of stew. Paused. Then said, "A terrible tragedy, of course. But you cannot discount that it is interesting to watch the divinity deal with the obvious mortality of a declining god. They go out of their way to pick young potentials so this kind of thing does not happen."

"Is that why you're really here?" wondered Kagee. Turning to glare at the imago sitting among his pantheon.

"I am here to be your bodyguard," Quasilun reminded them, as if that were all that mattered with nothing extra attached to it.

Phex hadn't realized that a person could eat stew with such profound rage, but Kagee managed it.

Quasilun looked at Phex. "You did well, of course."

"Why doesn't that feel like a compliment?" asked Phex, tired of Dyesi games.

Fandina gave the Dyesi version of a shocked gasp, crests flaring up and then flattening back.

Jinyesun gave Phex a frantic crest wiggle, urging caution.

The imago put its bowl carefully down, movements measured. As if it might startle Phex. "I had heard about what you and Missit could do together on a dais, of course. The true power of your dome, though. Remarkable." It was clearly not a compliment.

"You were told, yet you're still surprised?" Phex asked.

"It is different to hear a thing than to see it in full color." The imago's tone and crests were all carefully neutral. It was a little scary, how controlled this Dyesi could be.

"Phex, what happened tonight?" hissed Jinyesun.

Phex considered. "We all lost something."

Quasilun huffed out a Dyesi laugh. Everyone else looked confused. Phex ate his stew because Kagee had provided it for him and it was the right thing to do. He still wasn't hungry.

He worried he might throw it up later. He worried about Fortew. He worried that Tillam wasn't eating. He worried about Missit. He worried that his golden god couldn't sleep without Phex, just like Missit couldn't sing without Fortew. He worried that everyone was lost and lonely and out of balance. He worried that he'd been that angry. He worried that he cared.

They assumed a stable orbit around an empty asteroid a short distance away from the last dome. Everything on the spaceship cycled down into dimness, as if the ship were holding its breath. It too was waiting to see what would happen to Fortew. Phex and his pantheon went to sleep, since there was nothing else to do. Presumably, Tillam eventually did the same.

In the small hours of the night shift, Missit left his cot, padded through the empty hallways of the spaceship, and slipped in past the heavy skin and into Phex's bed, curling against him like he had long before on Divinity 36.

Phex shifted back and made a nest for him in the tiny cot so the god could use his shoulder as a pillow. So the boy behind the god could bathe in Phex's warmth and know that out there in the universe was one single person who cared for Missit himself and not just for the way Missit shone under a dome. Who cared not only that Fortew was dying but that Missit was losing his best friend.

Phex drifted off to sleep knowing they were both in a lot of trouble, that this had already gone a lot further than he thought it would. Deeply frightened that something he had thought transient was nested against him with a sense of entitled permanence. Phex was now scared of losing something he'd never thought he would get to keep in the first place. That fear was pitted against the other ones it inevitably carried with it. The fear of losing his pantheon. The fear of losing his place in the universe. The fear of losing divinity.

Perhaps all that anger of his on Tillam's dais had really been fear.

Phex was amazed that all these attachments had entered his life with such stealth. That he was holding them like fragile moments of starlight, and none of them would last even though he already wanted all of them to stay forever. He'd had no idea he was this greedy.

Now Phex began to fear that he had given himself away too easily to satisfy Missit's wanting, and his pantheon's, and the divinity's. Now he was left wanting in return, and that was a truly dangerous thing.

At breakfast the next morning, Tillam was present but subdued. No Fortew, of course, but the rest of Tillam was there.

Zil and Tern gave Phex funny looks, but he wasn't certain if that was due to his performance the night before or the fact that they knew Missit had spent the night in his bed.

Missit came in and sat next to him in a puff without hesitation.

Phex tilted his head in a telling way at Tern, who was pointedly glaring at him. He said to Missit, "They're very protective. Is this because you're the youngest or something else?"

Missit nibbled some toast. "You're overreacting. They don't mind. They know I like to cuddle someone when I sleep."

Phex was hit by both fear and worthlessness. The fear made him glance quickly around to see if any acolytes had overheard and inferred the worst. None had. No Quasilun, either. The worthlessness made him wonder if Missit really needed him at all. Or was he just a replacement bed warmer?

Missit continued talking blithely on. "I used to sleep with Fortew, too."

"Oh. Were you and he—?" Phex felt ill or something. That was unpleasant.

"No!" Missit gave a croaking kind of cry and latched onto Phex's hand. Squeezing. "No. Just good friends of many years. Brothers, I guess. I sleep better with someone. The acolytes know that. They won't assume anything else. They don't have the capacity." There was something sly in the way he said that. But also desperate. Nothing was ever simple with Missit.

"Can I please keep sleeping with you?"

Phex sighed and ate a piece of cold, slightly burned toast.

Tyve and Zil sat down opposite them and openly stared.

In fact, most of both Asterism and Tillam were staring at them. The Sapiens showed mixed annoyance and fear. The Dyesi looked mostly confused. Everyone knew, or guessed, that Missit had been in Phex's bed last night.

Kagee was different. He looked disappointed. Like he had expected better of Phex. Like Phex was weak.

"It's just sleeping," protested Phex, to his toast. Knowing exactly how defensive he sounded. It wasn't his choice where Missit ended up sleeping. There was nothing he could do about it.

He looked up and glared at all four Dyesi – from Fandina to Jinyesun to Melalan to Yorunlee. He wished he had crests to express his annoyance in a way that they would entirely understand. "If you people just believed in doors, this wouldn't be a problem."

Then Phex stood and took his mostly full plate back into the uncomfortable kitchen. Turned to see that all of them had twisted so they could still stare at him, even Missit. Like those flowers the infonet talked about, the ones that always kept their petals facing the sun.

He put his uneaten food into the recycling unit and the plate into the washer. He turned, leaned back, crossed his arms, felt overly warm and suddenly irritated. "What am I supposed to do here? I've tried to do everything you asked of me. All along. Everything you needed from me. Everything you wanted of me. All of you."

He wished he was back on Divinity 36 in his old kitchen.

There was a shake to his voice that he hated. This was some nascent form of the white-hot anger from the dais the night before. White because there was no color to it, just bitterness and frustration. At the divinity, at the pantheons, and at Missit. All of whom kept pushing.

Unspoken were Phex's other words, loud in the ensuing silence. *Am I supposed to kick him out? Am I supposed to reject him? Are you asking me to choose?*

Quasilun walked into the common area at that moment.

"Good," said Phex. "You talk some sense into them."

"What?" replied the imago, unruffled by confusion.

"Phex?" said Berril, voice small and scared.

Missit stood up to come after him.

Phex couldn't stand the look on his face. Those eyes flecked and wounded, that crooked smile absent. It all seemed like too much. It made Phex believe that he was the one willfully trying to diminish what they had by thinking of it as only sex and comfort. Made him feel like he was somehow taking advantage of Missit.

Phex didn't want to share a kitchen. Not even with Missit. Certainly not this one, polluted as it had become. He needed to go somewhere else where no one turned their faces toward him. Where no one needed or wanted anything from him for a while.

In that moment, he missed his dingy, tiny, lonely pod on Attacon 7. He missed the cafe that wanted nothing from him but to serve drinks and ignore the godsong overhead.

It was Tern who tugged Missit back to sitting, stopped him from approaching Phex.

Dimsum, being Dimsum, chose that moment to emit a huge belch from where she sat next to Tern's puff chair.

It broke the tension and everyone stopped looking at Phex.

Phex escaped to one of the grace practice studios. He never thought he would miss running the blades as a crudrat. But now he found himself remembering that time – the rhythmic patterns and flips of his youth. A language he thought had been grooved into his bones but now, he realized, he'd entirely forgotten.

The Dyesi had taken even that part of him – his corrupted past – and remade it into something divine. The only thing he got to have anymore that was entirely his was Missit in his arms. Maybe that was why he was so scared of it yet guarded it so jealously, even from himself. Because now even that was tainted. Even that was a matter for hard glares and for two pantheons to discuss. He hated feeling defensive. He hated this fear of the acolytes or Quasilun finding out. Finding out what, exactly? That he was capable of love? What was so terrible about that?

Phex understood then that part of his colorless anger was vested in this. That he'd found love but it was carved up and meted out and made small and painful by the demands of the divinity, the pantheon, and even his friends. That the things he was failing to protect included his own heart. He was angry because Missit needing him to hold him while he slept should be something precious between them, like godsong. Phex should be able to give such a simple gift to Missit without consequence. Without hardened looks and grave silences. It wasn't like he had anything else to give worthy of a god.

He was angry because he didn't just get to be in love with someone – it had to be boiled down and distilled into something too intense too quickly. Something toxic because of who they were.

But then, Phex had never gotten to be *just* anything, really.

Just a child without being a crudrat.

Just a kid without being a refugee.

Just a person without being a god.

Just in love without being a disappointment.

Just. Just. Just. A refrain like the beat of the blades against his memory.

Phex was back to practicing like nothing had happened a few hours later.

No one said anything to him about anything. He sang with Tillam in the morning and Asterism in the afternoon. He and Missit no longer had dance practice together. There would be no interstitial duet. From now on there must be an intermission between pantheons under the dome. Phex needed to rest between shows.

They were making plans to do everything without Fortew. To finish the tour without him. To replace him. Or that was what their practicing felt like.

That evening, everyone acted normal. Or at least carefully avoided the topic of Missit's sleeping arrangements. The pantheons had elected to reach a truce of some kind, where Missit got to do whatever Missit needed to do. No one mentioned Fortew. And everyone moved and spoke carefully around Phex, because they had hit up against something none of them realized he had, a breaking point.

Only Quasilun was too obtuse, or uncaring, to let the matter drop. "What was that about this morning, kid?" they asked Phex, after dinner.

"Stress, I suppose. It was a lot, stepping in to take on Fortew's role like that." Phex spoke casually because there was something about the way everyone else was so respectful to the imago that annoyed him. There was a twinkle in those big eyes that suggested Quasilun enjoyed this treatment.

"That's all?" The imago's crests twitched. A bright light

set in the ceiling shone through them, creating colorless rainbows on the floor at Phex's feet.

Despite his fear of Quasilun figuring out that he and Missit were… whatever he and Missit were, Phex couldn't help but like the imago. Quasilun was a practical, even-keeled person with no pretense. Phex found that admirable. In this, the imago was similar to the other bodyguards. It was a personality type Phex enjoyed, possibly because he wished he could be more like them himself. Or, on his best days, imagined he *was* like that.

"I was mad at the situation more than anything else."

"And you aren't anymore?" Quasilun wore a kind of close-fitting scaled jumpsuit made of the megafauna skins that formed the bulk of Dyesi fabric. Phex liked the outfit a lot. It was the first piece of clothing he'd ever encountered that he actively coveted.

"I like your uniform. Can I get one?" Phex asked, intentionally changing the subject.

"Phex? You're asking about clothing? Are you feeling well?" Tyve came over, mocking him gently.

Phex made a face at her, feeling relieved to be teased again. His pantheon had been so cautious around him all day. "It seems practical and comfortable."

"And sexy," added Tyve with pursed lips to hide a smile.

"Is it?" said both Phex and Quasilun at the same time.

"Seriously?" replied Berril, coming to Tyve's defense. "Yes, it is."

"Well, okay," said the imago. "Should I tell the divinity to look into putting these on gods?"

"Why not?" wondered Phex, privately hoping he could be one of the first.

"I don't think the nymphs would ever think to do such a thing. My attire is considered" —the imago looked at one of the acolytes lurking near the beverages— "old-fashioned."

Berril laughed. "Did we just compliment something grandpas wear or something?"

Yorunlee, who was sitting closest to them, looked over. "Pretty much. No offense, imago."

"None taken, youngling."

Missit wandered over, wearing Dimsum wrapped around his neck. He looked tired, which Phex found upsetting. What was the point in him sneaking into Phex's bed and causing all this fuss if the god still wasn't getting enough sleep? Phex wanted to pick Missit up and cuddle him on the couch puff, thread fingers through his hair, until they both just *stopped* for a while.

Instead, he glared at the golden god.

Dimsum trilled at Quasilun and put out a tentative paw.

The imago sneezed at her.

Much as she had taken an instant dislike to Phex, the murmel had developed an immediate affection for Quasilun. Not as great as her love for Missit but certainly preferential. Probably because the imago was sublimely uninterested in her or because she seemed to engender some kind of mild allergic reaction.

This did have an interesting side effect. Quasilun and Missit very rarely spent much time in the same room. Since Dimsum went wherever Missit went, with the noted exception of cantor practice booths late at night. And, Phex realized, his bed last night. Where had Dimsum been?

Missit said, "Sorry, imago, we'll go sit over there, shall we?"

"I think that would be best," replied the imago, sneezing again.

Missit sent Phex a longing look that meant he wanted be

followed. This just made Phex glare harder. Missit rubbed his eyes and sighed. But then Tern settled next to him and passed him a mug of tea. So, Phex felt a little better.

Phex decided to ask the imago a bodyguard question. "With both pantheons present in this room, how would you assess the power dynamics from a bodyguard perspective?"

"You are a smart one, aren't you, little blue? Are you asking for my professional risk-assessment analysis of Asterism and Tillam?"

Phex nodded. "Yes. Who would you rank the most dangerous? Of all of us here?"

"Bodyguards included?"

Phex nodded. There were a few bodyguards and crew as well as acolytes milling around. It was the dinner hour, and the galley and common area tended to get crowded.

Phex pushed, curious. "Would you put yourself at the top?"

"For physical power? Yes. For actual deadliness? Certainly not." The imago pointed at the other bodyguards, one by one, and then said, "Zil, Kagee, Tyve, you, then me."

"Why Zil first of the gods?"

"He can kill and would not hesitate to do so, but also he's out of training, hasn't really fought with his claws in a decade, so he could make a deadly mistake."

Phex nodded. "Lack of practice makes the man with the blade more dangerous, not less. Kagee next because he would not hesitate and possesses the capacity but is slightly less powerful than a Jakaa Nova?"

"Exactly."

Phex grinned. "But I'm near the bottom?"

Quasilun sipped a cup of corrosive dark. "You're still on the list."

Phex clicked encouragement.

The imago explained its reasoning. "You only fight if you think you have to protect others, never for yourself or the love of it. That's actually a deficit in ability. You might be physically tougher or deadlier, but if you will not use your full strength, it does not count as highly. In this, you are a little like one of us Dyesi. I think you *could* kill, though, which is why I placed you higher than me."

"Interesting," Phex nodded.

"You aren't surprised that I don't kill?"

Phex did not miss the fact that Quasilun had said *don't kill*, not *can't kill*. "You don't look like the nymphs but you are still Dyesi."

"Thank you for that." The imago looked genuinely grateful.

Phex nodded. "You specified physical power, what other kinds of power do you use to evaluate a room?"

Unsurprised by the question, the imago ticked them off on its six-fingered grey hands. "Political, social, emotional."

"Okay, who has the political clout in this room right now?"

Quasilun pointed out the acolytes and then Tillam's sifters – first Melalan and then Yorunlee – and then at Asterism's sifters – first Fandina and then Jinyesun. Phex assumed this had to do with the caves and the internal politics of Dyesi alliances and family strengths.

"Social power?" Phex asked, enjoying their game.

"Ah, well, that's relatively easy: you, then Fortew, whether he's here or not, then Fandina."

That surprised Phex a little, not the fact that the suns had been named first but the fact that Fandina was in there and not Missit.

"Why my sifter?" he asked.

"Fandina has leadership potential. I imagine when it

becomes an imago, it will also become the matriarch of a major cave – after instar, of course. You did not realize you had a leader in your pantheon?"

Phex considered. It did make sense. Fandina was very decisive and tended to make the decision for the pantheon if there was too much waffling. Also, it was good at controlling social situations. A skill that would only get better as it got older, because it was also clearly interested in group dynamics.

"And why me before Fortew?"

"Fortew is weak. You are holding both pantheons together with comparative ease. I know you don't think so, but you are doing a good job." Phex wondered if the imago was trying to make him feel better after that morning.

Quasilun continued. "You think being a sun doesn't count for much because you find it easy? Just because a thing comes naturally to you doesn't make it any less important to others. It's like your voice."

Phex clicked – *that* he understood.

"You want the rest of the social ranking?"

"No, I think I can figure that one out, it falls on pantheon lines, basically?"

"Are you going to ask about emotional power?"

Phex winced. The one he was least likely to grasp. Also the one that he thought the imago would have its own very Dyesi standards built around. Standards that likely would not match Phex's. Still, he was curious. "Is it me at the top again?" Because he couldn't take that revelation.

Quasilun huffed a Dyesi laugh. "Of course not."

Phex noted the amusement. The answer was the person in the room who was his opposite, then. "Missit?"

"Absolutely."

"Why?"

"Your words and actions carry the most weight, people want your attention and support, approval. That's social. For Missit, people want to see him happy. That's emotional power. They want to please him."

"I understand," said Phex, as he mentally lined up everyone else in the room according to that definition. Fortew would be next if he were present – after that, it was Berril, then Yorunlee, then Jinyesun, and then maybe Kagee? Or Zil? Phex wasn't sure after that. He would probably rank Kagee higher than most other people would. He wondered about Quasilun's order of emotional precedence.

"You do?" The imago was looking at him curiously.

"Of course. I want Missit happy."

"Do you?"

"You didn't know that?"

"I didn't know you were aware of that within yourself. It's quite mature for a Sapien of your age. Of all the Sapiens on this ship, your desires and loyalties are the hardest for me to fathom."

Phex was grateful for that insight. It meant the imago really did not realize what Phex had been upset about that morning.

Quasilun continued. "In part, I think that is why everyone around always yearns for your affection. You seem unattainable and mysterious."

"Even Missit?" Phex tested carefully.

"Especially him."

"Unfortunate," said Phex.

"Oh?"

"A god like Missit shouldn't have to yearn, he should already know."

"Know? Know what exactly?"

"That he already has everyone's affection."

"Including yours?"

Phex clicked.

"All of it?" The imago's dark eyes were suddenly sharp on Phex.

"Affection is not a finite thing to be portioned out in small amounts for fear it may diminish a whole." Phex was thinking of his pantheon. He was remembering his colorless anger.

The imago nodded. "A very mature sentiment. Usually, Dyesi do not come to this realization until imago state."

"What realization, exactly?"

"That to give love is like giving out light." Quasilun used the Dyesi word for *love* that was also their word for *beauty*.

Phex gave a bitter grimace. "Just shine it uselessly into the void?" Should he spend every day getting up onto that dais and pouring out song, color, pattern as if it were worthless but also the only thing worth living for?

He was thinking of Missit and the weariness on his lovely face when he stood on the dais lately. That loss lurking in him as he climbed off it. The exhaustion was there all the time now. A weariness Missit tried not to let anyone see, that Phex noticed because he was watching so closely. Those wide smiles slightly less wide. Those full, mobile lips just a little bit stiff. Which was why, in a desperate attempt to alleviate tension, Missit ended up in Phex's bed.

The imago looked at Phex with nothing but sympathy for his bitterness. "The point is not that the light you give is returned or reflected back, the point is that it is there, shining. The star is not important to the void, it is important to the ship that is looking for it."

Phex shook his head. "But does that matter to another star?" Perhaps he said that too unguardedly.

The imago looked back and forth between Phex and Missit.

The god in question glanced up and over at them, bright, flecked tired eyes drawn to Phex. Phex could see the yearning in them – of course he could. He was not blind to it. He wondered if the imago could see it too, and if in that moment the two of them had given everything away.

But Quasilun only said, "Everything becomes more dangerous when you each have your own gravitational pull."

There was a part of Phex that wondered if the imago was really there to protect Phex and Asterism. Wondered if Quasilun knew everything about them already – from Missit in his bed to Missit in the practice booth coiled naked around him – but simply believed it was unimportant. Light shining into a void. Perhaps the imago thought of them as it thought about the nymphs – careless youngsters, amusing in their insignificance. Silly little gods. Inconsequential stars. Perhaps Quasilun had other concerns, other reasons for being aboard their spaceship. Perhaps Phex's love was a tiny thing to Dyesi elders.

It was an idea in which Phex found great comfort. And for which he liked the imago even more.

14

ONCE IN A GREY DOME

Missit slept in Phex's bed every night from then on. Dimsum slept on the floor underneath, in blatant protest. Quasilun said nothing. The acolytes said nothing. And Dimsum, fortunately for everyone, said nothing either.

Phex wasn't sure if his pantheon had taken action on their behalf or if support had come from Tillam on high. Or if neither was necessary, and the Dyesi simply regarded co-sleeping as Missit's natural state, a necessity to be tolerated because of Fortew's absence and continued decline.

The divinity, as it turned out, had other, more important Phex-and-Missit issues to deal with.

Phex's second appearance with Tillam, and his first full performance filling in for Fortew, proved to be a much more difficult dome. He was better prepared and more confident in his role as Tillam's low cantor, but the crowd was cold and uncertain. The congregation might even be described as hostile.

Tillam's worshipers wanted Fortew, not some new demigod substitute. Asterism's worshipers didn't like seeing Phex sing with anyone but Kagee. It was as if he were caught cheating. Devotees of both pantheons felt betrayed. Phex lost believers because of it. So did Missit, although he could easily afford that.

And the divinity persisted in refusing to explain why Fortew was missing. Officially, their stance was that "he was exhausted, having pushed himself too much with this tour, but Tillam didn't want to stop the tour entirely." They stressed regularly that the divinity considered Phex a hero for stepping in.

But people believed in gods, not the word of acolytes. What wasn't godsong wasn't real, not to true worshipers. Any press release from the acolytes on the subject was regarded with deep suspicion.

Asterism, however, still managed to grow in popularity. There were some who joined their following simply because they were being pitted against Tillam in the popular press. A small but vocal contingent of worshipers took to the infonet to defend Phex, stepping in as needed on forums to act as vanguard. There were some counter flames from Tillam's base, and a few divine forums got shut down because of it. But that only added fuel to the fire.

Phex acting as Fortew was contentious at best and divisive at worst. But all this only happened with worshipers who hadn't seen them in person. Under a dome, no matter how hostile the worshipers started out, Phex and Missit singing together *always* caused godfix. And godfix won everyone over in the end. Anyone who managed to see Tillam live lost their hostility. Whichever side they came down on, whoever's worshipers they were, they left that dome grateful for the experience.

Slowly, gradually, that became the cry of the truly devout. Comments of support popped up more and more from those who now believed in both Missit *and* Phex. Who worshiped *both* Tillam and Asterism. Who accused others of being unfaithful because they were judging without seeing the dome in person.

They argued that no one knew how long Phex would be singing with Tillam, and shouldn't any true worshiper be grateful to be alive at this moment in time? A moment when two pantheons became one, sharing a low cantor? It was a historic moment. Something never before seen in all the divinity. Should they not be grateful and enjoy the uniqueness of Phex and Missit together? They would, after all, probably never get to have it again.

"There is something to it, isn't there?" said Kagee idly late one evening.

"What?" asked Fandina.

"Being loved like that. With such abandon." Kagee was looking almost thoughtful, a small silver philosopher curled in the exact center of a copper-colored puff.

"Isn't that why they call it worship?" wondered Phex, looking at Jin for confirmation.

Jinyesun wiggled its crests in reply.

"Do you like it, Phex, the adulation of thousands?" asked Missit, shifting against Phex, since they were sharing one of the larger puffs nearest the galley.

"Not as much as you do, but yes, I like it."

Missit clicked. "It's true, I love it. Crave it sometimes, I think. Like worshipers crave godfix. And I want to give it to them. But that scares me."

"Their obsession?"

"No, mine."

Phex was scared too. He was scared of the hunger of the worshipers. It was not a hunger he could cook for, satisfy with some practical solution. It was more intense. They would bleed him dry for what he couldn't give under that dome. They would bleed Missit dry for what he *could* give. Worshipers didn't even know exactly what it was they wanted from gods. They just *wanted*. Phex was scared for himself, but more he was scared for Missit, who had been doing this for so long – giving away parts of himself on the dais, handing out sound as if it were prayers for the dead.

Phex wondered how much of the self was in the human voice. In the colors they generated on Dyesi skin. Were they exhausted coming down from that dais because they were physically taxed by the performance, or because they actually lost parts of their souls up there? Was it god drop or soul drop? Were bits of themselves being sifted out into the air, like pollen on an unfamiliar world?

Their next tour stop was in Kill'ki Coalition space. Tyve was excited about it. She said her parents were nowhere near and she was actually not really familiar with this part of the territory, but still, the species in the congregations were all going to be familiar to her. There would probably be more of her believers, too, since in this sector, she was Asterism's most popular god.

The dome for their first performance was a new one. It occupied most of a small satellite moon along with a companion spaceport and some associated crowd control and provisioning warehousing. There was no city and no surrounding populace. There was also no atmosphere, only the artificial bubble generated for the dome itself.

From the outside, it wasn't pretty, either. It looked much as Phex imagined a cave would were it not underground, a kind of organic mound of rock, pockmarked by stardust and disinterest.

But inside, it was an amazing dome.

After practicing in it, Jinyesun said with puffy crests, "What a pleasure to sift this space. It reminds me of home."

Fandina clicked. "It's very honest to the originals, I agree. I like it very much."

"It's not pretty, though," said Kagee, bluntly.

"Agreed, rather ugly, actually. Well, to be fair, Dyesid Prime is not pretty either. Why do you think we admire prettiness so much in others? We have no beauty of our own, and no ability to generate it without a dome, without you," said Jin, sounding a little sad.

"But you yourselves are attractive to Sapiens," protested Berril.

"And that attraction has to do with… *beauty*?" The Dyesi word, the one that also meant love.

"Of course it does." Tyve widened her eyes, fluttering long black lashes at them.

Fandina looked genuinely perplexed. "Are you saying you find us Dyesi *beautiful*? Truly beautiful?"

Kagee laughed. "Are you being falsely modest? Of course we do."

Jin looked at Phex in desperate confusion, flushing various colors and wiggling crests. "Truly?"

Phex clicked confirmation.

"You read it on the infonet. You know that sifters in most pantheons have worshipers of other species." Pointed out Tyve.

Kagee added, "You get supplications regularly filled with offerings of love, and romance, and marriage. How is this a surprise?"

"We thought it was your fascination with sex. Or maybe a form of politeness to another species."

Phex said, being very clear, "Most Sapiens and even some of the Hominins find you wildly attractive *because we think you are very beautiful.*"

"Is attraction always coupled with beauty?" wondered Fandina.

"Not always," said Tyve, still amused by the Dyesi confusion.

Kagee said, "I find Phex beautiful, and I assure you, I do not want to sleep with him."

Phex tilted his chin at his friend. "Likewise."

"I have to think about this," said Jinyesun.

"You do that, pretty one," said Kagee in a flirtatious tone.

"Stop teasing," said Phex, mildly.

"Spoilsport," said Kagee.

Missit was waiting for Phex after he left the dais at the end of Asterism's set.

"You watched?"

"Just the final song. You are gods now. You held them in thrall."

That phrasing made Phex uncomfortable. But Missit was right – it had been godfix. He and Kagee could manage it for all of their original songs now. It was a good thing Kagee was already working on writing and creating three more.

"Where'd they go?" Missit asked, presumably about the rest of Phex's pantheon.

"Back to the ship. Quasilun took them. There's no VIP congregation tonight. This dome doesn't have the facilities, so they didn't need to stay."

Missit moved quickly over to him and stepped into his space. "You're unguarded?"

"I am. You aren't."

"Bob is out in the hall."

Phex knew that – he'd passed the cyborg on his way in. "And the rest of Tillam?"

"I actually don't know where they are. Can I sit on you?"

Why'd he ask if he was just going to do it anyway? Missit straddled Phex in the low puff couch.

Phex was embarrassed by how sweaty and sticky he was, recently having been on the dais. Missit didn't seem to mind. He sighed happily and nuzzled Phex's salty neck.

"You smell like dance practice. I miss dancing with you." They no longer bothered to practice their duet. It had been entirely removed from the performance rotation.

"You sleep with me every night," objected Phex, shifting to give Missit's knees more room.

"That's not the same thing and you know it."

"So pushy."

"It's part of my charm."

Phex grumbled, but he was too tired to do more than that. He needed to rest. He only had half an hour between shows to recover some of his energy. And Tillam always took more out of him than Asterism. He was comfortable with the songs but not the pantheon's dynamic. Asterism had become, if not *easy,* at least a pleasure. Tillam was hard work.

Phex slumped back into the soft knit of the massive couch. This one was particularly soft and a little fuzzy, in very muted blue-green. It reminded him of the puffs they'd had in their dorm room back on Divinity 36. He closed his eyes and let his head loll.

Missit was a warm sunbeam atop him. Barely any weight. *Was he still not eating properly?* His fingers patterned over Phex's neck. Tracing the drying sweat crystals there.

"Do you remember that time when I came bursting into the dressing room and you were fiddling with your socks?"

"Of course."

“I wanted to climb into your lap so bad.”

“So soon?” Phex opened his eyes slightly and stared at him.

Missit looked perfect and sublimely divine. Stage-ready makeup, costume exactly in place. His long, glossy gold hair was down and loose and brushed to a high shine, as it always was for a performance. He glittered, even in the low light of an underground room.

Phex’s hair was loose too. It probably needed a good comb-out before he went back up on that dais.

Missit leaned forward, that hair forming a curtain around them.

Phex knew that expression all too well.

“No kissing. You’ll get mussed.”

Missit grumbled and sat back.

“Have you eaten?”

“Yes.” Missit pouted.

“Did you have any protein at all today?”

“Phex, I’m fine. You’re the one who just came off the dais.” Missit was annoyed but he settled, straight-backed and elegant. Phex thought about him in a similar position, back arched and naked, and then realized he was the one in danger of getting mussed. So to speak. So, he continued firing questions at the god to distract himself.

“Did you hydrate properly?”

“Did you?” Missit gave a tiny sigh and climbed off his lap.

Phex felt bereft.

“Turn around and close your eyes.”

Phex was instantly suspicious. “Why?”

“If you’re not going to actually relax and keep fretting, I might as well brush your hair.”

Phex narrowed his eyes. He wasn't sure about this side of Missit.

Missit only glared back. "Behave, you."

Phex shifted. Annoyed by the stickiness of his jumpsuit. "I need a sonic clean and to change into my Tillam costume."

"Sit still for six minutes, you impossible man."

Phex did as told, closing his eyes, kneeling in the puff, enjoying the soft pull of a brush through his long blue hair. Missit was a lot gentler about it than the acolytes.

"Something nice happened to me as Bob and I were coming into the dome."

"Mmm?" Phex was getting dangerously sleepy.

"Just a worshiper."

Phex tensed.

"Properly vetted. They let a few of the most loyal form a little assembly line as Tillam arrived."

"What happened?"

"She said that listening to me got her through a lung transplant. That I gave her hope and helped her stay strong."

"She had crud lung?"

Missit's voice was wistful. "Like Fortew. And she was standing right there telling me this with so much hope and earnestness, breathing easily, voice strong. She looked and sounded fine, like nothing had ever happened. And apparently *my singing* actually helped her through all that."

Phex said, "People can make it through a lot if they have something to believe in."

"It's nice to be that for someone." Missit sounded genuinely happy about it. "I love being that for someone. Anyone. Strangers."

Millions.

Phex hoped this wasn't making Missit delusional about Fortew's prospects. Phex was pretty darn certain if Fortew was able to get a lung transplant, he would have already done so. But Phex didn't want to say anything when Missit sounded so happy for a change.

But that wasn't what Missit was getting at, as it turned out, because he said, "You're that for me, you know?"

That was a little too much for right now, right before a performance. Phex didn't know how to take that kind of statement.

He twisted and took the brush out of Missit's hand.

"Thank you," he said gravely, because the Dyesi had taught him to be polite. But neither of them knew whether he was thanking Missit for the brushing or the confession.

"I should get changed. The others will be here soon."

Missit came around and took the brush back from him, played with the coarse bristles, finding them suddenly fascinating. There was nothing special about it. It was just like all the others Phex had received from the acolytes. For a species who had no hair of their own, they were obsessed with hair care. Phex wondered what the brushes were made from. If, like the Dyesi curtains, they were the parts of some dead animal. It had a kind of horn or maybe tooth shape to it.

He stood and stretched out the kinks from sitting right after a performance and then went to find his next costume.

Missit watched him change with hungry eyes. Phex didn't mind – he liked being admired too. By Missit, anyway.

Missit said, golden voice soft, "You will keep hiding like that isolated moon. And I will keep trying to land."

Phex sighed. Missit was as inexorable as an actual ancient god – presiding over some small quadrant of a world long since faded into obscurity. It was as if he had latched on to some equally ancient form of love, one that had a ritualistic practice attached to it. One that required him to beat against Phex's resistance like waves against the stone of a lost temple. The waves always won, in the end, even if the name of the god that drove them ever forward had been forgotten.

Phex wondered why he even bothered to resist anymore. Was it just habit at this point? Did that isolated moon even exist? He fiddled with his new jumpsuit, the one that complemented and matched Missit's.

He moved back to the golden god and patted the side of his oval face, traced the sharp jaw, searched out the flecks in his eyes. "How do I warrant such relentlessness?"

"I think I was always looking for a foundation."

"And I'm foundational?" Phex felt himself crumbling, which seemed to put the lie into Missit's words. "I thought you said I was lonely and abandoned."

Missit gave his million-star smile. "You're a whole moon all for me, remember?"

"Cheesy."

Missit's lips were glossy and chapped and warm and many things, waiting on him, all at once.

Phex relented. Decided to muss him just a little. Enjoy the heat of him, the tiny, needy noises hummed out in that voice of a thousand domes. High-cantor want.

It was a risk. There were no acolytes at the moment but there were acolytes around. A bodyguard stood outside the open doorway. The rest of Tillam could arrive at any moment.

Phex drew back, shaking his head, genuinely confused. "Am I even worth your love?"

"Every moment of every second."

That was a little too earnest. So, Phex brushed Missit's cheek with his thumb and then moved quickly away. Ignoring Missit's soft whimper of loss.

"Drink something and fix your lip gloss," he said, by which he meant *I love you too, of course.*

"Grumpy," replied Missit, doing as instructed. Maybe understanding, maybe not.

Phex went to check his costume in the long mirror on the other side of the room. Remind himself of his role there in this place and time. Glared at the strangely stern and haughty god staring back at him. Forced himself not to see the loneliness of Missit's imaginary moon in his own reflected eyes. Tried to ready himself to fill in for the god that everyone wished he really was, even Missit.

The next morning, early, before the day started or the ship moved or anything was announced about their next tour stop. Before anyone told Phex what new crisis had hit the divine forums, or how many worshipers had been disappointed by his performance with Tillam the night before. Before he could even think that this might be a bad decision.

Before any of that, Phex uncoiled golden limbs from around himself, got up from his warm cot, picked up a very annoyed Dimsum, and tucked the murmel into his vacant spot.

Missit grumbled, in a not dissimilar tone to the murmel, but settled well enough with his arms around the blue beastie, hugging her close. Phex pulled the covers up and tucked them in, because Missit got cold easily.

Phex tried not to be hurt by how young Missit looked and how beautiful he was. Maybe the Dyesi were right – maybe love and beauty were actually the same thing.

Then Phex went to see Fortew.

Phex announced himself and his relationship to the room using proper formal Dyesi.

Fortew was sitting up in a luxury medi-bed looking rosy-cheeked, but the flush was likely fever, not health.

"Took you long enough," said Tillam's low cantor.

The real one.

He spoke using Galactic Common, not Dyesi.

Phex wasn't sure why he found it so odd, but he switched into it easily enough to respond. "Good morning, Fortew."

"Are you one of those who don't like to visit sick people?" Fortew asked. Phex wondered if that was insult or cheekiness, or if this was just how Fortew was. Had he really thought Phex should have visited sooner? They didn't know enough about each other's personalities.

Phex made his way over to the bed and stood looking down at the god's frail form. Fortew had never been very big, although he had taken up his fair share of space on a dais. Because he was very beautiful. Different from Missit – cuter, sweeter-seeming, less dangerous. Or perhaps that was only the way Phex saw him. Perhaps once, he had cut into people's hearts and called them lonely moons too. Perhaps once, on the dais, he had shone bright enough to hurt. Phex had just never noticed because from the start, even though that start was a tiny insignificant cafe dome with a statue on its counter, Phex had only ever seen Missit.

Fortew was beautiful in his fragility, like an ancient piece of glass, iridescent not like the Dyesi but with the translucent corruption of the incurable.

Phex considered. "No. I just didn't think you'd be interested in seeing me."

"So, it's a matter of worthiness? You're dating my little brother – of course I want to see you. Shouldn't you be asking my permission to court him?"

"Family?" said Phex, confused.

"What do you think a pantheon is, if not a family?"

"I have no frame of reference." Phex thought it meant home. Family seemed too lucky a thing to happen after childhood.

"Are you getting defensive?"

Phex frowned – *was he*?

"Tell me why I should let you keep Missit, when everything is at risk because of it."

"And whose fault is that?"

Fortew looked impressed. "You're disposed to blame me for dying young? That's oddly refreshing."

"It hurts him, what's happening to you. If I can't blame you for that, who can I blame?"

"Oh, certainly, it's just that no one else does. Or talks about it. I like it. You're on his side." Fortew's pouty lips twitched in genuine amusement.

"There are sides?" Phex tried to relax his stance, stand a little less like he expected to be hit and a little more like he expected to catch someone's leap.

Fortew cocked his head, pointed chin pert. "He'll be your responsibility when I'm gone, so you'll have to stay together. Can you keep up with both pantheons at once?"

Phex nodded. Forcing himself to remember how to act like a Sapien, not a Dyesi. "If I have to."

"And you're bitter, too." Fortew almost looked gleeful at this discovery.

"I exist in a space where your struggle with mortality has become almost entirely my problem."

"You think it would be easier to be together if you were not shared between the pantheons?" Fortew reached for a flask of water, but it was slightly out of reach, and his hand was shaking too much anyway. He hissed at himself in frustration.

Phex uncorked it and held it to his lips, casually. "Are you saying you're doing me a favor by dying?"

Fortew drank too small an amount and then turned his head away. "I regret to inform you I think very little on your feelings at all."

"Then why am I here?"

"You came to visit me, Phex, remember? Not the other way around." Fortew gestured down at his lower body. The medics had strapped him down, probably for safe transport through the upcoming fold, or maybe because he was at the stage were the tremors reached his legs.

But then Fortew explained, and it was neither. "I fall asleep, and when I do, it's nightmares. I keep thrashing and falling out of the cot. Then I'm too weak to get back into it myself."

Phex rubbed at his face because that made him want to cry.

"You're here because you want my blessing," said Fortew.

Phex looked at his hands instead of Fortew's pain. At the size of them, at their strength and health. He thought about how easy it was for him to catch Missit in a dance, how beautiful those dark silvery-blue hands looked against Missit's naked skin.

"Blessing for what?" he asked, knowing he sounded sullen. "To be Tillam's new sun? To be your replacement cantor?" Was that really why he was there?

"To be Missit's anchor."

Phex looked at Fortew's flushed perfect heart-shaped face, pointed chin, puffy lips, and big dark eyes. He wondered how much of that was manufactured Dyesi art and how much Fortew had been born with. Wondered if it mattered anymore that Fortew was so pretty when he was also so broken. "And do I have it?"

"If you have to choose, will you choose him?"

The eternal question. This was why Phex had waited so long to visit Fortew. He hadn't wanted to face another sun, knowing he would also be facing Tillam's conscience. "There's nothing else I can do. There's nothing else I'm good for now but being a god. I am what they made me. And the divinity, the Dyesi, they were the only ones who ever wanted me. Until Missit."

"Why are you telling me this?"

"So you fully understand what you're asking."

"Look at me, Phex. If you were lying here and looking back at yourself, what choice would you have wanted to make?"

Phex winced. "You're asking me to pick my own regrets. No one gets to do that in life." Especially not someone like him, who had always drifted through it, intent on survival and not ambition, or even hope.

Phex thought about the divinity and his pantheon. He thought about friendship and worship. He thought about being under the dome with either pantheon – and whether he actually liked it. Then he thought about what his voice could do to sifter skin, the colors. He thought about dancing with Missit, entwining blue and gold. He thought about running up the side of a dome and backflipping over Berril, grabbing her and hurling her into space. The explosion of her wings. The explosion of song when it was him and Kagee causing godfix in worshipers, or the power of it when it was him and Missit stunning acolytes into transfixed stillness. He thought about the control it gave him – he who had never had control over anything.

He enjoyed it all, but he didn't *love* any of it.

He thought about liquid gold in his arms and the joy in that warmth. *That* he loved. He thought of eyes flecked with pain and gold. He thought about all the faces turned toward him, and which face he always looked for in a crowd. The wide mouth full of honey and art and hopeless crooked smiles. Which one was *his* sun? Hot enough to burn like liquid metal, but still his favorite, the one he wanted to contain, for all it scalded. Phex wondered if he diminished himself, wanting to be no more than a vessel that held Missit's molten light. So that Missit, of all the gods, did not have to send his light into a void.

But even cataloguing all the things that the divinity had given him, the thing he liked the most and the thing he was best at, was being that vessel.

He wondered how he could even hesitate.

"I'd choose Missit." Because as much as he yearned to hold the golden god safe, the man who was that god yearned for him. Wanted him. Not for his voice, or his tricks, or the trick genetics had made of him. But because he saw something in Phex worthy of love, which gave Phex this terrible, scary idea that it might be true.

Fortew pursed his full lips and nodded. No clicks. No effort made to remember whose spaceship they were on or his years spent speaking a foreign tongue. Or singing in it. Like he'd forgotten all the little things that made him a god, sloughed them off like a nymph sloughed off a whole identity before instar.

"Then you have my blessing. You're steady and thoughtful. He's trouble. Someone responsible and stable like you *should* be looking after him." Fortew closed his eyes, relaxing back.

Phex's lips twitched in amusement. He didn't smile, though. Because he never really smiled. "Is that all I am?"

"We were never lovers, Missit and I. You know that, right? Always more than friends, though. I think that now, since I won't have a chance at anything with anyone else, that he was probably the love of my life."

Quasilun had said that there were as many ways to give love as there were to give light. Phex supposed this was what the imago had meant. "I'll look after him for you."

"Look after him for yourself or it has no meaning." Phex knew what Fortew meant. Because of Missit's love, Phex might learn to value himself. Might leave the shrine in the kitchen for the warmth of Missit in his lap on a couch puff surrounded by people. Might stop himself from being eaten by loneliness, his own or the fixed.

"Why not just say that at the beginning?" *Why this verbal dance?* wondered Phex, because he really hated this much talking.

Fortew cracked his eyelids and glared. "Go now. I'm tired."

Phex made his way to the door.

"Wait."

"Yes?"

"Could you find my sifters for me? I need to talk to them."

"Are they still yours?"

"Oh, *now* you're being cute?"

"I'll send Yorunlee and Melalan to you as soon as I can."

"No rush," said Fortew, "I'm not going anywhere."

They moved on to tour stop number seven then.

This series of performances were to take place on the other side of Kill'ki Coalition space, not too far from Attacon

7. It took four days to get there, and things aboard the tour ship quickly settled into a new routine.

Everyone had pretty much accepted the reality of their new situation, even the acolytes. Fortew would remain in his bed. Missit would remain in Phex's bed. Phex would remain in both pantheons. Practices would proceed each day in such a manner that Phex wasn't taxed overmuch. Tillam's worshipers would have to deal with an understudy, and the acolytes would have to deal with the continued fallout among believers that resulted.

All further congregations beyond dome performances, VIP or otherwise, were called off indefinitely. The divinity had decided that there would be too many questions asked if Asterism undertook direct contact with the public. It simply wasn't worth the risk for the goodwill it generated.

Without all the extra requirements of being gods and with only performances to worry about, Phex actually found their seventh set of domes comparatively easy and relaxing. Even though he was singing for both Asterism and Tillam back-to-back each night, at least there were no additional new variables to handle.

Tyve and Zil were both on point with their gracing. Clearly, the siblings were delighted to see so many Jakaa Nova in the massive congregations of worshipers and buoyed by their support.

Phex had rabid believers too – apparently, thousands had made the pilgrimage from Attacon sector specifically to see him. It felt almost as if there were more worshipers in the crowds supporting Asterism than Tillam in these domes, but that couldn't possibly be the case. *Could it?* Phex assumed that it was just that Asterism's fans were younger and newly recruited to the divinity, so more vocally enthusiastic than

Tillam's, who were a decade into this game and comparatively restrained as a result.

They performed three shows, with a day's break in between – for Phex's sake now, not Fortew's. Phex thought his pantheon had probably talked to the acolytes about not overworking him. He made a point of thanking them for that one night before bed, although he was pretty certain he could have handled it either way.

"It was me," said a sleepy golden voice from Phex's cot. "I asked them."

"You mean you ordered them to let Phex rest," replied Kagee, sounding odd about it – not angry but not pleased, either.

"Same difference." Missit rolled over, presenting his back to them. "Hurry up," he said to the wall but also, presumably, to Phex. "I'm cold."

Kagee looked at Phex. "Does he have to be such a *god* about everything?"

"I *am* a god," said Missit.

Phex ignored them both and went into the hygiene chamber to clean up.

Basically, everything was going as smoothly as Phex might have hoped. Fortunately, that remained the case right up until their final night in Coalition space.

Asterism's performance went fine, and as usual, Quasilun and a few local bodyguards took everyone from the pantheon but Phex back to the ship immediately afterward.

Tillam took to the dais and had a decent performance. Phex was clearly more tired than he liked to admit. He could hear the exhaustion in his own voice and see it in the dimming of the dome. Missit had been right to ask for the breaks.

Even with them, Missit had to bolster Phex a lot more

than usual. But on the (not so) bright side, there was no chance of them stunning any of the local acolytes into stillness. He and Missit could still hit godfix on most songs, but Phex didn't have the extra oomph needed to freeze the Dyesi in the audience. And, quite frankly, he didn't want to. Everyone always overreacted when they did that. And he didn't have anything to prove anymore.

It was a modern dome in a modern city on a modestly overpopulated planet. Which is to say this performance space felt a bit less like a cave and a bit more like a stadium or a cathedral. But the dome still responded beautifully to skinsift, so Phex was happy enough with the show. What he didn't realize was that its newer design presented some serious security issues.

With a dais that acted more like a stage, there were steps off to one side that led down into the lower levels and the throngs of worshipers there. These were, of course, blocked off and guarded by security. Local muscle, mostly Jakaa Nova, who were defended against fixation with huge, ridiculous-looking earmuffs strapped to their heads.

With the last notes of the last song still lingering as sparks of blues and greens shooting off and swirling into the pearlescent grey of a dormant dome, one of those security personnel acted completely out of character.

A Jakaa Nova turned and bounded up the stairs to join the six gods on the dais, just as they were making their final bows before a hasty exit.

It was one of those times when Phex had a weird surreal moment of wondering if this person was there to escort them off. Or maybe the muscle had just lost his way? It was as if Phex's brain, utterly exhausted from so many performances, couldn't really see what was happening as a threat.

Then he caught sight of Bob shouting, catapulting out of

the closest niche. Phex's brain reminded him that the cyborg barely ever spoke, but now Bob was using every single enhancement to amplify both volume and speed. Itrio was right there too. Bouncing fast in that way that looked creepy, contrasted to her heavy-gravity bulk. This particular dome layout meant their bodyguards had to get up those stairs to get onto the dais. But the local security had gone stiff against anyone going up there – because the crowd was boiling and murmuring, shocked out of both godfix and entertainment euphoria by a stranger on the dais.

Phex focused on the threat, exactly as all the bodyguards had instructed him. He forced his taxed muscles to remember what they had trained for late at night – after singing and dancing, cantor and grace, had come defense.

The security Jakaa Nova on his dais released his claws – wickedly sharp points of deadly keratin.

Phex's shock turned into adrenaline and he was moving before he could think to tell himself to do so.

In that particular moment, this man was no Jakaa Nova warrior – he was simply one of the fixed. Maybe his earmuffs had failed, or maybe the whole security getup had been fake from the start in order to infiltrate. It hardly mattered. Phex would have to stay out of reach of those claws and stop him no matter what. He mentally shrugged. What were Jakaa Nova claws but ten tiny blades, anyway?

The fixed looked as if he wanted to kill one of them. This wasn't a kidnapping or a drugging – this was obsession pushed into murder and elimination or consumption. Like Chef.

Phex didn't care which member of Tillam this fixed was after. The man would have to get through Phex.

The good thing about the fixed, if such a thing can be said, is that they were entirely focused on their target, the center of their obsessive desire. They cared only about whatever it was that their warped little minds had decided they must do to claim the god they believed in – destroy, maim, possess, it didn't matter. They just wanted that god. So, it wasn't like they were actually fighting with skill or planning strategically.

Phex did three of his long steps forward, leaned back, and lashed out with his dominant leg. Fast. Twice. One kick to the groin and the other to the face. The groin probably would have been enough, but Phex didn't like the expression on the Jakaa Nova's face. So, he hit him there, too.

The fixed stumbled, went down on one knee, but didn't stay down.

He came back up swinging with one set of claws and grasping with the other, intent on only one god.

Phex took a quick glance to the side, following the fixed's gaze, wondering which of Tillam he was actually after.

Missit.

15

THE DYESI COME IN JUDGMENT

Of course the fixed was after Missit.

Phex's ears roared, or maybe that was the worshipers. He leapt up to avoid a wild swipe. The Jakaa Nova wasn't even looking at him, too focused on Missit.

Phex landed, used his momentum to pivot, avoiding another swipe, and whipped his leg out high to kick the fixed again – to the side of the throat. This time with the full force of all his body weight behind it.

Probably because he was a singer, Phex always felt like the worst thing he could do to another being was attack their neck. But this was Missit's fixed. All standards fell to the wayside.

Phex barely noticed that two claws caught him across the calf on the way down. They shredded his costume and sank into his flesh, blood pouring hot and fast from the open gashes.

He felt nothing. Numbing agent in those claws, of course.

The calculating part of Phex's brain informed him to watch out and not slip in his own blood, because that would be embarrassing. He wondered if he should kneel on the bastard's back, keep him down, and just bleed all over him.

Fortunately, the Jakaa Nova stayed down and still without further help from Phex.

Phex wondered what would happen if that neck blow had actually killed the man. How would he feel? Should Quasilun have named Phex as the most dangerous person in that room back aboard the ship?

Had a god ever killed someone before?

But this fixed had been after Missit. *His Missit.* Turned out that made Phex really want to kill.

The roaring in his ears faded and he registered that there had been screams and panicked chaos but now the entire dome was eerily silent.

Phex was awash with calm focus and an odd kind of satisfaction. He should have felt drained – the bodyguards had warned him there was usually a crash after a fight. But Phex only felt energized – like he could sing again, like he could fight again. Euphoric.

He wondered if there was something wrong with him. Perhaps the Wheel had triggered his genetics for this, too – to fight, really fight, and stop, but then get up and fight again without the companion exhaustion rushing in to fill the void that adrenaline always left behind. If his response to battle was this strange kind of joy – what kind of monster did that make him?

Bob and Itrio were there, finally, although it had really only been seconds. The rest of Tillam's bodyguards soon followed. And then, last of all, Quasilun's huge form appeared – reassuring in that way only the imago had, as if it were older and more stable than everyone everywhere all the time, not just the Dyesi nymphs.

Phex was still wide awake and alert, but now he felt a lot

less scared. He hadn't even realized he was scared until the fear vanished.

Missit charged at him and leapt, hurling himself across the dais.

Phex plucked him easily out of the air – they'd practiced this move, after all. Missit wrapped arms and legs tightly around him – strangling his neck and his waist.

"Are you okay?" The god was repeating this over and over. His gaze searched Phex's face, looking for injury. Which Phex found mildly amusing, since it was his leg that still bled.

"Me? He was after you." Phex turned quickly so his body was shielding Missit from the fallen Jakaa Nova.

"Why are you such an idiot?" Missit's gold-flecked eyes were huge with worry.

"You're the one currently hugging me in front of millions of Tillam worshipers."

"So get us out of here!" ordered Missit.

Phex was accustomed to responding to instructions from Missit with alacrity. He found himself carrying the golden god across the dais toward the back hidden stairs.

The worshipers had found their voices again and were screaming in hysterical horror and anger, or possibly in ecstatic joy at witnessing such a scandal. Thousands, millions if the divinity hadn't throttled the beam, had just seen an attack of a fixed, Phex fighting him off, and Missit's insane display of affection and preferential treatment of a mere demigod.

"I'll deal with the fixed. You get your gods out of here," Quasilun barked at the bodyguards.

Phex hoped they had taken their earplugs out.

Bob came jogging up next to Phex, so he assumed yes. "Pass him over. You're losing a lot of blood and just did two performances in a row. There's no way you can carry him all the way to the ship."

Phex said, "I'm fine," and kept walking. Really, Jakaa Nova claws were amazing things – he felt no pain at all.

He caught a flash of dark red out the corner of his eye and instantly twisted to protect Missit.

"It's just me," said Zil sounding unhappy and scared.

Phex readjusted and kept walking.

"You should let someone else hold him. Your behavior doesn't look right, acolytes are watching." That was Melalan, giving out Dyesi cultural advice.

Phex thought it was absurd to even consider appearances and romantic relationships right now.

He patted Missit's back and hoisted him up farther so he wouldn't slip.

Missit pressed his face hard into Phex's neck and squeezed tighter.

"That just got beamed into I don't know how many domes, too late to worry about it now," said Tern, coming up on Melalan's other side.

"Divinity is going to have a whole new crisis to contend with. At least this will take the pressure off Fortew for a while," said Itrio.

Missit stayed quiet and clung to Phex, trembling slightly, which meant he really had been scared. Which made Phex angry all over again.

"Nice kick, by the way," said Itrio to Phex.

"Which one?"

"All of them."

Phex clicked. "You said to execute with intent to harm or why bother fighting at all."

"I did."

"Did I kill him?" Phex asked, sounding entirely dispassionate even to his own ears. What was *wrong* with him? Shouldn't the idea upset some part of him?

"Who cares if you did?" said Bob, sounding equally dispassionate, but then again, that was kind of how the cyborg always sounded.

Phex nearly made it all the way to the spaceship carrying Missit. But the blood loss finally caught up to him at the entrance ramp. He went completely dizzy, and his legs seemed to shift right out from under him.

Luckily, everyone had been expecting that. Bob grabbed Missit away while Itrio and Zil braced Phex.

Phex batted Zil off – his arms felt heavy and sluggish.

"Because I'm Jakaa Nova?" asked Zil, clearly hurt.

Phex snorted. "Don't want to get blood on your costume."

Itrio rolled her eyes and scooped him up, carrying him easily, like a baby. Heavy-gravity tinkers could do that to a person's muscles, make even Phex seem like a featherweight. Feeling ridiculous, and hoping there were no press lurking around the spaceship, Phex looped an arm around her neck and looked up at the night sky beyond the bubble. Dumb twinkling stars. Familiar ones. Like the ones on Attacon 7.

He wondered how he'd ended up there, in this exact moment of time and place, staring at the emptiness of space, feeling empty himself. Then realized he was getting highly philosophical, which actually was a bad sign.

"I think I'm going to faint from blood loss," he informed Itrio politely, making sure to articulate every word.

"Oh, are you?"

"I've been through this before." He noticed how slow and careful his own phrasing had become and could feel blackness creeping in around the sides of his eyes, which were rolling back in his head.

He felt himself convulse slightly, and this time, the

roaring in his ears was a welcome thing, as he knew it wasn't worshipers.

He smelled the warm copper scent of his own blood then. How had he forgotten that smell?

Then, nothingness.

Phex woke up in the ship's medical bay in a temporary cot they'd set up because Fortew was permanently occupying the main medi-bed.

Fortew was lying on his side and staring at him. "You're awake?"

Phex had a screaming headache, a very dry mouth, and stomach cramps. His entire body felt listless and weak. "I must have lost a lot of blood."

"They replaced it."

"Nice of them. Can I get a new head, too?" Phex massaged his temple with his free hand. The other one was attached to a wide array of tubes, cuffs, and wires. The bright white lights medics always seemed to require were too bright.

"How long was I out?"

"All night. It's morning and we've already left Coalition space. We are in Attacon sector now, waiting on you to wake up before we fold."

Phex appreciated such a thorough report. He noticed Fortew's wrist ident was blinking softly. He'd set it to follow something and report in. "What's the chatter?"

Fortew shook his arm, somewhat chipper. "The divine forums have gone completely insane. Clips from last night have been shared everywhere. From you fighting with the fixed. To you bleeding everywhere. To Missit's spectacularly ill-judged display of affection."

"The divinity must be losing its mind."

"The priors have already instituted maximum belief activation on your behalf. Countering agents are *everywhere*. I had no idea Asterism already had such a big believer base. And you are super popular – the mysterious blue-haired demigod of everyone's dreams, apparently. Stern, taciturn, yet caring."

Phex could see the archetypal promo scripts already. He closed his eyes.

Fortew's cheerful tone continued. Phex got an impression of what the god had been like before, possibly as much of a troublemaker as Missit in his own way. "The sacerdotes are still having a hell of a time with damage control, though, no matter how popular you are. No one has *ever* seen a god fight before. Let alone half-kill a Jakaa Nova and bleed all over a dais like some ancient warrior sacrifice. You know the Dyesi, they have no idea how to justify or defend violence. And you looked deadly up there, like there was no contest. Like you were picking on an enthusiastic worshiper."

"He was fixed." Phex opened his eyes so he could glare at Fortew, despite the lights and the headache.

"Oh, *we* all know that, the Dyesi and the gods, but the acolytes hate to even acknowledge that the fixed exist, let alone admit to how bad they can get. Works counter to their divine-expansion model. Makes the divinity look bad."

"I have put them in a very awkward position, I suppose."

"Exactly. To make *you* look good, they must explain how bad a true believer can get."

"Awkward." Phex wondered if that would be too much for the divine system to handle. If it would be easier to cut Phex free than explain the flaws that his presence now highlighted.

"Very. And then there's you bleeding everywhere. Gods

aren't supposed to be mortal, remember." Of course Fortew would notice that part. "Then you just carry Missit around like you aren't feeling a thing, so I guess that bit is not too bad. Because you went right back to looking godly. Or at least very badass."

"I *didn't* feel a thing."

"Hum?"

"Jakaa Nova claws have a numbing agent in them."

"Do they? Did I know that?"

Phex cocked an eyebrow at Fortew. "I don't know. Have you ever been slashed by one?"

"Nope." Fortew seemed gleeful. If anything, this whole scandal had perked him up. Phex supposed it was nice for him – the pressure was entirely off him for the first time in a long while.

"And Missit? How's he doing?" Phex asked.

"He's fine. Sleeping right over there with that vile blue monkey-creature of his. He refused to go back to his own bed, or yours, for that matter."

Phex rotated his head. Hard to do, as there were lots of shaped pillows stacked around him, designed to keep him immobilized, but he could see Missit curled in one corner of the room. Dimsum was a smug, dozing loaf on top of one hip. Missit hadn't even bothered to drag in a puff, just piled a bunch of brightly colored chunky throws on the floor, like a rainbow nest.

"No, I mean what about Missit hugging me? How are the acolytes handling that part?"

"Ah. Would we call that a *hug*?" Fortew was what, teasing him?

"Fortew." Phex made his voice low and grave and insistent. Wondering if that kind of authority would work on another low cantor. On another sun.

Fortew chuckled, which also made him cough and choke a bit. When he'd recovered, he said, "That was the worst of everything. Rumors are rampant that you two have been having an affair all along. That that's why Asterism was put on tour so quickly, because Missit wants his boy toy with him. That that's why you're replacing me. That I've been ousted because Missit is obsessed with you and wants you in his pantheon. And since he's the most popular member of Tillam, what he says, goes."

"Ridiculous!"

"Oh, but he *is* the most popular member of Tillam. He has about twice as many believers as any one of the rest of us. Always has done."

"That's not what I mean. I mean the rumors."

"Well, you know how believers get. Missit is meant to be *pure*. He's meant to belong to them. He's meant to love only them. He's meant to be an ideal, both attainable but also, somehow, still godly. So are you. They have to believe that you are free from romantic entanglements. There has to be this teeny-tiny hope that they could actually maybe really get with one of us, date us, fuck us, marry us. We can't have lovers of our own. That's not divine. That's not godly. It damages our reputations. It renders us mortal in their eyes."

Phex thought that Fortew's phrasing was very telling. That to their believers, what Phex and Missit had together somehow cheapened them both. It made him hate worshipers a little.

"Great gods are not meant to go charging across stages and cast themselves into some demigod's arms, except as part of a performance."

"So, Missit is taking most of the flak?"

Fortew shrugged. "Percentage-wise, it's probably about the same number of believers turning against each of you. But half of Missit's believers acting out against the divinity is five percent of the entire galactic worship base. The infonet is insane right now. There are wars getting less attention than that one clip of Missit leaping into your arms. Nice catch, by the way."

"And how's the divinity dealing with it?"

"Badly."

"Love is as much an anathema to them as violence," said Phex, thinking not just of what the Dyesi didn't see but what they couldn't even comprehend.

Fortew nodded. "I've always wondered if that was why they can't have either. As though, in all creatures – human, Sapien, Hominin – the one can't exist without the other."

Phex thought that was a horrible idea, and then remembered how much joy he had felt, kicking that fixed so hard he crumpled to the dais and making him stay there. It felt good to have protected Missit. He felt *good* about it. Not exactly like the joy of Missit arched and naked above him, but not all that different, either.

It made him feel queasy – on top of the stomach cramps.

"Show me the most popular clips?" he asked.

"You sure?"

Phex clicked.

Fortew beamed out the image into the space between their cots.

Phex watched Missit leap into his arms. It was a *very* nice catch. It looked like perfectly normal gracing to him, but he could get why it upset believers. Missit was far too comfortable in his arms. And the expression on Phex's own face, holding Missit close and safe. That looked a little too much like worship for anyone's comfort. Gods shouldn't look that way about other gods.

The next clip was Phex spinning into a wicked side kick

that hit the Jakaa Nova's throat. The one that had put the fixed down. It looked like Phex had used grace to kill someone. It was almost beautiful but also gave the impression that Phex had taken divine art and made it profoundly dirty. Corrupted the dome and all it stood for. As if he were the one who let violence onto the dais – simply because he was good at it. He'd used beauty, the Dyesi's *beauty* that was also love, for hatred.

That made Phex feel even more nauseous. He looked around for a bag. "Turn it off, please."

"The fixed isn't pressing charges," said Missit. He was standing, looking small and forlorn among the pile of blankets. Dimsum was wrapped around his neck.

"So, he lived?" Phex could not keep the relief from coloring his voice.

"Yeah. Not sure if that will make things easier or not." Missit came around between the two cots, fussed briefly over Fortew – rearranging the blankets, tucking them in about his friend's feet, glancing all the while, from under metallic eyelashes, at Phex.

He unwound Dimsum from his neck and encouraged her to join Fortew. She did, after a small grumble of protest.

Fortew grumbled too.

Missit swiveled, then stood still and quiet, looking hopefully down at Phex.

Phex shifted over as much as the cot would allow, toward the machinery, twisted onto his side with his bandaged leg on top, created too small a space. But it was more than enough of an offering, and Missit knew it.

Missit shuddered visibly and then climbed quickly in – making himself as small as he actually was but never looked, especially not on a dais. People forgot what a tiny, slender little thing the greatest golden god really was.

Phex's top arm was too fully tethered to medical gadgetry to hug Missit, so he just rested it carefully on his own hip.

Missit lay his head on top of Phex's other arm.

Fortew was still staring at them, so instead of nuzzling Missit's neck, Phex said, "I told you to keep your hair out of the way."

"Sorry, Phex," said Missit, sounding incredibly happy.

"Oh, I see," said Fortew, "You two are disgustingly sweet together. No wonder."

"No wonder what?" asked Missit, snuggling even closer to Phex, even though they were plastered against each other already.

"Be still," grumbled Phex, feeling relaxed and sleepy all of a sudden. His whole body ached, his leg was throbbing, and his mouth was dry, but the nausea had receded.

Fortew said, his voice cracking slightly, "I didn't think it was that kind of beauty."

Phex wasn't certain which of them Fortew was talking about or to, or if he meant them as a couple. But Phex had thought they'd already cleared this up. He had thought he'd made his position obvious to Fortew. But maybe not. And now, somehow, after what had just happened, it didn't seem like a courageous thing to say it out loud anymore. Even with Missit right there in front of him.

It seemed to be just another thing Phex would regularly have to deal with, like the fixed.

"I'm just not sure I'm very good at it," said Phex.

Poor Missit was confused. Phex and Fortew were literally and figuratively talking over his head. "Good at what?"

Phex switched to Galactic Common so he could use concrete words. "Loving someone."

Missit was dismissive. "Of course you are. You do it all the time."

"I do?"

Fortew looked equally surprised to hear this. "But he seems so aloof and cold."

Missit snorted. "Phex gives love out into the universe like he cooks for his pantheon. As if it is something that needs to get done and he's not sure if it tastes good but it's more important that everyone get fed. That's all that matters to him. Like he's slightly afraid they're going to turn their noses up at it, at him, and slightly delighted that they never do."

"Do I?" wondered Phex. Because was that love?

"You never noticed?" Missit bumped back against him, affectionately teasing.

Phex shook his head, brushing Missit's hair with his chin in the process, trying to think of times when he had given away love as if it was a necessary thing, to be supplied as if it were sustenance.

"Well, of course you didn't notice." Missit sounded resigned but practical. "You never do save enough for yourself."

"I don't… What?"

"Phex, just because you give away a thing doesn't make it worthless. Just because you save nothing for yourself doesn't make *you* worthless."

Phex was silent.

Fortew chuckled. "Aw, baby brother, when did you grow up and start appreciating people?"

"When someone *else* I loved decided to die on me," snapped back Missit.

Fortew winced. Then he said, "You're going to have to fight for it. You two, I mean."

"I thought we'd have more time," said Phex.

"So did I," replied Fortew, sarcastically. "We all always think we have more time. So, what are you going to do?

"Fight, of course," said Phex, because clearly, he could do that when pushed, and the whole universe now knew that about him. Plus, he wanted Missit. Not just because he was amazing, but because Missit thought he was Missit-worthy.

"Together, we'll fight all of them. The worshipers, the acolytes, all the divinity if we have to," agreed Missit.

"Is it weird that I think you might win?" said Fortew.

Phex only pressed his cheek more firmly against Missit's head, relishing the closeness, wondering if that golden hair would leave the impression of tiny lines in his skin.

Missit tilted to look up and back at him in what must be a very awkward and unflattering angle. "So, you're not mad at me about what happened?" He sounded genuinely concerned.

"On the dais? Why should I be? You can't control your fixed any more than the rest of us can."

"That's not what I meant. I meant hugging you in front of everyone. Like we're lovers."

"Oh, that. No. We *are* lovers, and you cannot control your nature any more than you can control the fixed."

"He wasn't one of mine, though." Missit relaxed again, in this he was confident.

"He was definitely obsessed with you. Never took his eyes off of you." Phex would have a hard time forgetting that. He wondered if he had a new nightmare to replace the blades that still, sometimes, haunted him.

"Yeah, but I wasn't his actual obsession, I was his target. The reason for his ire. The god he actually believed in was—"

"Me?" interrupted Fortew. "The forums are claiming he was one of mine."

"No," Missit said, "The acolytes let me monitor the resulting inquisition. He was one of Phex's."

"What?" said Phex and Fortew at the same time.

"That's why he's refusing to press charges or speak out against Phex. He believes in you, not me."

"Then why was he clawing at you?" wondered Phex.

"Because he decided I'm the reason you're in Tillam at all. Apparently, because we complement each other as cantor, and because we are so powerful together, he decided that I planned to oust Fortew and replace him with you. That I'm some kind of evil mastermind plotting to destroy Asterism for my own nefarious purposes."

Fortew said, "Well, that's the reasoning of a fixed for you. Entirely unreasonable."

Phex felt weirdly guilty that he'd beaten up one of his own worshipers.

Missit sounded almost amused. "He doesn't blame you for kicking him. Apparently, you've simply been *taken in by my wily ways*. He thought that if I were out of the picture, then Asterism would be able to become the biggest pantheon in all the divinity and you would be safe from me."

"Okay. Wow." Phex tried not to twitch in discomfort. "Do we know what the acolytes are going to do about this?"

"Which part?" wondered Fortew.

"All of it."

"Absolutely no clue."

Phex sighed, puffing up fine strands of Missit's hair. "Well, let's nap on it, shall we?"

"Very good idea," said Fortew.

Missit, who'd just woken up and was neither injured nor sick so not inclined to nap, said, "Wait, hey, guys?"

But Phex was already dozing off. Missit's weight against him now so familiar and beloved, it was like a drug that helped him to sleep, one his body could not process and get rid of quickly. Probably never could.

The divinity came up with an entirely novel solution to the whole situation. They decided to go public with the duet. To show the world that Missit's leap into Phex's arms was merely something well practiced for a special performance. It was the result of instinct, not passion.

The acolytes released and promoted high-production-value footage of Missit and Phex dancing and singing together in their old-fashioned duet. The special performances they'd previously reserved only for live congregations. The divinity made sure to emphasize how much it highlighted the synergy and balance of the two cantors – that this was something special, uniquely different from pantheon dynamics.

The acolytes also decided to have them start performing that duet again at their next show.

This decision made Phex nervous and Missit smug – because tour eight wasn't a tour stop like all the previous ones had been but a visit to the greatest dome of them all. Apex Dome near Dyesid Prime. And the reason they were headed home? The Divine Awards.

This was the place and a beam where, once every galactic year, the pantheons met and honored themselves – prettily dressed and sparkling, orbiting each other like true stars of the galaxy.

It was, without question, the most popular celebrity event of the year. Beamed live into every single dome and most households, with no exclusivity restrictions, it was available all over the infonet all at once. You didn't need to be in a dome to appreciate it, but most worshipers tried to be in at least a cupola.

And now Phex and Missit were to perform their duet at

the Divine Awards.

Missit had done the awards shows before, with Tillam of course. Several times. But this was different. Their duet was going to be the first of its kind at the Divine Awards. Phex had never faced up to something so high-pressure before, in front of a congregation made up entirely of acolytes, peers, and major gods.

Asterism was nominated for best demigod group and Tillam was up for a best godsong, for "Tillam's Lament." But neither pantheon had been slated to perform. So, Phex and Missit's duet was added to the roster at the last minute.

Phex was given three days to recover from his injury with all the medical power of the divine focused on his healing. Last time, when he'd been a crudrat struck down by a blade, it had taken him months to get over the blood loss and heal physically. And he'd lost much less blood back then. This time, after only a few days, it was as if nothing had ever happened to him.

The newly acquired medical team cut Phex lose and turned all their attention on Fortew in the vain hope that Tillam's low cantor could put in an appearance at the Divine Awards and pretend nothing was wrong.

Outrage over Phex's fight was still the talk of the infonet. The announcement of the duet hadn't assuaged it as much as the divinity hoped. Gossip was rampant. Worshipers and believers had organized into camps – those who supported Phex and Missit as a couple, those who did not, and those who thought it wasn't anyone's business.

Some of Phex's believers wrote to confess that they were staying up all night just to wage holy war in the divine forums. Phex thanked them for their service to his cause with his relic sticker, a soup ladle filled with blue fire, and wondered that he'd ever doubted that their faith was genuine.

It was no small thing, to fight a flame war on behalf of a mere demigod. Especially against Tillam's vast worshiper base.

It was generally hoped that Phex and Missit's actual performance would quiet all rumors, but in the meantime, the acolytes tried additional tactics.

The divinity forced the Jakaa Nova fixed to make a public statement of his obsession. He claimed all responsibility and said he was putting himself into a rehabilitation clinic for dome addicts. Since the only thing he was addicted to was godsong and there was no known cure for that, everyone who knew anything about the true nature of the fixed knew that this was all lies. This Jakaa Nova would either be locked away by his home sector for the rest of his life as clinically insane with no possibility of recovery, or he would be released and probably attack again. It was up to Coalition authorities to decide on his ultimate punishment. He was one of theirs, after all.

Meanwhile, most of the members of Tillam and Asterism rested and planned out their outfits for the awards show. While Phex and Missit went back to work practicing their duet. This time, everyone dropped in to watch. Even Fortew had himself carried over by Itrio so he could see the thing everyone talked about – from start to finish.

Phex wasn't entirely sure a spectacular display of compatibility on a dais would have the desired effect, but he did want to impress the other gods with his abilities – he couldn't deny that. He also wanted to show the acolytes that they hadn't made a mistake trusting him with the dome.

He was pretty sure he was in everyone's bad books right now. The three acolytes aboard the tour ship with them seemed half terrified of him – crests twitching and flattening whenever he moved too quickly or spoke too suddenly around them.

In consequence, Phex tried to stay still and liquid-grace in all the common areas, and spoke even less than he ever had before. He hated making people nervous.

Zil noticed and explained, quite kindly, “It’s the violence. They’ll get over it eventually.”

“They aren’t that way around the bodyguards, yet they’re the ones who taught me how to do what I did up there.”

“The Dyesi can compartmentalize and intellectualize the idea of those who are hired for protection. But if it had been one of the bodyguards, Itrio, for example, who did what you did to that fixed, the acolytes would be jumpy around her, too. Don’t take it personally.”

Phex nodded.

“Your sifters seem remarkably sanguine about it,” Zil pointed out, helpfully.

Phex said, “They weren’t there. They didn’t witness it under the dome. Tillam’s sifters *are* avoiding me.”

Zil chuckled. “That’s normal for them. They never liked you. This is an excuse.”

That hurt, because Phex had thought Melalan at least was coming around to enjoying his company.

Zil changed the subject. “Fortew says you two have something to tell us.”

“He does? What?”

“Something about that hug?”

“Uh?” Phex was at a loss. Fortew wanted him and Missit to admit to what, exactly? Having sex? Why? Hadn’t everyone guessed that by now?

“The two pantheons need to have a serious talk. So, we’re coming to Asterism’s quarters for FTL. It’s the only thing we could think of that would give us private time without bodyguards or acolytes around. Tern is arranging it.”

“I’m sorry… what?”

"Tern has an advanced degree in fold theory. You didn't know? He's a physicist. It's a matter of divine record."

Phex only nodded. Wondering briefly if Tern intended to change the nature of folding space so they could have a conversation about sex. But suspecting it was more that Tern would arrange the tech so Tillam must take refuge with them.

"Okay, so, we'll expect you?" Phex decided that ten years had given Tillam quite a bit of experience in how to manipulate divine restrictions to their own ends. So, he better accept what was coming.

Accordingly, when the alarm went off to prepare for the next fold, a small but chaotic crisis delayed matters.

Apparently, something had gone terribly wrong with all the safety straps in Tillam's quarters.

At first, they were told to strap down with the bodyguards, but Yorunlee made a fuss about that being *beneath* Tillam's dignity, plus the bodyguards were all too big to share cots comfortably and safely.

So, the acolytes, flustered and confused, agreed that the best solution was for Tillam to join Asterism in their cots and share the more luxurious and comfortable straps designed for gods.

Thus, Asterism and Tillam went two to a cot for the fold.

Phex and Missit, Tyve and Zil, Berril and Kagee, Jinyesun and Fandina, Melalan and Yorunlee, with Tern getting his own cot.

There was always time during a fold when everyone had to stay strapped in and bored while the mini scyther system ramped up. Then again when it ramped down out the other side. Afterward, the ship needed even more time to completely flush the DMPs.

Thus, the pantheons had quite a bit of private time together, safe in the assumption that everyone else on the spaceship was strapped down and could not overhear them. Plus, during a fold, any possible monitoring equipment would not function properly. A fold in space folded everything – it was one of the reasons the human brain had to be awake for the experience.

Tern was the one who broke the awkward silence. “Fortew tells us you two are actually in love with each other.”

Phex winced. Did the grace have to be so blunt in front of their four sifters? It seemed ugly said outright like that, in Tern’s flat tone. Phex almost preferred they just talk about the sex. *Love* seemed a lot more embarrassing.

Missit answered. Because of the two of them, he was always going to be braver in this matter. “It’s not as if he’s the air I breathe or anything trite like that.”

Missit paused and shifted against him, as if worried about how Phex would react. Phex distracted himself by testing the safety strap to make sure it wasn’t too tight or restricting Missit in any way.

Complete silence permeated their quarters. Everyone was listening intently. It was a lot worse than being on a dais in front of thousands.

Missit blithely kept talking. “How do I explain? Have you ever feared an empty dome? Not stage fright, but the opposite. That we’d show up with no worshipers to watch?”

Most everyone clicked affirmative. Phex supposed even he could understand that kind of fear. All the work they’d done for so long. As troubling as it was to have believers, it would be a whole lot worse if Asterism had no worshipers at all.

Missit pressed on. "So, that's similar to this feeling I had as a kid, when I looked at the stars. People usually smile and think, *Oh, how pretty, sparking pinpoints of light.* All I ever saw was the vastness between them, and that terrified me. Too much of space is nothingness. For me, Phex fits there, in the empty void between stars."

Phex thought that Missit himself was more like stardust stitched together by song, containing within him the fine craftsmanship of millennia and the hope of millions. But there was no way he was brave enough to say that privately to Missit, let alone in front of others. He'd admitted his feelings to Fortew, and it felt like that should be enough, shouldn't it?

"Is that love or companionship?" asked Fandina, sounding very confused.

"Didn't you say *desire* was usually wrapped up in Sapien notions of love?" asked Jinyesun.

Missit gave a little chuckle. "I wanted him from the moment we met, of course. Just look at him. And he wanted me too. After all, I'm me. But that wasn't ever all of it. Or even most of it. It was more this realization. For the first time, I met a whole other person and I thought, *He needs me.* Really needs me. Not for how I sing or what I look like, but for who I am."

"I did wonder how it worked," said, of all people, Berril. Her voice was high and kind of small but also hopeful. "I mean we love Phex, and we need him. But he does kind of float around, giving the impression of not actually needing any of us in return."

Kagee added, "Because he never wanted to be a god the way the rest of us did."

"True. But it turns out I always wanted to hold a god," said Phex, because that was a thing he'd realized recently was important.

"Any god would do?" asked Missit, sounding forlorn.

Was Missit unsure of him? Of them? That wouldn't do. How could Phex explain when words were his weakest means of communication?

"No! It's just…" Phex struggled to be brave about this, would rather be back on the dais facing down a fixed.

"Missit already has Tillam and its legions of worshipers. It feels like Missit taking Phex away from us is gluttony," said Tyve.

Phex bit his own lip hard. Wanted to cry. That was unfair to Missit.

"No." He almost whispered. Then louder, still shaky: "No. It's the opposite. He makes me feel like I deserved it." How did someone who spent his whole life being told he wasn't allowed to want anything for himself find the courage to beg for it? Beg for the privilege of loving from the only other people who'd ever been generous enough to accept him.

"Deserve what exactly, Phex?" Berril's voice was soft and kind.

"Love. Divinity. You. A pantheon. This. Any little bit of it. But mostly just him. Missit."

Silence.

Missit grabbed at Phex's forearms, pulling them tighter around him.

Phex tried desperately to explain, voice less shaky but coming fast and rough. "At first, I thought, *Who am I to get to be worshiped at all, let alone loved by a god?* Let alone Missit. But more, who am I to dare to love him back? It was Missit who taught me it's all right. That sometimes I get to ask for what I need, I don't always have to earn it."

"Fucking Phex," said Kagee, voice thick.

Yorunlee spoke then, sounding tired. "How can a god, even a young one, have so little self-worth?"

Fandina said, "Ever notice that Missit is the only person Phex ever really smiles around?"

Tyve gave a humorless chuckle. "And every time he does, he's surprised by it."

Missit said, "When we met, the first thing I thought was how lonely he seemed. No. That's not right. The first thing I thought was how hot he was. The next thing was how lonely. He reminded me of myself."

"And that's love?" asked Melalan.

"For Missit and Phex, it is," said Berril firmly, stalwart in her support.

"It's different than it would be for someone else?" asked Jinyesun, endearing in its attempt to understand what everyone meant by *love*.

"Cantors under the same dome, singing the same godsong, never cause the same colors – you *know* that. It's not that it is a different song, it's that the cantors themselves are different," Missit said finally.

There was a silence.

"Love is like godsong?" asked Fandina at last.

"Love is made of different colors depending on who's singing it, just like the dome," explained, of all people, Kagee.

"Ah, like skinsift."

There was a long pause while the Dyesi in the room processed this information.

Finally, Phex mustered all his courage and asked, "So, can I keep him? Missit, I mean. This. Us. Please?" His powerful voice, which could stun a Dyesi into stillness, sounded thin.

It was the first time Phex had ever asked for anything he really wanted, and it was probably the scariest moment of his life.

16

SONG OF ALL FEARS

"Let's vote, majority takes it," said Zil.

"I'm in favor," said Berril promptly because… Berril.

"I'm against," said Kagee. "It's Missit. Phex, it can't be good for you or Asterism in the long run. He'll always win. The divinity will see it done."

"This isn't a competition," objected Missit.

"You sure about that?"

Berril lashed out at Kagee. "Why are you always so against them?"

"Phex is going to get hurt!"

There was a muffled *oof* noise and some wild thrashing as, presumably, Berril kicked Kagee's shin. They were sharing Kagee's bunk opposite, and Phex could see them over Missit's shoulder, since they were lying on their sides, facing out.

"But, just like his past, it's not your pain to control. Phex has to make his own mistakes," said Tyve.

"I take it you're in favor, then?" Kagee asked Tyve.

Tyve clicked. "Missit makes Phex smile, Kagee. No one does that. Not even Berril. So, yeah, I'm in favor."

Zil said, "I'm in favor. I like the way he treats Missit, and I like how he fought for him on the stage. And I like how calm Missit is when they're together. He's such a little ball of angst and chaos most of the time. Phex is good for him. Grounds him."

Phex felt warm and proud and uncomfortable with the praise but also oddly honored.

"Thanks, Z," said Missit.

"Besides, it's your life to fuck up, kid," replied the Jakaa Nova, somewhat undermining his earlier support.

Everyone turned to Tern. Phex could feel Missit tense up against him. It was coming down to a simple majority. Assuming the Dyesi of their respective pantheons were all against the relationship because it was a *romantic* relationship and defied divine standards of godly behavior, Tern had the deciding vote.

Tern said, "I'm in favor."

Phex was a little surprised, also profoundly relieved.

"Really, why?" asked Melalan.

"My people have never put restrictions on love, except that Cotilax cannot love Mainspace and vice versa." He gave an ironic huff.

Phex winced in sympathy. Tern, for all his casual dismissal at the time, was from a divided sector. Tern could never tour his home space, had never performed for his own people. Tern knew all about separating whole planets that wanted to love each together.

Tern continued, "Screw the divine mandates. Let them be together. Who am I to stomp out affection when it's right there in front of me, just because it happens to be inconvenient? Frankly, we should all be so lucky as to get love at some point in our lives."

Berril's small voice come then, stronger now that she

knew others were on her side: "What right do we have to interfere, or find it gross, or stop it just because we think it'll end badly?" *That* last part was directed at Kagee. "*We* don't matter. It's not about *us*. It's about them."

"Ouch," said Kagee.

"What about us sifters, don't we get to vote?" asked Jinyesun.

"We assumed, as Dyesi, you would all be against us," said Missit.

"It's never been done before. Two gods pairing up. Uh, dating, I guess you would say." Melalan's voice and crests were neutral.

"You can't seriously believe that," scoffed Kagee.

Yorunlee said, "I think the four of us should talk about this among ourselves, but for now, we abstain from voting." Presumably, it spoke for all four sifters because it was the oldest.

Phex expected that to be the end of it.

But then the Dyesi started talking with each other right then and there. They were using a rapid tongue-swishing register that was entirely unlike the Dyesi everyone had learned. It didn't sound at all like frozen register, either. It wasn't another language, the Dyesi only had the one mother tongue, but it was so heavy in dialect or accented that it might as well have been.

Phex only understood one word in ten. And since the sifters were in the top two bunks, the conversation was, both literally and figuratively, well over his head.

The four kept talking like that, having a private conversation in the crowded room without pause, for many minutes.

But Missit was resting heavy against Phex, and Missit had grown up on Dyesid Prime.

"Do *you* understand what they're saying?" Phex asked.

Missit hissed a Dyesi negative. "They're using skinless register. I never learned it. Nor did my parents. It's not taught."

"Skinless?"

"The first lifestage before nymphs."

"Dyesi are born without skins?" Phex admitted to being slightly disgusted by the idea.

The sifters across the room had paused to listen to Missit's explanation, and huffed in amusement at this statement.

Missit laughed. "Ah, no. Sorry. It's actually just a thin, translucent skin with no sifting capacity, the name is kind of a joke about how delicate and fragile the Dyesi young are."

Phex swallowed. "Oh." He supposed it made sense that the children would have their own dialect – after all, the Dyesi had linguistic registers for everything else, including imagoes.

The four sifters went back to their conversation, clearly amused but happy to let Missit fix any misconceptions.

"You comfortable?" Phex asked Missit, because the fold warning was flashing and humming through the ship, shaking it slightly.

Missit twisted and tilted back so he could look up at him. "Perfect. You?"

Phex smiled down at him, so close. Feeling the certainty of Missit against him like a warmth in his bones. The warning lights gleaming off Missit's skin and reflected in his eyes.

"You're going to get so hurt," said Kagee.

Phex dragged his gaze off Missit's amazing face and glanced over.

Kagee – serious, sullen, sharp – was staring at them intently with those wide-set grey eyes. Had his eyes always been so sad? Phex had assumed Kagee was the way he was because he'd been hurt and rejected and mistreated by his planet. By constant violence and civil war. For the first time, Phex wondered if Kagee's spiky bitterness had more personal grounds. Had Kagee once had, and lost, his own Missit?

"Kagee," said Phex, "it took a lot for me to ask for this. For me to even think I could ask for Missit."

"Balls," said Kagee. "Trust you to turn loving Missit into a conduit for self-acceptance. It would be easier if you just wanted to screw the rules and him at the same time." He raised a hand and ran a thumb over his rings, spinning them in the strobing of pre-fold.

He jostled against the straps as Berril shoved him in annoyed encouragement.

Phex remembered then that Kagee too was trained to guard and defend. He wanted to protect Phex from Missit. Protect Asterism from the shrapnel of Tillam's pain.

"I promise I can do this, Kagee. Please," said Phex, finding it a lot easier to beg the second time. Wondering why he yearned so much for Kagee's support.

"Fine. Yes. I'll change my vote. I'm in favor. But don't ask me to pick up the damn pieces when it all goes horribly wrong." Kagee looked like he was trying not to cry.

"We all know you're an uncaring, callous loner," said Tyve, sounding proud of him.

"Good. Yes. Don't forget, I'm terrible and fierce. Berril, stop hugging me! Argh."

And then it was time to fold space.

If the four sifters had come to any decision, it wasn't made clear to the non-Dyesi. In fact, Phex and Missit were never verbally notified as to whether their relationship had been judged worthy or wanting.

Instead, the sifters decided to demonstrate their feelings

on the matter for all the divinity to see – publicly on the greatest dais of them all.

Everything about the Divine Awards was different from a normal dome performance, not the least of which was the dome itself.

Apex Dome was on Divinity 12, one of the many satellite moons that formed the rings of Dyesid Prime. It was designed specifically as an event dome for this exact thing, which meant it catered to acolyte taste on the interior, intergalactic-press taste on the exterior, and beam-specific spectacle over all.

Inside, it looked, acted, and behaved like a cave.

Outside, it looked, acted, and behaved like a cathedral.

There was even an old-fashioned red carpet of the type reserved for award shows since before the tinkers, although it too was made out of dracohor skin.

To a certain extent, landing on Divinity 12 felt a bit like going backward in time. As if Asterism had escaped the satellites of Dyesid to debut, gone out on tour, and now were right back where they started. Potentials fighting for godhood once more.

Pulling up to Apex Dome in their flash transport, there were a few die-hard worshipers waiting with banners and euphoric enthusiasm. None of them would be allowed inside the dome, but they had made the pilgrimage to Dyesi space in order to become one with the divinity.

They lined up either side of the grand entrance, which was basically a glorified drop-off zone, and got to see nothing more exciting than prettily dressed, nervous gods, grumpy bodyguards, and impassive acolytes exiting their vehicles and walking into the dome.

Still, screams, cheers, handwaving, and wild jumping met each new pantheon as it arrived. And there was plenty of press around to capture and beam out every second of it.

None of these worshipers or reporters would get to see the performance itself – attendance was tightly controlled and limited to earplugged bodyguards, acolytes, and gods alone. Even potentials were regarded as too much of a risk.

Because Apex Dome was also the most powerful in the Dyesi arsenal.

Every niche inside it would be occupied by bodyguards. Apex was probably the safest place in the galaxy to be a god in that moment. Phex was impossibly grateful to know that there would be no possibility of a fixed at this event.

As Asterism climbed out of their transport, there was some initial enthusiastic screaming from one contingent at the back. This was flattering. They were, after all, only a very new group of demigods. It was a true honor that any of their worshipers had managed to make their way to divinity home territory already. Tyve and Fandina bowed and waved happily. Berril unfurled her wings so everyone could gasp in awe.

But when Phex climbed out, the last one of the six, sentiment shifted. Some of the crowd seemed pleased to see him, but there was also a definite hissing from the watching Dyesi, and the press seemed suddenly hostile. One of them shouted a question at Phex, wondering where his *boyfriend* was. Another one asked why he wasn't appearing with Tillam, since *that* was clearly his group now.

It was pointed and mean-spirited but not unexpected.

Kagee looked like he wanted to kill someone.

Phex moved out of position and close to him, placing a

hand on the high cantor's lower back. "Stay calm. Our only job right now is to be pretty."

"At least that's something you're actually good at."

Phex ignored the barb for the pain that had caused it. "I'm right here, Kagee. I'm not going anywhere."

Kagee glared up at him out of the side of one eye but calmed down and took up his proper position for the sake of appearances without further comment, even trying to soften his expression for the beam.

Phex, for his part, ignored all questions, and posed for photos as was required of a god, making elegant obeisance to the area containing Asterism's small congregation.

There were so many different pantheons in attendance, the crowd was bound to be mixed believers. Phex had always known his chances of support were slim. He worried about Missit and Tillam, who would arrive later. He hoped his golden boy wasn't in for verbal abuse too. The medic had cleared Fortew to make an appearance, although he probably wouldn't be able to stay long. Maybe Fortew being there would help. But if the press had been cruel to Phex, they probably wouldn't let Missit off the hook, either – Fortew or no Fortew.

Phex thought Asterism did their best, and they certainly looked the part.

At his request, Phex, Tyve, and Fandina were wearing traditional Dyesi protector skins – scale-plated and gleaming in a reptilian way. Fandina said it was a touch old-fashioned but also kind of cool to bring them back in style for an award show – retro. Phex really liked the way they looked. His were all black with a silvery blue sheen, almost matched to his gunmetal skin. He thought he probably looked like hot oil at the bottom of a wok. Tyve's version was dark red and Fandina's a deep purple.

By contrast, Berril, Jinyesun, and Kagee were in filmy, floaty robes of an extremely light cloth. Also a little metallic, threaded with strands of the same material as Berril's hair. Jin had three robes layered in different shades of teal, cinched tight at the waist, highly flattering on that tall, elegant Dyesi frame. Kagee's were silver, grey, and black, and fitted tighter with less material so they didn't overwhelm his smaller body. Berril's outfit melded the style of the robes with the rest of Asterism. Hers was a halter design that showed off her wings, and while it was made of the same floaty material and wrapped like the two robes, it was made of fabric scales, like her wings and the skins. Those scales wafted as she moved – pure white and metallic pink.

Quasilun emerged from the transport after Asterism, and everyone hushed, even the press. Wearing dracohor body armor as well, the imago clearly belonged with the group, but colored a somber grey and easily twice anyone else's size, they didn't exactly *match* them.

Some of those assembled might have seen an imago before and knew what it meant, but the bodyguard was impressive no matter what. Quasilun ignored acolytes, press, and worshipers alike, and simply hustled Asterism inside Apex Dome.

The throngs of acolytes inside, waiting patiently for the awards to began, went into immediate respectful silence the moment they saw the imago.

Phex had never seen so many Dyesi assembled in one place before. Those not assigned some task or another were already seated expectantly, cross-legged on the floor, or on cushions, or soft squishy puffs. This time, all the puffs were soft grey like the dormant dome, presumably so as not to detract or interfere with the show. They were talking excitedly with each other, crests twitching. The awards show was obviously a treat for them.

Phex and Missit weren't scheduled to duet until the final third, so all of Asterism was led to their section of the dome. The six would sit together and watch the opening ceremony, initial awards, and performances.

It was kind of fun to be in the audience of a dome for a change. Much to Phex's delight, Errata performed in the first third. So did Xillon. Phex finally understood why they were considered the prettiest pantheon in the galaxy. They were truly breathtaking, especially their graces. Orrow performed in the middle third. Phex found it odd to see gods he'd sung with up on the dais, being all amazing and basking in the colors that resulted.

He wondered if it was weird for the gods performing, being unable to cause godfix. Neither he nor anyone around him was taken in by godsong. They enjoyed it, of course – these were the best of the best, award winners of the year.

Phex supposed that was just what happened when you became a god. The craft of the dome was what impressed him now. He could not stop himself from wondering how a pattern was made or how that exact color combination had been produced. He could no longer be carried away by the beauty or the sound, and the combination was to be appreciated in a wholly dispassionate way. A dome, for him, was now work, not art.

There was no godfix for anyone else in that audience, either.

Glancing over at Berril, Tyve, and Kagee, Phex thought that they looked like he felt – intrigued but not transported. Well, except Kagee. Being colorblind, Kagee had never experienced godfix before, so he would feel no sense of loss. He was just his normal grumpy self. Still, his pantheon seemed to have fun, especially Jinyesun and Fandina. The two Dyesi were puffy-crested with evident delight, big eyes focused on the dome. This was the Dyesi's greatest achievement, after all.

This was the thing *they* had given to galaxy. The best of the best was performing before them. They, too, could not experience godfix, but that didn't mean they weren't transported by the magic and privilege of a professional dome. Both of them occasionally sifted or even hummed along with the pantheon on the dais.

Asterism did not win the award for Best New Demigods. Phex was not surprised – they were still young and very new to the divinity. What fame they had was mostly the result of tagging along with Tillam and a certain amount of notoriety that he himself had accidentally generated.

"Give us a chance," Tyve said to a disappointed Kagee. "We don't really have enough godsongs out yet to win anything."

"It's my fault," added Phex. They had the fastest-growing believer base in divinity history – the acolytes had told them so. His recent scandal must have impacted the popular vote, the critics' response, and their chances with their peers.

"Shut up," said Kagee, now annoyed, but at least he no longer looked as unhappy as he had when they lost. "Stop being so damn self-sacrificing all the time. It's *not* your fault. You wanna blame someone? Blame me. I'm the one good at composition, I should write more songs faster."

"We're less than a year old!" protested Berril.

Phex side-eyed his light grace. "Yeah, but I beat a

worshiper unconscious on a dais. Of course it impacted our votes."

Kagee rolled his eyes. "You have all the fun. Next time, my turn."

Phex snorted. "Fine, but do it faster and with less blood. I think that was my biggest issue."

"Are you two finding humor in violence?" asked Fandina, sounding a little offended, crests slightly back.

"It's a bonding mechanism," explained Tyve.

"Sapiens are so weird," said Jinyesun, with feeling.

Fandina added, sounding like a slightly hysterical parent, "No killing and no more blood, either of you!"

"You're so demanding," said Kagee.

Berril brought them back to the point. "We *will* win next year." Phex hadn't realized she had such a competitive edge.

"We better get more original godsongs out before the awards, then," said Jinyesun, practically.

"I'm working on it!" winched Kagee.

"And try not to kill anyone," added Phex.

"No promises to work on that," shot back Kagee.

"He's joking," Tyve explained to their sifters.

"Is he, though?" wondered Jin.

A hush descended in their section of the dome. Quasilun's huge form cast a very long shadow as it moved to where they sat.

The imago crouched down next to Phex's puff so everyone's attention could refocus on the dais. "You're on call for your duet."

Phex craned his neck, looking over to where Tillam puffed in a completely different part of the dome. He couldn't make out if Missit was still there or not.

"Right, Phex, time to change everyone's opinion of you," said Tyve, with forced optimism.

"You really think one duet can do that?"

"The divinity does," said Fandina, firmly. "And they tend to know what they're doing, with a dome."

"Wish me luck, then."

Phex's pantheon clicked supportively.

Berril, sitting next to him, gave him a brief sideways hug, wings flashing green under the dome's opening color as a popular song commenced.

Quasilun swiveled, staying low, and said to Jinyesun, "You two still in?"

A curt nod from the Dyesi.

"Okay. It's a risk but you have my support. I'll be back after getting this one safely stashed beneath the dais."

Phex stood and followed Quasilun out of the dome and below the dais. "What was that about?" he asked once they were inside a tunnel.

"You'll find out soon enough."

Phex nodded. If the imago wanted to be mysterious, Phex couldn't stop it. It was a Dyesi's favorite game.

Missit was waiting for them in the vestry along with several acolytes and their performance costumes.

"You ready for this?" Phex asked, checking him over for signs of stress or mischievousness – which in Missit was occasionally the same thing.

Missit's grin was lopsided and very dear. "It just occurred to me that this is actually perfect for us. For the first time, we are performing for an audience rather than a congregation. This crowd does not expect godfix. Something experimental like our duet is perfect for them." His pretty face was bright with real excitement.

Phex was looking forward to it too, but he wasn't sure why. Perhaps he was merely being infected by Missit's enthusiasm. The golden god couldn't wait to show off this thing that only they did together. He was excited to surprise other gods, his peers, who had probably seen him only as one of Tillam over the years. Who had seen all his failures and successes, but only with his pantheon. They were hard to surprise under a dome. Missit was looking forward to the shock of it.

At first, Phex had seen this duet as just one more thing the divinity was making him do. For Missit, it had always been something special. Something unique that he could give to the dome that he had never given before – and after a decade of godsong, that was exciting for him. Phex was glad he could share that with Missit – novelty after years of sameness.

But for him, it had merely been an opportunity to be alone with Missit. And, when performing, the chance to do something he happened to be good at.

This time felt different. To the worshipers and the acolytes, Phex was about to try to prove his worthiness as a god, show that he could share a dais with Missit and not be diminished by it. But Phex also felt like he was trying to prove something to himself – he just wasn't sure what.

Missit twirled in place, waiting for Phex to change, so excited he couldn't stop moving.

Phex stripped and pulled on his performance costume, muffled his smile in the folds of the shiny fabric, worried his feelings were showing in that moment, and glad the acolytes couldn't really read Sapien affection.

"Assume your positions," said one of the Dyesi.

Phex and Missit made their way through the tight underground passageways toward a cave directly under the dais and the specialized stage lift waiting for them there.

Phex made sure Missit was ready on that lift. Then he climbed out of the underground system and took position against one side of the dome, melding in with the acolytes assembled there.

"What are you doing?" hissed one of them, confused.

"Are you not supposed to be on deck, demigod?" asked another, more polite.

"I don't need a lift or stairs to get onto a dais," explained Phex.

"What?" Crests flattened in confusion.

"Just watch. This is how the divinity spotted me."

The acolytes backed away. "As you say, demigod."

The opening music for their duet started to play.

Missit's golden head appeared and then the rest of him. For one long beat he stood entirely alone in the middle of the dais.

The music swelled and Phex took off running around the edge of the dome, and then, using three quick springs, he leapt straight up the side of the curved wall. Thrusting himself into a backflip, he landed in a crouch on the dais just in front of Missit.

The audience gasped.

Most of them would never have seen Phex do any gracing, let alone crudrat tricks.

Phex swirled in and around, coming behind to lift Missit up, as the god curled and then propelled himself forward, using Phex's bent leg as a springboard.

The first part of their duet was mostly dance while the music played. Then they started singing as they danced, softly as if they were only doing it for each other. First Missit and then Phex.

The dancing slowly shifted into just singing – first one and then the other of them, pausing and belting out the tune, until finally they came together for the first chorus.

As they sang the next verse, they danced together again,

but with less gracing and crudrat trickery, and more old-fashioned partner work. They mirrored each other in song even as they did the same with their bodies, intertwining harmonies and limbs simultaneously.

Phex had never seen a recording of this duet, but he was in very little doubt that what he and Missit could do together on that dais was remarkable. To him, it felt a little like sex, a performance that highlighted the sensuality of their partnership. Nothing blatant or shameful, just a kind of euphoric unity. And he had always known they were really good together at both. But this time, this time they were slicing themselves open for everyone to see what they were. Cutting themselves with the dais and the dome. Bleeding out love in the form of talent.

Dancing and singing like this came naturally to them as Sapiens but also as partners and lovers. This performance had little to do with the dome or the divinity, and because of that, it became a kind of beautiful heresy. Something that was entirely out of place under a Dyesi dome, yet entirely amazing to watch in *that* space. Their duet was alien to the alien place it inhabited while being entirely natural to the two bodies performing. It worked as a contrast, jarring with its strange loveliness. Like Phex's blue versus Missit's gold, the Dyesi dome versus human love.

Missit was like molten light in Phex's arms. The sound that their voices made without color was its own kind of magic – reverberating off the dormant dome but not impacting it in any way.

The audience sat in complete awed silence the entire time.

And right then, Phex realized what was happening.

Yes, he needed to show divinity that he could share a dais with Missit and not be made inferior. But he had also been trying to prove something to himself. That he could share love with Missit and not be lessened by it. That to give love was not to give it away and be diminished as a result. That to receive love was not to have to earn or deserve it. That his own happiness was no less vital or important than anyone else's. That he was obsessed with keeping Missit and Asterism safe because he was afraid of the pain of losing them. But that, in and of itself, meant he already had them and he already loved them. His love was an act of risk but also courage.

His worth was not in his ability as a cantor or grace or bodyguard or cook or even lover, but in the fact that he *wanted* to do those things even after names like *reject* and *crudrat* and *refugee* and *refuse* had been thrown at him. That he could still love. That he could send out light into the void, be it Missit's lonely heart or his pantheon or his believers or the empty spaces between stars.

They had just finished the second verse when something unplanned and entirely unexpected occurred.

Phex was too focused to really register that the dais had changed, that four iridescent figures had been lifted up to join them.

Jinyesun, Fandina, Melalan, and Yorunlee.

They were now six under the dome.

Phex didn't falter. He'd done too much, too often, and most of it unexpected in his brief career as a god. He was inured to surprise. Missit barely registered the sifters joining them either. Together, they simply continued with their duet.

But automatically, they both altered their voices for the next chorus. This time, they sang as if it were cantor. This time, they targeted Dyesi with music in the way that they did with godsong, forcing the ancient human melody to flow over sifting skin, melding their voices like they would for a pantheon.

Without true graces and only their own movements to interrupt the sift, the colors that resulted were almost patternless and blindingly bright – reds and golds and yellows. With four sifters, there was too much of everything. Missit and Phex's voices were interpreted differently by four sets of skins, and the dome became supersaturated with sounded color like a million sunbursts.

Phex thought about their pantheon cabal prior to the last fold. He thought that these four sifters were now visually representing the fact that every person understood love and beauty differently.

Phex didn't really have a chance to see what was happening to the dome itself, though. He could only feel its brightness and catch colors in his peripheral vision. He had to focus on singing and dancing – catching Missit, flipping him and then himself. The third verse was complicated and required all his focus.

It was in the last chorus that Phex caught Missit's eye and together they glanced up at the dome above them.

It was beautiful.

A kaleidoscope of colors, nothing clashing, just swirling and pouring in and out of each other, like a galaxy spiraling, like the pollen on those breezes that made Phex sneeze – melted gold and dancing stars from Missit's voice, and calm silver streams of empty moons and deep blue spaces from Phex's.

It wasn't a dome like the Dyesi thought of it, but it was *something.*

Like pillars, the four Dyesi on the dais with them did nothing more than stand and sift, turning what Phex and Missit were to each other into something for everyone to experience.

Phex hoped it worked. Whatever had convinced the four

Dyesi to show them this kind of succor, he hoped that was what everyone under that dome also saw and understood – both the colors and the pillars that supported them.

All too soon for everyone involved, it ended.

Phex and Missit stopped moving and stopped singing. Together, they knelt at the edge of the dais, looking out at the audience, their last notes soaring over skin and dome. The bright sunburst of their final harmony washed everything in golden light.

Squinting against it, Phex looked out, trying to see his pantheon, far away in the crowd.

Instead, he just saw Dyesi.

Thousands of them.

Every acolyte in that audience was standing. Every one of them in exactly the same position, crests high and waving softly, and skin sifted to match the dome. Blues and purples and greens, all turned gold. It was like they were automatons who had all been programmed to react in exactly the same way. Every. Single. One. It was as if they had fallen off the dome, like fruit from a tree that turned into Dyesi shape when it hit the ground.

It was incredibly eerie and highly unnatural-looking.

All those thousands of Dyesi standing paused, each one colored and positioned exactly the same as the next. Copies of themselves and each other and the dome.

Then the dome went grey.

As one, the Dyesi crumpled where they stood, wilted to the floor.

Melted like Missit's voice.

The only Dyesi left standing in the whole dome were the

four sifters on the dais and Quasilun, who Phex could make out lurking to one side, crests dispassionate.

Missit turned to Phex with awed eyes, "What just happened?"

"I have no idea."

"We forced the Dyesi to feel love," replied Yorunlee, as if that should be obvious.

"Doesn't look like they enjoyed it much," said Missit.

Jinyesun said, "From what I've read in your Sapien novels, first love is always painful. Is it not?"

"Jin, are you making a *joke*?" Phex was shocked.

"No. Wait. Am I?"

Phex stood, turned, and looked hard at Yorunlee, pretending he had crests. "Was that smart, what we just did?"

"No, but it was godly."

"The divinity may not like it when they finally figure out you are lovers, but now they respect you as a pair." Fandina looked almost smug. Phex wondered if this had all been its idea. It seemed like a Fandina-ish plan.

Melalan added, "And they must respect us as co-pantheons as a result."

Yorunlee said, sharp as ever, "We should get off the dais before they recover."

"Okay. Let's do that," Phex agreed, but he didn't join the others in using the stage lifts. Instead, he ran down the side of the dome closest to Quasilun.

He went and stood in front of Quasilun, facing the imago and waiting for… something. Praise? Criticism? Chastisement?

Quasilun said nothing.

Phex studied the imago's crests for clues.

Missit made his way over, while Yorunlee and Melalan

returned to Tillam's section, Jinyesun and Fandina settling back next to Kagee, Berril, and Tyve.

Missit and Phex, as one, moved to lean against the side of the dome just like Quasilun, turning to look where the imago looked, out over the fallen Dyesi.

Natural color was returning to nymphs' skin. Blues and purples and greens, making them look like wilted sea leaves washed up onto a shore after a storm.

For the first time, Phex realized, he wasn't afraid of them. Wasn't scared of the acolytes or of offending Dyesi sensibilities.

Missit slid his small hand into Phex's larger one, threading their fingers together.

"Look what we did," said the great god softly, in Galactic Common.

Missit wasn't talking about the dome or the Dyesi – he was talking about their pantheons. All of them, Asterism and Tillam, even the sifters had indicated their support one way or another.

They believed in him, not as worshipers but as people. As friends. Phex felt honored and lucky and amazed.

Some of the Dyesi began to pick themselves back up.

"Are they going to be all right?" Phex asked.

"This is normal," said the imago, somewhat dismissively.

"Normal for what, exactly?"

Quasilun looked away from the nymphs and down at them then. If the imago noted Missit's hand in Phex's, they weren't moved to comment or even flick a crest. "I wasn't sure it would work, when your Fandina told me the plan. And it may not yield up the results you desire, but one thing is certain. You and Missit and your pantheons will be kept together now. For as long as possible."

Phex felt the weight of the whole dome lift from his

shoulders. "Have we not shown them too much power? Won't fear drive them to separate us?"

Missit ran his thumb over the back of Phex's hand. "That is not how the Dyesi react to fear. To fear something is to seek to understand it so that it may be controlled, not to automatically try to destroy it."

The imago huffed in amusement. "Why do you think we started the divinity in the first place?"

Phex clicked understanding.

Quasilun looked away from them and back at the recovering nymphs. "You two, together, you are more than gods now. You are imagoes."

"Oh, dear, is everyone going to start using frozen register with us?"

Quasilun huffed again, and Missit laughed and squeezed his hand again.

Phex felt a very strange sensation then, one he didn't really know what to do with. A warmth that didn't come from Missit's melted gold but from Phex himself. A feeling that wasn't pride in his ability as a god or a protector. Heat from an unknown star inside of Phex. A thing that maybe once had been an abandoned moon.

"Oh," said Phex, surprised, "this is happiness."

EPILOGUE

Tillam were given the Immortal Achievement Award, which Phex found ironic since Fortew was no longer immortal. But Fortew managed to get up on the dais to accept it, and hopefully very few on the infonet noticed how much he leaned on Missit and Tern for support the entire time.

Back on their ship, changed into comfortable clothing, sitting in puffs and munching on tasty stew, the duet was all they talked about.

Apparently, it was all the infonet was talking about, too. The performance was being heralded as a revelation – the perfect combination of Dyesi entertainment and ancient human art. Missit and Phex were being called *the pair of the ages*, and no one was accusing them of being anything more than perfectly matched artistic talents.

The forums were full of professional analysts claiming how obvious it was that Phex would be protective under circumstances of such matched abilities. How they had known all along the relationship was one of perfect but platonic collaborators. Of course Phex would want to protect his partner, and of course Phex and Missit would be close when they could do such amazing things together.

As soon as they relaxed, the pantheons began hurling good-natured abuse at their four sifters.

"You could have warned us what you were going to do!" protested Missit, at Melalan.

"It was a performance, dear. You cannot deny us dramatic effect." The sifter looked quite smug.

"The surprise on your faces was priceless," agreed Yorunlee. Who Phex thought didn't have a sense of humor. Apparently, he was wrong.

Jinyesun said, "We wanted to show our support, and we thought this way would be fun."

Quasilun made a parentally chiding hissing noise at them. "Fun? Fun. You six caused massive full-scale group fugue. And you proved to the divinity exactly how powerful those two cantors are."

"But that is what earns respect. Is respect not a good thing?" wondered Fandina.

"Is that what it's called? *Fugue*?" Phex was happy to have the correct word at last.

"You knew something was different." Quasilun turned and focused on Phex, ignoring Fandina's question.

"We've caused fugue a couple times before. Once back in my potential days, when Missit first sang with me under a dome. We stunned the acolytes."

"It caused a bit of a fuss at the time," said Missit, looking up from his stew. Phex was happy to see him actually enjoying a meal for a change.

Quasilun seemed amused by the understatement. "I bet it did."

"This time was different. Every acolyte standing up and stuck in the same pose like that, creepy. That time on Divinity

36, they just kinda froze in their seats." Kagee said this as he cleaned his bowl.

Phex remembered his friend's smug grey face amongst the acolytes, all sitting so still. He thought about them standing this time, perfectly synced by his and Missit's voices. Were they fixated, perhaps? Or close to it? "Is fugue like godfix, only for Dyesi?"

"No. The two are materially different things. What you and Missit can do, that's something deeply primal. A survival instinct. A battle plan. You thought it was only freeze, but it can also activate a fight-or-flight response."

"You weren't stunned. Can Missit and I impact you at all?" Phex was curious, but also, he thought it was the right question to ask.

The imago looked proud of him. "No. But I can cause it."

"What?"

Quasilun tapped fine fingers to their smooth grayish cheeks. "Imagoes can't skinsift after instar, only the nymphs have this ability. But we can reflect the sift and we can sing. Who do you think were the first cantors?"

Phex considered Quasilun's almost-parental amusement over the whole incident. Over everything that the acolytes did and felt. Over the whole of the divinity. Like an elder regarding with good humor the antics of teenagers.

Different life stages, Jinyesun had said.

"You use it to control them, don't you? The nymphs. Control them as if they were unruly teenagers?"

Quasilun looked the Dyesi version of conspiratorial. If the imago had had eyebrows, they would have been quirked. "Something like that."

Phex realized then that Quasilun had used imago cantor to activate the fight response in the acolytes back on Earth 10. When he'd nearly been drugged and eaten alive. The acolytes had been forced into violence by Quasilun, on Phex's behalf.

If cantor could be used to freeze nymphs, it could also be used to turn them into warriors. Quasilun had used his voice to force the acolytes of Earth 10 to rescue Phex from Chef and the hysterical crowd.

Phex remembered now, just as he fainted, the sound of a bellowing cantor and the movement of blue streaks at the corners of his vision. Dyesi, fighting. Fighting hard, for possibly the first and last time in their very long lives. Quasilun had sung them into obedience. Which meant the dome wasn't strictly necessary, either. If an imago could do that, command all nymphs within range to freeze or fight or run, could Phex and Missit do that too?

"You don't need a dome." Phex wondered if his voice could command an army of Dyesi nymphs or only turn them into mindless cannon fodder for a short time.

"Ah, not strictly speaking, but we do need a cave-like structure, and without a proper dome, we can only control a few nymphs at a time. It's a defensive capacity. And it's something we protector imagoes carry with us. You two require a dome."

Phex looked at the imago for a long moment. Thinking about the classification of *protector*. Thinking about how the breeder imagoes lived their lives trapped in the caves, underground with their vulnerable skinless newborns, the megafauna having conquered the world above. "Nymphs were once needed to defend your caves, to protect the young and the breeders. That's why there are so many of them. That's why you can control them like that."

"Once upon a time, yes."

"Is skinsift a kind of protective camouflage?"

"Very good. Of course, none of it is necessary anymore.

Now we have technology, projectile weapons and the like, to defend against the megafauna. So, we let our nymphs out to play with what was once instinct, have their fun. Turn defense into art, as only nymphs can."

And the Dyesi nymphs had done what? Invented an entertainment system and taken over the entire known galaxy with it.

Phex stared at the imago, realizing that to Quasilun, to adult Dyesi in general, the divinity was just a game of gods and beauty. The nymphs were playing a sport of culture against the universe. This was their teenage pastime. Nymphs played with pantheons and domes like they were playing grown-up make-believe. Using Sapiens and other aliens to recreate an adult world on a large scale. But because they were not fully grown, they needed help for it, help from Sapiens and other aliens. But in reality, it was nothing more than a crude facsimile of what imagoes could do in their caves down below.

It wasn't that the imagoes didn't understand the nature of the divine – it was just that they didn't care.

The divinity, with its billions of worshipers, thousands of domes, and hundreds of gods, was of little consequence to Dyesid Prime. They had adult concerns and interests, no reason to leave their caves, let alone their planet. No reason to care what the nymphs did with their sifting skin and hypnotic domes, because to them it was nothing more than child's play.

Just like Phex's customers at the cafe, back on Attacon 7. The elders had always ceded the cupola to the youngsters in the evenings. Teenagers needed their designated spaces, room to grow and experiment. So, the Dyesi imagoes had ceded the galaxy to their nymphs.

Quasilun's attitude was simply *Look at our youngsters,*

having their fun. Aren't they cute? How little they know. How much they have to learn. It's so sweet that they think any of this matters and are so industrious about it.

"What can you do in a dome, imago?" Phex used the body language of extreme respect as well as frozen register, humbling himself before experience and indifference – Dyesi-style.

"Best if you never find that out, little blue." Quasilun nodded at him, Sapien-style, and stood, pearl-grey face as impassive as a dead dome.

The imago bent and patted Missit on the head. "You looked beautiful up there."

Missit blushed and lowered his gaze. "Thank you, imago."

"Don't stay up too late." With that, Quasilun left the galley area.

"Did you know any of that?" Phex moved Missit into his lap. Dimsum protested.

"No one wants your opinion," Missit told her, then answered Phex, "No, but my parents might have guessed at some point. From their studies. Why? Does it make a difference?"

Phex frowned, wondering why he felt troubled. There was a part of him that had thought, all along, even as he played the Dyesi game to win godhood, that perhaps the divinity was actually evil. That perhaps the Dyesi were intentionally taking over the galaxy for some deeply sinister reason. But to learn it was all a game? A galactic toy?

Why did that make him feel worse? Was it the careless nature of it all?

And why had the imago told him any of it? Him, who had a dangerous voice.

Had he just been warned not to use it?

fin

What happens to Phex, his pantheon, and Missit next?

Find out in *Dome 6*, the third and final book in the Tinkered Starsong series.

AUTHOR'S NOTE

Thank you so much for picking up *Demigod 12*. I hope you enjoyed this second installment of Phex's story. If you would like more Tinkered Starsong or have a favorite character, please say so in a review or tell a friend. I'm grateful for the time you take to do so.

Join Gail's newsletter, the Chirrup, for sneak peaks at cover art, sample chapters, and a *free* special high heat scene cut from Chapter 10 of this book. Find it and more at…

GailCarriger.com

ABOUT THE WRITERBEAST

New York Times bestselling author Gail Carriger (AKA G. L. Carriger) writes to cope with being raised in obscurity by an expatriate Brit and an incurable curmudgeon. She escaped small-town life and inadvertently acquired several degrees in higher learning, a fondness for cephalopods, and a chronic tea habit. She then traveled the historic cities of Europe, subsisting entirely on biscuits secreted in her handbag. She resides on the edge of the Pacific, surrounded by fantastic shoes, where she insists on tea imported from London.

Printed in Poland
by Amazon Fulfillment
Poland Sp. z o.o., Wrocław